Also by J. C. Cervantes

The Storm Runner

THE FIRE KEEPER

J. C. CERVANTES

RICK RIORDAN PRESENTS

DISNEP • HYPERION   LOS ANGELES   NEW YORK

First Edition, September 2019
1 3 5 7 9 10 8 6 4 2
Printed in the United States of America
FAC-020093-19214

This book is set in 11.85-pt Aldus Nova Pro, Bradley Hand ITC/Monotype;
Cocotte, Genplan Pro, Vonn Handwriting, Ammer Handwriting/Fontspring
Designed by Phil Buchanan

Library of Congress Cataloguing in Publication Data
Names: Cervantes, Jennifer, author.
Title: The Fire Keeper : a Storm Runner novel / by J. C. Cervantes.
Description: First edition. • Los Angeles ; New York : Rick Riordan Presents,
Disney Hyperion, 2019. • Sequel to: The Storm Runner. • Summary: Zane
Obispo faces an impossible choice—to save other godborns like himself from
the angry gods, or rescue his father, Hurakan, from his eternal prison.
Identifiers: LCCN 2018054205 • ISBN 9781368041881
Subjects: • CYAC: Maya mythology—Fiction. • People with disabilities—
Fiction. • Fathers and sons—Fiction. • Maya gods—Fiction.
Classification: LCC PZ7.C3198 Fir 2019 • DDC [Fic]—dc23
LC record available at https://lccn.loc.gov/2018054205

Reinforced binding
Follow @ReadRiordan
Visit www.DisneyBooks.com

For Julie Bear—the girl who adventured with spirit and returned with fire. This book is for you.
And for all the writers creating and waiting. Keep creating.

"The Prophecy of Fire was only the beginning.
But fire spreads. Until it burns everything in its path."

—Antonio Marcel De La Vega,
Venice Beach, California

I might be dead by the time this book finds you.
If it ever finds you.

Seven months ago, I sent out a secret message to any god-borns, hoping some might still be alive. I haven't heard back from anyone, which could mean (a) you're not out there, or (b) the magic hasn't found you. Or—and I don't even want to think about this alternative—(c) you exist and the magic has found you, but you've decided to ignore it. If that's the case, you've got muchos problemas.

Optimistic me wonders if I didn't write down *enough* for my message to have any power. Maybe it's like buying a lottery ticket—the more you try, the better your chances. Except my uncle Hondo has bought probably hundreds of tickets and all he ever won was a buck twenty-five.

So consider this my last-ditch effort, just in case something happens to me on the quest I'm about to take. I didn't want to leave you in the dark all alone.

I'm using magic ink that only godborns can see, the same kind I used for my last secret message, which was tacked on to the story I had to write for the Maya gods. They wanted me to bare my soul, for a couple of reasons. First, because they're mitoteros who can't keep their noses out of anything. Second, because they wanted to use my misadventure as a warning so no one else would ever defy them again. To make sure I didn't lie (I totally would have), they forced me to use special paper that would be able to tell if I wasn't writing the truth.

Knowing my story is in the gods' hands still keeps me up at night. There were some pretty embarrassing things in it that I would have preferred to keep private—like what I really think of Brooks.

The best thing about her? She's still willing to go along for the ride. She gets that I have to find my dad, Hurakan. He's a big jefe—a creator god, for gods' sake! He doesn't deserve to be crammed into some teeny tiny dark prison, choking on dust and memories just because he broke the Sacred Oath and claimed me as his son in front of the whole god council.

I owe him. Big-time. A favor for a favor.

Uno por otro.

And no matter how long it takes, and no matter what I have to do, I'm going to rescue him. Because if it weren't for him, I wouldn't be a godborn. I wouldn't have the blood of a creator *and* a destroyer.

I wouldn't be the Storm Runner.

So, do me a favor. If you find this and you hear that I died, could you punch the gods in their stupid faces for me?

Thanks,

Zane Obispo

P.S. I wrote this letter before everything happened. Before hell, before the Red Queen and the death magician and the evil bats. Before the end. I almost burned this note, but a certain someone said it marked the beginning and all stories need true beginnings. So here it is. The beginning of the end.

1

•

Killing one's enemies during Lent is probably
a mortal sin.

But what choice did I have? I didn't pick the timing of
all this. Maybe I'd get lucky and rescuing my dad wouldn't
involve meeting any evil forces of utter darkness. Or blood
spilling.

Knowing the Maya gods? Fat chance.

"Paddle harder!" I shouted.

Brooks sat in the front of the double kayak as rain pelted
both of us. We were paddling through a mangrove on the remote
island in Mexico where Ixtab, the queen of the underworld, had
stashed me and my peeps a few months ago. She did it to keep
us safe from the Maya gods, who thought I was dead—a fate
they felt I deserved for being the offspring of a human and a
god. Holbox was a pretty sweet place to live, unless you needed
to get anywhere quickly, like we did just then.

The island's mangrove was a winding, lush channel where
crocodiles and snakes hung out. Not my favorite kayaking
spot, to be honest, but it was the only way to reach the west
inlet.

That's where our "drop point" was. Jazz, our friend the
giant, was risking his life by supplying us with sensitive inside
information. He had to send it in secret, the old-fashioned

(epically slow) way so there'd be no trail leading back to him. I know what you're thinking—why not just send a text? Good idea, except that Ixtab's shadow magic was surrounding the island, to protect us from prying eyes, and it made things like smartphones and Wi-Fi go haywire. Plus, Jazz was under constant god surveillance. Any suspicious communication and the giant would buy himself a one-way ticket to Xib'alb'a. I felt for the guy.

We'd gotten the date and time of the drop from Old Man Pedro, who, on most days, you can find either painting a mural on the side of a building or sitting in the shade with a cerveza. When he's not doing those things, he's apparently coordinating these sorts of "messages."

"We could've just flown!" I hollered, trying to make a solid point.

"You know I don't fly in the rain!" Brooks shouted.

Right. We just kayak in it! I didn't know what her hang-up with water was. She'd gotten so much stronger as a shape-shifter, and get this: she could not only shift into a hawk, but a seriously grande hawk. I wished I had managed to master my powers like that. We both needed to be at our peak if we were going to succeed in this crazy quest.

"We only have two minutes," I called, my voice coming out in a strangled panic. "We're not going to make it!"

And we'd probably never get this chance again. Pedro had made that clear in his grouchy way. *You miss the drop, don't come crying to me.*

We were about to get the last piece of the puzzle—the exact location of my dad's prison. Supposedly, the gods had upped security and they moved him every month or two. He was due to be relocated again soon, and I had to bust him out before we lost track of him.

Too bad Fuego couldn't grow wings. That's what I'd named my combination walking cane/deadly spear, because it was as fast as fire. Back in the Old World, the Sparkstriker had pounded it with lightning, bound it with old magic, and infused it with my dad's blood. As a result, it was indestructible and had perfect aim. It also helped me walk without my usual limp, the result of one leg being shorter than the other. I usually only relied on that feature when I was running from a demon or something. My limp doesn't bother me like it used to—it's part of who I am.

When Fuego wasn't in cane or spear mode, it took the form of a letter opener (that was Ixtab's idea—why couldn't it change into something cool, like a dagger?), which I wore in my sock. That made things easier when I needed both hands. Like now.

Brooks gave me a murderous glare over her shoulder. "You so owe me, Obispo." The air glimmered blue, then green, and in an instant, she transformed into her giant-hawk self. She circled overhead with a loud cry (which I interpreted as *I really hate you right now*) and dropped low enough for me to be able to reach one of her thick talons.

Okay, so no piggyback ride today. I hesitated until she gave me her killer *take-it-or-leave-it* look. With a grunt, I grabbed hold of her slippery claw with both hands, and she took off. I must've looked like an idiot, dangling from her like a piece of soggy string cheese.

Whatever.

Brooks struggled against the hostile headwinds. The rain lashed us, and the sky darkened. She was seriously going to kill me when this was all over. But who could've forecast the stupid storm? I'm the Storm *Runner,* not the Storm *Predictor.*

You got this, I told her telepathically, trying to sound as cheerful and supportive as I could under the circumstances. (Note to godborns: Cheery optimism can be a butt saver when used just right.) Plus, there were a few crocodiles in the vicinity that looked hungry, and I didn't want to give Brooks any reason to drop me into their open mouths. Let's face it—she does sort of have a temper.

Maybe the storm will slow down the delivery, too, I said.

Stop talking. You're distracting me.

A minute later, Brooks swooped down to the inlet shore and dumped me like an old melon. I rolled across the packed white sand, missing a pointy piece of driftwood by a couple inches.

Brooks shifted back to her human form just as the storm raced away and the sky settled into a grayish calm. I wiped the sand off my arms. "Ha! We made it. Great flying...but, uh"—I lowered my voice—"not so good landing."

"It was a *brilliant* landing. You're alive, aren't you?" Brooks twisted her brown hair over her shoulder. It had gotten a shade lighter over the last few months with all the time we spent at the playa. "Let's see you do any better."

I should probably tell you the hard truth now, because you need to know in case it happens to you. After my dad, Hurakan, claimed me, and after I took down the god of death

with my mad fire skills, something happened to me. I couldn't
control my power again the way I had that day. I could only
make lemon-size fireballs that fizzled faster than Pop Rocks
on your tongue. So, being claimed by a godly parent doesn't
necessarily equal auto-awesome.

"The package is late." Brooks tapped her foot and looked
around. "Didn't Pedro say six thirty-two p.m. sharp?"

"What's that?" I asked, pointing up at the sky. A massive
red-feathered thing emerged from a thick cloud bank. "Could
that be the delivery dude?" I asked.

The bird (if you could call it that) had tiny chicken wings,
gangly long legs, an anvil-shaped head, and a beak that looked
more like a meat tenderizer. To say the thing was ugly would
be a huge understatement. I wondered how the poor bird had
gotten roped into this job.

Brooks squinted. "Is that a coconut in its claws?"

The bird zoomed toward the beach, then suddenly stopped
in midair and shuddered. I followed the bird's gaze behind me.
A wall of black mist rose up from the beach, slowly taking
the form of my hellhound, Rosie. For some people, it could
be pretty unnerving to have a dog twice the size of a lion that
could appear out of thin air. When I'd found her as a boxer-
dalmatian mutt wandering the New Mexico desert years ago,
she was just skin and bones barely weighing thirty pounds.
Ever since she went to the underworld and was "modified" by
Ixtab, Rosie's snout reached the top of my ribs, which says a
lot, because I'm practically six feet tall.

No wonder the chicken-winged bird was terrified. The

way Rosie was looking at it, you'd think she wanted the bird for a pre-dinner snack. She probably did.

"Rosie, back!" I commanded.

Ignoring me, the hellhound growled and bolted toward the ocean. She seriously needed to go to obedience school!

The bird's eyes went wide. *Eep!* it cried as it spun around and flew away.

"Hey, wait!" I shouted. "The coconut!"

For some reason, Jazz liked to send messages inside produce items. Last time it was a rotting avocado wishing us a Merry Christmas.

Eep! Eep! The bird was clearly too spooked to come back.

Brooks grunted. "Looks like we're going to have to go get the coconut ourselves."

I grabbed hold of her shoulders from behind, and she shifted into a hawk. A second later, we were airborne and whizzing toward the bird, which kept glancing over its shoulder with pure terror in its eyes.

Rosie leaped through the waves, howling and shooting streams of fire twenty feet into the air.

"STEAK!" I yelled.

That's the command to make her stop. Ha. She acted like she didn't even hear me. Faker.

It's her nature to hunt, Brooks said.

But could she not *hunt the delivery bird?*

The clouds thickened, masking the red creature. All I saw was its tail streaking through the gloom.

Rosie was keeping pace. "She won't hurt you!" I yelled to

the bird just as my dog hurled a torrent of fire epic enough to rival a dragon. "Just wait until we get home!" I shouted to Rosie.

Brooks was fast, though, and we were gaining. Thirty feet.

Twenty.

Fifteen.

And then something changed. I blinked to be sure. Up ahead, the ashy horizon had a long, ragged tear in it, just like in the Old World, when I'd thought the sky was going to rip open.

By the time I realized the seam was there, it was too late. The bird had disappeared through it.

The coconut tumbled into the sea.

And Brooks slammed against an invisible wall.

2
..

As I plunged toward the ocean, all I could think was *This is so going to hurt.*

Smack!

That was the sound of me belly flopping into the Caribbean.

I launched myself back up to the surface, where I sucked in a huge gulp of air. Okay, so my landing had been an epic fail. If Hondo were here, he would've busted a rib laughing and then shouted, *Splat's all, folks!* (Even though my uncle is a few years older than me, he usually acts younger.)

After recovering from her face-plant in the sky, Brooks had managed to swoop down and pluck the coconut from where it was bobbing on top of the water. Then she cruised over and picked me up. I grabbed the hairy orb from her other claw and gripped her outstretched wing to climb onto her back, where I clung to her slick feathers. I couldn't believe it. My dad's whole future could be inside this coconut.

What the heck happened? I asked telepathically. *What did you run into?*

It was crazy. . . . Some kind of barrier. But I couldn't see it!

I pinched the bridge of my nose and took a deep breath, not wanting to grasp the truth of what Brooks was telling me.

The shadow magic was supposed to keep the gods out, not *keep us in,* I said.

I mean, I hadn't left Holbox Island since we'd gotten here a few months ago, but that was because Ixtab had told me the second I stepped out from under the shadow magic's protection, I could get nabbed on the gods' radar and—*ripppp!*— off with my head.

I felt sick just thinking this island could be—was probably— some kind of prison. How could I ever rescue my dad if we were locked in ourselves?

Brooks flapped her wings angrily. *Why didn't we figure it out?*

That we're trapped here?

WHY we're trapped here. I mean, if you leave the island, then the gods will know you're alive, right? And they'll know Ixtab lied to them about you being dead. Of course she doesn't want to risk her own head. Ugh! We should have known not to trust a god.

She's trying to save her own butt!

Well, if she thinks she can keep me . . . us here—Brooks's bird muscles tensed—*she's got another think coming!*

Brooks was right. No way was Ixtab going to keep me here. Not when I finally knew—or was about to find out— where my dad was being held. If that red bird could find a hole, we could, too.

By the time we got back to our own stretch of playa, it was already getting dark. Rosie, of course, was nowhere to be seen. She knew I was mad at her. I mean, she had almost ruined our seven-months-in-the-making quest.

The scent of pollo adobado wafted from the house along with some of Hondo's Zen snorefest music. You read that right. He had turned over a new leaf since living on the island. Now he was all about visualization and meditation.

The coconut was clearly hollow, but I couldn't find a seam in the shell. I cracked it open by hitting it with Fuego and looked for the hidden message. Inside was a black obsidian disk no bigger than a quarter.

"Jazz protected the message in magician's stone?" Brooks said. "He takes this top secret stuff pretty seriously."

"Yep," I said. "He's a regular James Bond."

"Can't blame the guy," Brooks said. "The gods would gut him if they ever learned he was helping us."

I lay the black glass on a rock and jabbed it with Fuego in spear mode, splitting it in two. In the middle was a dark strip of paper that unfolded once, twice, three times until it was the size of a three-by-five notecard. I stumbled back. It wasn't that I was afraid of paper—it was that this was *exactly* how Ah-Puch, the god of death, had sprung to life before my eyes a few months ago.

My heart pounded as I picked up the message to check it out more closely.

"Well?" Brooks said.

"It's blank!"

"No way." Brooks snatched it away but held it out so we could both see it. That's when the paper began to shimmer silver, like flecks of twirling stardust. Then, slowly, words appeared on it as if an invisible hand were writing them.

WaTiki Indoor Waterpark Resort
314 N Elk Vale Rd, Rapid City, SD 57703
Midnight
March 24
Three demons

"My dad's hidden in a water park in South Dakota? Is this some kind of joke?"

Brooks frowned. "Three demons. That's nothing. We can totally take them." She tapped her fingers on her chin one at a time like she was counting. "Today is the twentieth, right? So that gives us four full days."

Rosie appeared on the playa just then, slinking over all chill like. She lowered her head, tucked back her ears, and let out a little whine. It was impossible for me to stay mad at her. Brooks was right—hunting was part of my dog's nature.

I'd been trying to retrain Rosie for the last seven months, and no matter what I tried, she refused to obey me, especially when it came to the commands for turning her flame throwing on and off. Ixtab had taught her to breathe fire every time she heard the word *dead*. It was handy whenever I needed to borrow some of Rosie's flames. But it wasn't so great when the word came up in casual conversation....

Rosie spat out a Milk Dud–size fireball and knocked it my way with her nose as a peace offering.

Snatching it up, I launched it down the beach. She raced after it so fast, she looked like a black streak of lightning.

"She's the best hellhound I've ever seen," Brooks said. "I

mean, her speed is, like, off the charts, and the way she can expand fire? Did you see how Rosie almost incinerated that bird? And *while* she was swimming!" Brooks looked at me, smiling like a proud mom at an art competition her kid had just won. She'd come a long way since the day she'd first met Rosie. "She's ready . . . and *you're* ready, Zane. We got this. *You* got this."

"Right," I lied. I imagined my dad worming around some tiny dark space, getting weaker and weaker, and it made me sick with guilt.

"I know you've been struggling with the fire thing. Maybe you've been trying too hard," Brooks said, digging a tube of mint ChapStick from her pocket and applying some. She smacked her lips together. "Or maybe you have to be, like, stressed out or in danger or something. Do you want me to shift into a hawk and attack you?"

"Uh—nice offer and all, but I'm good."

"Fine," she said with a shrug. "I'll be right back."

"Where are you going?"

"To check out that invisible wall." Then she became a hawk and flew away.

"I'll . . . uh . . . just be here waiting."

Rosie raced back with the fireball, groaned, and dropped the small flame at my feet. I reached up to scratch between her eyes (yes, she's that tall). *Thanks, girl,* I said. A side benefit to Rosie being a hellhound (other than breathing fire) is that I can talk to her telepathically, too.

She knew I needed to try harder. The problem was, I

couldn't just *make* fire the way Rosie could. I'd practiced for hundreds of hours, trying the exact way Hurakan had taught me in our one and only lesson on that day in the Empty.

Being with him, in a place he had literally created from scratch, was so mind-blowing I can't be totally sure, but I thought he'd said something about there coming a time when I wouldn't need an exterior source of heat—I'd be able to create my own. (Dumb me had thought that would happen the moment he claimed me in front of the other gods. Nope.)

He'd motioned toward the sun. *Draw on its power. Call it to you.*

I'd focused on what I used to call my bum leg, the one that's shorter than the other and carries all my godborn power. Hurakan was right. When I isolated my thoughts to this one part of me, what he called my "serpent leg," a strange energy had pulsed through my entire body. Of course, I'd been a *jaguar* in that moment, which may have had something to do with it.

Now feed the flame with your life source, he'd said.

When I'd tried, a terrible heat had overtaken me. Smoke came out of my nose. The burning snaked its way through me at unimaginable speed. I totally panicked.

Things hadn't gotten much better since then.

Rosie rolled the fireball onto her snout and tossed it to me. I caught the flame and spun it, letting it dance across my fingertips.

The moment felt tight as I let the heat seep beneath my skin so I could feed it with the power that pulsed in my leg. That was the only way to make fire bigger, stronger.

Rosie let out an encouraging whimper.

I focused hard until the flame grew to the size of a lemon. Sweat trickled down my neck. I took a deep breath, knowing concentration was the key. My trembling hands were engulfed in the flames, but my skin didn't burn.

I got this.

I got this.

I could still hear Hurakan's voice tangled in the wind of that memory like it was just yesterday: The fire *will destroy you if you don't release its power.*

I flung the fireball, letting out the searing heat inside me along with it. . . .

It fizzled over the waves like a dying sparkler. I stared down at my hands in frustration, wondering if I'd ever master fire.

A few minutes later, Brooks landed and shifted back.

"I just flew around the island," she said, catching her breath. "There's definitely some kind of barrier I can't get through, but . . ."

"What?"

"On the east side, I found a tiny hole. . . . I dragged my talon down the center, and it gave just a little."

"Perfect!" I said. "So, we can rip through it?"

Brooks pressed her lips together. "Not exactly. It closed up instantly."

"How . . . ?"

My mind shuffled through all the possibilities: Ixtab put up the wall to (a) protect us, (b) keep us on the island, (c) keep the gods out, or (d) all of the above. Whatever her reason, it didn't matter. I was getting off Isla Holbox, shadow magic or no shadow magic.

Ixtab had arranged something else, too. She'd transported a dormant volcano—my favorite, which I'd nicknamed the Beast—from where we used to live in New Mexico. She'd told me that inside it was my very own gateway to the underworld, in case of emergency. Ixtab had stressed (okay, maybe she'd threatened) *emergency* as in *only if the gods descend and try to gouge out your eyes*, so thankfully, I'd never had to use it. For half a second, I considered marching through that gateway to confront her directly, but then she'd know I was trying to leave and she might whip up even stronger magic to keep me here forever.

"Once they move Hurakan, we'll be back to square one, and Jazz already risked so much to get this intel," I said. "This might be my only chance to save my dad. We have to find a way off the island."

"What about the gateway map?" Brooks's eyes flashed with excitement.

Ms. Cab, my neighbor and a great Maya seer, had given us a magical map that revealed secret portals to other layers of the world. Correction—we'd *borrowed* it for our last quest, but we'd never been able to use it, because the lousy gods went and shut down all gateways.

"That's it!" I practically shouted. "Maybe the shadow magic is only around the perimeter of the island and *not* any gateway!" The thought of outsmarting Ixtab sent a thrill down my spine.

"I'll check when we get home," Brooks said, looking a little worried. "I just hope the shadow magic doesn't jam the map's frequency."

"We'll leave at dawn," I said with a lot more confidence than I felt.

"And if we can't get through?"

I gritted my teeth. "Then we'll storm hell."

At the mention of hell, Rosie whined and danced on her paws.

"Yes, you can come, too, Rosie," I said, patting her chest. "But you have to promise to listen. We have to work as a team. Got it?"

I didn't want to admit it, but I wasn't sure Rosie had ever forgiven me for letting her get turned into a hellhound. I mean, I *was* the one who had taken her into the volcano, where she'd been killed by a demon runner, sending her straight to the underworld. Deep down I was worried that some kind of trust had been broken between us. And that scared me.

At the same moment, Hondo called us from the back patio. "Yo, dinner's up. I cooked, so you get dish duty, Diablo!"

I turned to the palapa-roofed house where we now lived—Brooks included, except she got the casita attached to the courtyard, because, as Mom said, *Young girls need their privacy.*

Mom was on the patio, setting straw place mats on the table. She smiled and waved at us. She was happy—happier than when we lived in New Mexico. She loved Isla Holbox, with its sandy streets, brightly colored cafés, open-air shops, and the fruit and vegetable market. Me? I liked the beach and the Yum Balam nature reserve (named after the Maya jaguar lord), which also happens to be where my volcano is.

Little did Mom know I was about to incinerate her happiness by taking off on a mission that could mess up everything. I told myself it would all be okay. We'd find a way off the island in the morning—rip a hole in the sky if we had to. We'd fly under the gods' radar all the way to South Dakota, and everything would go as planned.

I was so wrong.

3

•••

Brooks's gateway map turned up nothing.
Zilch. Nada. The nearest gateway was in Cancún, and that was *beyond* the shadow magic barrier.

I lay in bed that night with a supersize headache. I thought I'd gone through every option, but then my mind landed on another. The last one—the jade. I still had the jaguar tooth my dad had given me, hanging around my neck on a brown leather cord. The amulet was fused with the most ancient and potent magic in the universe. I could use the tooth to spirit-jump to the Empty, and also to grant any power to whoever I gave it to. That was the irony, I guess. The power came in giving it away, which, to be honest, was so ungodlike.

I could give Brooks the ability to cancel Ixtab's shadow magic. But what if Hurakan's totem wasn't as strong as Ixtab's spell and we blew our one chance to use the jade's power?

That night my dreams were foggy, filled with faces and places I didn't know. Everything so out of reach. Until I heard a man's voice:

Time for the story to escalate.

I bolted upright, wide-awake. I peered through the dark. "Hello?"

There was no answer.

It must have been a dream, I told myself as I punched my pillow, ready to lie back down.

She's here.

Okay, *that* was definitely not a dream.

Throwing back the covers, I looked around. I could hear the waves crashing in the distance. That's when I felt a tug down in my gut, like the tide was pulling me closer.

I headed out to the beach.

Alone. (Unless you counted Fuego.)

Just a few months ago, Rosie would've been trotting happily beside me like on many restless nights back in New Mexico. But ever since she'd become a hellhound, she preferred sleeping inside the Beast. By the gateway. Near Ixtab. Maybe Rosie just wasn't meant to be with me anymore. Had we both changed that much? It was too painful to even think about.

Outside, the air was cool, and the moon was a milky half circle of gloom. The Caribbean glowed as if millions of blue stars burned under the water, thanks to bioluminescent phytoplankton—or what Brooks calls *sea sparkle.* It's a pretty awesome sight.

I rubbed the goose bumps off my arms as I dropped onto my butt on the empty shore, unable to shake the whispers. *Time for the story to escalate. She's here.* What was that supposed to mean?

Waves lapped within a few feet, and the horizon was black. I wondered if Pacific, the exiled goddess of time, was still out there. Was she okay? I knew she'd had to go deeper into hiding after delivering messages to me from Hurakan, but I wasn't exactly sure what "deeper" meant. I gripped the jade tooth she'd given me from my dad. I hadn't spirit-jumped back to the Empty since I'd demolished Ah-Puch, and even though I sort of wanted to check the place out again, I admit I was scared. Scared of what or who I might find there.

Shivering, I fished a matchbook from my pocket. My time was up. I had to master my fire skills—now. No way did I want to be the weak link in our rescue crew.

I struck a match, but a sea breeze blew out the flame. I tried again, cupping my hand around it. Playing with fire wasn't the hard part. It was pulling its energy inside and making it bigger, more useful.

A spark flew onto my jeans but left no mark. Thankfully, fire didn't incinerate my clothes. Ixtab had told me that my skin and anything touching it was nonflammable. Yeah, that was handy.

The tiny flame danced in the center of my palm. I tugged its energy into my hand, connecting to the power within my serpent leg while I willed the flame to grow bigger and bigger until it was the size of a lemon. That seemed to be my range—lemons!

With a deep breath, I expanded the fire another inch and then another. Strength pulsed in my back and arms as smoke streamed from my nose and eyes. My skin glowed as though lava were running through my veins. Heat seared my bones, growing so hot I thought I'd combust any second. And let me just say for the record that igniting into a blazing one-man bonfire is not my idea of a fun Friday night.

I panicked and quickly launched the mini meteor out over

the water. I watched it sail across the endless dark and...
caught a glimpse of something.

What the...?

I blinked and got to my feet. The fireball floated for a split
second, like someone had caught it. Then it fell into the sea.

Using the night vision I'd been born with, I could spot a
rowboat just beyond the breakers. The vessel rode the waves
closer and closer until I saw that there was something in the
boat. A hunched figure, wearing a hood. I peered closer. Was
it a fisherman?

When the boat rode up onto the sand, the hood dropped
away to reveal a mop of short dark hair. A girl.

Breath hitched in my throat.

I couldn't take my eyes off her.

Wait. That didn't sound right. I mean, it was *not* like when
I first met Brooks and saw her hundred-watt smile. This was
different.

The girl (she looked close to my age) just sat there, staring absently like a mannequin. Pale moonbeams cast dark
shadows across her thin face and wide catlike eyes. The boat
rocked as the waves hit it.

That's when Rosie came thundering down the beach,
snarling and growling like a maniac.

"Down, girl. Down!"

Her huge fangs glistened in the moonlight as she raced
ahead. In typical Rosie hellhound fashion, she wasn't listening to me. So I dropped Fuego and side-tackled her. "Stop!" I
hollered, my arms barely halfway around her thick body as
we rolled across the sand. "I said, DOWN!"

Still snarling, Rosie easily broke free of my grip, but she didn't advance any farther. Her black fur was sticking straight up along her spine, and for a second, I thought she might ignore me and incinerate this girl.

But then Rosie did something weird. She sniffed the air, relaxed her pose, and wandered over to the boat's bow, letting out breathy little whines.

If this girl were a threat, Rosie would for sure sniff it out. Just to be on the safe side, I picked up Fuego, ready to change my cane into spear mode. "What is she, Rosie?" I whispered, getting to my feet.

Rosie just kept sniffing and whining. Okay, so that meant the girl wasn't some assassin of the gods or a demon in disguise. Hopefully. Then I remembered the whisper I had heard. . . . *She's here.*

"Uh . . . you lost?" I asked, hoping the girl would snap out of it and say something. Anything. But she just kept staring ahead blankly. She had on a gray NASA T-shirt, some flannel pajama pants, and red cowboy boots. Who goes rowing in cowboy boots?

Was she even breathing?

I edged closer.

The girl collapsed like an empty pillowcase, smacking her head on the edge of the dinghy, where a long nail stuck out.

I leaped into the boat to check out the damage. Her forehead had a two-inch gash that was now bleeding. My stomach turned. (Yeah, I still hated blood.) Whimpering, Rosie leaned into the rowboat and pawed the girl gently. The she sniffed the wound and began to lick it.

"That's seriously disgusting," I told her as I watched the wound vanish. "Okay, that part's cool. But the whole licking thing? So gross!"

Ixtab had told me she'd discovered Rosie's "special" saliva when she was training her. *No other hellhound can do what she does. They're built to kill, not heal.*

A cool breeze swept across the beach as the girl opened her eyes slowly. I'll never forget the color—silvery blue, like a winter sky.

Oh boy, that's when things got tense. She shoved me away, scrambled out of the boat, crouched down, and, with a wave of her skinny arm, said, "AWAY!"

Come again? "Uh, you hit your head. Maybe you should sit down."

"Why are you still here? Where am I? Who are you? How...?" Her eyes darted around the dark beach. Her bobbed hair was jagged at the ends, like it had been cut with a razor. Then her eyes landed on Rosie and I expected her to go into freak-out mode, but instead she gasped. "Oh my gods! Is that Rosie? The hellhound?"

My defenses went up like a stone wall. "How do you know Rosie?"

Her expression went from fear to *I'm-going-to-Disneyland* excited in a single blink. "I don't believe it! If that's Rosie, then you're Zane, and I found you! I really found you. Just wait until Abuelo hears about this. He's going to go bananas."

"Whoa! How do you know my name? Who sent you?" I gripped my spear tighter, because even though she was small and looked pretty harmless, demons were masters of disguise.

Rosie rolled on the ground, stretching her legs all casual like. Whatever. The girl reached out a skinny finger and poked my arm. "Increíble."

I stepped back. "What's your deal?"

"Just making sure you're real and not one of my dreams." She reached down and scratched Rosie's belly like they were long-lost friends.

"Look," I said, "you can't just show up in the middle of the night and tell me you know me and Rosie . . . and . . . you better start talking."

She wiped her hair out of her eyes. "I knew magic was real, but this?"

"Magic. Right. How about we start with your name and why you're in your pajamas. In a rowboat. In the middle of the night."

She ran over to the boat, reached in, and pulled something out. A book?

"What is that?" I asked.

She lifted her icy gaze. "Your story . . ." Her voice dropped to an excited whisper. "The one the gods made you write."

4

••••

How had this girl gotten her hands on my story?

The gods had made it available to all the Maya sobrenaturals, of course. As for the "real" world, Jazz had promised to print and spread around the copies with my secret message so it could reach any possible godborns. But as time went on and I didn't hear from anyone, a part of me believed what Ixtab had told me: No godborns had survived.

"How did you get that?" I asked the girl. My heart was thumping frantically between excitement and fear.

She stood and said, "The library. Duh."

So Jazz had come through. I never should've doubted the giant.

The girl came closer. Her pajama pants were tucked into her boots. "Is this the island"—she flipped through the book until she found what she was looking for—"Holbox?" She pronounced it like most people do, *Hole-Box.*

"It's *ohl-bosch,*" I said. "It's Mayan for Black Hole and... never mind. Who *are* you?"

With a quick nod, she blurted, "Renata. Ren Santiago."

I was hoping for more than her name, but it was a start. "Okay, Ren... why are you here?"

She studied the book—my book—still gripped in her small hands. She looked up at me. "You called me here."

"Uh, I've never seen you before in my life."

She turned to the last page of the book and recited: "'If you can read this, you've got magic in your blood. Only another godborn would be able to see the words on these last few pages. Which is why I took the risk to write down the whole truth.'"

My mind flew in a gazillion directions as she continued. "'I was hoping to find you,'" she read more forcefully this time. "'Take it from me—someday, when you least expect it, the magic will call to you.'" She closed the book and gave me a smirk. "*You* called me."

In that moment, I had no words other than Brooks's "HOLY K!" The shout echoed over the crashing waves. And that was only the beginning. I pretty much word-vomited after that: "How'd you get here? How'd the magic call? Where are you from? Tell me everything, and start at the beginning."

Ren didn't answer. Not at first. Instead, she studied me carefully. "You're the son of—"

"Right," I interrupted. "Now, back to *my* questions?"

"So, I'm a godborn, too." She shook her head in disbelief. "That's what the book said. Only another godborn could read . . ." Her voice trailed off.

"Yeah, I wrote it. I know what it says. Let's start over. How'd you get here?" Maybe she was like Hondo and could only answer one question at a time.

"If you're being literal," she said, "the magic *called* me. The boat *brought* me."

That's when I noticed the boat had no oars, no motor. And if she had the blood of a god, how had she gotten through Ixtab's shadow magic? Or were only full-blooded gods locked out?

Rosie rolled onto her belly and began licking her paws. Maybe I wasn't asking the right questions. I tried again, my pulse racing. "Okay, so you read the book, the hidden words, and then what happened?"

Ren looked around with wide eyes. "This is amazing. I can't believe I'm here!"

I pushed my hair back, trying not to look *totally* impatient. This is how Brooks must've felt when she dropped into my boring life to try to explain that I was in the middle of some ancient prophecy. Except she was way better at this than I was. "Ren!"

She held her hands up. "Cálmate. I heard music. My dad's viola."

Then a terrible thought occurred to me. What if Ren was lying? What if she was just trying to infiltrate the island? I couldn't help it. It was too good to be true that another godborn had survived. I mean, it had been six whole months and nothing. Now, the night before I was going to leave on my quest to save Hurakan, she shows up? It didn't matter that she looked nice enough. If being part of the Prophecy of Fire—the one that destined me to release the god of death, darkness, and destruction—had taught me anything, it was that, in the Maya world, what you see is *not* what you get. Remember that.

"Take my hand," I said, stretching it toward Ren. "If you're a true godborn, then . . ."

"Telepathy," she said quietly as she placed her palm on mine. I opened my mind to her. *If you're a godborn, hop on one leg.*

She jerked free and frowned. "I'm not a circus animal!"

Rosie groaned, hiding her eyes behind her massive paws.

"Oh crap!" I hollered. "You really *are* a godborn. Or at least some kind of supernatural! It's the only way you could—"

"Read your mind."

"I *let* you. Big difference."

Ren tugged off her boots and wet socks and started to pace around barefoot. "Am I the first godborn to show up?"

"So far." *First?* Oh man, how many were out there?

Ren said, "That means, if there are others, then they haven't heard the call yet, or maybe..."

Wasn't this supposed to be *my* interrogation? "Let's just stick to you. Tell me everything, and don't leave out any details."

She cleared her throat and said, "After I finished the book—which was really good, by the way—I closed it and waited. I mean, not that I believe everything I read, but I totally know magic when I see it. Except nothing happened. I thought it was all a joke, and that was super depressing. But then tonight... I opened the book again and reread the last page—out loud this time—and within like five minutes, this song started to play. My dad's favorite." She sounded a little sad. "The music was far away, but then it got closer and closer. I could feel it pulling me like invisible hands. That's when I heard little feet scratching on my roof. At first I thought it was some cats or birds or something, but to be honest, the screeching freaked me out. I was going to wake my abuelo, but I thought, what could he do? So, I put on my boots and went to check things out. That's when the sky cracked open and these things..."

"Things?"

"Some kind of little flying creatures. I think they were hairy, but it was pretty dark." She said this so matter-of-factly you'd think she was used to bizarre happenings.

My mouth went dry. If some supernatural creatures had found her, then did the gods know about her? But how could they?

Ren went on. "I thought I was having another one of my nightmares, but these dudes were definitely real, because... they didn't leave when I told them to."

"Yeah," I grunted. "Monsters don't usually leave just because you ask."

She studied me for a second, then went on. "That's when my abuelo woke up and told me 'It's happening, and those beasts want to stop you.'"

"What... what was happening?"

"My destiny."

"Destiny."

"Are you going to let me tell this or not?"

"Right. Go on."

"We got in the car and raced through town, following the music," she said. "I didn't know my abuelo could drive like that. I kept asking him what I was supposed to do, and all he said was 'Follow the magic and don't look back.' So, I told him which way to drive. That's when we got to Sievers Cove."

"Where's that?"

"In Galveston." Her words came in a rush. "I got to the water, and an empty boat was waiting there. My abuelo gave me a blessing and told me to hurry. It was awful. I didn't want to leave him—I was scared those things would hurt him, but he said they weren't there for him. They were there for my magic. So, I got in the boat and promised I'd call when I got to wherever." She waved her hand through the air. "But then there were no oars and no way to get moving and those things were coming, and they had glowing eyes, and all I could think was, I do not want to die in my pajamas."

"*That's* what you were worried about?"

She rolled her eyes. "Thankfully, that didn't happen, because the boat started to move all by itself. And when I looked back to wave at my grandfather, a thick fog surrounded me, and I couldn't see anything. I was thinking this could be bad, but the music—my dad's music—calmed me. That's when I . . ." She hesitated for the first time. "I had an episode." Before I could even ask, she added, "The docs call them 'absence seizures,' but none of their medicine works. I totally zone out, lose all track of time, and I don't know what's going on around me. I've had them ever since I can remember. They don't hurt or anything. But they usually happen when I'm super stressed."

So that was her version of my bum leg—her supposed "weakness," which was really the key to her godborn power.

Rosie got to her feet and shook her massive body, sending flecks of sand flying everywhere. Then she took off down the beach like she'd spotted something to eat. I called after her, but she didn't listen. Typical.

I wanted to make sure I was following Ren's story. "You said your grandpa believes in magic, and he helped you get to the water, where the music was leading you, and—"

"He doesn't just believe it—he says our family *is* magic. That it's part of our heritage."

"Because of the Maya gods?"

"No, my dad's side is magic as in brujo. I had no idea my mom was a goddess!" Her face fell. "What . . . what do you think that makes me?"

"A witchy godborn?" Was there such a thing?

Ren tapped her knees with her fingers and let out a swish of air. "My abuelo used to tell me stories about my parents. How my dad fell in love with the 'wrong' woman." She made air quotes around the word *wrong*. "He called her some bad names. And said that someday I'd understand who I was and what kind of power was in me."

"Did he ever say anything about the Maya gods?"

"Nothing."

"What else did he say about your mom?"

"Just that she left us. She broke my dad's heart." She folded her arms over her chest. "He didn't like to talk about her."

Didn't? "What about your dad?" I asked. "What does he say?"

She scooped some sand into a small hill. "He died," she said softly. "A few years ago."

I felt bad for asking, but I had to know as much about her as possible if I was going to help her. Except I had no idea *how* to help her. I mean, when I put out the godborn call, I hadn't exactly thought about what I'd do *if* a godborn answered. "Hey, I'm sorry."

With a shrug, she added, "My dad used to tell me to ignore my abuelo and all the magic talk. He didn't like it. I think he was just trying to protect me. Him and Abuelo used to fight about it all the time. But I knew..." Her cool eyes zeroed in on me. "I knew I had magic in me, even if I couldn't do any cool tricks. And then I found your book and..."

Rosie lumbered back with a stack of driftwood in her mouth. Dropping the bundle onto the sand, she ignited it with her eyes.

"Thanks, Rosie," Ren said, warming her hands by the flames.

"Okay." I paced, trying to piece a godborn timeline together. "How old are you?"

"I turned thirteen a couple weeks ago."

I'd turned fourteen in December—she was younger than me by almost a year. That meant some goddess broke the Sacred Oath *after* Hurakan had.

"So you were never in hiding?" I asked. "Like a witness protection program or anything like that?"

Ren laughed. "I don't think Ixtab told you the truth about that. I've never been in hiding."

I had to remember that Ren had read the book. She knew everything there was to know about the Prophecy of Fire and my whole adventure. It was nice not having to explain the madness. I sat next to the fire. Even though I couldn't control my fire skills, something about a blaze always drew me in. Without thinking, I pulled a flame to me and began tossing it between my hands like a baseball.

"That's pretty awesome"—Ren's eyes were locked on my hands—"how you can use fire like that."

It was weird that Ren knew so much about me—practically

my whole life story—and yet I knew hardly anything about her, except that she had a magic-believing abuelo. I threw the fireball down the beach, and Rosie tore after it, bringing it back to me a second later.

The flames' flickering shadows played across the sand. Ren got to her feet. The shadows froze.

Then they leaned closer to her.

"Ren?"

"Yeah?"

"Uh . . . can you sit back down?"

"Why?"

I kept my eyes on the sombras that didn't follow her movement but instead seemed to loom over her. My pulse quickened. Maybe it was Ixtab's shadow magic? "I just need to test something."

The second Ren plunked onto the sand, the shapeless shadows wrapped around her. "What's wrong?" she asked.

I hesitated to say anything out loud. Who knew who might be listening, and we obviously weren't alone. "Do you see them?" I whispered.

Ren peered at me across the fire. "You mean the shadows? You can see them?"

I could barely nod. A giant lump throbbed in my throat. Who *was* this girl?

"They come and go," she said casually. "Abuelo calls them part of my magic. Sometimes they listen to me, sometimes they don't. Wanna see?" She closed her eyes. The shapeless shadows rose higher and higher until they looked like tall poles, wings sprouting from each of them. Then they collapsed just as quickly and disappeared. Ren opened her eyes. "See? Not very magical or useful, if you ask me."

"Can your grandpa do stuff with shadows?"

Ren shook her head. "Supposedly, magic doesn't run consistently through my family. And my dad hated the whole idea of it, so he wouldn't teach me. But I don't even know if the shadows are part of the magic, or being a godborn, or . . ." She let out a long sigh. "It's super frustrating not knowing who you really are."

It reminded me how I couldn't control fire very well. "So, you go into trances when you're stressed, shadows sometimes follow you, and you can sometimes make shapes out of them. Do they talk to you or anything?"

"I wish," Ren said.

Ren was right. We needed to know who her godly parent was, except I wasn't sure where to even begin looking. We couldn't exactly take out a want ad or put up a billboard. The gods had made it clear they wanted to be rid of godborns. (Like I said, jerks, right?)

So even if we found Ren's mom, it wasn't like we could throw a reunion party. Plus, I was leaving to go on my quest in just a few hours. Ren's problems were going to have to be put on hold. We'd call her abuelo, and then she'd have to wait here until I got back from this quest to figure out next steps.

Ren yawned loudly, and her eyelids drooped. "Now what?"

I tossed a broken shell into the water, thinking I could hardly wait to tell Brooks about Ren. She was going to flip. What would she think of this girl?

"The gods want to kill godborns, so . . . for now, you have

to stay on this island. We should figure out what those little flying creatures were and how they knew about you...or... No, we should definitely try to find out if you were followed."

"I should tell you..." She yawned again and laid her head on the sand. "The shadows...they can come out of..."

"Out of what?" But when I turned, the girl was fast asleep. "Ren?"

Then came an *eeekscritch*. From inside the boat.

Rosie and I launched to our feet simultaneously.

Eeekscritch.

I changed Fuego back into the spear as black smoke curled from Rosie's nose.

Crap!

Ren had definitely been followed.

5

Swirls of red fire burned at the center of Rosie's
eyes, which meant that whatever was inside that boat wasn't
here for surfing lessons. And with my luck, it was probably
gigantic and murderous and bloodthirsty.

Clouds of black smoke trailed from Rosie's nose, and her
ears were standing at attention as I gripped my spear and
stalked toward the rowboat. The shallow waves tipped it back
and forth. My palms were slick with sweat.

The warm water soaked my sneakers as a west wind raced
toward us. Craning my neck, I peered inside the dinghy just
so I wouldn't have to get any closer than I had to. But there
was nothing inside. Cero.

I'd have thought I was hearing things, except Rosie's killer
senses told me *something* was here. Was the something invisible? I didn't know if that was better or worse.

"What do you sense, Rosie?" I whispered. Her hackles
stood on end, and a low, deadly growl sounded from deep in
her throat.

Then that horrible *eekscritch* sound, like metallic branches
scraping glass, ricocheted across the beach, and I couldn't be
sure where it was coming from. But Rosie kept her laser focus
on the boat. Which, by the terrible way, was still swaying like
an invisible hand was rocking it.

That's when a small shadow, no bigger than a fist, slid over the boat's edge and began to grow into a tall column.

Before I could blink twice, three shadow monsters emerged from the column, spreading their colossal wings. Long insect-like arms and legs sprouted from their swollen, pulsing bodies.

Rosie's dark roar echoed over the thrashing sea.

"DEAD!" I screamed.

Rosie exploded into killer-hellhound mode, shooting fireballs out of her mouth and eyes. But the flames made contact with absolutely nothing (unless you count the now-blazing dinghy). I mean, how do you kill shadows? Shadows that were morphing and growing faster than I could say *dead*?

I threw my spear and, with flawless accuracy, it zipped right through the center monster's bulbous gut, causing a giant hole that closed before Fuego could circle back to me. There was no blood, no guts, and the thing kept growing!

Then it started to laugh. This deep chain-smoker-about-to-hack-up-his-lungs laugh.

I glanced over my shoulder at Ren. She was still curled up on the sand. How was she sleeping through all this? She was so helpless like that—I had to protect her.

The monsters rose to at least twenty feet. Pointed reptilian-like tails thrashed through the sea, causing massive waves.

Eeeeeek. Eeeeeek.

I covered my ears. Their high-frequency cries pierced my brain like an ice pick. Rosie launched herself at one of the beasts, bouncing off it and into a huge swell.

"Rosie!"

The monsters lunged at me.

At the same moment, Brooks in hawk form swooped down from the dark sky. Her enormous wings (which, by the way, I know for a fact can crush boulders) did nothing to stop the shadows. How was it that the forms could create massive waves and attack us, but we couldn't manage to even touch them?

One monster swiped Brooks away, sending her crashing into the violent black sea.

Clutching Fuego tightly, I dove beneath the waves, panic choking every breath. Brooks had gotten better at swimming after all my lessons, but she still hated the water and, in this kind of freak-out mode, she could drown.

I thrust my arms and legs through the water. Something smashed into me, sending me spiraling under. When I came up for air, Brooks was in human form, flailing, her head barely above the surface.

"Something's got my leg!" she screamed.

"Hang on!" I plunged beneath the dark sea and saw that vines of seaweed were wrapped around Brooks's thigh. Using my spear, I sliced through the slick ropes, and when I came up, she clung to me. "Get on my shoulders," I hollered.

For once, she didn't argue. She climbed up, and with one thrust, I hurled her into the air, where she changed back into hawk form. She circled high above the shadow monsters, which had raised their massive tails like they were getting ready to pound me.

Instinctively, I lifted my spear, ready to launch it, when . . .

"NO!" Ren's voice carried through the dark. I spun to see her standing on the shore, arms outstretched. Her ragged hair blew in the wind.

As if time had stopped, the sea stilled.

The shadows' tails froze in mid-strike.

Then they broke into a million pieces. Bit by bit they fluttered into the sea like ash.

Rosie was right behind me as I rushed back to Ren, snatching up Fuego.

"Are . . . are you okay? How . . . did you stop them?"

Brooks landed with a rush of air and changed into her human form. "What the holy Xib'alb'a, Zane? Who is this? And what were those things?" Her eyes blazed. Yup, she was furious. And scared.

Ren gawked at Brooks. "You're . . . you're Brooks. The nawal."

Brooks shot me a glare. "Spill it, Obispo."

I told her everything. I sort of expected her to gasp or something when she found out Ren was a godborn, but she just kept her poker face and asked the girl, "Where did those shadow things come from?"

Okay, no time for *Nice to meet you.*

"Did they follow you here?" I asked. "Or were they the shadows from earlier?" But hadn't Ren said those were harmless?

Ren chewed her bottom lip. "They didn't follow me."

"How can you be sure?" I said.

"Because I created them."

"Whoa!" I stepped back, pushing a mop of wet hair off my forehead.

"You *what*?!" Brooks cried.

"It's not what you think," Ren argued. "I tried to tell you before I fell asleep. The shadows come out of my dreams. The monsters . . . they aren't exactly real. . . ."

"Hang on!" I tugged off my soaked shoes. "What do you mean they weren't real? They nearly caused a tidal wave! They tried to drown us. Dreams don't do *that*."

Ren wrapped her arms around her waist. "I mean, they're real, but . . ." She shook her head. "Remember the shadows earlier? How I couldn't control them?"

I nodded.

Brooks scowled at me.

Ren said, "Well, they show up in my dreams, too, and sometimes they sort of come into this world, but once I wake up and tell them to leave, they vanish. The first time it happened, I was maybe five. Abuelo told me not to be afraid, to use my power to control the shadows. But no matter how hard I try, I can't make them do anything except leave. . . ." Her voice trailed off and was swallowed by the pounding surf.

I knew the feeling of having a power I couldn't use.

"So, the shadows," Brooks said evenly. "Are they always monsters?"

"Not always," Ren said. "After my dad died, I woke up from a dream about him . . . and I caught a glimpse of a shadow—I knew it was him. But the second I saw him here, in this world, he vanished."

I thought about Hurakan, how I would give anything to meet him in the Empty again or even to dream about him. It wouldn't be long before I rescued him and . . . Okay, I wasn't sure what would happen after that. I guess I hadn't thought about *after*.

Brooks frowned. "Have your dreams—nightmares, whatever—ever hurt someone?"

"No," Ren said. "And Abuelo told me that only those with magic in their blood can see them."

That explained why Mom and Hondo and the rest of the island's residents hadn't woken up. "I don't think they come from your dreams, Ren," I said. "I think they're shadows that are already here."

Brooks paced, rubbing her chin. "And maybe they kind of take shape as you dream."

"That's what those monsters did," I said. "It was like they were protecting you."

Brooks glanced at me. Uh-oh. She had that *this-isn't-good* look, and the last time I saw that, we were almost choked to death by a bunch of demon runners at a Jack in the Box.

My head was pounding, and my eyes were blurry. "We should get some rest," I said. Then I added quickly, "I mean, as long as you don't have any more nightmares with monsters or anything else that could kill us."

"I'll try," Ren said. "It doesn't happen that much, I swear. But if it does, just throw water on my face or something."

I was hoping Brooks (having been a sobrenatural a lot longer than me) would have some answers. Any answer.

Okay, maybe an answer that sounded exactly like *There's absolutely nothing to worry about.* That would've totally been my preference.

We headed toward the house.

"You're just like Zane described you in the book," Ren said to Brooks. "So—"

"So *brave*," I blurted. Geez, why didn't she just ask for Brooks's autograph already?

"Brave," Brooks echoed, staring me down with her fierce eyes. Luckily, she hadn't read the book. I hoped she'd never *ever* get her hands on it. I really needed to burn that thing! I looked around for it and saw that it was half-buried under the sand near the dying campfire. I'd go back and toss it in the embers later, when the girls weren't around.

Ren and Rosie strode ahead and out of earshot.

"Brooks, you really have no clue about those shadows?"

"I'm not a Maya encyclopedia of the supernatural, Zane."

"Someone should really write *that* book."

"I've never even heard of anything like this," Brooks muttered. She stopped walking and turned to me. "What do we do now? Abandon our plans?"

"No. We're going through with them," I said. "She can stay at my house. We just have to make sure she calls her grandpa first, to let him know she's safe. And then hope my mom doesn't freak out."

"Because some godborn just showed up?"

"Because we're going to rip a hole in the sky so we can go on a quest that could get us killed."

"*If* we can rip a hole."

"Just be ready," I said. "I'll figure it out."

Brooks blew a curl off her face. "Ren can sleep at my place." Then she added, "But only if Rosie stands guard."

I laughed it off to make Brooks feel better, but as we walked up the beach, all I kept thinking was *Even a hellhound can't kill a nightmare.*

6

With Rosie stationed at Brooks's door as killer-hellhound-watchdog, I slept in the hammock just outside the casita. Well, I didn't exactly sleep. My mind kept replaying the fight with the colossal shadow monsters. Between that, Rosie's hellish snoring, and thinking about how to rescue Hurakan within four days and what to do with Ren in the meantime, I didn't get any rest until the sun began to rise. The next thing I heard was "Hey, wake your flojo butt up."

That was Hondo smacking my leg as he stood over me.

I startled, tipping the hammock and dumping myself onto the sand-covered patio. "What time is it?" I said, clumsily getting to my feet. I glanced over at Brooks's door. Rosie was no longer there. Did that mean Brooks and Ren were gone, too?

"Where's Rosie?" I grabbed Fuego from the hammock and leaned against it.

Why couldn't everyone at least stay put until I figured things out?

"I saw her chasing a seagull down the beach earlier," he said. "It's after nine. Why'd you sleep out here? I mean, I know you have a thing for Brooks, but this is kind of stalkerish, dude."

"Nine?!" I raced across the courtyard, stumbling over the water hose. "Why didn't someone wake me?"

"You have a hot date or something?" Hondo followed me all the way into my room, laughing.

"It's not like that."

"Then what's it like?"

It's like this, I wanted to say. *Massive shadow beasts stormed into this world because some godborn shadow witch showed up in a boat with no oars. And today is the day I'm leaving to save my dad, who is trapped in a water park in South Dakota, but there's an invisible wall keeping me on this island that I have to find a way to bust through.*

I'd thought about that stupid wall all night. There was no way I'd get through it without the jade, but something was telling me to save the amulet's power. We just might need it on this quest. So, I had come up with another possible solution. A dangerous, crazy, *hope-I-don't-get-my-head-eaten-off-by-a-demon* solution. Now all I had to do was convince Brooks.

"Hey, Earth to Zane." Hondo waved his hand in front of my face, snapping me out of my daydream. "What's your problem?"

"Who said I had a problem?" I grabbed a T-shirt out of my dresser drawer and tugged it over my head.

"Uh-huh. Don't forget you've got afternoon duty at the shop."

"You think you could take my shift?" I poked around the room for my sneakers. A knot of guilt settled in my gut. I hadn't thought about how I'd say good-bye to my mom. The last time I set out on a quest, I'd only left her a note, and she was pretty furiosa with me afterward.

Hondo stepped in front of me. "Give it up, bro. What's

going on?" I'd grown another two inches the last couple of months, so Hondo seemed even shorter than before. But it didn't make him any less intimidating.

"What?" I asked innocently.

"I saw the burned-out boat."

I tried to look casual. "Oh, the boat—ha, yeah, that was Rosie. She . . . uh . . . she got a little too excited."

"I guess we owe someone a new boat, then?"

Oops! What was I supposed to say to *that*? "It . . . I found it abandoned last night. Had a hole in the hull. Total hunk of junk. I bet someone was just trying to dump the thing."

Hondo rubbed the stubble on his chin. "If the boat had a hole, how did it get there?"

"How should I know? Maybe it got the hole right before it got to shore, or . . ." I gave a light shrug. "Or maybe it was magic."

"Magic . . ." Hondo muttered as he reached behind him, pulled something out of his waistband, and flashed Ren's book. "Like this?"

I stared at the libro. *Crap!* I'd forgotten to go back for it last night.

I tried to snatch the book, but Hondo swept it out of reach before I could even touch it. His reflexes were quicker than ever. He'd once been a champion wrestler, and he'd taught me all sorts of moves that, let's be honest, saved my butt from plenty of demons—and a few bullies, too. But these last few months, he'd been training like I'd never seen him train before. It was like he was on his own mission. He got up at dawn to run, lift weights, and practice ninja moves like backflips and one-armed handstands. He even started yoga to become more flexible but made me promise not to tell anyone. Maybe he secretly wanted to try out for *American Ninja Warrior* or something.

"Good description of me as a tank, by the way," Hondo said. "You really think I'm that strong?"

Okay, he'd read the book. "Truth paper wouldn't let me lie, remember? So, everything in there is one hundred percent true."

"I scanned most of it—went right to the parts about me. Then I got to the chapter about those poisonous meatballs that sent me into sleep-hell mode...." His smile turned into a frown. "Just reading about it made me feel like I was reliving the nightmare." He clenched his jaw. "If I ever meet up with those sons of—those loser twins again..."

I nodded. "Can I have the book back? I, uh..." I didn't want Brooks to get her hands on it. What would she think if she saw all that stuff I'd written about her being beautiful, and like the sun, and pretty much the fiercest, most incredible person I'd ever met?

"I got you, bro. You don't want Brooks to read it," Hondo said. "I bet she wouldn't be surprised. I mean, the way you look at her? I thought I taught you how to be cool, man."

My head felt like it was on fire. I didn't want to talk about this anymore. I had bigger things on my mind, like saving my dad, and dream barriers, and living nightmares, and stupid invisible walls.

"You should burn that thing," I finally said.

"Dude! That'd be, like, sacrilegious. You're not supposed to burn books."

"You don't even read."

He held up the libro and flashed a smile. "I do now. I can't wait to get to the part about me storming the Old World."

"Whatever." I turned to leave, but Hondo jumped in front of me, blocking the door.

"Brooks is still zonked out, if that's where you're headed, so just a warning to stay away. You know she sleeps like the dead and hates being woken up," he said. "But I met the new girl."

I tried not to look stunned as I stopped in my tracks and gazed down at Hondo. I mean, what was I expecting, that I'd bring Ren here and no one would notice her? I guess I just thought I could introduce her myself. "Right. Ren."

"I was doing my morning training—"

"You mean yoga."

Hondo blew a frustrated breath. "I mean *training on the beach*, and that's when I saw her out on the playa, staring out at the sea like some sad ghost. Like she was waiting for someone."

Yeah, like an army of shadow monsters, I thought. "Where is she now?"

"She went to town with your mom, to check things out."

Ren was with Mom? I groaned. That meant Ren would tell her everything. It's a gift my mom has—she can get the truth out of anyone. And once Mom found out Ren was a godborn, she'd ask a million questions, questions that might lead to her trying to keep me here. Believe me, her guilt trips were far more effective than *any* invisible wall.

"So, who is she?" Hondo asked.

It wasn't that I didn't *want* to tell Hondo about Ren or even my plan to save my dad. But I'd learned from Brooks that knowledge can put people's lives in danger.

"Uh—she got here last night. She . . . she's just a girl."

"Right." His eyes narrowed suspiciously. "Comrades don't keep secrets from one another."

I heard Mom's footsteps coming down the hall. "Zane?" A second later, she barged into the room, knocking Hondo in the shoulder before he jumped out of the way. She had on a light blue shirt that was embroidered with yellow thread: MAYA JOURNEYS (that's the super-original name Hondo gave our business, which had started out as a bike and surf shop and had recently expanded to include island tours). Her hair was tucked under her matching blue baseball cap. "Has anyone seen Rosie? I've got some raw chicken necks for her."

"Haven't seen her," Hondo said.

Mom threw her hands on her hips. "Hondo, I thought you'd replaced the tram's tires. We need the vehicle for a tour group from Canada today. Zane, you're scheduled for this afternoon. Okay? And before you even ask, it's not for windsurfing. It's for an island expedition."

Even though driving the big golf cart was fun, I hated giving tours. Mostly because I'd circled the twenty-six miles that was Isla Holbox a thousand million times. But never once had I taken tourists to the Beast. First, because they couldn't see it if they wanted to (thanks to shadow magic), and second, it pretty much hid a gateway to hell, and I didn't think our liability insurance would cover that.

Mom stared at Hondo like she was waiting for something. "The tires?"

"I'm on it," Hondo said to Mom. Then he turned to me. "I almost forgot—Ms. Cab called. Said it was important." Then, with a halfhearted salute, he said. "Later...comrade."

After Hondo left, Mom turned back to me. "We need to talk. About Ren."

I craned my neck down the hall. "Where is she?"

"I took her on a little walking tour around town. We started chatting—about last night." She gave me the Mom look that said *I know what you're up to.*

"Okay, but where is Ren now?" I asked, trying to avoid what Mom really wanted to talk about. "Did she go back to Brooks's?"

"She's at Antonia's."

"Ms. Cab's?! Why?"

I hadn't even decided how to help Ren yet, and already she had confided in my mom and cozied up to Ms. Cab, who was filling her head with who knew what. And I didn't have time to chase this girl all over town.

"Ren said she wanted to meet her," Mom stated simply, like she always followed teenagers' directions. *Not!* "But the more important thing is," she added, trying to keep her voice calm, "why didn't you tell me you put out a call to other godborns? What were you thinking, Zane?"

"Why didn't you tell me my dad was a Maya god?" I regretted the words as soon as I said them. I knew Mom had just been trying to protect me.

"I've told you all I know, Zane."

She was right. Once we got settled on the island, Mom had spilled everything about my dad, including how much she had loved him even if it wasn't meant to be.

She tilted her head. "I just don't want there to be any more secrets between us."

Thanks, Ren. Didn't the girl know better after reading my story? Couldn't she see that my mom was the biggest worrier of all time across the span of human history?

"I . . . I had to warn other godborns, Mom. They deserve to know the truth. And I thought that maybe I could help them. Hang on—did Ren call her grandpa?"

"They were on the phone for some time. And then . . ."

"Then what?"

"I invited him down. He's on his way as we speak."

"Mom! He could be followed. He can't just fly here!"

"Well, he is." She let out a frustrated sigh. "We'll figure it out once he gets here. Right now, I have to get to the shop. Please, Zane, promise me you won't do anything crazy or dangerous with Ren."

I felt rotten. Worse than rotten. How could I make a promise there was no way I was going to keep? "Okay," I lied. "I won't do anything crazy with Ren." I mean, *crazy* is totally subjective, right? And not the same thing as dangerous. And Ren wasn't coming, so . . .

Mom glanced around my room. "How about picking this place up?"

Here's the thing about being part god. You sort of think you shouldn't have to clean up your room and have dish duty and all the other chores that are so boring. But Mom didn't care that I was a godborn who could shoot fire (sort of). To her, I was "still her son who needed raising." Whatever.

"Sure, Mom." Better not to argue, which would only make her stick around longer.

She tugged on my chin and was gone. As soon as she left, I shoved the piles of clothes and other junk under the bed, got ready in thirty seconds, and hurried over to Brooks's.

How could she sleep at a time like this?

I pounded on the door with Fuego's jade handle.

Silence.

"Brooks!" *Pound. Pound. Pound.*

The door swung open.

Brooks stood there in a pair of cotton pajama pants and a plain yellow T-shirt. Her hair was a heap of tangled curls. "Holy K, Zane! It's nine thirty. Why didn't you wake me?" She skip-hopped on one leg while slipping an ankle boot on the other.

"Um ... you're putting on your boots, but you're still in your pajamas," I pointed out.

"No kidding, Obispo! Who has time to get dressed when we're supposed to be..." She stopped herself and looked around. "Where's Ren?"

I explained everything that had happened while she was snoring away.

Brooks tied her unruly hair up into a sloppy ponytail and folded her arms across her chest. "She's at Cab's? Good. I'm sure they'll have loads to talk about. And we're wasting time standing around here."

"We have to go get her."

Brooks frowned. "We have a quest. And in case you forgot, it's got an expiration date."

"Brooks, we can't leave without . . . I mean, we don't even know if she was followed, or what those monsters chasing her were . . . and now her grandpa is coming down."

"Great. Then she's not alone. Now can we get going already? I have some ideas about how to get across that stupid barrier."

"Really?"

"Burn it down. Rosie can do the honors."

My shoulders slumped. "Pretty sure fire isn't going to destroy the shadow magic."

"Then how?" Brooks's nostrils flared. "Ooh . . . I know," she said sarcastically. "Why don't you just march into hell and ask Ixtab to let you off the island?"

"Are you coming to Ms. Cab's or not?"

"She doesn't trust nawals, remember?" Brooks's eyes searched mine. "I'll pack the backpacks. And you have exactly thirty minutes."

7

Fuego and I hurried down the playa.

Sandpipers skittered across the sand, seagulls and pelicans circled in the air, palm leaves rustled in the breeze, and the sunlight created shimmering trails across the clear blue sea. A few small fishing boats lingered past the waves. Ixtab had picked a pretty stellar hiding spot for us, but as beautiful as the "black hole" was, I guess I always knew deep down I wasn't going to hide out there forever.

I headed toward town, crossing the main road that led to Ms. Cab's. A few dozen tourists and locals cruised the main road in their shorts, flip-flops, and straw hats. People sat at outdoor tables, where stray dogs relaxed in the shade. The smells of coffee, fresh-baked pan dulce, and tortillas hung in the air. My stomach grumbled.

Ms. Cab's casita was neon pink with a palapa roof and surrounded by a dozen leaning palm trees that, to be honest, looked like they were made of rubber and could catapult cannon balls. A green hand-painted sign hung on the rickety wooden gate: CASA DEL ESPÍRITU. House of the spirit.

When Ms. Cab didn't answer the door, I headed around the side to the back patio, which opened to a shadowy jungle. I stared up at the crowd of colorful birds of all sizes peering down at me from the trees like they wanted to peck out my eyes. Now that Ms. Cab's mission to protect me was over, she'd found a *new* mission—to rescue hurt birds. Ever since Ixtab had turned her into a chicken for a short time, Ms. Cab could actually speak bird, which helped them trust her.

Just then, Ms. Cab stepped out of the wide doorway, where sheer drapes fluttered in the breeze. "Zane Obispo, our next guest."

Why did Ms. Cab's voice sound funny? It was like she'd been screaming to jams all night. And what was with that weird greeting? *Our next guest?*

I peered behind her. "Hey, Ms. Cab. Where's Ren?"

"Take your place in that chair," Ms. Cab said, pouring me a glass of iced tea (was that dirt or sand twirling in between the ice cubes?). At the center of the small circular patio table was a plate of chocolate squares. "Homemade chocolate made from fresh-roasted cacao beans. Have some," she said, adjusting a gold cuff on her wrist.

Her face was darker than usual. She must have done some intense sun-worshipping recently.

I almost drooled as I snapped off a square of chocolate. "Is Ren still here?"

"Oh, yes. The girl with tangled hair and tangled thoughts. She went to the market for me. She'll return shortly. Sit. We need to talk."

I set Fuego down and planted myself in a worn equipale chair, thinking, *Ren's just gotten here and already she's an errand girl?* The chair's leather creaked.

Ms. Cab sat like she had a stiff back. "Would you like to hear about my vision? It's a juicy one."

"Sure."

Ms. Cab was a nik' wachinel, a Maya seer, and she'd been assigned the job of watching over me since I was born. She was my neighbor back in New Mexico, where she'd worked as a phone psychic. But she'd never been what you'd call a *good* psychic. She was pretty hit-or-miss and hadn't even foreseen Rosie getting killed by that stupid demon runner and being sent to Xib'alb'a. But on Holbox, Cab's seer powers had dried up completely, because she couldn't see anything past the shadow magic that surrounded the island.

I chose my words carefully. "But, uh . . . doesn't the shadow magic mess with your sight?"

"Pish to shadow magic and the gods! Their days on prime-time are over, Zane. Why aren't you eating the chocolate? I worked all day in the kitchen for you."

Primetime?

I took a bite of the candy, and my mouth pretty much exploded—it was sweet, fiery, nutty, and bitter all at the same time. It slipped down my throat like velvet.

"Yes, that's good." Ms. Cab smiled as she patted her fore-head with a white napkin. When she set it down, it was streaked dark brown. It reminded me of that self-tanning lotion one of Hondo's old wrestling buddies used to slather on before a match. Why was she using that stuff?

"So, tell me, Zane." Her tone shifted to concerned guidance counselor. "How will you ever leave?"

My heart rolled over. She knew! How? Brooks would never tell anyone. And Ren hadn't heard about our plan. . . . I had underestimated Ms. Cab's seeing ability. But I still tried to throw her off track. "I don't know what you're talking about...."

"Denial is an ugly thing. But I'm here to help." She tilted her head and nodded sympathetically. "Sometimes people don't know where else to turn." Her left eye twitched like a gnat had flown into it.

I wasn't about to confide in Ms. Cab. She wasn't my protector anymore. "Like I said, I wasn't planning on doing..." My brain stumbled on the next word, and I felt suddenly lost, like I couldn't remember what I was trying to say. Wait, what had Ms. Cab just told me?

Ms. Cab took a swig of tea and banged her glass down on the wooden table. My hands began to tremble uncontrollably. What was wrong with me? *Focus, Zane. Focus.*

"And they said you were smart, that you'd be difficult." Ms. Cab leaned closer. "But you're like all the others."

Others? "Ms. Cab, you're not making sense." Had she been drinking? My tongue felt suddenly thick and numb, like I'd been sucking on ice cubes all morning. Why were words so hard to form? I looked down at the plate of chocolate squares, wondering what she'd put in them.

Ms. Cab's mouth parted into a barely there smile. "I know things, Zane. Big things. Are you calling me stupid?"

"What? No...I just..." The words lodged in the back of my throat, and a sudden brain freeze gripped me. I squeezed my eyes closed and swallowed a few times, waiting for it to pass.

"Are you all right, Zane?"

I nodded automatically, but I definitely wasn't all right.

Ms. Cab removed a piece of paper from her pocket. Her hands were so dried and cracked it looked like she hadn't used moisturizer in a thousand years. "I wrote it down so I would not forget anything important."

"I . . . I really gotta go."

"*Go?*" Ms. Cab snorted. "Don't you see, Zane? You can never leave."

"*Never leave,*" a parrot echoed. "*Never leave.*"

My stomach clenched. I suddenly felt light-headed and weighed down at the same time.

"Now, let me try and read this." She held up the paper, and her face twisted, her eyes shifted, and her jaw clenched. "Why don't you read it to me?" She pushed the sheet across the table.

I looked down and began reading the words silently.

"Out loud," she demanded.

The words blurred in and out of focus. "'Ixtab didn't want to save you,'" I read. "'She wanted to hide you, to keep you from realizing your true potential and power.'" I looked up at Ms. Cab.

"Go on," she chirped. "You're doing fine. A definite C-plus for effort."

"This doesn't make sense," I said.

"Just finish."

I didn't want to read more, but the words came out of my mouth anyway. "'She crafted this whole illusion. Zane, you must know she's the queen of trickery. It's all been a trap. Ha. Ha.'"

"A round of applause, ladies and gentlemen!" Ms. Cab whooped and loosened the belt of her yellow dress. That's when I noticed streaks of mud across the tie. "Two big blows," she said. "Ixtab betrayed you, and we have something you want. And the most delicious part? You have no way of getting it, no way off this island. Where is the justice in this world?"

Anger raced through my veins, and just as suddenly, I felt a sharp pain in my back, like I'd been stabbed with an ice dagger. I gasped and with a single thought, I changed Fuego into spear status.

"No need for violence," Ms. Cab said.

I wanted to launch Fuego at this version of Ms. Cab, but my legs buckled. Actually, just my human leg buckled. I stood on my shorter, storm runner leg, wondering if it was strong enough to hop me out of there.

Ms. Cab laughed.

"Who are you?" I demanded. "Where's the real Ms. Cab?" She had to be some supernatural in disguise.

Cold sweat dripped down my face, and my insides felt like a giant fist was wringing them out. Uncontrollable shivers gripped me as my mind stumbled over all my memories of Ixtab and everything she'd ever told me. How she had once pretended to be my enemy and had sent an alux and demon runners after me to trick the gods into thinking she was on their side. How she'd made the gods believe I was dead, and how she'd given me the truth paper to write my story on.

A rush of cold snaked through me. I looked down at my hands. Ropy black veins bulged beneath my skin. I could feel the freezing sludge pushing through my veins, forcing my heart to work overtime. I panted, still clutching my gut in agony as I collapsed to the ground.

"Almost there," Ms. Cab said softly. "Just let it come, Zane."

This demon version of Ms. Cab reached into her dress pocket and pulled out a small red bird. Was it stuffed? All I could do was lie there frozen, staring up at her with eyes I could barely move. Using a small knife from the table, she split the bird's chest open, and a flurry of tiny winged beetles escaped.

Their shells sparkled green like they had emeralds growing on their backs.

The bedazzled beetles swarmed me, climbing all over my body, their teeny feet stepping across every inch of my skin, up my cheeks and across my scalp. I used to think snakes were the most repulsive creatures in the world. I was so wrong.

I wanted to scream. The freezing cold was pulling me under, to a place I didn't think I'd ever escape. For half a second, I imagined jumping to the Empty. The jade tooth was always tied around my neck, but what good would that do? My spirit would be safe while my body would still be here fossilizing at Monster Cab's feet.

"Map him well, little friends," she practically sang to the beetles.

Map . . . ?

Monster Cab drew closer, stooping to watch her insects stomp all over me, flutter their glittering wings near my eyes, and poke their spindly legs inside my ears.

Ms. Cab said, "Almost done."

I only needed her to come a few inches closer. *Come on. That's it.*

The second she was within striking distance, I swept my

storm runner leg across the intruder's ankles, bringing her to the ground with a loud thud. The beetles on my leg startled and buzzed into the air. Good first move, but what now? I couldn't exactly fight her off while I was lying there like a corpse. Stiffly, she got back to her feet and popped her spine with a loud *craccckkk*.

"*Tsk, tsk, tsk,*" she uttered, waving her finger. "I'm not the enemy, Zane."

Right. Because friends feed friends to bugs!

The beetles swarmed all around her before settling back on my storm runner leg. Then, out of nowhere, a hazy image floated in front of me, but it was like I was in a train and the scenery was humming by too fast for me to catch all the details: rolling gray-green hills with outcroppings of deep red rocks. A stream rushing through a deep canyon. Flecks of floating cotton. Then the images slowed long enough for me to see a plot of dirt. Written on it were the words *Help us. Before it's too late.* Cold sweat dripped into my eyes and the pictures vanished.

My muscles hardened, my blood slowed. I was turning into a human Popsicle. I needed heat, but the sun was tucked behind the thicket of trees. I managed to close my eyes, and with single-minded concentration, I channeled my energies from my godborn leg, drawing on its power. Then I felt it. A heat source was nearby.

Rosie.

Yes!

Fake Cab looked around wildly like she could sense Rosie, too.

"Now!" she screamed to the insects.

A second later, Rosie stalked around the corner, smoke curling from her nose as she grunted wildly. Right behind my hellhound was Brooks, her eyes ablaze. "Where's Zane?"

If she'd only looked down, she would have seen me frozen like a wax statue on the ground.

The winged beetles lifted in a frenzy, and I could feel pinpricks in my hands like I was thawing out. But it wasn't happening fast enough. In a flurry of arm gestures, Monster Cab directed the insects back into the stuffed bird's chest.

"¡Ándale!" she cried as she closed up the bird's chest with a single tap of her bracelet. Then she tossed the bird into the air, and the thing flew away.

"Tell me!" Brooks hollered. "Or I release the hellhound."

Cab inched back and began to pant. She swayed, clutched her stomach. Her eyes grew three sizes too big. "What's happening? Where am I?" She rubbed her forehead nervously. Was she turning back into the real Ms. Cab?

I heard footsteps. Clipped and confident. Mr. O appeared, carrying a paper sack. "I brought mangoes," he announced cheerily.

"Get back, Mr. Ortiz!" Brooks ordered.

"Zane?" Ms. Cab rushed over to me. "When did you get here? Are you all right?"

My words finally came. "No! You just tried to freeze me and feed me to your bugs!"

Ms. Cab shook her head. "What are you talking about? Why would I do such a thing?"

Brooks noticed me for the first time. "Zane! You okay?"

I managed a small nod as Brooks's eyes flew back to Ms. Cab.

Mr. O asked, "Por qué you are on the floor?"

With an epic roar, Rosie lunged twenty feet and landed within a foot of me and Ms. Cab.

"Rosie?" Ms. Cab said softly.

Brooks stood at my dog's side scowling.

A dangerous growl sounded from Rosie's throat. Brooks leaned closer, keeping her hawk eyes leveled on Ms. Cab. Then, in an even but angry voice, she said, "DEAD."

Flames erupted from Rosie's eyes and mouth. I rolled to my knees.

Just in time to see a cyclone of blue fire swallow Ms. Cab.

8

Mr. O cried, "¡Mi amor!"

Mangoes tumbled across the patio. Birds scattered from the trees. Bright blue flames engulfed Ms. Cab as her screams rose into the air.

"No!" I threw myself on top of her to try to extinguish the blaze. The moment I grabbed hold of her, the flames twisted tightly around me, a hurricane of heat. I could feel my strength returning, and all the cold melted away as the fire raced through my blood, healing me.

But where was Ms. Cab? Time slowed—maybe it stopped. The blue fire began to pulse. And then came the same whispering voice I'd heard last night.

Eating the chocolate was a bad idea.

Who are you? I asked telepathically.

You'll find out soon enough.

The flames died, and the first thing I saw was Monster Cab. Her face was melting off in waxy-looking chunks. I jumped back, watching in stunned silence as columns of shadowy smoke rose into the air.

"¿Qué es eso?" Mr. O breathed. "Where is mi amor?"

"An imposter," Brooks hissed. "I knew it."

The thing's skin dripped to the ground in a sizzling heap of goop that smelled like canned spinach and burning hair.

All that was left of Monster Cab was a lumpy statue made of hard, cracked mud, its expression frozen with terrified eyes and a wide contorted mouth.

My head was spinning. My ears rang, and my bones vibrated. Who was that guy talking to me? *You'll find out soon enough?* I already didn't like him.

Brooks rushed over and socked me in the arm. "I told you not to come here!"

A loud racket came from inside the house, like someone had knocked over a whole shelf of encyclopedias. We all rushed in. The small sala was quiet. Muddy footprints led us around the stacks of books and into the sunny blue kitchen, where the refrigerator was lying on its side. And behind it? Ren and the real Ms. Cab were sitting on the floor, tied back-to-back. Their hands and feet were bound, and their mouths were gagged with dishcloths.

"Ren!" I blurted.

"¡Mi amor!" Mr. O cried.

We freed them quickly and helped them up. Ren rubbed her wrists. "It's all my fault. . . . I should have waited—"

"For us!" Brooks grumbled.

Mr. O put his arm around Ms. Cab. "Antonia . . . Gracias a Dios."

Ms. Cab looked like she might hug him, but then she scowled and marched back outside to take a look at the burned statue. "First I'm turned into a chicken, then I'm gagged and tied up by a mud person who left tracks all over my house!"

Ren stared at what was left of the creepy version of Ms. Cab. "I even tried to get the shadows to untie us, but nothing worked," she said. She was wearing some of Brooks's clothes: a plain green T-shirt and a pair of jean shorts that were too big and hung loosely on her small frame.

"What happened to you anyways, Zane?" Brooks said with a huff.

"I . . . It . . . poisoned me!" My mind was still spinning.

"That thing could've killed you guys," Brooks said, looking from me to Ren and Ms. Cab.

"Why *didn't* it kill you, Ms. Cab?" I hated to be so blunt, but that was usually the way things happened in the Maya world.

"When a mud person impersonates someone," Ms. Cab said, "they need to keep that human alive and close by." She shook her head. "Really, Zane! How could you not notice it wasn't me?"

Maybe because it looked just like you! I wanted to shout. Except for the brown makeup and cracking skin. Okay, maybe I should've noticed sooner. "Uh, sorry?"

"That fake Ms. Cab," Ren groaned. "She tricked me, too. Told me she had information to help me."

"Yeah, well get used to it," Brooks warned. "Maya supernaturals can be wicked cunning."

Rosie sniffed around, her ears pricking and her muscles flexing.

I leaned against Fuego, feeling a little weak. "Anyone want to tell me what the heck a mud person is and where this one came from?"

Brooks said, "Do you remember the Maya gods' first creation?"

"They made humans from mud," I said. "But the people ended up being dumb and weak, so the gods destroyed them." Then it clicked. "Are you saying . . . this was some ancient mud person?"

"No," Brooks said. "This one was freshly made, but the question is, who created it and why?"

"Obviously, the gods," I said, because they were usually behind evil stuff.

Ms. Cab shook her head. "This work is too sloppy for the gods," she said. "Definitely a supernatural, though, because that thing was coated with so much raw magic, it rattled my very bones." Rubbing her forehead, she added, "I haven't heard of an attempt at a mud person in over a century, mostly because they're so unreliable—which tells me that whoever sent this one is an amateur."

Ha! It had seemed pretty legit to me. "Yep, that rules out the gods."

"Someone wanted to get to Zane . . ." muttered Brooks, still puzzling it out.

It creeped me out that a supernatural had laid a trap for me. How had they found me? I glanced at Ren, who was petting Rosie. Did the godborn have something to do with it?

Ms. Cab went on to tell us how she'd woken up at midnight to the mud monster standing over her bed. She'd tried to fight it off, but it overpowered her. The thing tied her up, took her exact measurements, and stole her voice. "Then it stayed up all night watching infomercials and talk shows," she cried. "It was absolute torture listening to it practice talking in the mirror."

So *that's* why the creature had seemed like a really bad talk show host. I'd never get used to what seemed to be the *unlimited* boundaries of Maya magic. And what was up with those creepy beetles? And those images that had flashed through my mind? I was now sure they were of places in New Mexico.

Ms. Cab collapsed into a chair as her birds returned to the trees, squawking and flapping their wings wildly. "Yes, I know, but I'm safe now," she told them. Then she turned to the rest of us. "If some wicked force came for Zane, then he's been compromised. Someone knows he's alive, and one way or another they will find their way onto this isla. And if they discover Ren's a godborn, too..."

My mouth fell open. "You can see that...?"

Mr. O let out a low whistle. "La otra godborn..."

Ren looked at me. "When our hands were tied together, I felt so helpless. Then I remembered how you had used telepathy, Zane, so I... I tried it. I mean, Ms. Cab and I had to make an escape plan."

Rosie grumbled while Brooks patted her and looked around suspiciously.

"At first the telepathy didn't work," Ren continued. "But I concentrated really hard, and then Ms. Cab's voice flew into my mind like... like the wind. I told her about me."

"Tengo muchas preguntas," said Mr. O. "First, why was that thing here?"

Ms. Cab removed some seed from her pocket and scattered it on the ground for the birds. "Tell us everything, Zane."

A few minutes later, I'd recounted all the grisly details of what had happened between me and the mud thing.

Brooks went over to the table, and examined a chocolate square. "Clever."

Mr. O lifted the plate and spilled the remaining candy into his sack. "I will test it. See what I can learn." Even though Mr. O didn't have his greenhouse anymore, he still grew peppers, and he'd expanded to herbs and other plants. If anyone could figure out the poison's properties, it was him.

Ren raised an eyebrow. "What were the bugs mapping?"

"I don't know," Ms. Cab said. Her face filled with more fear than when we were planning to stop the god of death. At least then we knew what we were up against. But now? There was something infinitely more terrifying in the *not* knowing.

"Maybe it's some sort of magic spell," Ren guessed. "Or ceremony."

"Magic," Brooks uttered, still rubbing Rosie's neck absently. "I've heard about these Maya magicians who found an old pool of mud deep in the jungle. Some believed it was left over from the first mud humans, and supposedly it had all this power." She shook her head, scowling. "Gods never pick up their messes."

"That's right!" Ms. Cab said like a lightbulb had turned on in her mind. "The high priests discovered that some of the gods' creation powers lingered in the pool, so they worked with magicians and made potions from it. But, as far as I knew, it was used up a hundred years ago."

"Please tell me they didn't bathe in the leftover people." My stomach felt like it was eating itself.

Ren's face went white. "Or that the mud wasn't in that chocolate Zane ate, because that would mean . . ."

"I didn't eat anyone!" I shouted.

"Think of it as a mud pie," Brooks teased.

Mr. O patted my shoulder. "No te preocupes."

Easy for him to tell me not to worry. He didn't just eat an ancient mud person!

"Gross," Ren uttered.

"But I still don't get what 'mapping' means," Brooks said.

"Or why I saw flashes of New Mexico," I reminded them.

"Maybe your brain was in shock," Ren said, "and it was trying to make you feel better with pictures of home?"

Home. Was New Mexico still home? Ren's guess wasn't bad, but I knew there was more to it than that. "Then why were those words written in the sand?"

Frowning, Brooks said, "Maybe mapping has something to do with going back to New Mexico? Or maybe the frequency is all jammed up and . . ."

"We are thinking wrong." Mr. O rubbed his chin thoughtfully. "When I created my peppers, I wrote down notes, instructions so I could understand how the peppers worked, how they grew. I was not trying to get somewhere in the world. I was trying to get somewhere in my *mind*. To understand."

Everyone was silent. The birds pecked at the seed on the ground. A warm breeze rustled through the trees. Then it hit me.

"Someone wants to know how my powers work." Yeah, well, whoever wanted this Zane map was going to be way disappointed when they found out I couldn't do anything more than make fire lemons.

"Uh, Zane . . ." Brooks began like she had something awful to tell me.

Ms. Cab said, "Dios mío."

"Someone wants my powers, don't they?"

Ren pushed her bangs out of her face and frowned. "Rotten thieves."

"Muy rotten," Mr. O echoed.

"But they failed," I said. "I mean, I can still touch fire. When I went to extinguish the flames, they didn't burn me— they actually healed me."

Brooks twisted her mouth and folded her arms. She looked up at me. "You know what this means, right?"

"What?" I wanted to know, but I didn't want to know. "What does it mean?"

"Whoever did this is going to come back to finish the job."

Why did Brooks always have to be so fatalistic?

Rosie growled and bared her massive fangs. I swear, it was like she was itching for a fight. Man, she had really changed from the skinny fraidy-cat dog I once knew.

Ms. Cab ran her hands over her disheveled hair. "I need my eyes. My powers!"

Since we'd been on the island, she hadn't taken out her box of creepy moving eyeballs that let her see the future. There was no point, because they didn't work with Ixtab's shadow magic (more like *prison* magic).

Brooks grunted in frustration. "I don't know about you, but I'm sick of looking at this stupid mud thing!" The air shimmered green and blue as she shifted into a hawk, spread her wings, and crushed the statue to dust with her sharp talons. It was a magnificent sight.

Ren gasped. "Whoa! That's way more awesome in person!"

Stooping, Ms. Cab ran her fingers slowly through the pile of dirt that remained. "Do you ... do you hear the voices?"

Voices in the dirt? I guess that was no weirder than the voice I'd heard in the fire. But I heard nothing this time.

Mr. O and Ren stepped closer. Brooks shifted back to human and exchanged a *what-now?* glance with me as Ms. Cab grabbed a handful of mud, closed her eyes, and hummed a weird tune. When all the bits of clay had sifted through her fingers, she opened her eyes.

"Did you see something, amor?" Mr. O asked.

Ms. Cab's mouth fell open as she stepped back. The birds went crazy. A startling wind blew across the patio, sending dirt swirling into the air. Rosie threw her head back and howled. Yup, Ms. Cab had definitely seen something. But how?

"What ... what's wrong?" Ren asked softly.

Ms. Cab's gaze met mine. "I heard a message from ... the ancestors."

"Ancestors?" I asked.

"They are an ancient lineage of great seers." Ms. Cab's voice was tight. "A powerful source. They must have worked very hard to reach me through the shadow magic. Or someone helped them reach me. . . ." Her voice trailed off.

"What's the message?" I asked, wondering if it would be as obvious as *Eating the chocolate was a bad idea.*

Ms. Cab hesitated, then said, "'In the dark, you shall

choose the path, but beware. All roads lead to the gods' angry wrath.'"

"Great," Brooks groaned.

"That's it?" I said. "Whichever path I pick, the gods are going to be mad?"

"What kind of prophecy is that?" Ren asked.

Ms. Cab grimaced. "I lost communication, but not before they could tell me one more thing."

"What?!" we all cried in unison.

I held my breath, praying she was going to say something like *Zane will succeed in rescuing Hurakan and no one will die.*

"'The Prophecy of Fire was only the beginning.'"

My heart took a nosedive. Those were the exact words I'd heard from the tarot-card-reading dude back in Venice, California. The one with two gold front teeth, silver-rimmed shades, and my future in his pocket. I wished now that I'd stopped to talk to him and found out more, but at the time I'd thought he was just some street peddler.

My memory stretched back to that day. What else had he said? And then I remembered:

Fire spreads. Until it burns everything in its path.

9

····

I left Ms. Cab's with a sour feeling in my stomach and a question that grated on my bones: How could the Prophecy of Fire be the beginning? And if the ancestors were so all-seeing great, why couldn't they just tell me who wanted to steal my so-called powers?

"Zane, why are you walking so fast? Where are you going?" Brooks hurried beside me.

"Xib'alb'a," I said, even more convinced that my pre-Cab idea was the best solution to our getting off the island. Now, more than ever, we needed to bust out, rescue my dad, and get the answers we'd never find here.

"We're going to the underworld?" Ren said with way too much excitement in her voice.

"Not *we*," I said.

Brooks's eyes flashed amber. "Are you crazy?! You think you can waltz up to the queen of the underworld and ask her to let you off the island? I was just kidding when I suggested it! Zane? Are you paying attention? You want her to know what you're up to? She'll for sure double the shadow magic, and we'll never get out of here."

"You still have the gateway map, right?"

"Yeah, but it's . . ." She rushed alongside me. "It's in my pack at home."

"We have to get it."

"Why?"

I glanced at Rosie. Maybe we could send her for the back-pack. I couldn't risk going myself and running into my mom. For all I knew, Ms. Cab had already called her and told her everything. "Because the map will show us a gateway down in the underworld. A gateway to South Dakota," I said as I marched toward the mouth of the jungle. "That's why I want to go there, not to see Ixtab."

Rosie walked between Ren and me. I could sense that she felt protective of the girl. It made my heart hurt. Would things ever go back to how they used to be between us? What if they never did? It was too depressing to think about.

"But what if you run into her?" Ren asked.

"That would suck," I said. "But I bet hell is a big place. Chances are she won't even know we're there."

"Zane!" Brooks said, looking frantic. "This is the stupidest, craziest idea you've ever had. We need a plan, backup plans, exit strategies."

"There's no time!" I argued. "We have just three and a half days left. This is our one and only chance. Like you said, if whoever it is that wants my power comes back here, I'll never rescue my dad. I have to go—now."

Ren looked both excited and stunned. "Hey, do you think there's evidence of aliens in Xib'alb'a?"

"What does that have to do with anything?" Brooks asked, sounding exasperated.

"I have a blog," she said. "*Eyes in the Sky.* Ever heard of it?

No? Well, I keep a record of UFO sightings, alien encounters, and other stuff. You wouldn't believe how many people email me. I mean, a lot of the reports are fake, but some are totally real. You should see the photos I get."

Brooks nodded like it wasn't entirely crazy until Ren got to the part about some old guy from Palenque named King Pakal and his sarcophagus. "The carvings clearly show him sitting in a spaceship," she said excitedly. "Scholars have argued forever about these aliens that visited ancient civilizations like the Egyptians and stuff. And I don't know. I just think the sky and the stars have a lot of secrets."

"Spaceship," Brooks repeated in a monotone. "Secrets."

Ren smiled. "Exactly. Amazing, right?"

"Good for King Pakal," I said to Ren. "But right now, we have to get into hell, and you need to go to my house and wait for your grandpa."

Brooks turned her attention back to me. "If she ... If Ixtab catches us . . ."

"We'll come up with an excuse for why we're there."

"Uh-huh . . . like we just wanted a tour of the place." Brooks's voice was thick with sarcasm. Just once, couldn't she say *Good thinking*?

I got a small nugget of satisfaction out of the idea of using Ixtab's own kingdom to bypass her shadow magic. The mud person's note had said Ixtab didn't want me to have my full powers. Was that true? Then why didn't she off me all those months ago, when I was sitting in a cell in the underworld?

A light rain began to fall. My chest tightened as we cut

toward a narrow side street lined with brightly painted houses. I couldn't shake the voice in the fire and now the ancestors' message.

Brooks grabbed my arm, jerking me to a stop. "Couldn't we just try high-speed crashing through the wall?"

Then it hit me. Brooks hated the underworld because it's where her sister had gone to avoid marrying the hero twin Xb'alamkej, aka Jordan the jerk, losing her freedom in the deal. Maybe Brooks thought she'd get stuck there, too. "It's okay, Brooks. You don't have to come with me."

"Zane Obispo, if you think you can tell me what to do—"

"You're both wrong," Ren said.

Brooks and I whirled toward Ren as she leaned against one of the murals that decorated the walls of Isla Holbox. The painting was a yellow-and-pink fantastical sea creature with branch-like antlers. "Don't you get it?" she said. "The enemy— whoever it is—wants you guys to argue, because it makes you weaker. We have to stick together now." She walked ahead, and Rosie followed.

"That's not the way home," I called out.

Brooks whispered, "Who *is* she?" as we hurried to catch up to Ren.

"You guys lived through the Prophecy of Fire because you stuck together, right?" Ren said as we entered the mouth of the jungle.

"And because we had a *plan*," Brooks said.

Ren kept plowing forward. Rosie trotted beside her, exhaling trails of smoke.

"Hey," I said. "You don't even know the way."

"Then you lead." But Ren didn't slow down. We kept pace through the dense foliage. "I came all this way," she said. "The magic called; *you* called. And I made it across the ocean for a reason," she added. "The night before you got attacked? And just before the ancestors told you that the Prophecy of Fire was only the beginning? Doesn't seem like a coincidence to me. You need me. Besides," she said with a half shrug, "Ixtab could be my mom for all I know. You're not the only one who wants answers, Zane."

Ixtab? Ren's mom? Was that possible? The queen of the underworld didn't exactly seem like mom material. But then I remembered her getting a little choked up when she had told me about the godborns, as if she had lost someone.... And there *was* the whole shadowy-ish connection between her and Ren.

"You can't just walk up to the queen of hell and ask her if she's your long-lost mom," I argued. "And your grandpa's on his way here."

Ren stopped in her tracks. "And?"

"And," Brooks said, "don't you think he'll be a little peeved when you're *not* here?"

Ren shook her head. "He said I have a big destiny that I'd understand someday. He'd *want* me to go on this quest, to follow the magic all the way through. I promise not to say anything to Ixtab—if we run into her, that is. Just let me poke around, see what I can find."

"You could get hurt, Ren," I said. "That mud monster? That was nothing."

Ren pinned me with her wintry eyes. "I'm safer with you."

"She has a good point," Brooks said, suddenly changing gears.

What the heck?

A long grunt of agreement emerged from Rosie. *Traitor.*

"We're talking the underworld here," I said. "It's a dark and dangerous place, and the demons—they run wild there." Okay, I made that last part up, but it *could* be true. I just thought maybe I could scare Ren off. "Plus, you're not"—I stopped myself before Rosie went into dragon mode and burned down the jungle—"D-E-A-D, and you can't go to Xib'alb'a unless . . ."

"You're not *D-E-A-D*, either," Ren said. "So that means the emergency entrance must be for the living."

"Ixtab never said the entrance was for *four*." It's not that I wanted to go alone. Believe me, I didn't. But what if Ren got hurt? That kind of guilt could drown a person.

"Let's take a vote." Brooks shifted her arms into massive wings that she stretched overhead. Was she trying to intimidate me? It was so not working. "I say she comes with us to Xib'alb'a. She *is* a godborn after all, and she deserves to find out the truth about her mom."

A rustling in the trees drew our attention. Hondo emerged, out of breath. Leaves poked out of his thick hair.

"H-Hondo," I stammered. "What are you doing here?"

"Followed Rosie's smoke trails, and, uh, you guys are kind of loud." Hondo turned his eyes on Ren as he caught his breath. "So, you're a godborn, eh?"

"How . . . how did you know?" I asked.

"You'd have to be an idiot not to put it together," Hondo said. "I mean, I wake up and there's this mysterious girl whose name just happens to be scribbled in the tell-all book, and then there was the burned-up boat, and you were acting all weird, Zane. Besides, your mom sort of told me. And then there was this." He tugged Brooks's backpack from behind him.

"Hey!" Brooks snatched the pack away.

"Looks like someone's going monster hunting." Hondo smiled. "Can I carry the ax?"

"No one's going monster hunting," I said. At least, I hoped we'd get through this without seeing *any* monsters. Yeah, I know, I'm still overly optimistic.

Brooks glanced inside the pack like she was making sure everything was in its place. "Where's the demon flashlight, Hondo?"

He fished it out of his pocket. "I need it more than you do. You're a hawk with killer talons!"

"True." Brooks nodded. "Keep it."

"Can I have one of those?" Ren asked, stretching her neck to get a view inside the pack.

"Wait a second—*you* have the book, Hondo?" Brooks said.

"I looked for that thing all morning," Ren said.

"It's not a very good read," Hondo offered, doing his worst to hide his smile. "I wouldn't bother if I were you, Brooks. I mean, you were there for everything. It's kinda boring, actually. Zane's not much of a writer." He hooked his arm around my shoulders. "Right, Zane?"

I loved my uncle for trying to protect me, but seriously? Did he have to insult me at the same time?

"I thought the book was . . ." Ren hesitated. "Adventurous, kinda scary. Gross in some parts. Really sweet in others."

"Sweet?" Brooks let out a small laugh. "Zane, I don't remember any *sweet* parts. Mostly demons, blood, hair, and guts."

That was totally true, but had she already forgotten that night on the boat when she fell asleep on my shoulder? Or how about . . .

Ren glanced at me. I tried to give her a look: *Don't say another word.* But she just kept on blabbering. "The part when you guys got the enchantment and you had on that really pretty dress and when Zane saw—"

"You described my dress?" Brooks asked me.

"Dress?" I said. "I don't remember, and we have bigger things to worry about than my writing." I could strangle Ren. The girl had *zero* filter and was kind of clueless. Didn't she get my eye signals?

"Yeah, like you guys telling me where you're going," Hondo said. "And don't even try to act all innocent, *comrade.*"

"Xib'alb'a," Ren volunteered.

"Living the dream," Hondo muttered. "And *why*, exactly, are you going to hell?"

I groaned. "Just tell him everything, why don't you."

Hondo knuckle-rubbed his scruffy cheek. "You're definitely going to need a *hero* like me on this quest."

"I'd feel a lot better if Hondo was around," Ren said. "He totally saved you guys last time."

Hondo smiled wide and pointed at Ren. "I like her."

I knew there was no talking him out of it. No way would he give up the chance to fight. I mean, he lived for combat, and I could tell he was going stir-crazy on the island. He'd already held wrestling matches with anyone dumb enough to fight him, and—big surprise—he beat them all. Yeah, you could say his training was paying off big-time.

"Wait," I said. "Aren't you supposed to be leading a tour about now?"

"Uh, yeah, but the golf cart isn't exactly built for speed, and I sort of had a blowout."

"You were supposed to change the tires!"

Hondo rubbed his chin. "Worse, I left a bunch of Canadians alone in the jungle. You think they'll give us a bad review on TripAdvisor?"

Ren let out a small laugh. I just sighed.

"So, about the book . . ." Brooks said.

"You heard Hondo," I said. "It's totally boring." Man, she wasn't going to let this go. My cheeks were getting hotter by the second, and things were getting more complicated. Not only did I have to find a gateway through hell, rescue my dad, and figure out who had sent the mud person, I had to keep the book out of Brooks's hands.

"Besides," I added, "we should be focused on getting off this island."

"And I'm here to help one hundred and fifty percent," Hondo said. I swear he was practically dancing in place.

"You mean one hundred," Ren said.

"Huh?"

"You said one-fifty, and that's not really possible."

"Yeah, well, lots of things aren't possible." Hondo rolled his eyes at me. "I'm rethinking whether I like her."

A minute later, we'd filled Hondo in on everything that

had happened. He just shook his head and repeated certain words, like *Bugs? Mapping? Mud freak?* When we got to the part about Ren bringing monsters from her dreams, he held his hand up and asked her, "Hang on. Can you bring stuff other than monsters? Like, say, a winning lottery ticket, or a ninja sword, or something like that?"

Ren sighed. "I don't think so, but I never tried."

"I could teach you some mind techniques I've been studying," he said. "I bet it would help unlock your unconscious so you could manifest whatever you wanted. See? You guys need me. So, what's the vote? Are Ren and I coming with? I vote definitely yes."

"Me too," Ren said, high-fiving Hondo like they were football buddies. Whatever.

"Four to one, Zane." Brooks quirked an eyebrow.

Everyone (Rosie included) stared at me with expectant eyes, telling me I'd already lost.

My cheesy uncle flexed a bicep, winked at it, and said, "Well then, vámonos. Let's get this hell tour started."

10

Time passes differently in other realms like Xib'alb'a, the Old World, and the Empty. What was three hours there could be more like a whole day in the real world—or three seconds. I had to get through the underworld as quickly as possible to (a) reach my dad in time and (b) avoid worrying my mom.

"Hondo, you need to tell my mom we're leaving," I said.

Don't judge. You would totally take the chicken way out, too, if you knew my mom.

"Yeah, right," Hondo said. "I can't go home. She's already going to kill me for messing up the tour. Hell is definitely safer."

"She'd for sure try to stop you from going," Ren said to me. "Just write her a note."

"Last time I did that, she nearly ripped out my eyelashes one at a time," I said.

Brooks nodded. "You have to tell her, Zane."

"No way," I said. "Ren's right. She'll only try and stop me." So I went with a firm plan B.

Let Ms. Cab tell her.

I borrowed a pen from Brooks's pack and scribbled a *shorter-the-better* note on a receipt Hondo had in his pocket.

*Tell my mom what's up. We had to go see about some stuff.
Be back soon. P.S. Don't worry.*

I gave it to Rosie and told her to deliver it to Ms. Cab. Rosie
looked at me with her big brown eyes and groaned like she
didn't want the job, either.

"You can teleport anywhere," I said. "Just drop the note in
her box or something. Then disappear real quick-like."

My dog rolled her eyes and vanished into a trail of black
mist. If she could talk, I'm pretty sure she would've told me
*You're a wuss, and you owe me a lifetime supply of chicken
bones.*

If I didn't die on this quest, Mom was for sure going to
murder me. I only hoped Rosie wouldn't get distracted by a
flamingo or a plastic shopping bag blowing in the wind.

We journeyed through the maze that was the jungle, the
dense canopy of tangled trees blocking out the sunlight. I
cleared a path with Fuego.

"Zane?" Brooks halted in her tracks and pointed at Ren,
who stood frozen with her eyes glazed over. She wasn't blinking, and her pupils were dilated so huge, the blue of her irises
was almost gone.

"Ren?" I rushed over, hoping she wasn't going to collapse
or anything. But she just stood there like a statue. "She's in
one of her trances," I said.

Hondo's eyes bugged out. "She looks like a zombie."

From every direction came chirps and screeches. The shadows around us seemed to grow darker. Brooks pushed past
me, drawing closer to Ren. "How long will she stay like this?"

"How should I know?"

Rubbing his chin, Hondo studied her. "Maybe she's like those monks who can make themselves look dead but really they're just meditating."

"Pretty sure she isn't meditating," I said.

"You think she's going to bring more shadow monsters?" Hondo snapped his fingers in her face.

That would be a great way to ruin a perfectly nice hike to the underworld, I thought.

"She's so defenseless," Brooks said in a low voice. Then she reached into her pack for a water bottle.

"What are you doing?"

"She said to throw water on her face."

"If she's *asleep.* She never said anything about her seizures, trances, whatever they are. What if waking her is dangerous?" I asked. "Like, maybe she has to come out of it on her own?"

"Fine. I'll carry her," Hondo offered. "She looks like she weighs all of eighty pounds."

Rosie materialized at the same moment. For once, she had perfect timing.

"Put her on Rosie's back," I said.

Hondo lifted Ren up and placed her gently on Rosie's shoulders. "Don't let her fall, girl."

"Was Ms. Cab angry?" I asked my dog. I walked at her side, my hand around Ren's waist to keep her from sliding off. Rosie threw me a side-glance and narrowed her eyes like she was saying, *Please. I've got this.*

The jungle grew thicker and darker, crowding around us like a living thing that knew we were here uninvited. Our footfalls were light, barely crunching the twigs and leaves scattered across the ground. But my mind was heavy, replaying everything that had happened. All of it was pretty terrifying. Ren showing up right before the mud monster. The whispering voice. That stupid ancestor message of doom! I wanted to punch it in the face.

Then the tip of the Beast came into view and my heart did a strange flip. Anyone else would see only a wall of tangled rain forest. But I could spot a black cone rising a couple hundred yards out of the earth to meet the sky.

Hondo glanced around when we came to a stop. "This is a dead end, guys."

"It's behind the forest." I separated some thick leafy branches, and we descended into the darkness.

"Uh..." Hondo breathed. "This seems totally sketch." This was my uncle's first time here. Just like in New Mexico, he'd never been interested in the volcano—or maybe he understood it was my special spot. And he'd kill me for saying this, but the guy hated small, tight spaces. That had only gotten worse after the hero twins poisoned him and sent him to a dark, torturous place where his worst nightmares came true. Hondo had never talked about it, but I was pretty sure he'd been in a cold, gloomy box with the walls pressing in on him while grating music shook his eardrums. I had no doubt that all his recent meditation stuff was so he would never feel that vulnerable again. He was training his brain to withstand even his worst fears. Maybe when this was all over he could teach me a thing or two.

Rosie rushed ahead, her giant feet stomping the ground persistently. I was about to remind my hellhound she was lugging Ren on her back, but somehow, the girl stayed on securely.

A few minutes later, we came to a clearing where only pinpricks of sunlight came through overgrown trees the size of skyscrapers.

Hondo looked up. "Where is it?"

"It's hidden behind a veil of shadow magic," Brooks said.

"Just follow me," I said.

We hiked the last twenty yards up the path. Once we were within a few feet, Hondo gasped. "That volcano just appeared out of thin air!"

"You're just close enough now to see it," I said.

"Seems like a weakness in the magic," he muttered.

"If you weren't with supernaturals, you'd never be able to see it," Brooks countered.

The volcano's entry point wasn't concealed with brush like back in New Mexico. Instead, it was enchanted. Only a supernatural could open the stone panel.

Rosie nosed the door and it slid open with a swish of cool air.

Ren stirred, then sat up and rubbed her eyes.

"Hey, you okay?" I asked.

She glanced around, looking disoriented. "I *hate* this! How am I supposed to help you if I zone out at the worst times?"

"You said it happens when you're stressed?" I asked.

Ren nodded. "I'm a little freaked about—"

"The underworld?" Hondo said with a big exhale. "Me too."

"About Ixtab maybe being my mom," Ren corrected.

"You'll get it under control," I said, wondering how her

trances were tied to her godborn powers. My leg was directly connected to Hurakan, who was also sometimes called One Leg or Serpent Leg. Maybe Ren's mom had some kind of nickname, too?

Hondo twisted his mouth and rubbed his chin. "Ren, if you go into trances when you're stressed, get ready to have a lot, because we're heading into Maya madness territory."

"She knows that, Hondo!" I growled. "And I'm pretty sure that isn't helping."

"All I'm saying," he added, "is that she needs to be able to handle stress. Meditation would help."

"I'll try anything," Ren said. "I can't just become a zombie in the middle of some big moment or fight."

"I'll train you," Hondo whispered to her.

"Can we just get inside?" Brooks shouldered her pack and got on all fours to lead the way.

Hondo scrunched down to navigate the tight opening. "What is this, the elf entrance?"

"It's so dark," Ren exclaimed, following closely behind Rosie, who had to belly-crawl so she wouldn't hit her head. Flames blazed in the hellhound's eyes, illuminating the space. "Thanks, Rosie."

"You mean . . . you can't see in the dark?" I asked, bringing up the rear.

Ren hesitated, then said, "That's a Zane thing."

Rosie snorted.

The passage was tight. Ahead of me, Hondo's breathing quickened and he began to chant under his breath, but I couldn't make out the words.

"We're almost there," I said. I called the heat from Rosie's eyes and made a small fireball for more light.

I heard Hondo's sigh of relief as we emerged into an open chamber. Our shadows loomed across the craggy walls. Ren spun around with her head tilted back. "It looks just like how you described it."

"Really?" Brooks said sarcastically. "I thought Zane was such a *terrible* writer." She elbowed Hondo, who just shrugged and rolled his neck back and forth like he had a cramp.

Rosie blew out a stream of smoke and lumbered across the chamber, where she stopped in front of three passages, each branching off in a different direction. I knew this place so well I could walk it blindfolded. Rosie, too. We'd spent years exploring the volcano back in New Mexico before I knew who I really was.

I stared down the passage on the far right. That was where the demon runner had tricked Brooks and me and led us into the sacrifice chamber. A place I'd avoided ever since.

Please don't let that be the gateway to hell, I prayed.

"Dude," Hondo said, "you pick some creepy places to hang out."

"How many caves are in this place?" Ren asked like she was interviewing me for her alien blog.

"A lot." I shrugged. "It's like a maze that goes on forever."

"So which one goes to Xib'alb'a?" asked Brooks.

I didn't want to admit the truth—that I had no idea where the door to hell was.

It wasn't like Ixtab had given me a map. She'd never mentioned the entrance's exact location, only that it was inside the

Beast. And even though I'd been back here a bunch of times, I never poked around for the passageway to the underworld, mostly because she'd threatened me with torture if I ever used it for anything but the direst situation.

"I don't see any emergency exit signs," Hondo said.

"*Entrance*," Brooks corrected. "Not exit."

"Depends on how you look at it," Hondo mumbled. He kept taking deep breaths and placing his hands together like he was saying a prayer.

"You okay?" I asked.

"Gotta prepare the mind, calm the nerves," he said. "It's all about controlling the breath. And *seeing* the outcome you want. I see a tall, beautiful woman opening the door and saying, 'Hey, come on in for some Flamin' Hot Cheetos and salsa.' Then she gives us everything we want, we get to fight a demon or two for fun, and we go home with a trophy."

"Trophy?" Brooks let out a light laugh. "Pretty sure hell doesn't give out trophies."

"It's my vision, and your negative energy is jamming my good-vibe frequency, Brooks," Hondo said.

"I like it," Ren whispered to Hondo. "Could use a little more detail, but pretty solid as far as visions go."

Brooks rolled her eyes and Rosie gave a short grunt like she was trying to say *This is hell, not fairyland.*

"Rosie will show us the way," I said. "Right, girl?"

The hellhound escorted us down the corridor to the left. The passage led to a web of narrow caves, tight crawly spaces, and inclines so steep I couldn't investigate them, even with Fuego. Just as we were about to cut right, Rosie stopped, backed up, and stared at the wall to our left. But there was no door, no opening, not even a sliver of light.

"Are you sure this is it, girl?"

She lifted her chin, and her eyes glowed red as she focused on the trio behind me and whined.

"Back up, everyone." Rosie grabbed my fireball between her jaws and nudged my cane. I knew what she wanted me to do. I changed Fuego into its awesome glowing blue spear self and stepped back the entire ten feet the passage allowed. With a deep breath, I launched the weapon, worried it didn't have enough distance to gain momentum.

The passage lengthened, and the wall opened wide when the spear hit it. I blinked as bright light streamed into the cave. When my eyes adjusted, I saw a snowy meadow in front of us. There was an icy rush of a stream, and snowflakes tumbled down from above.

Pale shapes glided through a few leafless trees like white shadows or ghosts.

"Holy K!" Brooks said as we teetered on the edge of this strange world.

"Holy hell," Hondo uttered.

"Increíble!" Ren said.

"We're going in there, aren't we?" Hondo shivered. "Someone could have told me to bring a coat."

"Just tell yourself it isn't cold," Brooks teased.

"This doesn't feel right," Ren said.

"Then we're in the right place," I said as Fuego appeared back in my hand and I stepped into snow up to my ankles.

11

My heart pounded as we inched across the meadow toward a dead forest. "What is this place?"

"It's like the North Pole or something." White fog streamed from Hondo's mouth. "I thought hell was all fire and brimstone."

Brooks pressed her lips into a line and glanced around suspiciously.

Looking stunned, Ren stood a few feet behind everyone like she was too afraid to take another step toward the strange forest. "I really don't think that's the way," she said.

"How would you know?" Brooks said to her.

"I just have a sixth sense about stuff like this. I can always sniff out a fake alien report, too."

The snow beneath my feet shifted to reveal an ice lake. "Guys."

Brooks's and Hondo's gazes followed mine.

"Please tell me there's not water underneath this," Brooks muttered softly, like she was afraid her words could puncture the ice.

"Nobody move," I said, stopping in my tracks. I looked at Rosie. Smoke curled from her nose. Her muscles were flexed.

"Let's just back up slowly," Brooks said.

"Backing up is the wrong direction," I reminded her.

"Water is always the wrong direction!"

I glanced over my shoulder. Ren stood at the edge of the meadow, shaking her head and gesturing for us to come back. Her mouth was moving, but I couldn't hear what she was saying.

The snow was falling heavier now, big thick snowflakes that stuck to my lashes and blocked my view of Ren. The gloomy sky seemed to press in on us as an arctic breeze swept through.

"Ren!" I shouted.

Her muffled voice traveled to me, but still I couldn't make out the words.

Then I heard the sound of a whip being cracked. A hairline fracture traveled through the ice, stopping only inches away from our feet.

"It's going to break," Hondo warned. "We gotta bolt."

"Running will for sure make it break," I argued. Why would Ixtab give me such a dangerous entrance to hell? Maybe she was so confident in her shadow magic she never thought I'd need it.

"Zane." Brooks pointed to my feet. "You're . . . you're melting the ice."

Water pooled around my feet. It had to be a result of the fire I'd pulled inside of me a few minutes ago. *Crap! Crappity crap!*

"Dude, really?" Hondo rubbed his arms.

"What do you want me to do?" I groaned.

"Don't be so hot!" Brooks said.

Hondo raised his eyebrows and let out a shivering laugh.

Brooks threw Hondo a scowl as I lifted my feet one at a time, trying to shake the heat out. Rosie gave me a look like *Not happening.*

"Zane, we can't stand here all day," Brooks said.

"I've got an idea!"

I had just called Rosie over to hitch a ride, when Hondo said, "This place feels muy dead."

The stillness of the moment was shattered. Upon hearing the word *dead,* Rosie launched a massive fire stream from her nose and mouth directly into the ice.

"STEAK!" I yelled, but it was too late.

Brooks's *NO* echoed across the forest as the ice collapsed and we were plunged into the freezing dark....

I totally expected violent waters, but instead I got a g-force drop through a howling tornado of wind and ice. Hail stabbed me like a million needles as my screams echoed. Fuego slipped out of my hand.

Brooks, in hawk form, dove past me with Hondo clinging to her back.

"Zane," he hollered. "Grab hold!"

I grasped one of her talons, struggling to get a good grip. I swung mightily as she flew through the air. Her widespread wings acted as shields against the ice daggers.

Kee-eeeee-ar! she cried.

Rosie tumbled past me, howling with such ferocity the ice walls shook. Streams of fire spewed from her mouth, melting the falling hail. Then I did a double take. I couldn't believe it— Rosie had sprouted wings! Huge black wings. How in the...?

Brooks flew back up, up, up.

Freezing rain pounded us. I'd never been so cold. My fingers were so numb I wasn't sure I could keep holding on.

"There's no opening!" Hondo yelled when we got back to just under the surface of the ice lake. "It's frozen over again!"

"Where's Ren?" I screamed. Had she fallen past us?

Rosie's howl carried from below. Brooks beat the ice ceiling with her massive wings with zero success. "We can't leave Rosie behind!" I hollered.

With a loud shriek, Brooks swooped down—actually, she flipped 180 degrees and went into a dive that nearly made me heave. But, lucky me, I didn't upchuck. That came *after* we landed on the icy surface below.

After I saw all the eyes.

Fuego zipped back to me as I took in the eyeballs (big and squishy with black irises). They were packed into the ice walls, shifting back and forth like they were following our every move. They didn't have lids or lashes or anything resembling *normal* or *human*. For all I knew, they belonged to demons.

I gagged, readied Fuego, and scanned the place. Which, by the way, was so *not* a good entrance to hell. I mean, Ixtab could've totally given me an elevator and ixnayed the creepy polar chamber and ogling walls.

Rosie appeared beside me, whining and dancing in place. I shouldn't have looked down to where she was fixated. But I did. That's right. More eyeballs were lodged beneath a thin layer of ice right under our feet.

I jumped back, gagged, then barfed.

Hondo climbed off Brooks's back and swayed, his face looking a little green. "Dude, hold it together, man."

I tried to warn him, but it was too late. He stared at the eyeballs looking up at him. He might've yelped. Then he hurled, too. Twice as much as I had, by the way.

Brooks had already shifted back. She wrinkled her nose and hooked one arm under Hondo's while I held up his other side. "You okay?" I asked.

"Are those ojos real?" he slurred.

"Don't look at them," Brooks said.

"¡Están por todas partes!" he cried. "¡Odio los ojos!"

He was right. The eyes were everywhere, and I hated them, too.

It was always obvious when my uncle hit his freaked-out threshold, because Spanish came pouring out of his mouth.

"How about we don't stand in the vomit?" Brooks grimaced.

We stepped back a good five feet. The ice chamber was only about fifteen by fifteen.

Brooks and Hondo started shivering uncontrollably. I pulled Rosie's heat inside of me and created a tiny fire between my hands that everyone huddled around to try and warm themselves. That's when the jade tooth around my neck vibrated. I held my breath, hoping I hadn't imagined it. There it was again. Was it Hurakan trying to communicate with me?

"What happened to Ren?" I asked after the jade went still. Had she tumbled into this subzero hell, or had something even worse befallen her?

"*She* was smart enough not to follow us." Brooks blew warm air on her hands and nestled close. Which I didn't mind, exactly.

"Are you sure?" I said, looking up. "What if she went into one of her trances again and she's stuck up there, and..."

Brooks frowned at me. "I'm sure she's fine, Zane. And even if she did, she's better off up there than down *here*."

Hondo wore a stunned expression. "Did I just fly?"

"Technically," Brooks said, "*I* just flew."

Hondo hunched closer to the flame. "Who knew getting into hell would be so hard? I mean, shouldn't it be the opposite?"

A cracking sound caught our attention and a set of doors slid open in the ice wall. Ren stepped out, wide-eyed and panting, as if she'd climbed Mount Everest. "You're okay!" she shouted. "I told you that wasn't the way!"

The doors closed and disappeared behind her.

"There's an elevator?" Hondo snarled. His lips were turning blue. "Are you k-k-k-kidding me?"

"There *was* an elevator," I muttered.

"I tried to tell you about it," Ren said. "I didn't see the button at first. It was actually a rock, but it totally looked out of place," she explained. "Super-slow elevator, though. And there was a creepy voice that kept singing '*Welcome to the dark side. One way only. What goes down doesn't come up.*'"

Brooks glared at me. "I'm following her from now on."

I threw my hands in the air, dissolving the mini fire. "Like I was supposed to know I had a private elevator to hell?"

"*This* is the und-d-der-r-wor-rld?" Hondo's teeth chattered.

"It's gotta be Rattle House." Brooks rubbed her hands together before tugging the gateway map out of her backpack.

"One of the six fatal houses?" I said.

"Fatal?" Hondo echoed.

"Yeah," I said as I drew more fire from Rosie to warm everyone. "The first is Dark House—so dark it drives people crazy. The second is this place. The third is Jaguar House, filled with hungry razor-toothed cats ready to rip out your throat."

"Man," Hondo groaned. "What's up with the Maya gods and blood and guts?"

Brooks drew closer, her hawk eyes glowing amber. "The fourth is the worst, if you ask me. Bat House, filled with the bloodthirsty shrieking things." She shivered a little as she studied the map. "They like to suck your blood nice and slow."

"Dude, can you make the fire a little bigger?" Hondo asked, closing his eyes and taking deep breaths.

"What are you doing?" I asked him.

"Trying to meditate away the cold."

"Is it working?"

"No."

Rosie whined and danced as she stared down at the shifting eyes in the ice, trying to stamp them out with her massive paws.

"You're afraid of the eyes?" I asked her.

Rosie groaned her agreement, and then, without warning, a torrent of fire erupted from her mouth, aimed directly at the floor.

"STOP! STEAK!" I yelled. "You want to melt the floor and let them loose?"

"Uh, that would be a huge NO!" Hondo cried, opening his eyes.

Surprisingly, Rosie listened to me this time; I scratched her neck.

Ren rubbed her arms vigorously, scanning the miserable space no bigger than my bedroom. "Uh, guys . . . I don't think there's a way out of here."

Anger pulsed beneath my skin that this . . . *this* was my entrance to the underworld? What happened to the nice, newly renovated apartment Ixtab and I had hung out in before?

"These houses are just places to test people's strength," I said, looking around for an exit. But why would Ixtab want to test me more than I'd already been tested? "The twins got through here somehow. . . ."

"The twins," Hondo repeated, venom in his voice. "Well, if those morons could find a way out, so can we." He rushed around the room, tapping his knuckles on the icy walls, looking disgusted.

Rosie hurried behind him.

"Well?" I peered over the edge of the map Brooks was holding. The wrinkled paper was a mess of crisscrossing lines in all different colors, connecting flashing blue squares. I remembered the first time I saw this thing and how it was like staring at a long scientific formula. Ms. Cab had explained that these magic maps are rare and the squares mark the gateways to different places and layers of the world.

"Whoa," Ren breathed. "All the place names keep changing. I just saw Boise Tortillería and now . . . the letters are some kind of hieroglyphs."

"Look for one that's blinking slowly. They blink faster when they're going to close soon," I said, as if I could read the thing. Thankfully, Brooks could, sort of. Hopefully enough to get us to the other side of hell and close to South Dakota.

"Er... we've got a problem," Brooks said.

"Other than freezing to death in hell?" Hondo shouted as he continued looking for a way out.

"There's no rhyme or reason to this." Brooks pressed her lips together. "It's like the map's going haywire...."

"Maybe it doesn't work in Xib'alb'a," Ren said.

"It has to work!" The map was our only ticket off the island.

"Stop looking at me!" Hondo shouted at the roving eyes.

"No one's looking at you," came a familiar voice.

We all spun to see a young woman step through a panel in the ice wall that closed behind her with a *swish*. She wore loose black cargo pants with ties at the hems and a black long-sleeved shirt. Her hair was tied into a high ponytail that drew her face back so tightly it looked like her skin might crack if she smiled. No chance of that happening, though. It was Brooks's fierce (and super-demanding) older sister.

Hondo leaned over and whispered in my ear. "Dude, it's her—the one who jammed a lightning bolt into Ixtab's back."

"Quinn?" Brooks raced over. "I thought you were in hiding, undercover...."

She gave Brooks a quick hug. "Things have changed. And you guys aren't supposed to be here," she said to everyone but me and Rosie. "This entrance is for Obispo and the hellhound only. In case of an emergency."

"It's a total emergency," I said. "And her name's Rosie."

Quinn shrugged. "Right. Zane, you're an idiot, and you, Brooks, you should know better than to think you can come to Xib'alb'a. If the lower-level demons get one whiff of you guys, zombie madness will break out! You want to get your faces eaten off?"

Brooks stuck her chin in the air. "*You're* here."

"I'm full—" Quinn stopped herself. I knew she was about to say she wasn't a half-breed nawal like Brooks. "Come on, we need to get out of here before the next storm hits. They come every five minutes, and they get more violent each time."

"If it's so dangerous, why use this place as an entrance?" I asked.

"The six deadly houses are part of the oldest areas of the underworld," Quinn said. "Ixtab couldn't have you waltzing down Main Street, could she?" She smirked. "But you were supposed to use the elevator, genius." She gave a hard stare at Ren like she was noticing her for the first time. "Who's the girl?"

Ren shuffled her feet. "Er...I'm—"

"Her name's Ren," Brooks said.

"I can smell she's not entirely human," Quinn said.

Ren nodded like she was about to spill her guts, but before she could, Quinn added, "Okay, so three half-breeds, a hellhound, and a full...human." Her gaze shifted to Hondo, who was smiling. *Smiling!*

He pushed his hair back and folded his arms casually, but I could tell he was just trying to act cool to impress Quinn. I was pretty sure it would take a lot more than flexing biceps to impress *her.* "So how about we check out of Rattle Hell Hotel," Hondo said.

"Ixtab's not going to like that you brought them with you, Zane," Quinn said. "Do you know how dangerous this place can be?"

I swallowed the lump in my throat. "Uh . . . she can't know we're here."

Quinn looked like she might grip my throat with her bare hands. "There's no way to avoid the queen."

"Please, Quinn," Brooks said softly. "We need help. . . ."

"No one comes to the underworld for help," Quinn spat.

"We do," I said. "Please. Just get us through a gateway . . . without Ixtab knowing."

Quinn's eyes found the map still clutched in Brooks's hand. "That's a pretty rare and valuable thing, little sister."

Brooks pushed her hair behind her ears and stood taller. "And it's yours if you help us."

I wanted to shout *NO!* We needed that map to get home once we rescued my dad. The longer I was off the island, the higher the chances of the gods finding me. But when I saw Quinn consider the trade, I held back. It was more important to get to South Dakota. We'd figure out how to get home after. Plus, I was pretty sure Brooks had a backup plan. She was probably born with one!

"You'd give me this map," Quinn said flatly.

"And then we'll be gone," I added.

"Loooong gone." Hondo mimicked throwing a football to make his point.

Rosie practically nodded.

Quinn eyed Hondo up and down. Then she flashed a quick glance at Brooks. "Fine, it's your death. Follow me," she said. "You all need some dry, warm, non-human-smelling clothes."

We followed Quinn to the door she'd just come from. Beyond it, an escalator ascended into the darkness.

"Hell has elevators *and* escalators?" Ren said, looking up to what had to be a thousand floors.

Hondo tapped me on the shoulder. "How do we know this doesn't lead to Bloodsucking House or Rip Out Your Guts House?"

"We don't." And with that, I stepped onto the escalator.

12

We ended up in a long hallway that reminded
me of some run-down hotel. It reeked like rotting beans.
"What's that *smell?*" Ren asked, covering her nose with her
sleeve.

"Pus River is just beyond these walls," Quinn said. "Hang
out here long enough and you get used to it."

"Kind of like the dairy farms back home," Hondo muttered to me.

Right. Except there was a big difference between cow
manure and a river filled with oozing, contaminated yellow pus!

"We don't have to cross that river, right?" I asked.

Hondo cleared his throat and spoke loudly. Too loudly.
"A little pus never hurt anybody." Then he turned to me and
made a gagging face.

Rosie groaned. But Quinn seemed oblivious to Hondo's
attempts to get her attention. She walked ahead at a clipped
pace, her head bent close to Brooks, whispering. I'm sure they
had a lot of catching up to do. They hadn't been in contact
since we were in the Old World seven months ago.

"NO!" Quinn said to Brooks, quieting her voice a second
later.

The worn velvety carpet was purple with big dark stains,

which I was way hoping wasn't blood. The walls were made of rough stone and covered in graffiti: a massive snake biting off someone's head (bad memories), a crazed skeleton spearing a hellhound, an enormous hairy bat baring fangs dripping with blood. At the center was Ixtab, surrounded by hellhounds, holding a decapitated head toward the stormy sky. Yeah, you could call this place Nightmare Hall.

Quinn must have seen us staring, because she said over her shoulder, "That's a battle scene from the old war days when Ixtab took over."

Ren tugged on my arm. "What do you think the chances of Ixtab being my mom are?"

I was about to tell her she could do worse, when Quinn, still huddled with Brooks, hollered, "You can't be serious!" She whirled to face us. "A mud person? That's not possible!"

"Yeah, well, that's what people say about aliens, too," Ren said. "And guess what? Where do you think the Maya gods came from?"

Quinn swung her ponytail back and forth as she sauntered ahead. "Please tell me you're not one of *those* people," she said to Ren. "Let me guess. An ancient astronaut? Humans are so gullible. They'll believe anything."

Ren opened her mouth to argue, when I shot her a *chill-out* look. She scowled, and I could tell she was battling with herself. I knew the feeling. My mouth was always a few steps ahead of my brain, too. Ren's cheeks reddened, and just when I thought she'd gotten herself under control, she blurted, "I've seen pictures of the carvings on King Pakal's sarcophagus. He's totally driving a spaceship. His hands are on levers and his feet are on pedals. And..." she went on excitedly, "his mouth is connected to what looks like a breathing tube!"

"Seriously?" Hondo said. "The Maya gods are aliens? That explains why the demons look so bug-eyed and they have those weird-shaped heads."

Quinn snorted, then mumbled to herself as she picked up her pace.

I said to Ren, "Maybe cool it on the conspiracy stuff while we're down here?"

She rolled her eyes and muttered, "It's totally true."

A minute later, we stood in a dim, cavernous warehouse with dark corners and rows and rows of dusty shelves. It kinda looked like Home Depot, but instead of tools and toilets, this place was filled with spears, clubs, axes, strange feathered masks and headdresses, and tiny clay statues. There was even a whole row of little golden frog figurines.

"What is this place?" Brooks asked.

"Junkyard Row," Quinn said. "All the stuff no one in Xib'alb'a needs or uses gets sent here, and Clementino, the junk warden, gets orders on what to burn and when. The problem is, he's *way* too nostalgic and, as you can see, he keeps more than he destroys." She picked up an old flip-style cell phone. "It's also stuff left over from the deceased. You wouldn't believe what they show up with in their pockets."

That was sort of depressing to think about.

"We're supposed to get our new clothes *here*, in a junk-yard?" I muttered to Hondo.

He just shrugged, looking around in awe. "These weapons

are seriously sick! You think I could take a few?" he asked
Quinn. "And maybe a feathered mask?"

"They're broken, useless," Quinn told him. "Plus, touch
anything in here and you'll have a curse on your head, which I
wouldn't recommend. Maya curses are the worst—they really
stick. Clementino!" she called as she stalked down one of the
shadowy aisles. "Oh, where is that foolish man? Don't just
stand there," she barked at us, "follow me!"

We did as we were told. Even hellhound Rosie, but she
totally snorted a few trails of smoke in defiance.

"I saw that," I whispered.

When we reached the back of the warehouse, a small
old man (and by small, I mean, like, five feet tall, hunched
rounded shoulders, and skinny toothpick legs) came out of
double wooden doors with painted panels showing a bloodletting ceremony. I'd read about those in my book about the
Maya. In an effort to communicate with their ancestors and
the gods, people had stabbed their skin to release blood.

My guts tightened.

Quinn took the man aside for a whispering convo. Then
they came back and Clementino gave us a wide toothy smile.
His teeth were humongous, like he wore a set of fake chom-
pers size extra large. They didn't fit in his scrawny face. Had
he stolen them from some dead person's mouth? "Time to get
ready," he announced.

"No one's draining my blood!" Brooks declared with a
frown.

Clementino grabbed for her backpack. "Hey!" she cried.
"That's mine."

"Can't take anything into Xib'alb'a until it's been sanitized," he said. "It's a serious health hazard."

"Uh, everyone here is already dead," Hondo said. Luckily, Rosie was too busy sniffing around to hear the word as a command. "And I really like the shirt I'm wearing."

"There are worse things than being dead," Clementino said, smacking his lips together. "Take me for example. Perfectly happy pawnshop owner until the day a dirty rotten demon decides he doesn't like me. Next thing I know, I'm being hauled here." With a dramatic sigh, he added, "I think he was jealous of my teeth."

"Sounds like a raw deal," I said, remembering how Rosie had been whisked to the underworld, too.

"How was I supposed to know you should never win in a poker game against a demon?" Clementino went on. "I had a straight flush and—"

"Enough story time," Quinn butted in. "Give him the pack, Brooks."

Clementino grabbed my arm and whispered, "Demons are notorious cheats—and sore losers. But you didn't hear that from me."

Quinn turned to Hondo. "No one's going anywhere in the underworld until you scrub down and get rid of that human stench."

"But these are my lucky boots!" Ren cried. "Can I get them back later?"

"If there *is* a later," Clementino said way too gleefully. "Who's first?"

Hondo's hand shot up. Then he leaned closer to Clementino. "What exactly *is* a scrub-down?"

"Agua caliente, magic foam, and a pinch of ancient bone dust," the old man said. "I'll have you smelling like the dead in two minutes flat."

Hondo groaned. "Can we *not* do the bone dust?"

"Look," I said to Clementino, "we don't really have time for foam and dust or whatever."

Ren nodded emphatically. "I'm allergic to dust. Makes me have sneezing fits."

Quinn cursed under her breath and said, "Why do I always get the impossible tasks?" She pushed us toward some stalls with hanging curtains in the front. "¡Ándele! Get undressed in there. I'll pick out some dry clothes for you while you bathe."

"Not many clothes here," Clementino mumbled to Quinn. "I just burned all the snakeskins. And those demon hides? All gone. But I might have something. . . ."

"What was wrong with our own clothes?" Hondo shouted from the dressing room next to mine.

There was no way I was going to put on a demon hide. It was bad enough that I'd just been forced to roll around in a bunch of dead skin cells. And after that I'd had to sit in a giant clay pot filled with hot foamy water that had some very suspicious bubbles. Finally, I got peppered with ancient bone dust, and I choked so hard on it I thought I'd cough up a lung.

It was definitely a low moment.

Or at least that's what I thought until I stood in the dressing room, wearing a gray animal pelt (which looked a lot like rat fur) as underwear, my body coated in bone dust. At least old Clem hadn't put Fuego and my jade tooth through his "fumigation" once I told him where they'd come from.

Clementino and Quinn whispered outside the tattered drape.

"This is all you have?" she said.

"I burn the clothes left over from the dead," Clementino said. "These came from the food court on level eight after those shameful souls went vegan."

"I vote we exit on the vegan level," Hondo called out. He popped his head in between the curtains separating our changing areas. "That means they won't eat off our faces, right?"

"Pretty much."

A second later, Clementino's wrinkled hand popped through the closed drape. "I accidentally destroyed your clothes during fumigation. Oops. Here. You're lucky I hadn't burned these yet."

I took what he offered. *Lucky?* "Is this a joke?" I stared down at the multicolored wide-striped polo shirt and electric-blue polyester shorts. Seriously? Quinn expected me to wear a Hot Dog on a Stick uniform?

"No *way!*" Hondo shouted. "This looks like something that *Blue's Clues* dude would wear."

I frowned. "You watch *Blue's Clues?*"

"When I was a kid, okay? The old show!"

Okay, I know throwing on some stupid fast-food uniform

with big old fat stripes was the least of my worries, but I hadn't exactly imagined rescuing my dad in *this* outfit.

"You could always walk around naked," Quinn said, not even trying to mute her stupid laugh.

Hondo and I came out of our dressing rooms at the same time in matching uniforms, except my shorts practically hung to my knees. Hondo's shirt was too tight, and it had a ketchup smear right in the center.

Rosie lay down and buried her head under her paws. "Be glad you're a hellhound," I mumbled.

Quinn stood there, holding matching baseball caps.

"I don't do hats," Hondo said, trying to look cool.

With a sigh, Quinn said, "Fine by me. But it's to cover any leftover scent of your hair. Bone dust only lasts so long. We could just shave your head if you prefer."

Hondo took the hat.

Then Quinn handed each of us a pair of white sneakers. "These are the only sizes Clem had, so hopefully they fit."

I shoved my feet into the mustard-and-grease-stained sneakers, which were a half size too small, especially on my bigger left foot.

Clementino eyed us up and down, then said to Quinn, "Too bad they can't go see Ixchel's apprentice. They could use sprucing up."

I remembered reading about Ixchel, the goddess of healing, the moon, beauty, and other stuff. She was also called the lady of the rainbow. "The goddess has an apprentice for makeovers?" I asked.

Clementino nodded, stroking his white stubbly chin.

"Way up on level nine, for the souls who need a little extra something. Most newly deceased people have the worst self-esteem, so they get a makeover at the spa. You know, to help them adjust."

"Unless souls enter on the lowest level of Xib'alb'a," Quinn said. "Then they just get their eyes gouged out."

"Uh...what level are *we* on?" Hondo asked casually.

"The lowest," Quinn said with a smug smile.

Rosie lifted her head from the corner where she'd been snoozing (I know, who could snooze at a time like this?) and smirked.

"What? You entered on a higher floor when you died? Well, we can't all be hellhounds!" I argued as I planted the stupid cap on my head.

Brooks and Ren were waiting for us back at the bloodletting doors. I could feel my cheeks getting hotter as I went over. This was so humiliating! The only thing that didn't make me melt into the ground was the fact that Brooks was wearing the girl version of the uniform: a sleeveless striped shirt, and a hat that looked like an upside-down popcorn bucket. She and Ren were twinning, except somehow Ren's red boots hadn't been destroyed in Clem's dumb fumigation process (she said it was because they were made Texas-strong). I was glad to see that Brooks's backpack hung off her right shoulder.

I opened my mouth to speak, but Brooks said, "Say one word, Obispo, and I'll drop you a hundred feet."

Brooks was totally strong enough to make good on her promise, so I kept my mouth shut.

Quinn called Rosie over and whispered something in her ear, and the hellhound took off running. "Hey!" I called after her. "Rosie!"

"Stop wigging, Obispo," Quinn said. "You'll see her again."

"How long do I have to stay in this stupid uniform?" Hondo licked his finger and rubbed at a ketchup stain.

"For as long as you're here," Quinn snorted. "And to be honest, even the fried-hot-dog smell and bone dust can't cover *your* human scent," she said to Hondo. "You sure you want to risk bringing him along, Zane?"

"Hondo comes with us."

"It's your funeral."

Quinn turned to Clementino. "Thanks, Clem. I owe you one."

Clementino rubbed his bone-dust-covered hands together. "A deal's a deal. You'll put in a good word for me? Get me into that high stakes poker game up on level six?" He flashed another toothy grin.

"You really think you can beat demons on their own turf?" Quinn asked.

With the flick of his wrist, a king of diamonds card appeared in his hand. "They don't call me One-Eyed Ax for nothing."

I'd played enough card games to know that the king of diamonds is depicted with one eye and an ax. Great. We'd just relied on a dead gambler to conceal us from the underworld's monsters.

Clem turned to the rest of us and snickered. "May your

journey be ... lucky." He disappeared behind the bloodletting doors. "You're going to need all the luck you can get," he shouted from the other side.

Brooks said to Quinn, "Maybe it's not a good idea to trust someone called One-Eyed Ax."

"Desperate people don't get to choose whom to trust," Quinn said. "Let's go."

Brooks rolled her eyes and tugged on her hat as we followed her sister out of the dim warehouse. "I hate it here."

Hondo asked, "Where are we going now?"

Quinn looked back over her shoulder. "Pus River."

13

Here's when things went from semi-smooth to Maya mayhem. (Always expect mayhem in our world.)

Sporting our Hot Dog on a Stick polyester, we followed Quinn up a couple flights of corroded metal stairs. "You found a gateway?" I asked her.

"No, I just thought a tour of Pus River would be super fun."

Once we got to the top, Quinn stopped at a claw-slashed door and faced us like some kind of general. "Anyone afraid of heights?"

Water dripped off the stairwell (at least I *hoped* it was water) as we all shook our heads.

"So, is this, uh . . . the river place . . . ? Is that what's behind the door?" Hondo asked, trying to look chill, but I could tell he was nervous.

Quinn gave an annoyed smirk. "We'll be flying the rest of the way. But don't relax yet. If any of the beasts below get a whiff of you, things could get hairy and bloody, and they'll notify Ixtab of your presence in less than a second." She exhaled. "That's why I sent Rosie ahead. She can act as our on-the-ground defense, just in case. Now, a few rules." She flashed three fingers. "Don't talk. Don't breathe too much. And, oh, for sure *do not* sneeze or cough. Got it?"

"Why can't we breathe?" I asked.

"I said don't breathe *too much*. Unless you want to inhale poisonous gas. Let's go." Quinn shoved the door open.

Stepping through the door was like being dropped into a painting created with every possible shade of red. Below was a wasteland of rocks, canyons, craters, and what looked like dried-up lake beds. Red dust covered everything. The blood-shot sky was streaked with trails of silvery dust. The air was thin and hot and dry.

"Obispo and Human," Quinn said, pointing to me and Hondo, "you're with me. Ren, you go with Brooks." Quinn quickly changed into a giant white eagle with brown-speckled wings. Brooks followed her sister's lead and morphed into her hawk self.

Everyone climbed onto the birds' backs, and after a stomach-dropping takeoff (with Quinn in the lead, of course), we were soaring through the toxic air.

My jade tooth vibrated once against my neck. I tugged on it. *Hurakan? Is that you?* I know it sounds crazy, but it felt like he was trying to communicate with me. *Hello?* He didn't answer.

Hondo spoke low in my ear: "This is freaking awesome." He acted like we weren't flying over hell and trying to blend in so we didn't get our faces eaten off.

I gripped Quinn's neck and opened my mind to hers.

We don't have to, like, swim in Pus River, right?

It's the only gateway out of here. Take it or leave it.

How close will it get us to South Dakota?

Quinn shook her head. Even as an eagle she could sigh

and roll her eyes. *I'll get you as close as I can. Tell muscle-head back there to quit making so much noise.*

I was so busy scoping out the landscape below I didn't notice the thing flying up behind us until it was so close there was no mistaking the familiar, best-forgotten beast.

Red bulging eyes, no nose, and a mouth filled with long, sharp fangs.

A demon runner! With *wings!*

Quinn! Demons!

She swiveled her head, cursed, then turned up the speed. *Just act cool. He'll fly right by. Unless he picked up the human's scent. I told you not to bring him!*

But we're covered in bone dust!

Even bone dust can't completely cover THIS human.

Act cool. Act cool. Act cool. What were the other rules? *Barely breathe.* Total fail. I was practically hyperventilating.

The demon runner's spiderweb wings stretched wide beyond his bloated, hairy body. When the heck did demon runners get wings? Maybe it was a hell thing? The monster sniffed the air. Once. Twice.

Uh-oh. *That* couldn't be good.

Brooks was cruising to our right and hadn't spotted the demon yet, or maybe she just wanted to pretend it wasn't there. Ren was busy taking in the red world, probably looking for aliens.

Just as I turned to whisper to Hondo to stay calm, he saw the creature and did the worst possible thing. He screamed, "Demon!"

Idiot! Quinn said. *Hold on!*

The scream started a chain reaction. Ren shrieked. Brooks's panicked war cry was strangled by the thin, hot air.

Quinn went into a nosedive. Straight for a mountain of rock.

Quinn!

The demon runner released a screech that shook the dust loose from the sky. That's when things got even uglier, because, instead of one demon, we now had two more on our tails!

Same hellish red eyes, same long fangs, same bloated hairy bodies. Same grossness!

I gripped Fuego. Could my spear take out three demon runners?

No, Zane! ordered Quinn. *We're almost there.*

No, you don't want these monsters hanging with us? Or no, don't throw the spear?

God, Obispo. Do you always have to be so dense? If you throw that spear, it will alert an entire army. Never mind that you can't kill a demon runner that's already in Xib'alb'a! Don't you know anything?

I glanced over at Brooks. She was flying directly into the headwinds, unblinking. Her eyes were ablaze, and her talons were flexed and ready to tear out someone's eyes. Ren was leaning into her like some kind of jockey racing for her life. Quinn released a series of low-pitched whistles. Brooks nodded and responded with some screeches. They could bird-speak?

The demon runners were only a few feet away, shrieking and clawing at the air with their hooked feet.

Hondo launched his Hot Dog on a Stick hat at one and pumped his fist when it hit.

Quinn reached back and snapped her beak at Hondo, missing his fingers by an inch. "Hey!" he hollered as she let out an ear-piercing cry. A second later, a familiar roar echoed from far below. Rosie?

At the same moment, Quinn and Brooks made a figure eight, looping across each other's paths like acrobatic super-birds. Something about this move confused the demons, because they stopped in midair and stared like they weren't sure which direction to go.

That's when Rosie appeared. Her massive black wings batted the demons out of the air like they were nothing more than gnats. Bright orange-and-yellow flames raged from her eyes and mouth as she roared like a dragon.

Since when did Rosie get wings? I asked Quinn.

Only in Xib'alb'a.

"That's my girl!" I yelled.

"Kill 'em good, Rosie!" Hondo shouted.

But every time Rosie swatted a demon runner out of the sky, the stupid monster would just shake it off and come right back.

Hondo death-gripped me with one hand and pointed with the other. "Quinn's trying to kill us."

I can't say I didn't agree with Hondo, because we were basically racing toward a mountain of solid rock that was sure to crush our skulls.

Detour! Quinn said.

"Quinn!" I screamed. "The mountain!"

You might want to close your eyes for this, she said. Then she zoomed us toward our deaths.

No way. If I was going to die in Xib'alb'a, I didn't want this place to be the last thing I saw.

Instead, I looked at Brooks.

Then Quinn slammed into the mountainside.

14

••••

I braced myself for impact, but it never came.
The mountain turned into a thick fog at the last possible second. I glanced over my shoulder to see if we were being followed. Guess the demons didn't make it. Relief flooded my locked muscles, and I nearly tumbled off Quinn.

Hondo's fingers dug into my back as he yowled in my ear. "We're alive!"

Please tell him to shut up, Quinn said.

My insides felt like they'd been scooped out with a shovel. *What . . . ? How did we make it?*

I opened a passageway for us at the last second. Ha! Those demon runners are going to have migraines for a week.

Clean, cool air filled my lungs as I glanced over at Brooks, who was soaring with wide wings, like she was made for the sky. Thankfully, Ren was wide-awake. Rosie raced past us, howling in triumph.

We soared through the fog and emerged into an alien landscape very different from the one we had just escaped. Four reddish-pink suns hung low in the sky. A gilded jungle stretched out before us. The trees' leaves, trunks, and branches were made of a glimmering metal that reflected a rainbow of colors.

"This place is paradise!" Hondo said breathlessly. "I told you . . . you have to *visualize* the outcome you want. You think all that gold is real?"

That's when I realized that Hondo was built for this strange and amazing and dangerous life. He'd never been meant for janitorial work or even running tours on Holbox. I mean, I knew he was happy on the island, but here he was 100 percent alive.

This doesn't look like Pus River, I told Quinn. *Or South Dakota.*

Change of plans.

What? Why?

Those demons have already told Ixtab you're here.

Panic gripped me. *Then we have to run!*

¡No, menso! Do that and you'll be dead in less than five seconds. You have no choice. You have to face her now.

Are you insane?

Listen, Mr. I-Don't-Have-a-Single-Strategic-Bone-in-My-Body. Our plan's been thwarted, which means you have to pretend you intended to come see her.

My insides coiled into a tight ball. *And say what?*

I'm sure you'll think of something.

My mind raced, trying to come up with a list of excuses, but then terror took over as I imagined Ixtab seeing right through me and ripping my heart out with one hand.

"This place is sick," Hondo hollered. "I thought we were going to Pus River, not King Midas's hideout."

Midas? Quinn said. *Tell him the Greeks had nothing on the Maya! We were the first great engineers, architects, and* astronomers. And *we developed one of the most accurate calendar systems in human history.*

Okaaayyy, no more mention of the Greeks.

Quinn let out a loud cry that Brooks seemed to understand. Brooks's eyes narrowed with some kind of shock, then determination. I figured Quinn had told her about our little change of plans.

As we descended farther, the suns melted into the horizon, casting a pinkish glow across the gilded jungle. The trees gave way to a huge complex that was dominated by nine golden Maya pyramids arranged in a circle. For a second, I thought the layout looked a little like Puksí'ikal, the heart of the Old World. But that place was drab and gray, and cobwebs choked the trees. This place . . . it was dripping with vibrant gold.

At the center of the complex were silvery demon runners with sharklike skin and thick white braids hanging down their backs. They sparred with axes, swords, and spears, showing off their fancy footwork on what looked like a shiny marble floor. Some stood at the far end and shot arrows from blowguns aimed at rubber dummies fifty or more yards away. These weren't the demons that had just chased us. This was Ixtab's elite army.

"Quinn, those dummies are moving."

Really, Obispo . . . you can be so dim-witted. In real life, targets never stand still. So, of course the demons would practice on things that move. You should see the flying dummies!

With eyes glowing silvery blue, the demons all turned to watch us descend. The place went as silent as the midnight desert when we came in for a smooth landing. We hopped off Quinn and Brooks, and the sisters shifted back into their human forms.

Quinn raised her right arm and the demons went back to their sparring. Wow. If she had that kind of authority, I wondered why she hadn't called off the demons that had pursued us a few minutes earlier. Was there, like, some kind of demon hierarchy?

I followed Quinn's gaze to an impressive square temple on a pyramid that seemed to stretch a hundred stories high. A giant waterfall surged from the top terrace down the other nine, splashing into a pool at the bottom.

Hondo was right. This place was amazing, like one of those fancy resorts you see on TV. Except for all the demon combat, that is.

Two soldiers wrestled a few feet away from us, grunting like they'd been at it all day. Hondo shook his head and whispered to me. "See the one on the left? Good offensive sugar stance." I knew that term from his training. It's basically where one leg is in front and the other's in the rear, making it easy to switch from defensive mode to attack mode.

"But that one on the right?" he continued. "She should be in defensive square stance, and she's not even close to squatting low enough. Check out the footwork."

Hondo was spot-on, because a couple seconds later, the sugar-stance demon outmaneuvered the other one and dropped her to the dirt, pressing an ax to her throat.

"I need to get me one of those axes," Hondo whispered.

While Brooks told Ren about the change of plans, I leaned closer to my uncle to do the same.

He cursed a few times, but I barely paid attention, because my entire focus was on Ixtab. She stood at the edge of one of the lower terraces, barking orders at some guy, waving her arms angrily. I couldn't make out her words until she shouted, "Then find the little beast!"

At the same moment, she glanced at us. Our eyes met, but she didn't give me a welcome-back smile or even a tiny wave hello. Nope—the newest landlord of hell scowled at me, then disappeared only to materialize in front of us a second later.

Here's the thing about the goddess of Xib'alb'a: she's striking. Her eyes are bright sapphires and her face is sculpted perfectly, like a mask. But you somehow know that if you dig deeper there's another mask and another and another, and you get the creepy sense that you're never seeing Ixtab's true face.

"Well, well, well," she sang. "If it isn't the willful son of fire. I was wondering how long it would be before you showed up." A barely there smile tugged at her lips as she took in our outfits. Her gaze swept over us, landing on Rosie. Then came the real smile.

Whatever.

Rosie lowered her eyes and then her chest and head, like she was bowing.

"No need for such formality, Rosie." Ixtab nodded once and added, "But I, too, am glad you're back."

My insides twisted.

The goddess sauntered over in her white silk pants and fitted black tank top. She wore diamond earrings bigger than any rapper's and a row of at least six gold bracelets. "How about a nice snake head or two?" Ixtab asked Rosie in a syrupy sweet voice.

"Gross!" I cried. "She doesn't eat snake heads."

Ixtab said, "*All* hellhounds eat snakes. It's one of their favorite treats." She called a demon over and told her to take Rosie for some "sustenance." I was about to argue but stopped when I saw how fast Rosie was wagging her nub tail. My heart split into a million pieces. Did I even know her anymore?

As I watched Rosie go, Ixtab's smile flipped into a frown. "How dare you bring these miscreants into my kingdom, Zane."

Keep it cool, Zane. Keep it cool. "Er . . . sorry," I said, though what I really wanted to shout was *How dare I? You lied to me! You locked us up on that island.* But if I did that, then she'd know we'd reached the wall, and she might suspect we were trying to escape. Ixtab was the queen of deception, and she'd see right through a lie.

Ixtab eyed each of us, lingering a little longer on Ren. Did she know just by looking that Ren was a godborn, too? Or that maybe she was her daughter? "And who are you?"

Ren's cool eyes widened. "I'm Renata."

"She's a godborn," Hondo blurted.

Ixtab drew back her shoulders and studied Ren like she could see into her soul or something. Maybe she could.

I socked Hondo in the shoulder. "Dude!"

"Ow . . . What'd you hit me for?"

"Way to hold back some information in case we needed to, like, negotiate or something."

"Oh, Zane," Ixtab said. "I suspected she was a godborn the moment I saw her. Do you think we gods are that stupid?"

Was I supposed to answer that?

"Tell me, Renata," Ixtab practically purred. "What do you think of the underworld?"

Ren shuffled her feet and looked Ixtab right in the eye like she was checking her out, too. *Please don't say something stupid*, I thought.

"Have you noticed how much your demons look like aliens?" Ren said.

I buried my face in my hands and took a deep breath so I wouldn't strangle her.

Ixtab replied coolly, "I'll come back to you in a moment." Then she shifted her gaze to me. "Why are you here?"

"Uh...I, uh, had some questions."

Brooks stared at the sky, her nostrils flaring.

At the same moment, Quinn snatched an arrow that was sailing through the air, right at Hondo. I hadn't even seen it coming.

"Whoa!" His dark eyes grew ten sizes. "Thanks."

She shot him a side glare. "I should've let it skewer you."

With a slow grin, Hondo waggled his eyebrows at me as if to say *She totally likes me*.

Ixtab said, "The middle of the field is probably not the safest place for you to stand. Come."

Oh, good. She cared about our safety. Excellent sign. Plus, I was glad for the extra time to think up an excuse for why we'd come here. My brain churned out the possibilities.

I could ask her about the mud person and mapping. Seemed like a perfectly legit reason to cruise to Xib'alb'a. Then we could scram out the back exit of Pus River. Maybe this wasn't such a bad thing. I'd not only get to South Dakota, but I'd get there with some answers.

We made the steep climb up the nine terraces, which Ixtab told us represented each of the nine layers of the underworld. At least until she "finished the new upper level."

Then she said, more to herself than us, "Heaven gets thirteen layers, so surely the underworld is worthy of one more."

We finally reached the top. Sheer white drapes hung in neat rows across the temple's ten-foot opening. The curtains parted as we approached. We found ourselves in the most luxurious room/temple/penthouse I'd ever seen. The light pink walls looked like they had been hand-plastered in a swirling pattern. Along the gold-trimmed ceiling were jaguar heads carved out of jade and other gemstones I didn't recognize. There were ornate chairs with thick-fringed pillows and granite tables with scrolled feet.

Hondo let out a low whistle as he looked around. Brooks twisted a stray curl, acting totally uninterested, but I could tell she was impressed, too. Quinn just stood at attention like the trained warrior she was. And Ren nosed around with her face way too close to all the delicate statues, which were probably worth millions of dollars.

Ixtab looked my uncle and me up and down and huffed. Then she spoke into a bracelet. "Get Itzel up to my private chamber immediately."

Hondo, Brooks, and I exchanged glances. A second later an

old woman walked in. She was wearing a raggedy dress that looked pretty much like a burlap chile sack. She was nothing but gray and ash tones and looked like a sketch that hadn't been completely filled in.

"Get some decent clothes for our guests," Ixtab ordered. "Something that isn't going to drive my demons mad with hunger."

"But that's what *these* clothes were supposed to prevent," I said.

Ixtab raised a perfectly groomed eyebrow. "Clementino is an amateur. I don't know why Quinn bothers with him. Everyone knows bone dust only lasts so long, and surely she realized you'd be here longer than thirty minutes."

Quinn didn't so much as flinch. Me? I was having a mini heart attack, worried that Ixtab was onto us and picturing our heads on tonight's dinner menu.

Ixtab glanced back at Itzel. "They look preposterous, and I can't take that wretched hot-dog smell."

Seriously? She lived in pus-smelling Xib'alb'a! Of course, she probably never visited the lowest level of the underworld.

Itzel huffed. "First it was the demon-soldier uniforms. Now you expect my creations to cover these . . . these . . ." She shuddered like Ixtab was asking her to drain Blood River with a straw. "I am the world's best designer. I have influenced the most artistic minds in history. I am not about to outfit these putrid humans, who, no matter what, will end up on every worst-dressed list. No." She shook her head. "I will not have my name associated with such trash."

Ixtab sighed. "Would you rather fit the giants?"

Itzel eyed each of us with beady eyes. "I have a good mind to stuff you in paisley."

"Something discreet," Ixtab said.

"Yeah," Hondo said. "I definitely don't do paisley."

"Fine," Itzel crabbed. "Polka dots it is." Then she huffed and stomped off.

Brooks looked at me and shrugged. I only hoped Itzel had better taste than what *she* was wearing.

"Now, Zane," Ixtab said, "why are you here?"

I had to proceed cautiously. Ixtab was cunning and had pulled off the greatest Maya con of all time by duping the gods into thinking I was dead. It would be too easy to walk into a trap, so I had to be on guard. I unfolded bits and pieces of what had happened at Cab's. Ixtab listened without a single emotion on her face. Not even a twitch. Was she breathing? "So ... uh ..." I hated that my voice trembled. "I need to know who made the mud person and why they'd want to map me or—"

"I've never heard of mapping." She glanced at her watch, frowned, and tapped the screen. "Sounds preposterous."

"We think they were trying to steal Zane's powers," Ren said.

"Doubtful." Ixtab tapped a finger along her sculpted chin. "The better question is how they penetrated *my* shadow magic."

The magic that imprisoned us on the island, you mean? I wanted to scream, but I couldn't afford to (a) make her mad or (b) give her any clue that I was planning to rescue my dad. "So, if the mud freak wasn't there to steal my powers," I said, "why was it there?"

"That is quite inconsequential right now." Ixtab's face reddened. "How dare anyone defy me and touch my magic! I've spread myself too thin, doing renovations on nine levels of the underworld simultaneously. Nine! And we're adding a tenth level! Did I mention that I'm also expected to manage the souls, feed the demons, train..." She took a deep breath. "When I find whoever did this..." she said with a growl. Her honey-streaked hair began to shift to blue demon status, but just as quickly she got her temper back under control. "I will have to do some investigating. It could be just a rogue group. We get those from time to time. Lesser gods are always annoyed about something. But not to worry—they never succeed."

"But how did they know I was alive?"

Ixtab's expression gave away nothing, but I could tell she was doing some deep goddess thinking. "Don't touch that!" she barked at Ren, who was stroking the head of a tiny golden crocodile statue.

Ren jerked her hand back.

Ixtab scowled as she circled the girl, studying her carefully. "Small for a child of a great Maya god. And yet so much..."

"So much what?" I asked.

"I will ask the questions," Ixtab said. "Tell me, *Renata*... Where did you come from, and how is it that your skin buzzes with so much magic? Before you speak"—Ixtab held up a perfectly manicured finger with shiny black polish—"I should be fair and tell you that a single lie equals a two-year swim in Blood River. Two lies? Well, let's hope it doesn't come to that bloody mess."

I was for sure going to be sick.

Ren looked from me to Brooks to Hondo. "Uh... Texas," she managed.

"Texas," Ixtab repeated. "Ah, yes... 'Remember the Alamo.' Such a terrible siege! I am so good at inspiring revenge, which is the only reason the Texans eventually won the war. Nakon will tell you otherwise, but we all know what an exaggerator he is."

"Er, but..." Ren faltered. "Aren't you... like, *from* Mexico?"

Ixtab waved her hand through the air. "I am from wherever the power is. Now, *Renata from Texas*, it is no coincidence that you appeared on the island the night before this wicked perpetrator appeared, so perhaps you have the answers."

"That's what I said!" Ren beamed. Then her face fell. "Wait. I don't have any answers...."

"Then prove to me that you're not cloaked in magic and you really are a godborn." Before anyone could blink, Ixtab closed the six-foot gap between her and Ren and grabbed hold of her hand.

Ixtab's face was unreadable, but it was clear they were using telepathy. I was dying to know what they were saying. There was some nodding, a few gasps, and then Ixtab withdrew and blinked several times in astonishment. She turned to me with laser focus.

"Well?" I asked Ren. "Is she your mom?"

Ren looked away and shook her head.

"*You...*" Ixtab hissed at me. "This is *your* fault. You're the reason... YOU put out a call to godborns?"

Note to godborns: If/when you put together a team for a

quest, make sure you tell the members to keep their big fat mouths shut!

"My fault?" I could feel my cheeks reddening. "You told her?" I said to Ren.

"No! She . . . It kind of fell out of my brain."

Crap! What else dribbled out?

Ixtab drew closer to me. But no way was I going to let her intimidate me, not for another second. Nope. I had a lot to say. And it sounded like . . . "I, uh . . . I had to be sure!"

"Who gave you the right to use the magic of Itzam-yée' on such a stupid and reckless idea?" Uh-oh. Ixtab's eyes burned with blue flames. "Do you have any idea what you've done, Zane?"

"Yeah, I found a way to call to the godborns! Now maybe you can find other survivors."

"No, Zane." Ixtab stepped so close I could see her perfect pores. "You made the godborns *visible* to the gods."

15

How could one nugget of truth cause such a massive shock wave? In that moment, Ms. Cab's words came crashing down on me: *Magic is so mercurial. One can never fully gauge its temperament or understand its logic.*

"You mean...the magic in the paper...it betrayed me?" I cried.

Ixtab scowled, and I could swear her eyes flashed in Ren's direction before she said, "*This* is why we need to reopen SHIHOM!"

"Shy...huh?"

"The Shaman Institute of Higher-Order Magic!"

"I'd for sure go to that school." Ren's whole face lit up.

"How was I supposed to know—?"

Ixtab cut me off. "Imbeciles like you need to learn to respect magic's properties." She pinched the bridge of her nose. "You need to understand that a wild beast lives at the center of *all* magic and it *cannot* be tamed. Not by gods. Not by anyone."

"Yeah, well, I didn't get the almighty Maya training, okay?" I felt sick. If there were more godborns out there, and they were visible to the gods, they'd be murdered in their sleep. And it would be *my* fault. How did things go from bad to worse to *the universe is collapsing in three, two, one* so fast?

Ren gasped. "That's what those little flying things were,

Zane. The night I was attacked, before I came to the island. The gods—they must've sent them."

Ixtab rolled her eyes. "If the gods were aware of your pathetic existence, I'd know about it. But there is no doubt that *someone* picked up on your energy. The magic spinning around a newly awakened godborn is powerful. Someone is willing to go to great lengths to find you."

If they found Ren, then . . . I seriously didn't want to follow my mind to the conclusion that was begging to be heard. But I couldn't get the image of the message out of my mind. *Help us. Before it's too late.* "I think . . ." I swallowed hard. "I think they already have. And other godborns, too."

Ixtab glared at me with her scorching sapphire eyes and said slowly, "You're absolutely correct. For once."

This was definitely one time I didn't want to be right. I would've much rather she said something like *Oh, no, Zane. Those mud freaks are all liars. Can't trust a thing they say.* But it wasn't like I could trust *her,* either. I wanted to ask Ixtab why she'd told me all those months ago that no other godborns had survived. Had she lied to me then, or had she really been in the dark?

Brooks beat me to the punch. "How do you know all this?"

Ixtab flashed an annoyed look. "I am the goddess of the underworld. I trained the greatest Maya army of the dead. I have eyes and ears everywhere."

"Aliens," Ren whispered to me with a confident nod.

Ixtab said to Quinn, "Take the others downstairs. I need to talk to Zane alone."

"No!" Brooks shouted.

"I don't have much time..." I started saying to Ixtab.

"You came all this way," Ixtab purred while glaring at Brooks. "We will take as long as necessary to get to the bottom of this."

Heat crawled up my spine and neck, tingling my scalp. I had to get out of there, and soon, to reach my dad before he was moved. But I also wanted to find out about the godborns. I figured I owed them at least that much.

I grabbed hold of Brooks's hand. *Go. I'll meet you back here in thirty minutes. Then we'll get to the gateway.*

Brooks released my hand just as Quinn took her by the arm. Quinn whispered something in her ear that somehow settled Brooks down enough to follow. Okay, she *stomp-*followed. Ren was right behind both of them, glancing over her shoulder at me with worried eyes.

Hondo lifted his chin and looked at me defiantly. "Do you want me to stay?"

"Do you want me to burn you into a pile of ash?" Ixtab said.

"I'm not leaving Zane alone."

"It's cool," I told my uncle. "I'll meet up with you...later." He didn't move an inch. "Really," I said. "It's okay."

Reluctantly, he headed out, but he kept looking back until he disappeared down the steps.

After they were gone, Ixtab took me up an elevator that led to a rooftop patio. Golden vines grew across smooth jade trellises, and at the far end was a square arch. Beyond it was a pool of murky water that floated five feet above the ground, in midair. Steam rose from it in spirals. For a second, I thought I could hear faint whispers coming from the water.

"Whoa!" I breathed. "That's—"

"A scrying pool," Ixtab said, leading me past it to the roof's edge. "Souls live inside the sacred waters and help me see things." Ixtab paced, her gaze on the floor. "Two days ago, I received news that kids—*certain* kids who had magic swirling all about them—had been abducted. Of course, I thought nothing of it, chalked it up to a magician's prank. I mean, who cares about a bunch of snot-nosed brats? I had no idea we were talking about godborns until I learned about your call to them just now."

"Abducted?" I needed to sit down for this. Maybe even lie down. But I did neither. I was too stunned to move.

"That's not the point," she said. "The point is that they were all taken under the same circumstances—in their beds while they slept. Absolutely vile." Ixtab shook her head. "At least take them with their eyes wide open!"

"Could it be more mud people? And if someone is rounding up godborns, why not take me?"

"No one could take you past the shadow magic around Holbox, even if they wanted to."

A terrible dread pressed in on me, and before I could stop the words, they burst out. "That island . . . it's a prison?" I quickly added the question mark so she wouldn't know I had already figured out her scheme to lock me up forever.

"It saved your life, didn't it?" Ixtab tugged on her bracelets. "You know nothing of prison. That island is a sanctuary. Did you think I could risk you waltzing off and getting caught by the gods? How long do you think it would take them to realize that it was I who had shielded you, kept you alive? And as much as I *marginally* respect you, I am not about to give up my queendom and my life for you. So, yes, I put some security measures in place. And look, your life has been spared by that so-called prison. How about some gratitude?"

She had a point. A terrible, logical point. Ixtab didn't owe me anything, and she'd already saved me once. Now, more than ever, I knew she'd never lift the shadow magic. I had to get to Pus River and fast. "You could've told me."

She lowered her voice, and I thought I heard a note of gloom in it. "Sometimes knowledge brings nothing but despair, Zane."

She ushered me to the pool and removed her gold watch. Staring at it, she frowned, tossed it onto a lounge chair, and spoke into one of her bracelets. "Note to self: Call the time-keeper for watch repair." She gave me a syrupy smile. "Now, where were we? Oh, yes." She dipped her hand into the water. It hissed, and black steam curled into the air.

Images appeared like I was watching a movie.

First was the girl. About my age, with caramel-colored cropped hair, brown skin, and hooded, suspicious eyes. She walked down a littered school hallway with her head partway down but her gaze turned up.

"She seems mad." Or scared. I knew the look. I'd seen plenty of kids at my old school walking the halls on guard, like they were waiting for a brick to fall on their head. Or maybe a bully to jump them. It's no way for anyone to have to live.

The scene changed to a different one, of the same girl in bed, a green comforter pulled to her chin. Winged shadows raced across the walls. I felt a scream building inside of me, like I wanted to warn her. But then a large swollen hand reached for her. She woke up wide-eyed, her cry stifled.

The girl vanished, only to be replaced by a boy walking outside. He looked maybe fourteen or fifteen, with a sharp chin and small green eyes. His bleached hair was cut close to his head and a scar ran across his chin. He wore a bomber jacket as he cruised down a city street. The wind pounded him, and winged shadows followed. Were those the flying creatures Ren had told me about?

In the next scene, I saw that boy in bed, tossing and turning when the same hand appeared in the frame. A beefy arm hooked around the kid's neck. But this guy didn't scream. He fought back, punching and kicking like a madman.

That's when I saw something else.

"Hang on!" I shouted.

With the wave of her hand, Ixtab froze the image. "What is it?"

"Look! There's a gold cuff on the kidnapper's wrist, and—"

"Lots of people wear cuffs, Zane."

"The mud monster that attacked me had that same bracelet!" I stepped closer, wishing I'd taken a better look at Ms. Cab's. "Can you make it bigger?"

Ixtab flicked her wrist and the picture magnified. I now saw that the bracelet was engraved with the image of a creature with big googly eyes. Its lower jaw was missing, and it had a knife-like tongue. And all over its upper body were gaping mouths filled with sharp teeth. Its clothing from the waist down was made of crossed bones and skulls. Chills ran up my legs. "It . . . it looks like a monster."

Ixtab ran her slender finger along her chin, and smoke curled from her eyes as she whispered, "Tlaltecuhtli."

"Tlahl-tek-oot-lee? Who the heck's that?"

"The Mexica earth goddess, whose name means *the one who gives and devours life.*"

My mind was spinning. "What's meh-shee-ka?"

"You might be more familiar with the term *Aztec,* which means *someone from Aztlán,* but the Mexica never called themselves Aztec." She sighed.

Sure, I'd heard of Aztec (Mexica) gods, but I'd never given them much thought. "And where's Aztlán?"

"It's a mythical place the Mexica believe is their homeland," she said. "And those that wear this bracelet worship the goddess...." Ixtab rolled her eyes. "If you want to call Tlaltecuhtli that. I mean, let's be real. The Mexica came hundreds of years after the Maya, and we are clearly the superior pantheon."

"Hang on," I said. "Mexica gods are still around?"

"Not exactly," she said.

"Then what *exactly?*"

Ixtab quickly explained how some Spanish explorer named Cortés warred with the Mexica empire and pretty much killed them off. "With no sacrifices to keep the gods strong," she said, "they died off with their people. Now, where were we?"

"But why would someone worship an extinct god?"

"Pish. Happens all the time."

Sounded pretty convenient for the Maya, if you ask me.

I watched in stunned silence as image after image appeared in the water. Kids of different sizes and colors, all around my age, going about their lives in places that ranged from city streets to back-country roads, until they were plucked out of them, one by one. By the time Ixtab's slideshow was over, I'd seen ten godborns in total.

"We have to help them!" I cried. I admit it was a pretty bold declaration, because I had zero idea how.

An inky cloud bloomed and darkened the water.

Ixtab threw her hands up. "I don't even know where they are now, which is infuriating, and it tells me powerful magic is masking them."

"Yeah, magic from the devourer Mexica lady!"

"Are your ears broken? I told you, she's dead," Ixtab said. "No, there's another piece we aren't seeing. It doesn't make any sense. The only remaining Mexica are a few ghost royals, and they don't have this kind of power. Plus, they wouldn't be so foolish as to mess with the Maya gods. After all, it's due to our generosity that they're even still walking this earth."

"Hang on!" A memory bloomed. "When you left me on the island, didn't you say something about going to see a king?"

"Yes," said Ixtab. "The council met with the Mexica ghosts several months ago. Mostly to take pity on them. They are souls who couldn't or wouldn't meet the challenges of their underworld, Mictlan. With no underworld of their own, and no place here in Xib'alb'a, they are in a state of limbo."

"I get that my magic made the godborns visible to the *Maya* gods. But how could the Mexica know about them, too? Especially if they're just ghosts?" I asked. "Unless . . ."

"Unless what?"

"Unless some Maya god is a traitor."

Ixtab studied me. A muscle in her right cheek twitched. "What Maya god would be stupid enough to . . . ?"

"It wouldn't exactly be the first time," I said, remembering my dad's defiance of the Sacred Oath, and Ah-Puch's plan to end the world. Then there were the hero twins, and probably lots more examples I didn't even know about.

Ixtab's eyes roved the rooftop, and I could tell she was playing out limitless scenarios in her mind. "Zane, tell me more about the mud person. There has to be a detail Quinn left out, something you forgot to mention?"

I walked to the edge of the roof and back, worried Ixtab could see my secret plan to escape and save my dad. I thought about the ancestors' message about all paths leading to angry gods and wasn't sure if I could trust Ixtab with it. Hadn't Monster Cab told me the goddess wanted to prevent me from accessing my powers? And what about the blurry images of New Mexico I'd seen? Did those have anything to do with this?

Just then, Quinn showed up on the roof and said, "Forgive my interruption, mi reina, but you have an important message."

"I'll take it in the temple," Ixtab said. "We're not done here, Zane," she added before disappearing in a puff of blue smoke.

Quinn rushed to my side. She glanced over her shoulder, clearly worried, then looked back at me. "Something is very wrong."

"No kidding—"

"Zane!" She frowned and twisted her fingers together

anxiously. "You don't get it. My powers . . . they're changing, and—"

"What do you mean?"

"Brooks's are, too."

I stared at her, stunned. "Changing how?"

"They feel different—weaker, sickly. At first, I thought it was nothing, but . . ." She took hold of my shoulders, gripping hard. *You guys have to go. Please. Take Brooks far, far away from here, before it gets any worse.*

Her desperate tone made every muscle in my body tense. Who did she think was listening in on us?

You're not making any sense.

Why do you think all those demons are down there training? Because they like to kill things?

Gods, you're annoying!

Me? I'm not the one talking in circles.

She took a deep breath and loosened her grip slightly. *The Sparkstriker sent me on this mission, here to Xib'alb'a . . . undercover.*

Shouldn't that be a secret? I mean, she wasn't very good at being undercover if she was telling me her spy status.

I trust you not to tell anyone. Not even Brooks. She grabbed both my hands in hers and squeezed them like a vise. Her jaw tightened. *Soon we may not be able to shape-shift anymore.*

How . . . ? Crap! Is Ixtab behind all this? She'd taken away Brooks's powers before.

No. No god is capable of draining all the sobrenaturales' powers at the same time.

Do you think it has to do with the godborns being abducted?

From the look on Quinn's face, I could tell she didn't know anything about that, so I filled her in quickly.

It can't be a coincidence, she said. *Don't tell Ixtab about the sobrenaturales. We don't want the gods catching wind of our... situation.*

Why not?

They love weakness and would use it to their advantage, believe me, she said. *Just promise me you won't let Brooks do anything stupid. She'll listen to you.*

Uh, that's not exactly true.

At that moment, Ixtab reappeared. She looked into each of our faces and then solemnly said to Quinn, "It has begun."

16

Nothing good can come from the words *It has begun.* Especially when you're standing in hell with the queen of Xib'alb'a and a double agent who happens to be the sister of the girl you... uh, never mind.

"Call the Warriors together for a meeting," Ixtab commanded.

Quinn gave a single nod to Ixtab and left. Ixtab turned to me, and the heat of her stare was enough to melt my face off. "Come with me."

"What's begun?" I hated the tremor in my voice. (Hey, heroes get scared, too, you know!)

Blue flames erupted in Ixtab's eyes. "That is none of your concern."

Before I could argue or run, she swept her arm in front of herself and the entire setting vanished faster than the strike of a match. We emerged in a dark stone tunnel that smelled like metal and rotting flesh. The ground moved beneath us, and I realized we were standing in a small, rickety rowboat. The vessel was gilded with intertwining solid gold snakes that I really hoped wouldn't come to life.

A distant torch cast a faint light that glistened off the top of the blackish, oily... I gagged. Yep. We were floating on Blood River. "Why... why are we here?"

Ixtab picked up a long oar, its tip crafted with jade and gold. She placed the oar over the side and dragged it gently through the still blood. I might have gagged again. "I don't get down here very often," she said. "But it's quiet and there are no prying eyes or ears. We cannot be too careful."

Right. Because who in their right mind would ever hang out *here*? I needed to swallow the lump in my throat, but I was sure I'd throw up all over the place if I did. I sat down on the center bench.

"The magic you put out in the world," Ixtab said as we glided through the blood, "it connected you to the godborns. You are now linked, and we can use that to our advantage."

Our advantage? What was that supposed to mean?

Look, I wasn't about to argue with her. Even though I wanted to shout *You're wrong!* my best bet was to listen, agree, and get the hell out of hell. I was supposed to meet Brooks in fifteen minutes. "Uh...okay."

"Here," she said. "Take the oar."

"That's okay."

"It wasn't a request."

I was for sure going to be sick. I took the oar from her and propelled it through the river, which, by the awful way, was thick and thick, and did I mention *thick*?

Ixtab sat on a small bench at the stern. Her eyes glowed in the dark. I kept glancing over my shoulder so I could see if she tried to lunge at me or something. "Well?" she asked.

"Well what?"

"Do you feel the connection to the godborns?"

I thought about the whispering voice that had told me

Time for the story to escalate, and *She's here,* and *Eating the chocolate was a bad idea.* The voice had said I would find out who was talking soon enough. But it hadn't sounded like a godborn—more like a crafty sobrenatural or some other Maya creature I didn't know about and maybe didn't want to know.

"Um, I . . . I don't think so."

"You don't think so," Ixtab said evenly. I could tell she was trying to keep her temper in check. "You might not even be aware of the connection yet. Think harder!"

The oar glided through the blood, which had to have been pretty deep, because never once did it touch bottom. Whose blood was this, anyway? I wondered. Everyone who had ever died?

"Well, there is one thing . . ." I said, remembering the images of New Mexico that had flown past my brain.

Ixtab stood. "Tell me."

Uh-oh. Her nostrils flared, allowing even more smoke to curl out. Yep, I told her what she wanted to know. That seemed to bring her blood pressure down a few notches. "New Mexico? Are you certain?"

"I think I know my own state. But the images changed so fast I have no idea about the exact location. It has to be a message from the godborns. To come find them."

"And to hurry."

"Are you positive it's just ten kids in trouble? We have to make sure no more are taken!"

Ixtab smirked. "You're lucky I am somewhat sympathetic," she said, tugging on one of her bracelets. "I've ordered the magic pages in your book destroyed. I have a team out there as we speak, hunting them down so no other godborns are awakened, discovered, and abducted."

"How will you find all those books? I mean, there could be hundreds. . . ." Knowing Jazz, he had printed thousands.

"The paper is from the World Tree, remember?" As an aside, she said, "I knew there was a black market for it, but clearly I haven't been paying close enough attention." A deep scowl made her face look older as she went on. "Anyway, where are the tree's roots?" She wasn't really asking. "Right here in Xib'alb'a. My demons and hounds have the best senses. Believe me, they can trace anything that comes from their backyard. It won't take long."

I don't know if it was the fact that I was rowing through blood or that I was locked in a dark tunnel with the goddess of the underworld, but I felt a surge of bravery. So I took the plunge (that's a metaphor, by the way) and asked her, "How do you know they're godborns, anyway? You told me none had survived. . . ."

"Hmph. Your half-mortal mind couldn't *begin* to comprehend the secrets I am privy to, the secrets I keep, the whispers that swirl around the dead. Why do you think Ah-Puch wanted so desperately to hold on to his throne? Because he liked the place?" She let out a bitter laugh that echoed across the stone walls. "No, he wanted the power that comes with the underworld. Believe me, Zane. The dead know much more than the living do."

And apparently she wasn't going to tell me any of her secrets, especially those about the godborns.

"But why would anyone bother taking the godborns if

they haven't been claimed?" I asked. "It doesn't make sense. I mean, I was claimed and I still don't have much power, so they mapped me for nothing." It was hard to admit, but if Ixtab was the queen of secrets, she probably already knew.

"Zane!" she shouted. "I will excuse you this once, because it isn't your fault that part of your brain is human. Such a shame. Try not to think in such obvious ways. It's too easy to surmise that the abductors are trying to steal the godborns' powers. No, their goals are bigger and viler than that. But one thing is certain—your magical connection to the godborns means you are the answer."

Bigger and viler? As in they're also draining sobrenaturals of *their* power?

Then another thought occurred to me. "If the godborns are visible to the gods, then that means you can find them without me."

"The books' pages will soon be destroyed, severing the magical connection, and ten godborns have already been taken and hidden from us. You received those mental images for a reason. You must be the one to rescue them."

"Rescue?" Pump the brakes. Who said anything about a rescue? "Me?" I dropped the oar into Blood River. "Oops."

Ixtab waved her hand and the boat stopped. "Yes, you," she said.

"Why do you even care about the godborns' welfare?" How did I know she wasn't tricking me into rescuing them so she could use them for some other evil purpose?

What can I say? Once I get started, my imagination runs away with me. But, hey, those were seriously valid points, given that she was the queen of trickery. I don't know why I bothered asking, though. She was a pro at giving only crumbs of information, making you think you're in the know when really you're just wandering around in the dark.

Ixtab raised an eyebrow. "Because you put them in this predicament."

Sometimes the truth sucks.

I tried to deflect it. "Is it because you have a kid out there?"

Ixtab didn't even flinch. Nor did she give me a fiery blink or a stony stare. Just: "Remember who you're talking to, godborn. Try to stay on track for once—and that track is rescuing the godborns."

Right. But how was I supposed to rescue the godborns *and* Hurakan? Yeah, I know, I owed them for getting them into this lousy mess, but I couldn't give up my one opportunity to save my dad, could I? He was being transferred in three human-world days (who knew how much time had passed while we were in Xib'alb'a), and I might never get this chance again.

"I—I—" The realization hit me between the eyes mid-stutter. "Wait a second. What happened to me staying off the grid?"

"I have a solution for that."

Was this my ticket to freedom? Hondo had taught me tons about fighting—both physically and with the mind. If he were here, I knew he'd tell me that in battle you look for advantages. And I was being handed one on a silver platter. Next he'd tell me that alliances matter—who you side with can mean the difference between defeat or victory. And last he'd say, *There* are two kinds of battles. *Those that are won, and those that are lost. The winner is always the one who is best at deception.*

You're probably rolling your eyes, thinking, *No way can you outdeceive the goddess of the underworld.* Maybe not, but I could at least try negotiating.

"I'll help. . . . My friends and I will rescue the godborns. But I want something in return."

Ixtab narrowed her eyes. "Go on."

I swallowed hard, hoping she wouldn't shove me into the blood. "You need to bust my dad out of prison."

"Ah." Ixtab closed her eyes and took a deep breath before opening them. "I'm sorry, but I cannot help you there."

"Why not? A rescue for a rescue. It's totally fair. Can't you just send some of your demons to do it?"

"Who cares about fair? Fair is you saving those whom you have put at grave risk. Fair is allowing me to take a couple weeks of vacation. Fair is . . ." She tilted her head and softened her voice. "Even if I were willing to save your father, how long do you think it would take the other gods to determine I was the one who defied them? I'd lose not only my crown but the head wearing it, and you'd spend the rest of your life running in fear. Is that what you want?"

"What I want?" Ribbons of steam began to rise off the river. "I didn't want any of this!"

"So it is with destiny," Ixtab said with no sympathy in her tone.

I swallowed my anger and took a deep breath, but it was difficult in the humid air. "What about the other gods who helped me? Like Kukuulkaan. Once the gods read my story, they knew he betrayed them, right? Did anything bad happen to him?"

"No, because I tore out certain pages."

"To protect him? Because he's your friend?"

"Because I need his vote on the council." She plunged her hand in the river and muttered something I couldn't hear. The blood boiled. Red steam billowed out of it in a vortex, and bright orange flames shot from the top. "Place your hand in the river," she said.

It took a nanosecond for her words to reach the logical part of my brain. "No way! That's, like, thousand-year-old blood and . . ." The burning instinct to run flooded every cell in my body. But there was nowhere to go, nowhere to hide.

Ixtab sighed and waved her hand. Gone was the sulfur smell, replaced with the scent of the desert after a summer rain. The blood turned to crystal blue water, like the Caribbean, and I suddenly missed my island.

I peered into the water. No piranhas or other flesh-eating monsters. As a matter of fact, it was totally clear and empty. "How do I know that this isn't a hallucination and the water isn't really blood and some monster isn't lurking down there, waiting to eat me for lunch?"

"Don't be ridiculous. Nothing wants to eat you. I just need to draw out your life force."

Oh. Well, that was so much better. "Whoa! That sounds bad."

Ixtab stroked her chin. "Haven't you learned by now that if I wanted you dead, all it would take is a simple blink? Maybe two or three, but it would be easy, especially since you're trespassing in my kingdom. Do as I say. This is the only way to strengthen your connection to the godborns."

"Right, thanks for the life-drain offer and all, but I think . . . no."

She sighed, and a crown of blue fire floated above Ixtab's head. The gold snakes in the boat's frame began to hiss, and with a single wave of her hand, I was lifted off my feet and . . . you guessed it.

Chucked into Blood River.

17

The water took hold of me as if it had hands and
teeth. I couldn't move an inch. A slow panic began to wind
up my feet. It climbed my legs, coiling tightly. The jade tooth
seared hot against my skin, vibrating stronger than it ever
had before.

Hurakan? I asked in my mind.

My lungs constricted. Air. I needed air.

Ixtab's voice broke through. *River of Blood, tell me, is he
the one?*

The one? I could feel my secrets (yes, you read that right)
peeling away from me like sunburned skin, and there was
nothing I could do to hold on to them.

Is he the one? Ixtab asked again, more forcefully this time.

The one who ditched school seventeen times? The one who
busted Hondo's taillight with his cane (total accident, BTW)?
The one who stole a pack of Sour Patch Kids from the dol-
lar store? The one who thought he could rescue his dad? The
one who . . . I fought to keep this secret hidden, but it was like
holding my breath. Eventually, I had to let it go.

The one who almost kissed Brooks last month at the
bonfire?

Emphasis on *almost*. It didn't happen, okay?

My heartbeat began to slow, my limbs drooped with

fatigue. My storm runner leg pulsed with electrical shocks like it was fighting off death. As I slipped into nothingness, the last thing I heard was the water's rasping voice. It spoke in a strange language I'd never heard, but somehow, I understood it.

He is the one, my queen.

When I woke up, I was back on Ixtab's rooftop patio, lying on a lounge chair with striped orange cushions that smelled like they'd just been sprayed with that citrus-scented tire cleaner Hondo likes. The sky was dark, and strings of tiny lights hung across the jade trellis above me. I had the same bared-soul feeling I had when Mom made me go to confession to tell Father Monroe all my sins.

Ixtab sat next to me, flipping through a fashion magazine. "Really, Zane. If you're going to pass out, save it for something big, not a simple life draining."

I sat up, rubbing my eyes, then scanned my body for any traces of blood. Thankfully, there were none. "You pushed me in! That was so not cool. Those were my secrets!"

"I needed to see inside your heart and mind, and that meant I had to trick your body into thinking it was dying so it would let go of the information I requested. Don't worry, I only examined what I needed. I left your little heart secrets intact," she said with a knowing smile that made my cheeks blaze.

"Or you could've just asked me." I swung my legs over the edge of the chair. "What time is it? I have to go."

Ixtab tossed her magazine aside. "If my wretched watch were working, I could tell you."

"Why did you ask 'Is he the one?'"

She hesitated a second too long, which told me that what was about to come out of her mouth was a lie at worst, a half-truth at best. "I needed to be sure you are the right one to try to rescue the godborns. No sense sending you into a death trap."

A terrible heat raced up my spine. "How am I supposed to rescue them if we don't know exactly where they are? I mean, New Mexico's a big place."

Ixtab waved her hand through the air and a gold lipstick tube appeared. She uncapped it and put on some of the red stuff. "You'll just have to work with the details you have. Did the image tell you anything specific?"

I considered the rolling gray-green hills with outcrops of deep-red rocks and the flecks of floating cotton. "They . . . they remind me of the southern part of the state."

"That's something," she muttered. "We have no idea how the godborns are being treated, or what's happening to them, so you must hurry. For all we know, they could be on death's door."

The world was unraveling inch by stupid inch, and Ixtab wasn't helping to weave it back together. "Even if I find them, how am I supposed to get in and out? There's, like, ten of them. . . . I mean, you have a plan, right?" I rubbed my forehead, trying to get rid of the massive headache coming on.

"Plan?" Ixtab laughed. "You think this is the only catastrophe I am dealing with right now? This is your mess to dig out of, Zane. I am sure you can figure it out. If not . . . *tsk, tsk, tsk* . . . well, let's not think such things."

Gee, thanks. "But there's still the problem of the gods picking me up on their radar. Or Ren. Who knows how long this will take, and the longer we're out there, the more likely they'll find us."

"Ren isn't at risk."

"What? Wait a second . . ." I stepped closer. "You know who her mom is, don't you?"

"I do not," she said. "But before you explode that human head of yours trying to figure things out, just know this: she has protective magic around her that you do not. I cannot say any more than that."

So, what, I got the dud godborn genes? Then I remembered that Ren said she had magic in her family history. Is that what Ixtab meant?

"As for you," Ixtab went on, "I have a solution to protect you."

"Good. Protection is good. Are you going to give me an invisibility cloak"—how cool would that be—"or more shadow magic or something?"

"I have to kill you."

I jerked my spear up and jumped back. "Are you crazy?"

"Oh, calm down. It's a temporary death, for three measly days. To make you undetectable to the gods. Mostly."

"I'd prefer *totally* undetectable. And to stay alive."

"Please! I am *not* a miracle worker, for Xib'alb'a's sake. It's impossible to smother every ounce of your life, Zane, without actually killing you. This way, the traces of your godborn essence will be so small, a god would have to be staring you in the face or actively looking for you—and they *aren't* looking for you, since they think you're dead. Now, are you in, or are you out?"

Why did I have the feeling Ixtab wasn't telling me the whole truth? "Why only three days?"

"The magic usually only lasts forty-eight hours, but I'm feeling generous. If you don't return to Xib'alb'a by then, the death magic will consume you and you'll be permanently dead. But don't worry, Zane. If that happens, I won't give you a terrible assignment here in the underworld. I'll even throw in a penthouse in level three."

No way. I wasn't about to leave my mom and Hondo and Rosie and Brooks. My jade tooth suddenly got hot and vibrated again. I couldn't help but notice that the vibrations had only begun here in the underworld and they were getting stronger as time went on. "If I agree—and I'm not saying I am—what am I supposed to do with the godborns once I rescue them?"

"I will find a place to hide them," Ixtab said. "But we can worry about that if, er, *when* you succeed. Now, do we have a deal?"

"A deal means I get something in return. Something more than just protection."

Ixtab smiled. Her eyes ignited into blue flames. "Ah, the son of fire. So bold. So stubborn. So like his father. Come now, I have souls to reap and demons to train. What's your decision?"

My jade vibrated with such force I nearly jumped. Hurakan was definitely trying to get my attention. "I need an hour with my team. To decide."

I couldn't just let the godborns rot, but I couldn't let my dad languish in prison, either. I didn't know if I would ever get this kind of intel about his location again.

I had to find out what Hurakan wanted, and there was only one way to do that.

18

Back at the temple, Brooks was pacing the penthouse's stone floors. Hondo was swinging punches in the air with his eyes closed. And Ren? She was opening drawers and poking her nose inside (no doubt looking for proof of aliens). Quinn was nowhere to be seen.

"Zane!" Brooks hurried over as soon as I stepped off the elevator. "That was more like an hour. We have to talk."

"No kidding!" I said, but I marched straight toward Ren. "What did you and Ixtab talk about in your telepathy session?" I asked her. I knew there was something Ixtab wasn't telling me about this whole mess, about Ren's magic. But I expected a fellow godborn to give it to me straight.

She hesitated. I barely knew her, but it was obvious she was choosing her words carefully, or worse, thinking up a lie.

But before she could speak, the designer Itzel appeared. "I have your clothes." Except her hands were empty.

"Where?" Ren asked, rushing over like she was glad for the interruption.

"You already made them?" Brooks asked.

Who cared what we were wearing! I had to talk to Ren, and then Brooks—alone—and after that it was time for me to jump to the Empty. "I don't think..." I started, and the jade buzzed again.

Itzel must have read my mind, because she said, "Oh, but you *should* care, Mr. Tacky-Tack. Stay in your hot-dog threads and wait for the flesh-hungry demons to sniff you out and eat you alive. Ha! Maybe their hunt tonight will lead them right back to you. Wouldn't that be ironic?" Her tilted smile was more of a sneer. "Or you could wear my clothes, a coveted Itzel design that will give you half a chance of staying alive here and above."

So she knew we were headed back to the human world. But how would her designs keep us alive beyond Xib'alb'a? Maybe Ixtab wouldn't have to kill me temporarily after all. . . .

Her coal-like eyes glistened beneath the chandeliers. "If it were up to me, I'd prefer you get eaten. You aren't worthy of wearing my creations. But Ixtab has spoken."

Hondo rubbed his hands together. "Sounds good to me. This polyester shirt is giving me a rash."

I expected Itzel to take us down to some fitting room, but instead, she opened her mouth. It expanded so much, a billboard could've fit inside. A cloud of purple mist swirled from her throat and wrapped around each of us.

I couldn't see anything through the mist, but I heard Itzel. "Perfect," she said. "I am so good. Should get a crown or something. The measurements are exact. As I expected, of course."

A second later, the cloud disappeared. We were still in our old outfits, but in each of our hands was a tied burlap sack.

"Well?" Itzel said. "Don't act so ungrateful. Open them!"

Inside my sack was a pair of jeans, a dark purple T-shirt, and a pair of gray sneakers. *This* was her idea of high fashion?

Hondo dumped his stash out on the floor. A pair of

shredded jeans and . . . he held up a gray long-sleeved button-down shirt. "I hate buttons," he whispered to me. "Does she think I'm an accountant or something?"

Ren tugged out a long yellow hoodie that laced up the front, and a pair of black track pants with white stripes down the side. I could tell by her face that she was as underwhelmed as the rest of us. "These pants don't have any pockets," she muttered.

I looked over at Brooks, who was scowling. She had gotten a pair of dark green leggings, a shiny black bomber jacket, and a plain white tee.

Itzel grimaced. "It's all wrong."

Hondo nodded. "I figured we had the wrong clothes. I don't do sleeves. Or buttons."

"Not the garments. *You*," Itzel said. "You're all wrong." She rolled her eyes. "These are meant to keep your sorry human butts from getting stabbed and killed. Nothing can penetrate this fabric—not daggers, not teeth, not fire. Why I should waste them on you is beyond me."

"But they're just . . . plain clothes," Ren said.

"*Plain* is being generous," Hondo huffed.

"The material," Brooks said, inspecting her leggings. "It's different."

Looking closer at the shirt in my hand, I saw Brooks was right. There was a give to the fabric, and it had the thickness of a wetsuit. But the material looked familiar. "Is this . . . ?" I couldn't get the words out. I mean, I liked the whole idea of not getting stabbed to death and all, but . . . Chills ran up my legs.

"Demon skin?" Brooks finished the sentence for me.

"You think I'd waste perfectly good demon skin on the likes of you? No. It's synthetic. No demons were harmed in its creation." Itzel grabbed Ren's track pants out of her hands, growling, "Ungrateful humans. No appreciation or taste. These fine threads also work as camouflage. Do you have any idea of the precision and craftsmanship that go into something of this caliber?"

"Isn't camo, like, green and, you know, army-looking?" I asked, wondering when Itzel last had her eyes checked.

"The most unimaginative species . . ." she muttered as she held the pants up to the chandelier. "This is enchanted camo!" Immediately, the pants blended in with the light fixture—as in you couldn't even see them in her hands.

"*That* is sick!" Hondo said.

Ren nodded enthusiastically. "Does this mean we're going to be invisible?"

Itzel rubbed her forehead like her skull was about to explode. "All you have to do is tug on any button—you all have at least one." She glared at Hondo. "But you can only use the disguise device three times. Maybe four—I don't remember the exact number. The camouflage effect puts incredible stress on the fabric."

"Then what happens?" Brooks asked.

"The clothing combusts, of course," Itzel said.

"Of course," I mumbled.

Hondo was still wearing a huge smile. "You said dagger-proof, right?"

"These garments are the sole property of the House of Itzel," she explained. "Consider this a loan." She gave a loud sniff. "And if anyone asks you where you got them, for the love of all that is couture, do not say I designed them. I would never live it down."

After we all got dressed in our private rooms, I met Brooks in the jungle behind the complex. I'd talk to Ren later. Time was running out and I had to get back to Ixtab with my decision soon. I knew I'd have to take her up on the offer of the "death" protection. I also had to find out what Hurakan wanted.

Moonlight glinted off the golden tree Brooks was leaning against, and for half a second, she looked like she was just a normal girl waiting for a bus. Except she was as far from normal as Pluto was from the sun.

"What took you so long with Ixtab?" she said.

"A lot has happened." I thought about Quinn's message of doom. "Why didn't you tell me your powers are fading?"

Brooks stiffened. "Because you'd give me that freaked-out look you're giving me right now. And I only felt it when we got here. I can't fly as well as usual, and it takes tons of concentration to stay in hawk form when usually it's easy."

"But Rosie seems fine."

"She's a hellhound. Quinn said it's only affecting people born as a sobrenatural, like shape-shifters, seers, magicians...." Her voice trailed off.

"How could all the sobrenaturals be getting weaker at the same time?"

"Sobrenaturales."

"Huh?"

"You said 'sobrenaturals.'"

I sucked in a sharp breath. "And why does that even matter right now? Can we get back to the sobrenaturals losing power?"

"I don't know how we could be getting weaker at the same time. I mean, not even a god could take away all of our powers. Maybe it's a virus or..." She was grasping at straws.

"There's a virus that attacks magic?"

"No, but it sounds better than some massively powerful evil monster being behind all this. Anyway, let's just get to the gateway. Now."

"There's, um, some things I need to do first," I said. I told her what had happened with Ixtab.

Brooks blew out a long breath and frowned. "Abducted? Mexica ghosts?! No way can you let her make you dead, even if it's only for three days. That's craziness!"

I poked Fuego into the dirt. "It's not *dead* dead.... More like a death spell."

Brooks looked up at me and for half a second her warm amber eyes softened, and I thought she might actually hug me. She didn't. "I can't let you die, Zane."

I knew it would be hard to convince her. "Brooks, I owe the godborns. It's my fault they're in trouble. Plus, the spell will keep me off the gods' radar. And, if I'm fast, I can use the death magic to stay undetectable long enough to..." My voice dropped to a whisper. "To still rescue my dad."

"That's *if* you somehow find the godborns and get them out of their prison without anyone noticing in less than three days." She paced, twisting a curl around her pinkie. "It's one thing to rescue Hurakan. That's, like, one person, not ten.

And I'd much rather go up against three demons than some unknown army made up of who-knows-what kind of monsters. It's too risky, Zane."

She was right. At least I knew the monsters who were holding Hurakan. We needed reinforcements, but where would they come from if all the sobrenaturals were losing their powers?

"Everything is connected," I said, wishing I had all the pieces to the puzzle. "The mud person, the kidnappings, the sobrenaturals..." I clenched my fist around Fuego.

"You look like your head is about to explode," Brooks said.

"We need backup to save the godborns."

"We need a whole plan. No one just marches into battle. I mean, I could lose my powers in the middle of this rescue, Zane. Where would that leave us?"

My cheeks reddened. I knew what she was thinking, because I was thinking it, too. If only I had control over my fire abilities, we might not need her strength as much.

My jade tooth sent a jolt of energy beneath my skin, startling me from my thoughts. "I need a favor."

"I will *not* let you become a zombie." Brooks's voice trembled. "There has to be another way. It's too chancy. You could get caught and not make it back here, or Ixtab's gateway could close, or so many other things could go wrong."

"Brooks..."

She looked up at me, and her eyes fell on the jade tooth I was still gripping. "You're going back to the Empty, aren't you?"

"I have to."

"Why?"

"I...I think Hurakan wants me to. Ever since I got here, the tooth has been vibrating like he's trying to communicate with me. I think he has something important to tell me. Maybe he has some answers."

"That's crazy. He's in prison, as in *extra* lockdown. No way can he travel to the Empty. *But,* if he could..." I could practically see the wheels spinning in her head. "He could maybe tell you where they plan to move him to so we might still be able to rescue him. I mean, just in case..."

"Which is why I have to try."

Could I do this? Go back to the place where I'd ended Ah-Puch? I know it sounds totally paranoid (remember, these are the Maya gods we're talking about here), but I had this horrible image in my head that the second I returned, the god of death would be there in all his serpentine, maggoty glory, waiting to bite off my head. It was the reason I hadn't gone back before this. But Hurakan wouldn't call me there if it was dangerous, would he?

"Could you, um, watch over my body while I'm there, to make sure no one flays it, or eats it for dinner?" I asked Brooks. "Oh, and don't let me stay gone longer than thirty minutes." I handed Fuego to her for safekeeping.

"You really ask for the world, Obispo." Brooks rolled her eyes and socked me in the arm. "Just hurry back."

I spun wildly through nothingness, through whispers that formed no words. A distant wind howled, a door slammed closed. Glass shattered. And when the world came to a stop, I opened my eyes to the Empty.

I stood at the top of my dad's pyramid, looking out across the sea through feline eyes. I loved this feeling of strength that only came when I was in jaguar form, the only form I could take while in this secret world Hurakan had built.

I peered around, hoping to see him. But I was alone. Had he not summoned me here? And then I realized that the Empty—*this* Empty—wasn't the lush landscape at the tip of the sea that I remembered. This world was tattered, torn at the edges, like it was made of tissue paper.

Shreds of sky blew in the wind. The sea was colorless.

It's dying, I thought.

I felt a hundred shades of miserable. Out of the corner of my eye, I could see the abyss—the unfinished part of the Empty where I'd sent Puke Face spiraling into the fire.

I admit it. I was more than scared to be here.

Then came a familiar voice.

I hoped you'd come back.

19
••••

I jumped to my feet, excited and relieved.
Hurakan?

We don't have much time. His voice, raspy and weak, was coming from somewhere in the jungle below.

My heart raced. I couldn't get the words out fast enough. *I know where you're being imprisoned! I'm coming to save you.*

That doesn't matter now, he said.

How could it not matter? I launched myself down the pyramid steps and into the trees, racing toward the sound of his voice.

It's too late for me. Zane, you must listen. When I die, this place will die, too. We won't get this chance again.

What do you mean too late? Die? Gods can't die!

Your human mind thinks of death as the end. For me, it means something else.

Then you won't really die?

Silence hit me from all directions. I came to an abrupt stop. Cobwebs were taking over the dying trees, just like we'd seen in the Old World. Wispy white trails fluttered in the sea breeze.

Hurakan?

Crap! Was he gone already? Had I wasted our one chance

to talk? A deep and terrible roar emerged from my throat, reverberating across the jungle.

Zane. His voice was now a whisper. Something flickered in my peripheral vision and then...Hurakan stepped out from behind a tree. In the form of a man. I stopped breathing. He looked part solid, part ghost. He wore a loose-fitting black shirt-and-pants set that reminded me of the scrubs doctors wear, and his face was thin, his eyes sunken.

In the same instant, he transformed me back into human form.

"Whoa!" I looked down at my hands, then back to Hurakan. "Why aren't we panthers?"

The first time we met here, Hurakan had told me we had to take the shape of jaguars in order to relate to each other, because we were strangers. Once we had some familiarity, an emotional connection, we could take a different form.

Oh. *OH.*

Imagine someone igniting a thousand sticks of dynamite inside your heart. That's what this realization felt like.

But he clearly wasn't well. Hurakan coughed as the outline of his shape faded in and out. A raging fury burned inside my bones. I wanted to slowly gut the gods for what they'd done to my father.

I hurried over to help him stand. Once he steadied himself, he let go and said, "I wish I could have been here to train you. But...other things got in the way." He took a wheezing breath, grimacing like his ribs were busted and it hurt to inhale. "Like prison walls."

"So not funny," I said.

He half smiled anyway. "Dad joke."

Who knew Hurakan had a sense of humor?

"I've been waiting... hoping you'd show up here, Zane."

"Waiting? I didn't think you could still access the Empty. And the jade—you didn't call me until today," I said.

Hurakan's eyes found mine. "I don't have a connection to the jade anymore." He frowned. "So, no, I didn't call you here."

"But then..." Every cell in my body froze. "Who did?"

Hurakan's face was suddenly cold, unmoving. "There isn't time for us to solve that mystery. Events have been set in motion, and you must do something—"

"Save the godborns?" I cut in. "You're not the only one who broke the Sacred Oath." I don't know why, but for some reason I felt it was important for me to tell him. I quickly explained everything Ixtab and I had figured out.

He didn't even flinch at the mention of the godborns. With great effort, he said, "You will need your greatest powers for what lies ahead. Which is why you must listen." He began to fade.

Desperation crawled up my spine. "No... wait!"

It was too late. He had faded to nothing, but his voice lingered on the sea breeze. *Get to the pyramid. The top step. Now!*

I bolted back toward the pyramid, taking long strides. Here in the Empty I had no limp, and I could race with the speed and power of a jaguar, even in human form. But as I did, the ground shifted beneath my feet. The Empty began to tilt. I lost my footing and had to grab a tree branch to steady myself. My hands slipped, and I went spinning toward an ocean cliff and away from the pyramid.

Hurry, Zane.

With every ounce of strength I had, I redoubled my efforts and launched myself toward another tree, trying to get a hand- and foothold. A moment later, the world righted itself enough so that I could run again. And I did. Like I'd never run in my life. Not as a human or a jaguar. As a godborn.

I flew up the stairs until I reached the top. Bits of gray sky fell around me like ash. The ground rumbled. The top stone step was broken, and a piece of thick parchment was sticking out of a crack. I unrolled it to find a message.

Dear Zane,

By the time you read this, I will have claimed you in front of the council, giving you access to your full powers. I will have been imprisoned. And hopefully you will have destroyed Ah-Puch as we know him.

I looked up. *As we know him?* Hurakan had written this before the battle at the Old World.

I continued reading as ash sprinkled onto the page.

With the hope that my plan worked, you survived, and you are now living under Ixtab's protection, I write this message. I fear the future is a bleak one.

The Empty trembled and I felt a strong tug back to the underworld.

No! Not yet! I scanned the note faster.

> I know this is not what you want to hear, but the Prophecy of Fire was only the beginning.

"Why do people keep saying that?"

> I wrote this letter unsure if I'd ever have the chance to tell you in person.

My throat began to close up.

> I know it is in your nature to want to rescue me. Don't. You will only be wasting your time, for it has been written. And so it shall be.

"Written? What's been written? What does that even mean?" I was so sick of half-truths and unclear messages. Why couldn't one stinking, lousy god give it to me straight?

"Give up this pursuit to save me, to save anyone but yourself." Hurakan's image once again flickered in front of me. "Do you understand?"

"No!" I shouted. "I need *you* to understand. I *have* to save the godborns. It's my fault they're in this mess. But I don't know where they are, and..." I hesitated, thinking it might not be a good idea to tell him about the whole death-magic deal with Ixtab. "How am I supposed to rescue them if I can't even control fire, and all the sobrenaturals' powers are fading, and—"

"What did you say?" Hurakan looked stricken. "About powers fading?"

"The sobrenaturals' powers ... they're being drained."

"The Fire Keeper," he whispered.

"The what?" My mind churned in dangerous circles, making me suddenly light-headed.

A defeated expression swept across his face. "He tends the eternal flame. His whereabouts are known only to Itzam-yée, the deity bird that nests in the great World Tree."

"So, this fire-keeper person just watches a flame all day?" I asked. "What does he have to do with any of this?"

"He makes sure the flame never goes out. It's the source of tremendous power." Hurakan hesitated. "Most think he is a myth. If the gods or other malos were aware of his existence, the Fire Keeper would know no peace. He'd be hunted for all eternidad."

"Is he like a seer?" I asked.

"The Fire Keeper can read each lick of the flame, each glimmer in the embers. He sees what no one else can—places, people, events—with perfect clarity. Choices and outcomes. He can even manipulate the future."

"Manipulate it like change it?"

"At great cost, but it can be done."

My pulse raced. Maybe the Fire Keeper could tell me where the godborns were, and who was holding them. . . . Maybe he could tell me a lot of stuff that would help my quest. He might even be able to change my dad's future. "What does he have to do with the sobrenaturals?" I asked.

"How did I not see it?" Hurakan muttered to himself.

"The Fire Keeper is the key. He . . ." Gripping the temple wall with both hands, he drew a heaving breath like he'd just been punched in the gut.

"He what?"

Hurakan vanished yet again.

"Hurakan?" The echo of my voice was only met by silence. "Hurakan!" Frustration rose up inside me with so much pressure I thought I'd combust. A sudden gust of wind ripped through the jungle.

Run, Zane. Far away, Hurakan said. *And don't look back.*

"I'm not running!" I shouted. I was sick of living a lie, sick of being stuck in a prison I didn't create. Sick of pretending to live a life that wasn't even mine.

There is no victory in pride.

"There's no victory in running away, either."

In the next breath, I felt a sudden and familiar mind-numbing rush. I was out of time. The world began to swirl in a haze of mist and shadow, and the letter ignited into flames as I was ripped away from the Empty.

20

Brooks hovered over me, studying me with wide amber eyes, her tanned face only inches from mine. Her hands were pressed against my chest. "You were thrashing around," she said. "You've never done that before. I thought old Puke Face was there, ripping you to shreds."

"I could totally take him," I said. "But thanks for the vote of confidence."

"Holy K, Zane. Way to freak me out!" She was still hovering.

I was sure she could feel my heart pounding. I scooted away and rubbed my left cheek with the back of my hand. It stung like . . .

"I slapped you a few times to try and bring you back," Brooks said. "Sorry about that. How come your nose isn't bleeding from the jump?"

I sat up, gripping the jade, and replayed Hurakan's words. *I didn't call you here. . . .* Dread smashed against my skull like a two-ton hammer.

"You're zoning out, Obispo."

"Huh? Yeah. Sorry." We got to our feet. I gave Brooks the short version of what I'd learned, and ended with "If Hurakan didn't call me there, who did?"

"Maybe Pacific? I mean, she's the one who first gave you the tooth."

"But she's in hiding, and ... why would she want me to go to the Empty?" Something about that answer didn't feel right.

"You don't think ... it's Puke, do you?"

"No way! Don't even think it!" Ah-Puch didn't have any connection to the jade, and besides, he was spinning in an eternal vortex of fire.

Then I remembered some of his last words to me. *Once Hurakan is dead, this place will die, too. And with nothing left here to trap me, I'll head off to the underworld and I'll take back what's mine. So, any way you look at it, I win.*

Was that true? Or had he just been bluffing? The last thing I needed to worry about was the god of death coming back to finish me off.

"Maybe the jade's magic called you there by itself..." Brooks guessed. "Like, maybe it knows more than even Hurakan. ... I mean, it's totally possible."

I wished she were right, but something told me whatever the truth was, I wasn't going to like it. How had everything gotten so complicated? I'd gone to Xib'alb'a to sneak out through a gateway, and I felt more trapped than ever. What was the right thing to do? Save my dad, or rescue the godborns? How could I choose?

Brooks interrupted my thoughts. "What aren't you telling me?"

It was no use to try to act innocent. Brooks would see right through me. "He told me to run, Brooks."

"Why? That's so"—she made a face like she'd just taken a bite of something sour—"cowardly."

"Maybe it has to do with this *bleak* future."

Brooks folded her arms tightly. "Are you sure Hurakan said 'bleak'?"

"Yes."

"Like how sure?"

"Brooks."

She pushed her hair behind her ears. "Okay, okay. I hate bleak," she muttered as she quickly glanced over her shoulder, then back to me. She took hold of my hand and, using telepathy, said, *Let's put all the pieces together. According to the ancestors, the Prophecy of Fire was only the beginning, and no matter what path you choose, the gods are going to be furious. The sobrenaturales' powers are weakening, and we don't know why or how. The godborns are being abducted.*

Someone's eavesdropping on us, aren't they?

A demon to your right, but don't look. She's totally fake-acting busy.

I turned.

I said not to look!

That's always going to make me look!

Brooks rolled her eyes and continued. *There's some mythical dude called the Fire Keeper who can see stuff and change the future, which is seriously sick. Hurakan said the future is bleak and to run away. Man, the future must be worse than bleak if big bad storm god Hurakan wants you to run. Run to where? There's nowhere to hide if a prophecy has your name on it.*

No one said my name is on a prophecy.

Right. The ancestors were just hanging out in the dirt for nothing. Her eyes widened. *That's it!*

What?

We should go find the Fire Keeper and tell him to change the future. Bye-bye, bleak.

I stabbed Fuego into the ground. *I don't think it works that way. Plus, Hurakan said it costs a lot to change the future, which probably means blood or your head or something.*

Good point.

You forgot one thing, I said.

What?

Ixtab suddenly wants me to save a bunch of godborns, I said. *But at first she told me they were dead. Why should I believe her?*

Exactly—but something's missing. Are you sure you're telling me everything?

I was sure she could see the lie on my face before I even spoke the words. *Yes, I . . . I told you everything.* Quinn's secret that she was working undercover better be worth keeping, I thought. Man, I hated lying to Brooks, especially when we had promised we would never hide the truth from each other again.

What if we split up? Brooks suggested. *I can get to your dad, and you can go find the godborns.*

If your nawal magic fails, you can't be out there alone fighting demons, I said.

She rolled her eyes. *I'm pretty good with deadly weapons, in case you've forgotten.*

We stick together.

Squeezing my hand tighter, she said, *The eavesdropper's
gone now.*

I nodded distractedly.

"You have that look," she said out loud.

"What look?"

"That *I've-made-up-my-mind* look," she said. Why was she
still holding my hand? Not that I was complaining or anything. She traced her thumb over mine and I sort of leaned
closer, just barely—I'm talking half an inch. She dropped my
hand and stepped back. "You've already decided to use the
death magic, haven't you?"

"I have to. Whatever we do next, at least the spell will keep
me safe from the gods." I gulped as I nodded, thinking Brooks
was going to lay into me, maybe even shove me against the
tree, but she didn't do either. Instead, she studied me carefully,
then said, "Next time? Telepath faster."

I hadn't told Brooks that the Empty was dying. There
might not be a next time for us . . . or the world. It was too
depressing to say out loud, and I was pretty sick of being the
guy with bad news.

Grunts and shouts from the demon soldiers echoed across
the jungle. It was obvious now why they were training so
hard. There was going to be a big battle. I wondered if that's
what had Hurakan so spooked.

We left the jungle and ran back to the temple, where Hondo
and Ren were waiting.

"Where's Ixtab?" I tried to catch my breath.

"She was here," Hondo said. "Left a few minutes ago for the battlefield and didn't look too happy. Hey, you okay?"

Questions flew at me, questions I didn't have time to process, think about, or answer. Brooks gave Hondo and Ren the SparkNotes version as I rushed out to the platform and scanned the area. There. Ixtab stood near the waterfall across the field. I raced down the steps, followed by Hondo, Ren, and Brooks. We weaved between the sparring demons, who glared at us with murderous eyes, and made our way toward the waterfall.

"You can't die!" Hondo shouted after me.

"Told you!" Brooks said.

I ran ahead, ignoring them both, thinking about Hurakan's plea to trust him. "Ixtab!"

The demons' shouts and grunts and clanging weapons were too loud for her to hear me. Ren tripped over a spear. Hondo helped her up without missing a stride.

By the time we got to the waterfall, a minute later, Ixtab was gone.

"Where'd she go?" I asked. I needed that death magic!

Brooks started to say something, when I spotted a flaming arrow zinging across the field. I watched in paralyzed horror as it zoomed right toward her back.

"NO!" I threw my hand up and leaped through the air, knocking her out of the way just as the arrow veered right. We tumbled to the ground, me landing on top of her.

"Zane! What's wrong with you?"

I propped myself up and looked down at her reddened

face. "The arrow—it was going to hit you! Are you okay? Are you hurt?"

With a grunt, she shoved me off and rolled away. "What arrow?"

I pointed at the weapon, its flame now sputtering on the ground. "That one." I looked around to see who had shot it. It was impossible to tell. Arrows zinged all over the place, and I realized we had just gotten caught in the middle of another drill. Or maybe the demon who fired it had wanted a moving target.

"Our clothes are like armor," Ren whispered to me. "Remember?"

Hondo helped me to my feet. "Dude, I thought you said fire doesn't listen to you."

I went over to the arrow and was about to stomp out the fire with my foot, when I heard familiar faint whispers, but I couldn't make out a single word.

"You made the arrow change course," Ren said. "I mean, it all happened so fast, but you screamed and . . . it turned at the last minute."

"I knew it!" Brooks said. "You have to be stressed out for the fire to listen to you. Let's do it again. Maybe have a demon charge you or something."

"But I didn't even try," I muttered. "And no, I'd rather not get attacked by another demon."

It was like Ren said—everything had happened quickly. I hadn't even *thought* about the fire, only that I couldn't let Brooks get hurt. I picked up the arrow. As the flame died, I pulled its heat inside me and let it expand. Power raced through my body so fast I was sure I'd explode. The fire blasted out of my fingertips like a huge firecracker, throwing me back at least ten feet. I landed on my side with a bone-aching thud.

"Zane!" Brooks shouted, running over as I rolled to my feet.

"Are you okay?" Hondo said.

"That was awesome." Ren was smiling. "Even the demons ran for cover."

Trembling, I stared in shock at my fingertips—they were still smoking.

Quinn marched over, glowering. "Are you trying to blow up Xib'alb'a? We're practicing our kill shots here and you're shooting fire missiles?!"

"I...I didn't mean..." I shook off the surprise, trying to stay focused. I wondered if I had gained power from being in Xib'alb'a, or did it have something to do with seeing Hurakan again? Stretching my fingers, I could still feel the aftershock of the eruption. Amazing!

At the same moment, Ixtab materialized in a column of blue mist. Rosie was right behind her.

"Did you decide?" she asked.

I cleared my throat and looked from Hondo to Brooks to Ren and back to Ixtab.

"Yes. I'm ready to die."

21

.
.

I need to pause right here.

Mostly because what happened next was pretty much the beginning—or end—of everything, depending on how you look at it. It's hard to explain, but it was sort of like this: Imagine you've spent your whole life as a sea creature and then one day you break the surface and discover you have lungs. And all of a sudden the world above is different and scary and so much clearer than it was under the water. Even if you don't like what you see, you know you can't ever go back to living in the ocean again, because, well, now you have stupid lungs.

Here's the bottom line: Things were about to change big-time, and life was never going to be the same. Not for me or my friends or my family or any godborn. Sorry about that. If you want to murder me, take a number.

Ixtab had changed into a long black silk dress that touched the terrace's stone floor. *This* is how she dressed for a Desesperadas meeting? Didn't look very desperate to me. "You've made the right choice," she said.

"Don't do it," Brooks whispered.

Ren's eyes widened. "Zane, what if . . . ?" She didn't finish, because there were too many *what if*s to consider. What if I wasn't strong enough? What if I didn't succeed? What if the godborns died because of me? What if I became permanently dead? I thought about the ancestors' message: *In the dark, you shall choose the path, but beware. All roads lead to the gods' angry wrath.* Was I doomed no matter what?

Maybe it was the fire power I'd just felt, or the fact that I was standing in hell, but I decided in that moment to ignore the prophecy. Why should the ancestors get to call all the shots? They weren't going to rule me anymore.

Rosie let out a small whimper as a spear sailed overhead. Hondo mumbled to her, "Those demons don't have very good aim, do they, girl?"

Ixtab straightened. "Are you ready, godborn?"

"Zane..." Brooks warned.

There was no more time to think about it. Before I could chicken out, I shook Ixtab's hand.

Hondo came over and hooked his arm around my neck. "I got your back, Diablo." He looked at Rosie and whispered, "Dead or alive." Then he turned to Ixtab. "If he doesn't live through this? I'll hunt you down."

I love my stupidly brave uncle, but it's never a great idea to threaten the queen of the underworld. I for sure thought Ixtab would shoot fire at him or choke him with her gold chain.

Instead, she ignored him and said to me, "You will only have one opportunity to return to Xib'alb'a. This will open a gateway where none exists." She handed me something about the size of a quarter. It was blue and a little spongy. Was it... a kernel of corn?

"What am I supposed to do with this?" I stared at the seed in my hand.

"Even small, seemingly insignificant things can be powerful," she said. "Maize is sacred to the Maya, Zane. Quinn will give you instructions on how to use it, and no matter what, do not misplace it." She spun toward Quinn. "You know what to do. Please do not dally with death boy like last time." And then she was gone.

Death boy? Dally?

All eyes were on Quinn. I have to admit, she looked flustered, and I had a feeling it had to do with whoever this "death boy" was. She spun and marched up the steps toward the waterfall.

"Hey!" I called after her. "Where are we going?" But she didn't answer. I couldn't wait to get her alone and learn more about the secrets she'd discovered about Ixtab.

"Does this mean we get to skip Pus River?" Hondo said.

Ren followed on my heels. I slowed to let her catch up. "What did you and Ixtab talk about when you used telepathy?" I asked her again.

Ren kept her gaze straight ahead. "She's not my mom."

"Yeah, you already said that. Does she know who is?"

"She didn't say."

I wanted to ask more, but we'd come to an overlook deck halfway up the stairs. A narrow twenty-foot bridge extended from it, leading straight *into* the pounding cascade. "After you," Quinn shouted over the crashing water.

Scratching his chin, Hondo said, "Uh . . . you want us to

walk into that hundred-foot waterfall that looks like it could snap our bones? Are you kidding?"

"I never kid." Quinn's face was granite. "That's where we have to go for Zane's death ceremony."

Rosie sniffed the ground and then sat on her haunches like she was waiting to see what we were going to do.

"I don't do water," Brooks said, backing up.

Quinn's expression softened, and I could tell she wanted to say something to Brooks but was holding back. Then, with a knowing nod, she said "I'll go first" and stepped onto the bridge.

"Isn't there another way to wherever we're going?" I asked.

"Pus River," Quinn said over her shoulder.

Hondo nodded way too eagerly. "Come on, guys. We can do this. It's just a waterfall. A baby one, too." He walked next to Ren and leaned in to tell her, "Remember what I showed you. . . . Visualize, take deep breaths, meditate."

Ren seemed uncertain as the two of them walked off after Quinn, who had already disappeared behind the curtain of water. When they reached the end of the bridge, Hondo took Ren's hand and shouted, "Geronimo!" Right before they pushed through the torrent, I could swear it stood still for a nanosecond.

But when I asked Brooks if she'd seen it, she just gave me a *why-do-we-have-to-do-this?* look.

Rosie was next. She stretched her front leg in front of her body and let out a massive yawn. Then she stepped into the waterfall like it was the flap of a doggy door.

Brooks tilted her chin up, clenched her jaw, and said, "One day, Obispo, we will go on a quest that involves zero water!"

I trailed Brooks, wondering what her deal was. But the falls pounded so loudly I could barely hear myself think. Brooks waited for me at the end of the bridge.

"On three?" I said, taking her trembling hand.

But before I could even count to one, she closed her eyes and jerked me into the roaring water.

22

.

..

I was expecting a crushed skull, busted teeth, or a vomit-inducing free fall into some death pit. Instead, I stepped (totally dry, by the way) into a wedding reception, where pink and green strobe lights flashed across a garden plaza. I spotted the bride and groom jamming on the dance floor. Glasses clinked. The crowd's chatter and laughter bounced off the perfectly pruned, rounded trees. A few guys stood in the corner doing shots and slamming their fists on the table while the sun melted into the dusky sky.

"Where in the heck are we?" I asked Brooks, looking around for the others.

"I'd say hell, except we just came from there."

Quinn grabbed us and hauled us behind a tree. I was glad to see Hondo, Rosie, and Ren waiting there. Hondo kept trying to get a waiter's attention, and Ren bounced to the beat.

"I hate weddings!" Quinn shouted over the music.

"What is this place?" Brooks asked.

Quinn shook her head. "How many times do I have to answer the same question?"

"San Miguel de Allende," Hondo said to me, looking around. "Hey, señor! How about a drink?" he hollered at a waiter carrying a tray of what might have been champagne.

The guy didn't hear him, or maybe he was just ignoring my uncle.

"San Miguel de huh?" I asked.

"Mexico, you uncultured swine," Quinn said.

The place smelled like a million different soups blended together with garlic, carne, and spices I couldn't name. Rosie kept sniffing the air and licking her big chops. How could she already be hungry? Hadn't she just feasted on snake heads?

The plaza was surrounded by little shops, and at the far end was a massive cathedral with pink Gothic-looking spires and towers that poked the dim sky.

"I've got strange news and bad news," Quinn said.

"Give us the strange first," Ren suggested. Everyone nodded. Even Rosie.

Quinn pointed to a clock on one of the towers. "Only a couple of hours have gone by in the upper realm since you arrived in Xib'alb'a. More time should have passed here. I've been keeping track, and you've actually been away for ten hours." She shook her head. "But it's like eight hours were erased, or time stood still or something."

Stood still . . . like the waterfall.

"As if we could trust any clock in hell," Hondo muttered.

I didn't care where the extra time had come from—it meant I still had three whole days to find the godborns and get to my dad. "And the bad?" I asked.

"Aside from Zane having to get killed," Hondo said.

Quinn turned in a circle, looking super confused. "This isn't right."

"Is that the bad news?" Brooks asked.

"We need to be over there." Quinn pointed left. "Or is it there?" she muttered. "Yes, definitely over there. Come on." She took off in the direction of the church.

"Are you lost?" I asked, trailing her. Because that's what it looked like. And no offense, but I really thought that the person leading me to my death should have at least *some* sense of direction.

"No, I am *not*," Quinn said. "I haven't been here since last year, and the door can sometimes move, okay? *That's* the bad news."

"Lost is definitely bad," Brooks muttered to me.

Rosie sniffed the cobblestone road. Her nub tail wagged as she trotted ahead, weaving between a couple of toddlers sharing a churro. One pointed, wide-eyed, while tugging on his mom's sweater, and I swear it was like he could see Rosie in her hellhound form.

"Hey, can we stop in the churro shop?" Ren asked as we passed. I felt suddenly hungry, too.

"No," Quinn said over her shoulder. "There's no time to spare."

"Distract her. I'll catch up," Hondo whispered in my ear before ducking into the panadería.

We turned right at the corner, and as we passed by the cathedral's iron gates, I glanced up. Gargoyles lurked on the corners of the building, their eyes frozen wide as if they were on the verge of a scream. That's when I felt a strange tug. At first, I ignored it, but there it was again. Like some-thing...or someone...was calling me inside. Was this Hurakan's sign?

I slowed my pace. "Do you hear that?" I asked Brooks.

"The really bad party music?"

If Mom were there, she'd drag me inside to light a candle and say a prayer. But she wasn't there. I know it had been less than a day, but I missed her and felt lousy that I hadn't said good-bye. I wandered through the gates and told Rosie to stay and keep watch for Hondo so we didn't lose him. Brooks and Ren followed me while Quinn circled back, shouting some choice words at us.

Inside, the place was empty. A crystal chandelier cast a dim flickering light across the vaulted brick ceilings and stone floors. Yellow flowers were tied to the ends of each pew, probably left over from the wedding.

Brooks's voice dropped to a whisper. "Zane, what are you doing?"

"Do you want last rites or something?" Ren asked. "You know, before you die?"

Yeah, *that* was a depressing thought. I stood very still, waiting. Listening to the distant whispers. Where were they coming from? I made my way toward an altar where dozens of votive candles burned in little red glasses under a painted statue of Mary.

Even Quinn kept her voice to a hush, although it was clear she was furious. "Where's that uncle of yours, and why are we here, Zane? We have to go! Every second you wander around without protection is a second closer to you losing your head for real."

I signaled for everyone to be quiet. When I got to the altar, the whispers grew louder. That's when I knew. The voices . . . they were coming from the tiny flames.

I couldn't make out the voices or separate one from the next, but every few seconds I'd catch a name, like *Ignacio* or *Charles*, or a few words, like *make him marry me*, or *heal her*.

"I can hear them," I said quietly.

"The candles?" Ren asked.

"The prayers," I said.

"That's creepy," Quinn said, crossing her arms. "And voyeuristic. And creepy."

Brooks tugged my arm. "You shouldn't listen, Zane. Isn't that, like, sacrilegious or bad luck or something?"

"Definitely bad luck," Ren said. "I heard about a guy who erased people's prayers from the book of intentions and got cursed for it."

"Cursed?" I swallowed the lump in my throat.

"He went bald, like overnight," Ren said. "And he was only eighteen."

I ran my hands over my hair. Ren and Brooks were right. Listening to even *pieces* of people's prayers felt wrong. Plus, I really wasn't in the market for bad luck *or* curses.

"Zane, we have to go," Quinn warned. "Fausto's not exactly patient."

I was about to ask who Fausto was, when Hondo and Rosie burst into the church. Hondo held out a dozen half-wrapped churros and smiled. "For the win, right?"

We all took one. Even cranky Quinn. Rosie got four.

Before we left, I struck a match, lit an unused candle, and

said a silent prayer. *Please help me find the godborns and save my dad and, oh yeah, please don't let me go bald or have some other horrific curse fall on my head or anyone else's. Okay? Uh, thanks.*

Exiting the back of the church, we found ourselves on a narrow cobblestone street lined with tightly packed houses. The rising moon cast a cool glow over the yellow, red, and blue facades. Bougainvillea spilled over the rooftops and garnished the carved wooden gates of each house.

Every few feet, Quinn would stop and press her hand on one of the gates. Some had angel stone reliefs hanging above them and others had lion-head knockers. "Where is that door?" she muttered. "I'm sure it's here. Or over there? He probably moved it again. Uggh! Not funny."

I'd never seen Quinn so flustered. I mean, she'd been completely cool and in control when we'd flown over the Old World together, hunting the god of death. But now? You'd think she was getting ready to sing at the Super Bowl half-time show.

"Maybe if you tell us what you're looking for we can help," Brooks said impatiently.

"Finally!" Quinn smiled (shocking, I know), stopping in front of a brown puerta in a wall in front of a house. She traced her fingers over the wood panels. Two painted words materialized on the wood: EL GRITO.

"Cool trick." Hondo licked some sugar off his fingertips. "But why would anyone name their house the Scream?" He shot me a wary look.

Ren whispered, "Because people scream a lot in there?"

My stomach turned in on itself as I stepped closer. I saw that the gate had eight panels and inside each one was a carving I was sure hadn't been there before: a round face with a wide-open mouth and terrified eyes. Perfect.

Brooks scowled, shouldering past me. "I don't like this. I thought we were here to . . ." She hesitated, choosing her words carefully, especially with Rosie there. "We only need to make Zane kind of D-E-A-D, Quinn," she said in a low voice as if I wasn't standing right next to her.

Quinn knocked twice on three different panels, like some kind of code, and said, "We *are* here to make Zane D-E-A-D."

"*Fake* D-E-A-D," I reminded her.

Quinn ignored me. "Brooks, did you think I was going to smother him with a pillow? This is a precise art. One wrong move and it's lights-out forever. And now we're late!"

"Whoa!" I held my hand up in protest. "What do you mean, 'lights-out forever'? Ixtab said there were side effects, but she didn't say anything about me actually *dying* in the process!"

"I say we take our chances with the gods." Ren elbowed me. "If they find us, I bet we could outrun them."

Hondo shook his head. "As crazy as it sounds, this is the better strategy to give you the best chance of survival, Zane. But whoever is doing this"—his dark eyes met Quinn's—"they better be a pro."

Quinn sighed. "It's not like I'm bringing him to some street vendor selling dark magic. Puh-lease! Fausto's the best. Obnoxious, but the best."

Leaning closer to Brooks, I muttered, "Street vendors sell dark magic?"

She gave me a light shrug and twisted her hair around her pinkie, which was never a good sign. I hated when she was nervous, because it usually meant I should be freaking out.

I felt slightly dizzy as the gate clicked and opened slowly like it was automated. I looked from worried face to worried face. A cool breeze drifted from the courtyard inside, but it was too dark to make anything out.

Just as my foot crossed the threshold, a shrill scream pierced the air. We all jumped back. Everyone except Quinn. "Sorry," she said. "I forgot to tell you about that little welcome. It's just a recording. Part of the stupid ambience."

"Any other *stupid* surprises?" Brooks asked.

Quinn twisted her mouth, and in this dim light, she looked like Brooks minus the nose freckles. "Nope. I think that's the only one," she said. "But who knows with Fausto. He thinks he's funny, but he's totally not."

"Who is this Fausto dude, anyway?" I asked, not sure I even wanted to meet the guy.

"An expert death magician, among other things." Quinn walked through the gate.

Great! My executioner was a prankster mago?

Hondo hooked his arm around my neck, tightening his grip. "Don't worry, kid. No one's going to do any death-magic-mojo-kung-fu on you unless it feels right."

Brooks took my hand. *You don't have to do this.*

For once Brooks was wrong. Too many people were counting on me. I had to follow through.

I stepped inside El Grito.

23

•

•••

We entered a narrow outdoor passage where moonlight spilled between the trellises above. It led to a shadowed garden with a grove of purple-flowered trees.

"Are those heads hanging from the trees?" Ren asked with horror.

Good thing I could see so clearly through the dark or I might have lost it. "They're masks," I said. Every branch was filled with them, dangling by what looked like fishing wire and twisting in the breeze. Beyond the garden was a big stone house with at least four stories. Thorny vines climbed the walls.

"Whoa!" Hondo breathed. "This place is like . . . king status. But the masks? No me gustan."

"I don't like them, either," I muttered. Rosie grunted in agreement.

Ren had already headed over to examine one of them. She tapped a flesh-colored mask that had slits for eyes and a gaping hole for a mouth. "These could be alien faces, if you ask me."

I went over to get a better look. All the masks were different. Some were jade mosaics, others were painted papier-mâché with horns and pointed eyebrows, and the rest were

made of wood and stone. But all of them were in the middle
of a scream. Even the wolves, lions, and jaguars.

I was so focused on the masks, I almost didn't notice the
guy step out from between the trees. He was about Hondo's
age, had shoulder-length blondish hair, a pierced nose and
eyebrow, and his arms were covered in tattoos—mostly
knives, dragons, and broken hearts. He wore jeans, a gray
tank top, and an apron splattered with paint.

"Hey, Fausto," Quinn said, barely looking at the guy. "Is
everything ready?"

Fausto came over and gave Quinn a giant hug. She
stiffened.

"Man, what's it been, like a year?" he said. "I hope you're
staying awhile this time."

Quinn blushed. Yeah, you read that right. The cranky ice
queen blushed.

Hondo cleared his throat and stood taller. His head
whacked a wolf mask. "We're not staying."

Fausto snapped his attention to Hondo. A slow smile crept
up. "I wasn't asking *you*, was I?"

I could tell Hondo wanted to deck the guy, but before he
could say anything, Quinn stepped between them and said,
"Fausto, you know why we're here."

Brooks added, "And we're sort of in a hurry. We've got
places to be."

Right. Like New Mexico. My plan was to get to the godborns first. My dad had three days before he was transferred.
The godborns might not have three hours, and like Ixtab had

said, who knew how they were being treated—or if they were already hurt.

Rosie yawned and collapsed under a tree. I was about to die and all she could think about was sleep?

Fausto wiped his paint-stained fingers on his apron and scanned each of us. "So, who's the lucky victim?"

I half raised a hand. "Uh . . . that would be me."

Fausto studied me. "Nice spear," he said, glancing down at Fuego, which was still in cane mode, so how did he know? Must've had something to do with him being a mago.

"Thanks," I said, keeping my eye on Ren, who had wandered away, still checking out the masks. Moon shadows rose up from the ground, surrounding her like a blanket. I wondered why they had been MIA in Xib'alb'a.

"Okay, Zane," Fausto said. "This is how it's going to work. You choose a mask, you put it on, you die. Any questions?"

"Hang on." Brooks held up her hand. "We need a little more information. Like, who are you, what are your credentials, and how in the heck do the masks—?"

"Make me D-E-A-D?" I asked.

Fausto ignored me, keeping his focus on Quinn and Brooks. "This has to be your little sister, Quinn."

"Quit stalling, Fausto." Quinn gave him a hard stare.

"People always want to hurry death magic," he muttered. Then he answered us. "The masks are supernatural artistic perfection made by me and every generation of my family before me. There's only been one mess-up—okay, maybe two, and it was, like, three generations ago, some distant uncle. I've got a one hundred percent success rate, which basically means the death magic will kill you enough, but not so much your heart stops beating."

"What do you mean 'kill me *enough*'?" I said. "You're either D-E-A-D or you're not."

"Oy...Let me explain in terms you might understand." Fausto scratched his chin.

Brooks frowned, and I could tell she already hated the guy.

"Think of it as anesthesia," Fausto went on. "You get enough, and it takes you under. You get too much, and you're a goner." He gestured to a group of trees. "Those are battle masks over there, and beyond that, ceremony masks. And that tree there?" He nodded to the closest and the only one without purple flowers. "Those are all death masks. Worn by great warriors, priests, kings, and queens—worn by their corpses, actually, and infused with my death magic."

"You want me to put on a mask a D-E-A-D person wore?"

"Seems pretty morbid, if you ask me," Hondo said.

"I *didn't* ask you," Fausto said.

Hondo tensed. I could totally tell he was imagining putting Fausto in a chokehold. Just when I thought he'd lose his cool, Quinn wrapped her arm around Hondo and squeezed. I swear my uncle grew like three inches.

Fausto's eyes narrowed to barely there slits. "Really, Quinn?" he said, offering a painted-on smile. "Trading down for a human now?"

Quinn batted her eyes all cool-like, and as she opened her mouth to say something (probably sarcastic and annoying), I jumped in. "They hate each other," I said. "Fight all the time."

Leave it to stupid adults to ruin everything. If Quinn made Fausto mad, he could make a mistake, and then I'd be a goner. No thanks.

Quinn must have recognized her mistake, because she quickly shoved Hondo away and said, "As if."

Brooks rolled her eyes as Hondo smiled wider. I thought he'd collapse under the weight of Quinn's rejection, but nope. He winked at me like he was saying *See? She likes me.*

"Can we just get on with this?" Quinn asked.

With a sly grin, Fausto said, "As soon as I get my payment."

"After we see you don't one hundred percent kill him," Brooks said.

"Fair enough," Fausto said.

"So, what do you mean the masks were worn by corpses?" Did no one else catch *that?* "Like, did you steal these masks off their cold bodies?"

"It's not like they need them once they're dearly departed, dude. And it *is* my magic."

I really hoped he had cleaned/disinfected/fumigated these things. My stomach was in knots. "Does it matter which one I pick?"

"For sure. Pick the wrong one and you'll be decapitated." He busted up laughing. "Don't look so wrecked, dude. It was a joke." Rosie lifted her head and growled at Fausto, who held his hands up defensively. "Sheesh. No sense of humor. Go on, amigo. You can't choose wrong."

Yeah, tell that to the ancestors. I went over to the death-mask tree and looked up. My stomach clenched as I scanned the faces, looking for the least creepy one. Brooks stood by

me and said, "How about that one?" She pointed to a plain
wooden mask, but my eyes were already drawn to a simple
jade one. The eye holes were large, and so were the nostrils,
but the mouth was closed. And there was something about
its plain expression that felt... harmless.

Was this the right one? I wondered. As if by way of an
answer, a sudden heat pulsed in my blood, slow at first, then
searing hot. I looked down at my hands. My palms were glowing. Before anyone else noticed, I clenched them.

Hondo spoke in a low, soothing voice. "Visualize the right
one. You have to see it in your mind's eye."

Ren walked over. Two shadows followed her closely. They
circled the mask as if they were inspecting it. "I like it," she
whispered. "Do you think King Pakal's death mask is here,
too?"

I reached up and unhooked the mask from the wire. It was
heavier than I expected. The heat racing through me faded.

Fausto eyed Ren. I wondered if he could see her shadows,
but if he could, he didn't say anything. He turned back to me
and raised an eyebrow. "Interesting choice."

The way he said *interesting* didn't make me think interesting. It made me think *wouldn't have been my choice.* "Who did
it belong to?" I asked.

"The Red Queen."

"Who's that?" Brooks asked.

"A noblewoman from, like, the year 600," Fausto said.
"Some archaeologists found her tomb in 1994, and ever since
they've been trying to figure out who she was. But those
morons will never know the truth."

"Which is?" I asked.

"Alien," Ren muttered.

Heat pulsed down my arms and into my legs, erupting in a tiny flame at my feet.

"Whoa," Fausto said.

I watched the flame float up like a leaf lost in the wind. And just as it died, I heard the same man's voice: *Excellent choice.* I nearly dropped the mask.

Everyone stared at me expectantly, and I could tell they hadn't heard the whisper. Ren's shadows wrapped around her as I looked down at the Red Queen's mask. Quickly, I tugged Quinn to the side, out of everyone's earshot, and spoke in a low voice. "What if Fausto's powers are weakening, too? What if he messes this up?"

"I already asked," she said. "He *is* losing his power, but the magic is already in the masks, so you're covered."

That made me feel oh so much better. *Not!*

"You have no choice but to do this, Zane, if you want to survive in the human world. Or would you rather go back to Holbox?"

No, I wasn't going to run away, despite Hurakan's advice to do just that. "Let's get this over with."

We rejoined everyone, and just as I lifted the mask toward my face, Fausto shouted, "Hang on!"

"What!"

"I forgot. I'm supposed to tell you about the potential side effects, which seriously takes all the fun out of it." He recited the long list in such rapid succession he sounded like one of those TV ads for drugs you'd rather not have to take.

"Migraines, diarrhea, vomiting, tooth and hair loss, insomnia, kidney failure, high blood pressure, nightmares. Let's see . . . what else?"

There was *more*?

"Oh, and acne. Some people break out. But I totally disinfect all the masks to help avoid zits."

"Not to mention the gross remains of skin and hair and bodily—" Brooks caught herself and zipped it.

"Dude," Hondo muttered to me. "You sure this is worth it?"

I met Brooks's gaze. If only we could use telepathy without touching. Not that I needed it right now. I could tell she was thinking, *THIS IS SO NOT WORTH IT.*

But I had no choice. I had to avoid the gods' detection. Then something occurred to me: "How exactly does this prevent the gods from seeing me? Does it make me invisible to them?" I asked Fausto.

He shook his head. "The gods are good at sniffing out life essence, but if yours is only at two percent, you won't even register. I mean, unless you walk right up to one, which I wouldn't recommend."

He for sure didn't need to worry about that.

"Other than hiding from the gods, why else would someone use death magic?" Ren asked.

That was a good question. I imagined Fausto didn't get tons of customers.

His eyes grew big like Ren had taken him by surprise. "To hide their magic, why else?"

Why would someone want to hide their magic? I wondered as I raised the Red Queen's mask and took a deep breath.

Brooks death-gripped my hand. Her eyes flashed amber. *You better still be Zane after this.*

Right. What if the Red Queen possessed me or something? Or what if a part of her came back with me? Just the thought of it gave me the creeps.

Brooks hugged me, but it didn't help as much as I would've hoped.

I managed a weak smile as I stepped back and, with a shudder, pressed the mask to my face.

24

•
••••

My legs buckled. The world dissolved. And I
found myself in a small vaulted chamber about half the size
of my bedroom. A single wall torch illuminated the space,
which was taken up by a rectangular stone sarcophagus. To
my right was a doorway that gave access to the chamber. Red
powder was scattered across the sandy floor.

This was not what I was expecting. I mean, I didn't feel
dead. Maybe this death magic was going to be easier than I
thought.

"Hello?" I called out, steadying myself with Fuego. My
voice echoed.

A shimmering cloud appeared on top of the sarcophagus,
and an older woman materialized out of it. She had olive skin,
black hair tied up in a tight bun, and a band of jade stones
around her forehead. "Zane Obispo," she said with a smile.
"Oh, I haven't had a visitor in so long. So few choose my death
mask, but I can tell just by looking that you are smarter than
most."

I didn't know what to make of her or this place. "Er . . . am
I dead yet?"

"*I* am dead. You are soon to be masked by death. I should
introduce myself."

"You're the Red Queen?" I guessed.

"I am, and *you* must hurry. I can only be here for one minute and thirty seconds. Now, the rules: I cannot provide any information unless you ask the right questions, and you cannot ask the same question twice or more than one question at a time. One minute fifteen seconds."

My throat throbbed painfully. I tried not to think about the fact that I was standing in an ancient tomb with a dead queen. "I thought... aren't you supposed to, you know... make me dead?" No one had said anything about a question-and-answer period.

"Here you stand before the great Red Queen and you choose to waste time. I offer you an answer to any question, and by the looks of you, you need answers. I didn't come all this way for a single death deed. I am fulfilling a debt, and you're wasting time."

There was no time to ask about her debt. "I heard a voice in the fire—it whispered to me."

"That is not a question."

"Why did the voice whisper to me?"

The Red Queen extended her small hand and called a piece of the torch's light to her. The fire sphere floated above her palm. "To tell you something."

I was about to argue that *that* was the worst answer of all time, like *Alice in Wonderland* bad, but we were on a tight schedule. Then it struck me—what if the voice that had been whispering to me all this time was the Fire Keeper dude? What else had he said? *Time for the story to escalate.* Had he been creeping on me since the night Ren got to the island? At

Ms. Cab's I had asked him who he was, and he'd said, *You'll find out soon enough.*

"Who does the voice belong to?" I asked.

"I'm not good at voices. Do you have a recording?"

"You said you would offer an answer to any question."

"That *was* my answer." The Red Queen glared at me. "Look at me like that again and I will lock you in this sarcophagus with only worms for company."

Okaaay, on to the next question. "Can you guys really change the future?"

"'You guys' does not make sense to me."

I sucked in a big breath, trying to keep my cool. "Can fire keepers change the future?"

"Indeed."

A wild, off-the-charts hope grew in an instant. Maybe Brooks's idea wasn't so loca. If I could get this Fire Keeper to change the future, I could control what happened to the godborns *and* my dad, and I wouldn't need to be in two places at once. I mean, there was a reason Hurakan had mentioned him to me and I had picked *this* mask. But if I was wrong...

"Do you know where the *current* Fire Keeper is?"

She smiled and said, "Of course. I am his great ancestor, after all! He is where he is. One minute."

That migraine side effect Fausto had warned me about? It was already jamming its knuckles into my skull. I had to choose my words more carefully. "Where do I find him?"

I was hoping the queen/ex–fire keeper was going to tell me *Down the block,* but instead she closed her eyes and said, "I can see him now at Land's End, where two worlds meet."

That was it? Where two worlds meet? "Do you have an address?"

The Red Queen's face went slack like she wanted to say *Are you kidding me?* She swiped her hands together, dousing the flame. "I see places, settings . . . *not* addresses."

My mind couldn't keep up with all the thoughts racing in and out. "I'm supposed to save the godborns and my dad, and I only have three days, and I have a feeling that maybe the Fire Keeper can help me . . . but you don't even have an address . . ." I took a deep breath. "What am I supposed to do?"

"I should have been clearer," she said. "I cannot address matters of conscience and the heart." Her eyes were deep brown with lines around them that gave her a grandmotherly look. "Only you can answer that question."

Seriously? She'd made such a big deal about answering *any* question and now there were more stupid rules. "Fine," I said. "Would it be a smart choice to use my time to find him?"

"You are the son of fire." The Red Queen pressed her lips into a thin line. "You are connected in ways only the Fire Keeper can divulge to you."

"Will he change the future for me?"

"If you go see him, the future will change."

That wasn't what I had asked. As if she could see my disappointment, she added, "A better future indeed."

Something fluttered inside of me. This was it. *This* was how I could save my dad and the godborns! I mean, a better future was a heck of a lot better than a "bleak" one.

"How do I find him without an address?"

"Ask the flame. Forty seconds."

What flame? I wanted to scream, but I had a more important question. "Do you know anything about the sobrenaturals' powers being drained?"

"I know *many* things about it." The Red Queen held up her small hand. "We are out of time." She looked at the wall behind me and sighed. "I told him what you asked me to. Well, it's not my fault. He should know. Fine. But my debt is now paid."

I whirled around. "Who are you talking to?"

"You. There is one more very important piece I apparently must tell you," she said with a grunt. "If you choose to search for the Fire Keeper, you must travel alone to see him." Her eyes shot to the wall again. "Happy now?" I realized she was talking to the torch.

My cheeks felt like they'd been slapped with a hot towel. "I can't just leave my friends behind." No way. Wasn't happening. We were a team.

The Red Queen stood next to me. The top of her head didn't even come to my shoulders. "The final steps in the journey of fire must always be taken alone. And the Fire Keeper's identity and location must be kept secret at all costs."

The tomb began to evaporate.

"Wait! What would happen if they came anyway?" I had to know.

"Unless your friends are gods or have the blood of the gods, great misfortunes will fall upon your quest and upon their heads. Perhaps even a nasty curse or two."

Of course! What would a good old Maya quest be without misfortunes and curses?

"Your time is up." The Red Queen whispered, "Son of fire. Of storm. Of the creator. Of the destroyer. Do you seek death?"

I only *thought* the word *yes* before she said, "Then death is yours."

25

—

A sudden heat charged through my blood and
bones so fast I couldn't take a breath. It felt like I'd been
shocked with a million volts of electricity, and every cell in
my body was splitting open and regenerating. Like every bone
was breaking and reconnecting. Like my brain was exploding
and being pieced back together. Forget the side effects, there
should have been a warning label for the actual death part:
Dying sucks!

The next thing I knew, I was lying on the grass under the
trees in Fausto's garden. A sharp pain stabbed behind my eyes
as the world slowly came back into focus. I could feel the Red
Queen's mask in my hand. I was relieved it hadn't become
stuck to my face or something creepy like that. My eyes darted
around, making sure the Red Queen hadn't hitched a ride back
with me. Thankfully, I only saw my friends and Fausto.

Ren stared at me with horror.

"Dude," Hondo said. "You look . . . kinda sick and pale and
sweaty."

"You guys can see me?" I asked.

"You're not a ghost, idiot," Quinn said.

"Phew—glad it worked." Fausto rubbed his brow. "Hate to
mess up my ninety-percent perfection rate."

"Ninety?!" I thought Brooks might lunge for the guy's throat. "What happened to one hundred?"

"I'm really bad with numbers, okay?"

"How do you feel?" Brooks knelt next to me, biting her lower lip. "You just vanished. What happened?"

"I feel like I was crushed under an eighteen-wheeler." I checked for my pulse. Relief flooded my body when I could feel the *thump, thump, thump*. I got to my feet shakily, leaning on Fuego. "I saw her—the Red Queen." I didn't tell them about our little Q and A session. It would only raise suspicions.

Hondo said, "A D-E-A-D queen in a tomb? Bro, that's seriously creepy."

Brooks didn't take her eyes off me and I could tell she was thinking I was hiding something.

"You should plan to stay the night here," Fausto said.

Hondo looked like he was about to argue, when Quinn put her hand on my shoulder and said, "You're going to be exhausted and weak for a while. It's part of the death magic. And everyone else should rest, too. We can leave at dawn."

"Less than three days, two rescues?" Hondo muttered, dragging his hands down his face. He didn't say the word I knew was on the tip of his tongue. *Impossible.*

Rosie came over, sniffed me, then backed up with a growl. A thin trail of smoke floated from her eyes.

"Hey, girl, it's me." I stretched out a trembling hand, which only made her retreat farther. I felt suddenly hollow, like someone had carved out my insides.

Brooks patted Rosie reassuringly and whispered something in her ear. Ren narrowed her gaze and studied me like she could see something the others couldn't. But I was too tired to ask her what it was.

We made our way through the dim orchard toward the house. As we slipped between the gloomy shadows, my heart felt so small I wasn't sure it was there anymore. I knew what I had to do. And everyone was going to hate me for it.

Hurakan's voice echoed across my dream. *Run, Zane. Far away. And don't look back.*

I woke up in a cold sweat. "Hurakan?"

There was no answer.

The clock on the nightstand read 4:03 a.m. I peered through the dark at the small bedroom. The stone walls pressed in on me. There was no window and the air felt thin, like I was trapped in a coffin.

Dawn would be here soon. It was time to go. So, I got up, grabbed my shoes and Fuego, and started for the door. I stopped by the wall mirror and took a peek. *Crap!* I looked worse than I had earlier. My face was pale and my eyes were sunken, shaded by dark circles. I basically looked like a walking zombie with super-chapped lips.

The good news (if there was any) was that I didn't feel sick. As a matter of fact, I felt rested and ready to do this thing. I'd used Fausto's computer the night before to email my mom that we were all okay and to google images of New Mexico. Every picture confirmed that the godborns had to be in the southern part of the state. Of all the places in all the world, I couldn't figure out why the abductors would take them to where I used to live.

Next, I'd done some research on Land's End. I'd found out that it could be a place in England (though I doubted a Maya fire keeper would hole up there) or San Francisco (a possibility). It could also be a clothing store (but I was pretty sure the Fire Keeper didn't live in a retail outlet). My last choice was the southernmost tip of the Baja Peninsula, also known as the Arch of Cabo San Lucas, where the Sea of Cortés and the Pacific Ocean meet. I figured Land's End *had* to be Cabo. The Red Queen had said *where two worlds meet*—and, hey, oceans were the same thing as worlds.

I'd given this plenty of thought. If the Fire Keeper could see people and places like Hurakan described, he could tell me the exact location of the godborns. Then I would ask him to change the future to one where I rescued them *and* Hurakan. I know what you're thinking—it was a big risk on an even bigger *if*. But there was a reason the Fire Keeper had been whispering to me and had given instructions to the Red Queen, right? Plus, when I'd asked Her Majesty if the Fire Keeper could change the future, she had said, *Indeed*, as in yes, definitely, done deal. Or, as Hondo would say, *Slam dunk!*

With my hand on the doorknob, I froze. Guilt gnawed at me. Here I was leaving in the middle of the night like some kind of deserter while everyone slept.

I'd sat through dinner, picking at my chicken wings, sure Brooks knew that something was wrong. After dinner, she'd asked me point-blank why I was being so quiet. I'd just blamed it on the death magic, but I could tell she didn't totally believe me.

Look, what choice did I have? I knew she and Hondo

and even Rosie would never let me leave without them. The bottom line was, I couldn't risk curses on their heads. But I couldn't leave without saying good-bye, either. I snagged a piece of paper and pencil nub out of the nightstand.

Hey guys,
     When you read this, I'll be long gone, and you'll be hating me pretty hard. I'm sorry. I can't take you with me. If I did, you'd be cursed, and I can't let that happen. I didn't make the rules. Please don't worry. This is a genius, for-sure plan. I'll meet you back on the isla.

I didn't know what else to say, and I suddenly felt hollow and alone. I stalked down the hall and stood outside Brooks's door. Carefully, I slipped into her room. My eyes cut through the dark until I found what I was looking for: the backpack slumped at the foot of her bed. Silently, I stalked over, squatted, and holding my breath, unzipped the pack tooth by tooth. I only hoped she hadn't given the gateway map to Quinn yet. Relief flooded my chest when I found it.

Brooks rolled over with a loud exhale.

I froze. My heart thudded in my ears. If she caught me in here, checking out the gateway map so I could sneak off without her, I wouldn't have to worry about the death magic becoming permanent. She'd kill me herself.

The map flashed to life with blinking squares so bright I was sure they'd wake Brooks. Good thing she slept like a vampire. There was a gateway opening at a bus station about a mile away. From experience (which wasn't much), I figured the gateway would likely be closing in about forty-five minutes. I could get there in fifteen. That would give me a window of error. I put the map back so they'd have a way to get home.

I stood and went to the door, stopping only to leave the note on the dresser. I didn't risk a glance at Brooks. I knew without looking that her face was hidden behind a heap of tangles and her arms were thrown up over her head, because that's how she always slept. Like someone ready to spring and pounce.

Outside, mist crept over the silent earth like ghost breath. I had no idea where Rosie had decided to curl up last night and all I kept thinking was *Please don't be at the gate.*

I swept past the hanging masks, careful not to disturb them, because who knew what kinds of powers they had. I mean, if the Red Queen's mask could make me dead, what could the battle masks and ceremonial masks do?

My eyes darted around the dark, waiting for Rosie to leap out and pin me to the ground while she howled for everyone to wake up. Luckily, she was nowhere to be seen, which was weird, since she had the sharpest senses in the universe. My dog could sniff out a cockroach ten miles away. As I opened the door to the street, I thought, *This was too easy,* and something about that made me muy nervioso.

A shifting shadow drew my attention. I stopped in mid-step just as an orange cat slinked from behind a flowerpot and hissed at me. The air sparked and shimmered around the cat until it was . . .

"Quinn?"

"Going somewhere?"

For a split second, I wondered if I could lie to her and get away with it. Probably not. "Uh . . . since when are you a cat?"

"I take all sorts of forms, but the smaller the form, the less energy I have to use. And like I told you, I'm not exactly myself these days."

I remembered Brooks explaining that a lot of shape-shifters can take a bunch of different forms and she was bummed because she could only shift into a hawk.

"You can't stop me," I said.

"You said you'd keep Brooks safe, Obispo."

"This *is* me keeping her safe. You have to trust me." I wanted to tell her *Don't worry—I can change the future.* Okay, technically the Fire Keeper could, but the Red Queen had said I was connected to him in powerful ways. And the best part of my plan was that no one had to storm a castle and get killed.

I thought Quinn would stick me in a headlock and drag me back into El Grito. "I do trust you," she said. "The Red Queen must have told you something big enough that you're willing to leave your team behind."

I nodded as a terrible bitterness clenched my insides. "She did. It's foolproof."

Quinn smirked. "My dad used to tell me anyone who believes something is foolproof is likely to be proven a fool."

"If you're here to try and stop me, don't."

"I'm not. I'm here to tell you something." Quinn shifted uneasily. "I shouldn't, but it's rotten not to, and if it were me, I'd want to know."

Why did I have the feeling that whatever she said next

was going to change the course of everything forever? "Know what?"

"Your dad . . . he's not going to be transferred."

"They're leaving him where he is?"

She shook her head slowly. "He's going to be executed."

A cold terror climbed up my legs, and a lump the size of a glacier formed in my throat. I couldn't breathe, couldn't think, couldn't stop my eyes from stinging. "No! Why? Ixtab said they'd never kill him—that they . . . they might need his powers someday."

"Seems they've changed their minds," she said. "Invitations have already been delivered. They want to make *this* execution public."

Right, because the last time they'd scheduled an execution it was for Pacific, the goddess of time. My dad had rescued her and sent her into hiding deep under the ocean. My stomach churned. Only the gods would send out invites to an execution! (Like I said, they're total and complete jerks.)

Quinn handed me a piece of paper. "I'm sorry."

I read the invitation silently.

BEHEADING PARTY!

YOU'RE INVITED TO THE EXECUTION OF THE HEART OF THE SKY,

ONE-LEG, OTHERWISE KNOWN AS THE TRAITOR HURAKAN

MARCH 24

ROASTING BEGINS AT ELEVEN P.M. SHARP.

BRING YOUR BEST AND WORST HURAKAN STORIES

EXECUTION WILL TAKE PLACE AT MIDNIGHT

PYRAMID OF THE MAGICIAN

So they'd changed his transfer date to an execution date. My hand trembled and a sharp pain shot up my godborn leg. I handed the invite back to Quinn. "Why are you telling me now?"

"Because it might change what you do next. If it were me, I'd want to know before I did whatever it is you're about to do."

"My dad doesn't deserve to die just because he broke some stupid oath." Why had the gods changed their minds? And why were they so scared of godborns, anyway? Now more than ever I knew I had to get to the Fire Keeper. He had to stop my dad's execution.

"A lot of people don't deserve a lot of things, Zane." Her expression tightened. "Just make sure you have a backup plan. No matter *how* foolproof you think this one is."

She sounded like Brooks, and she was right. What if the Fire Keeper could only alter one future event, or what if I couldn't find him, or . . . No. He had whispered to *me*. The Red Queen had said he would help.

"Can you do me a favor?" I asked. "Can you make sure Brooks doesn't hate me . . . for leaving?"

Quinn let out a light laugh. "As if I could control anything my sister feels or does."

Despite Quinn's rough edges, I could tell she loved her sister. I guess that was why she'd let Brooks keep the map.

Glancing up at the sky, she added, "But if anything happens to her, I'll hunt you down and peck out your eyes."

"Aren't you going to be with her?"

"I have to leave."

My stomach rolled over. "To go where?"

"You don't really think I'm going to answer that, do you?" She shifted into a cat and darted off into a dark alley.

"Quinn, wait!" But there was no sign of her.

Now I felt even more guilty for leaving Brooks, Hondo, and Ren behind. Quinn could have helped protect and guide them. But then I realized that I was the one who posed the threat to them, and that made me feel even worse than guilty.

Well, at least they had each other and the gateway map. They could get back to Holbox, where it was safe.

I followed the narrow cobblestone road that wound down toward the parroquia's pink spires, and all I kept thinking was *Execution. Execution. Execution.*

I emerged onto the plaza, where garden lights illuminated the church, casting lean shadows against its pitted walls and towers. As I walked through the little jardín to the edge of the square, Rosie materialized from a wall of smoke.

I stopped in my tracks. "Hi, girl. Nice night for a walk, huh?"

Her eyes glowed red and she bared her teeth.

I knew there was no fooling her. "You think you can stop me?"

As an answer, my dog shot fire at me. I ducked, batting the flame down to the concrete like a tossed pillow. It fizzled out. "Really?" I said.

Rosie studied my face as if she didn't recognize me. Not completely, anyway. "It's okay," I said. "I'm not really *D-E-A-D.*"

She peered at me with her shining brown eyes, and if she could talk, I swear she would have told me she didn't want to be dead, either. I'd never admitted this to anyone, maybe not even to myself, but I missed the old Rosie with her black spots, goofy smile, and small stature. Getting her back from Xib'alb'a had been a dream come true, but things had never been the same between us since. It was all my fault for ever letting her anywhere near demon runners.

Finally Rosie accepted me. She groaned, then pawed my shoe.

"You can't go with me, girl. Bad things could happen, and you could get cursed...." I scratched her head, realizing she already *was* cursed. And maybe we needed each other now more than ever. I glanced at the tall clock at the center of the jardín. Its hands were frozen on 4:25.

Just then, Rosie's ears perked straight up as her eyes fixed on something behind me.

I turned to see Ren curled up asleep on a bench beyond the church's iron gates. I was torn between checking on her and backing away. The last thing I needed was for her to wake up and ask me what I was doing there. But before I could make the decision, I noticed two shadows lingering beneath the bench. Were they sleeping, too?

Nope. Slowly, the shadows rose up, lengthening as they took the shape of human figures with glowing white eyes. I stood still, thinking maybe Ren's shadows were like wild animals and it was better not to make any sudden movements.

The good news was that they hadn't seen us. I placed my hand on Rosie's shoulder. *Don't move, girl. Stay quiet.*

The bad news was that my dog growled and shot a short stream of fire from her eyes. What part of *quiet* did she not get? "Rosie! STEAK."

Too late. The shadows were already glaring at us. They drifted toward us between the iron bars. A nervous laugh bubbled out of me. "Steak...It's a command....See? She stopped."

The shadows floated closer, growing to at least seven feet, and in the blink of an eye, they joined into one figure—a skinny long-limbed man with a top hat, walking on stilts. Honest. I don't make this stuff up, okay?

Top Hat opened his mouth and the sound that came out was like a million vibrating cicada bugs.

Clickzzclickzzclickzz

Rosie was snarling, her massive fangs glinting in the moonlight. Man, she looked ferocious.

My brain did a one-eighty. In times like these, I was super glad she was a hellhound.

26

"Hey, Ren!" I called. I knew she was having a nightmare and wasn't intentionally trying to kill us, but . . . "Now might be a good time to wake up!"

She didn't even stir. Typical!

I crept backward, gripping Fuego. Not that my spear would do me any good. Last time I met up with Ren's shadow monsters, Fuego was an epic fail and sailed right through them. Rosie launched another trail of fire, which, of course, didn't deter Top Hat, either.

"Hey, uh . . ." I said shakily. "I'm not going to hurt Ren. I'm her friend. Just ask her—she'll tell you."

But Top Hat kept gliding closer—slowly, like he wanted to prolong my terror. Rosie's hackles stood at attention as she stepped in front of me protectively. My mind shuffled through the possibilities . . . tall skinny dude in a top hat with no weapon. How much damage could he do to a 98 percent dead godborn anyway?

Top Hat extended his spindly arms. They grew longer and longer like one of those stretchy action figures.

"Hold him off, Rosie."

She lowered her chin to the ground and snarled at the

shadow. Ducking, I lunged behind a trash can, out of Top
Hat's line of sight. Just as I stood to race toward Ren and
shake her awake, I heard a strangled yelp. Top Hat had Rosie
pinned with a stilt jammed against her throat. My hellhound
writhed beneath the shadow, her eyes shooting flames that
were swallowed by the darkness.

"Get off my dog!" I screamed. I took off running toward
the monster, instinctively launching Fuego through the air
before my limp returned and my knees buckled. Just like
last time, my spear sailed right through the form and looped
back to me. I drop-rolled to the ground, swiping at Top Hat's
remaining stilt with my leg. I connected with nada.

I think Top Hat might have chuckled.

The shadow reached for me. I tried to scramble away from
his grasp, but in a flash, he caught me, clutching my ribs so
tightly I couldn't move or breathe. He was so distracted with
me, Rosie was able to break free.

As my lungs were being crushed, I realized that even with
death magic, I *could* die.

"AWAY!" Ren's voice was the best thing I'd ever heard.

Instantly, the shadow vanished with one last hair-raising
clickzzclickzz.

"Zane!" Ren rushed over with Rosie right behind her. "Are
you okay?"

I got up onto all fours, gasping for air. Rosie patted my
back with her giant paw as I caught my breath. "Ren...you...
really"—*gasp*—"need to stop"—*wheeze*—"having nightmares
that want to kill everyone!"

"I wish I could. . . . I'm sorry. I think. . ." Ren looked frantic. "I think they are like guardians, like they somehow protect me?"

"Well, they're doing a really good job, but maybe you could tell them I'm not a threat?"

"Good thing Rosie woke me up."

"Good thing only sobrenaturals can see your shadows." I couldn't imagine some innocent person out for a morning stroll only to be shocked when a shadow gutted them.

"What're you guys doing out here, anyhow?" she asked.

"I could ask you the same thing." Awkwardly, I got to my feet. White spots floated in my vision, and my bones felt like burned rubber. If this was what it was like to be almost dead, I hated to think how awful being totally dead would feel.

"I couldn't breathe in that El Grito place," Ren said. "The house gave me the creeps, so I went for a walk after everyone went to bed, and I guess I fell asleep out here." She studied me, shaking her head. "You look terrible, Zane. Are you sure you're okay?"

"I don't feel as bad as I look," I said. "You should . . . er . . . get back to the house." I didn't have time to chat with Ren, not now.

She narrowed her cool eyes. "I don't believe you."

"I swear." I held up my hands. "I feel fine."

"That's not what I meant. I don't believe you told us everything the Red Queen said. I'm pretty good at sensing stuff. How do you think I sniff out fake alien reports?"

Were there any other kind? I stroked Rosie's neck, thinking how much I hated Ren's sixth sense. "I told you everything and, uh, I gotta go."

"Where?"

"On a walk. Clear my head." I started to move away, hoping she wouldn't follow. I just needed to get to the bus station before the gateway closed, and I figured I only had about twenty minutes to get there, thanks to Top Hat.

"I'll go with you," Ren said. "The sun will be up soon. Aren't we supposed to leave at dawn?"

"Right," I said, trying to think fast. "But I, uh...I sort of wanted to light a candle. You know, say a prayer before we take off." Man, I was such a mentiroso. And in front of a church, too! Mom would have a lot to say about that.

"I'll pray with you."

"Ren, I have to go somewhere alone...and you can't follow unless you want to be cursed."

She didn't even flinch. Actually, she seemed to be somewhere else and not listening to me at all.

"I need to tell you something." Ren tugged on her shirt. "It's really important, and I can't say it in front of everyone else. Not yet."

"Okay, but, uh, how about later? Like I said, I gotta go."

She looked up at me with tears in her eyes. "It's awful, Zane."

If anxiety had claws, it was shredding my insides. I sighed, giving in. "Okay...how about we walk and talk?"

Ren picked at a cuticle as we headed down a winding road

toward the bus station. She hesitated, like she was trying to
get the words just right. "Remember when I told you my
abuelo said I had magic in my blood? That it was part of my
heritage and destiny?"

"Yeah."

"On my dad's side . . . we come from a bloodline of brujos
that I guess . . . the Maya gods thought had croaked. Or at least
that's what Ixtab told me."

Rosie trotted ahead. I picked up the pace.

"Okay, so you're a godborn with witches in your family. . . ."
Then her words hit me. *The Maya gods thought had croaked.*
Why did I have the feeling that something really bad was
coming next?

"Ixtab told me that if the gods found out my family line
was still around, they'd murder us."

"Let me guess." I thought my head might explode. "Because
the gods don't want anyone else to have any power." Which
is why they hate us godborns so much. If I didn't know any
better, and if Quinn hadn't told me the gods didn't have the
power, I'd think they were the ones behind weakening all the
sobrenaturals.

Ren dragged her boots as she walked. "I mean, I knew
about my family's magic, or at least as much as my abuelo
had told me. I bet that's why my dad never wanted to talk
about it. He was trying to protect me." She grunted in frustration. I knew how she felt. It was terrible to be hunted for
something you didn't even do, just because of the family you
were born into.

"But what's the big deal?" I said, trying to make sense of it. "I mean, the gods don't have any problem with other sobrenaturals, like nawals and seers and stuff. Do they just have a thing against brujos?"

Ren looked up at me with her wintry blue eyes. "My dad's side of the family is Mexican."

I wasn't following. "My mom's Mexican, too. Why does that matter?"

"It's different for me...." She stared at the ground. "Our blood is..." Her voice trailed off, and in that tiny fraction of a life-stopping moment, she stopped and gasped. Her gaze was glued on something up ahead. "What. Is. That?" she whispered.

I looked up.

Rosie let out a deep, murderous growl.

About thirty yards away, a hunched figure emerged from a dark alleyway. Its shape flickered in and out of view, here one second, gone the next. It limped toward us, its bald head hanging so far to the left I thought it was in danger of rolling away. The figure's pale, grayish skin looked sickly in the fading moonlight. Terror gripped me so tightly I couldn't manage a single breath.

I jerked Ren into a dead-end crevice between two buildings, and we bunched together in the tight space. I peered around the corner. He kept coming. That's right—*he.*

Every atom in my body ignited.

Ren clutched my arm. *Zane?*

It's ... him.

Who?
I couldn't even get the name out telepathically.
Who, Zane?
It's Ah-Puch.

27

WHAT?! **Ren screamed in my head.** *The god of death? The guy you killed? Or obvs not, but how . . . ? Are you sure? Look again.*

I was sure. Even though the viejo looked nothing like Ah-Puch, I knew. I could feel it in the tremor in my bones and the burning in my blood, and even though the scar had vanished months ago, my wrist ached like those skeleton eyes he'd planted in me were still there.

It was magic-button time. Itzel had said all we had to do was twist a button on our enchanted clothes to camouflage ourselves. I didn't waste any time. *Bam!* I looked down and no more legs and body—only a lime-green building with gum wads.

Twist a button! I ordered Ren.

While she followed my lead, I pressed my other hand against Rosie's neck. *Girl, you need to disappear. We can't let him see or smell you.* My hellhound blinked at me with her murderous red eyes. I knew it was in her nature to fight, but now wasn't the time. What good would it do me to light Ah-Puch on fire (which obviously hadn't worked the first time) only to have him reappear in some other, more

dangerous form tomorrow or the next day? I just needed to
hope he hadn't seen us. *Stay close by, though,* I said as Rosie
vanished in a stream of smoke.

Zane! My buttons aren't working! Ren's telepathic voice
was all terror and panic. She was right. I could still see her.
Ah-Puch stood in front of our hiding spot only ten feet away.
He hadn't seemed to notice her. Yet.

At the same moment, three moon shadows peeled themselves from the ground and wrapped themselves around Ren
until she disappeared. Her hand squeezed mine.

I told the shadows to hide me, she said. *But now I can't see
anything. Is he still coming?*

I pressed myself against the wall. *He's just standing there.*
His image continued to flicker like a broken television screen.
Here one second, gone the next.

What do we do?

My pulse pounded in my ears. *Stay very still.*

Ah-Puch sniffed the air. I could sense Rosie nearby, but
that did nothing to stop the horror that was rising inside me
like a ferocious tide.

Ren squeezed my hand again. *What's he doing?*

I held my breath, watching helplessly. Ah-Puch was supposed to be burning in a stormy inferno. A terrible metallic
taste filled my mouth and throat. How in Xib'alb'a had he
gotten out? How was he *alive*? Oh my god! Had the Empty
finally disintegrated? Was my dad . . . ?

ZANE! Ren urged.

He's looking at the ground, and . . .

And what?

And his head is tilted like he's listening for something. Oh crap.

WHAT?

I didn't want to tell Ren that Ah-Puch glanced up just then and inhaled the air like some kind of wild animal hunting its prey. I held my breath.

He walked toward us. Three heart-stopping seconds went by. Then five.

Zane?

My legs trembled close to a ten on the Richter scale. I gripped Fuego tightly. I didn't care how helpless Ah-Puch looked, I was ready to use my spear. Then I remembered how weak he'd been when I let him out of his prison all those months ago. His crony, Muwan, had brought him a blood sacrifice to restore his strength. But she was dead now, so how was he going to . . . ?

He was within five feet of us now, his head hanging low and his breathing labored. His bony chest rose and fell with a faint rattle. He wore a stretched-out white T-shirt and baggy gray pants, a far cry from the fancy suit he'd worn when I first met him.

I froze.

Zane . . . tell me what's happening!

An avalanche of panic crushed my chest. Ah-Puch lifted his gaze. His eyes shimmered a sickly yellow. He inched closer, lifted his bony chin, and sniffed the air again. A slow smile crept across his wrinkled mouth. "Zane Obispo," he breathed. "Finally, we meet again."

Maybe he couldn't see me, but clearly he could smell me.

So much for stupid death magic! I admit it—I wanted to stay invisible. If Hondo were there, he would've told me to take away what he calls "the bully factor" and just face the god of death. Man, Hondo's advice always sounds so much better when you're not choking down fear.

And if I wanted to get to that gateway, I had to go through Ah-Puch. With shaky hands, I twisted the button again, and instantly my camouflage disappeared. It took every ounce of willpower I had to force any trace of terror from my body language. I released Ren's hand and stepped out from the crevice and into the road, planting Fuego firmly in the ground between us.

Ah-Puch was no taller than five feet—as opposed to his previous six feet five—and his skin was shriveled like a rotten apple. Three, maybe four, long, wispy hairs poked out of his bald head. Okay, this was not the Ah-Puch I remembered, but that didn't make him any less terrifying or dangerous. Like I told you before, what you see in the Maya world is not always what you get. Remember that.

"Aren't you going to say hello?" His voice was raspy and weak.

"Last time I saw you"—I forced the words, channeling my uncle's fearlessness—"you were a snake."

Ah-Puch nodded and blinked slowly. "I didn't . . . wouldn't choose this pathetic form unless it was absolutely necessary." He paused like he was waiting for me to ask the next question, or maybe he was just catching his breath. "Your magic is quite impressive, by the way. You look good wrapped in death."

"How . . . how did you know?"

"I am the *god* of death," he said, as if I needed reminding. "The *only* god the magic doesn't work on."

I risked a glance at Ren—or the shadows that completely enveloped her. Apparently Ah-Puch couldn't see her. I had to wonder, why weren't the shadows doing anything? Like attacking Ah-Puch. Smothering his ugly face! Where the heck was Top Hat now? Then I realized the monsters only came to life when she was asleep.

Rosie reappeared next to me, baring her massive fangs as black smoke trailed from her nose and eyes. I could tell she was just itching to tear Puke Face apart.

His eyes widened in surprise. "Ixtab let you keep the hellhound? How sweet."

Ah-Puch's apparent weakness gave me more confidence as I patted Rosie's neck. "Why are you here? *How* are you here?"

He walked a few feet toward the building and leaned against the wall. "A part of me is still spinning in that blasted inferno you trapped me in." He shook his head and closed his eyes, like the exertion of speaking was too much. "The Empty is growing weaker, and I managed to find a tiny fissure in its slow destruction, enough to free as much of myself as I could." He coughed a few times, then took a wheezing breath. I was relieved that the Empty wasn't gone completely. That meant Hurakan was still alive.

Rosie was in warrior stance, her burning eyes never leaving Ah-Puch.

Feeling bolder, I said, "Well, if you came for revenge . . ."

"Revenge?" He let out a sputtering chuckle. "Oh, no, Zane. I came for your help."

It took me a long second to process that. "You want *my* help?" Clearly, his brain had been fried to a finger-licking crisp.

I know you're wondering about the gateway that was going to close any minute—so was I. But what was I supposed to do, tackle the god of death? Leave Ren to defend herself alone? I was in shock, and no one thinks clearly under that kind of stress.

He held up a withered hand in surrender. "Hear me out. You recently went to the Empty."

I didn't confirm or deny it, figuring I owed him nada.

"And I heard you and Hurakan. There are other god-borns?" He shook his head. "What has the world come to? But that is not my concern. My only concern is me. You fought and beat the god of death. An impossible feat. And now, quite ironically, you are the only one who can restore me to my full strength and glory. So I've come for your help. To save my life."

"Are you borracho? I'd never help you! You can rot in that inferno."

"I can feel your father weakening. I heard him tell you that it was too late for him. Believe me, those were the words of a god on the verge of dying. Soon the Empty will be destroyed, and I will be free anyway," he said.

My heart seized. "He's not going to be executed, because—" I stopped myself, realizing my mistake too late.

"So the gods are making an example of him after all."

Crap! Why had I said anything? "The gods will never let you go free, even if the Empty *is* destroyed."

"You're smart, Zane. I like that about you. You must get it from your mother's side. Is all well with her?"

Rosie snarled. Froth dripped from her fangs.

This cordial Ah-Puch was definitely not the one I'd battled and defeated. "That's none of your business."

Ah-Puch squatted, then collapsed into a slumped-seated position. "If you help me, then I will help you," he said weakly. "It's why I called you to the Empty. But you were so busy with Hurakan, I couldn't get your attention."

"*You* called me there?"

"It appears, when you dragged me there using your little magic jade charm, a connection was created between us. It took me a while to figure it out. Sometimes, when the flames were ripping through me, I'd get a flash of your life. An island. The sea. Salsa. The girl. Ah . . . such emotion. Your life . . . that's what's kept me going all these months."

I thought my head was going to explode. "You've been spying on me?"

"It's not like I had anything else to do! And sadly, your pathetic human life was the only glimpse of hope I had." He managed a trembling smile. "And then hope surged when you appeared in the underworld, *my* kingdom—"

"*Ixtab's* kingdom."

"Fine. How is she, by the way? Never mind, I don't really care. She can have the burden of that wretched place." He coughed. "The point is that I was able to call to you once you were in Xib'alb'a, and now? You made finding you even easier once you died. Figuratively speaking."

That's the thing about Maya magic: there are always a cause and effect you never see coming.

"Well, you can go back to the Empty and rot."

Ah-Puch licked his dry lips and winced like he was in pain. Okay, I know this is going to sound loco, but I really did feel sorry for the guy. I mean, if I didn't know this was old Puke Face, I'd have thought he was someone's nice old gramps with one leg in the grave asking for his last bite of a bolillo and caldo.

I drew closer. Rosie was right by my side, still foaming at the mouth like she was ready to eat the god of death as a snack. I mean, he couldn't have weighed more than one hundred pounds.

"I . . . can . . . take you"—Ah-Puch's voice was barely a whisper—"to . . . the Fire Keeper."

So, he really *had* heard everything Hurakan and I had said. I suddenly remembered Ren was sitting a few feet away and could hear everything, too, but it's not like I could tell her not to listen or ask Ah-Puch to step inside the church so we could have a private conversation. The last thing I wanted to do was draw his attention to her.

I shook my head. "I don't need your help. Besides, no one knows where the Fire Keeper is."

Isn't that what the Red Queen had said? Thanks to her clue, I'd narrowed it down to Cabo San Lucas. Except by now the gateway at the bus station had closed. I felt like an elephant was sitting on my chest and I couldn't breathe.

"Except the Red Queen, right?" Ah-Puch went on. "So good to hear her voice again. Not really, but I'm trying to be polite." He took a shaky breath.

So he'd heard us in the tomb, too? Geez! "Yeah, well, you were king, like, four hundred years ago, and this is the new fire keeper. You're not exactly in the know anymore."

"I am at my best wherever there is death, and it seems you have plenty on your hands. And let's not forget, as the rightful king of Xib'alb'a, I know more secrets than you could ever imagine." Ah-Puch leaned back and closed his eyes. "You think the deceased no longer speak to their king?" He shivered. "The hourglass is running out. I'm the only one who can get you where you need to go. Shall we talk terms?"

"Like last time?" The memory of his betrayal made my insides boil. "When you promised to save Brooks *and* Rosie and you only saved Brooks?"

"I *did* save Rosie. Look at her. She's a magnificent creature."

"*Ixtab* saved her!"

Ah-Puch hooked his thumbs in his belt loops and gave his loose pants a tug. "Who do you think got her noticed at Intake, Zane? Me, that's who! But let's put that aside. In less than three minutes, this shell of a body will stop breathing. This opportunity will be lost, and you will never get to the Fire Keeper in time. And before you ask, yes, I heard pieces of your little talk with Ixtab down under. I know your death magic is only good for three days. During my reign, it lasted much longer, but who's counting?" He sneered. "Let me help you," he said. "I am a powerful ally—okay, not in this form, but I *can* help you. I'll even let you set the terms." He dropped to the ground and began to shiver.

"Zane, you can't just watch him die." I spun to find Ren standing behind me. Her shadows were gone, and she was completely visible. Rosie lifted her chin, knocking me in my shoulder like she was actually agreeing with Ren. "He didn't save you!" I told my dog. But what if he had? What if he really had kept his promise? "Ren, you have no idea what he is. *Who* he is."

"I read the book, remember?" she said with a huff. "Maybe he's changed after being stuck in fire for months." She went over and kneeled next to him. "You did terrible things," she said to the god of death, gently taking his hand. "You were evil. Prove to me we can trust you."

As they communicated telepathically, Ah-Puch's eyes fluttered and his breathing was labored. Then a spark of recognition flashed across his face like he suddenly realized who Ren was. Could he sense she was a godborn? Did he know who her mom might be? Whatever it was, he managed a weak smile, and I couldn't tell if it was pleasant or evil.

Ren looked up at me. "Who's the Fire Keeper?"

I glared at Ah-Puch. "So much for keeping secrets."

His breathing grew shallower. He coughed into his hand, streaking blood across his palm. "I can get you there in a matter of minutes, saving you precious time."

"Zane?" Ren looked up at me, her eyes pleading with me to do something to stop his suffering.

"If the Empty is going to die, why not just wait it out there?" I asked Ah-Puch, challenging his motivations.

"I always play my odds with great precision," he sputtered. "There is an infinitesimal chance your father will survive, and where..." He winced, sucked in a sharp breath, then continued. "Where would that leave me?"

Spinning in a blazing vortex where you belong, I thought.

Ren tugged on my sleeve. "Zane, please. Look at him."

What if Ah-Puch *could* help me? And if I could set the terms myself, then maybe I could reduce the risk. At that moment, I didn't have a whole lot of viable choices. "*If*—and it's a big if—if I said yes, then how could I make you better?" I asked hesitantly. "And don't tell me with blood, because you're not getting any."

"Many ways. The jade... for instance."

"No way!"

Ah-Puch was too frail to put up a fight. "Then the maize you carry from the underworld. I can smell it."

"You think I'd waste that on you? That's to open the gateway back to Xib'alb'a."

"If you give me just an ounce of strength, I can open any gateway you want...." His voice trailed off in a coughing fit, and I swear the guy was going to hack up a lung all over Ren's red boots. "Small daily doses," he said. "The risk is minimal, Zane, and if at the end of it all I fail..." He closed his eyes and clenched his jaw. "Then you do not have to restore me. But if we succeed, then you... must be... the one to... make me whole again."

"Because I ended you?"

His eyes met mine. "Because you have the oldest, most powerful magic in the universe hanging from your neck."

The jade. The one thing with the power to give anything I asked for, but only if it was for someone else.

"See?" Ren said. "You only need to heal him enough to help you . . . us."

I hated to burst her bubble, but there was no *us*.

Ah-Puch began to fade from sight. We were running out of time and I had to choose.

I know what you're thinking: *Didn't you learn from last time? This is the god of death! Let him rot.*

Except there was no other gateway opening anytime soon.

My heart was jamming to the beat of a really bad rap song as I squatted next to the god of death. The guy smelled like rotten chunks of cow liver. "Here's the deal," I said, trying to keep my voice from shaking, because you have to look *muy fuerte* when you're negotiating with a god. "You get me to the Fire Keeper today. Then you have to serve me as long as I need you. Until I let you go." Hey, if I was going to make a deal with the god of death, it was going to be for everything, and if things didn't pan out at the Fire Keeper's, I for sure would need some godly help.

"You won't hurt anyone," I added, "kill anyone, or devour anyone. You won't try and take back your kingdom from Ixtab, start any wars, or hurt the godborns or me. You will listen to everything I say, and at the end of the quest, *if* we succeed in all of the above, I will . . ." I hesitated, glancing at Ren. She tipped her head in agreement. With a deep and not-so-confident breath, I finished it. "I, Zane Obispo, will give you back your full strength."

Ah-Puch extended his withered hand. "I agree to your terms, godborn."

28

It only took three tiny bits of the maize kernel
to get Ah-Puch standing upright. And two more to add a few
more hairs to his head and stop his coughing. "You expect me
to open a gateway with five measly crumbs?" he complained.

"Pretty much." I stuffed the kernel back in my pocket and
turned to Ren. "I'm sorry, but you can't come with me. The Red
Queen was super clear. She said if I took anyone, the journey
would be filled with misfortunes and you could be cursed."

"Technically"—Ah-Puch raised a finger, smacking his
skinny dry lips—"that doesn't include a god, or anyone with
the blood of a god. Soooo . . ."

I shot him a *don't-make-me-regret-this* glare. I knew he
was right, but he didn't have to tell Ren that. There was no
reason to have her hanging out with Puke Face if she didn't
have to.

"I'm coming with you," Ren said. I started to argue, but
she added, "You're going to need me, Zane."

"You'll definitely need her," Ah-Puch said. "Trust me."

"I'll never trust you," I growled.

Ah-Puch smiled, showing a mouthful of twisted gray
teeth. "You already have."

I really hated this version of him. "We have a deal," I said.

"And that includes listening to me, so can you callarte for a whole second?"

Ah-Puch shrugged, inspecting his ragged nails while whistling a stupid tune.

"That includes whistling," I said.

Cupping a hand over his ear, he said, "Bad ears. What was that?"

Ren folded her arms. "Zane, you're not the big boss here, and I can help you with him." She lowered her voice. "Trust me."

The way she said *trust* told me she had a lot more to tell me about her magic. "Ren, I . . ."

Ren jammed her thumb in Ah-Puch's direction. "Unless you'd rather only have Mr. Hard-of-Hearing God of Death for company."

Rosie grumbled. "Sorry, girl. I know what good company you are." Ren scratched the hellhound's thick neck.

Okay, Ren had a point. I didn't want to think about doing all this with Puke Face as my only source of companionship. Plus, I wanted Ren to finish telling me whatever the *awful* thing was about her dad's side of the family. What was so dangerous about their blood that the gods wanted to murder them for it?

Turning to Ah-Puch, I ordered, "Open the gateway and take us to the Fire Keeper at Land's End—in Cabo San Lucas." I figured I had to be specific or risk getting sent to England. Or worse, stuck between the pages of a clothing catalog.

"Cabo what?" he asked, cupping his ear.

Running low on patience, I repeated myself, louder this time.

"You don't have to shout." Ah-Puch sighed. "I'm not your personal genie, you know." He raised a finger and slowly traced the shape of a large square.

Nothing happened.

The sun was beginning to creep into the sky.

"Where is it?" I asked impatiently. Brooks was probably waking up about now, and that meant she'd find the note in a matter of minutes. I hoped she and Hondo wouldn't freak when they learned Ren was gone, too. But it was all for the best.

My mind spun down a road paved with good excuses for leaving Brooks behind: I wouldn't have to feel guilty every time I looked at her because I was keeping another secret. She'd no longer be in physical danger or at risk of being placed under an awful curse. She'd never have to know I made a deal with Ah-Puch. There was another benefit, too, as much as I hated to admit it: I wouldn't have to listen to any more of her fatalism. I may even have been a little relieved to be away from Brooks's constant planning and overthinking.

Ah-Puch's voice jerked me back to the task at hand. "I must be too weak," he said, rubbing his bony chin.

"You're lying." Man, I wished I had made *no lies* one of my terms.

Ren patted Ah-Puch's arm. "Can you try again?" It was probably easier for her to be nice to him because reading about someone's evil isn't the same as *living* through someone's evil.

"Maybe a little more maize would help," he said.

"You've had enough," I said.

He jiggled a finger in his right ear. "Can you repeat?"

"I said, you've had enough!" I practically shouted.

"One more morsel isn't going to restore my full powers. We have a deal. Only you can make me whole again. Believe me, godborn, I'm not about to ruin my chances."

Reluctantly, I fished the kernel out of my pocket and scraped off another bit before handing it to Ah-Puch, who touched it to his mouth. Color rose in his cheeks. When he traced with his finger this time, the air crackled and sparked as a gateway opened and expanded big enough for us to step through. I expected to be able to see what was on the other side, but it was like trying to get a glimpse of the sky from fifty feet under the ocean.

"Could be a bumpy landing," Ah-Puch said. "We better hold hands."

"What do you mean, bumpy?" Ren asked.

"Better hurry," Ah-Puch said. "Gate's going to close."

Just as we connected our hands (which I totally didn't want to do with Ah-Puch, but I was the unlucky one in the middle) and were about to go through the gateway, I heard Brooks call my name. I looked over my shoulder and saw her about twenty feet away. She took a step toward me, then froze as her gaze fixed on Ah-Puch. I could tell she recognized him. She gasped as her eyes drifted to our linked hands. Everything happened so fast I can't be sure which came first: the confusion in her expression, the sting of betrayal in her blazing gold eyes, or the punch to my heart.

"Gate's closing," Ah-Puch hummed.

Rosie sniffed the edge of the gateway as Ren squeezed my hand. *We have to go,* she said.

Brooks shouted, "Zane!"

I wasn't even thinking when I tried to release Ah-Puch's hand and make a beeline for Brooks. All I wanted to do was make her feel better, make her understand. Make her not hate me. But I never got the chance, because Ah-Puch jerked me into the gateway.

Just for the record, I want to tell you that there are different kinds of misery. Like getting your nose busted by the school bully, or being stuffed in a toilet during gym. Then there's the misery of hurting a best friend so much it rips out your own heart. Yeah, that's what I was feeling as we stumbled onto a wide pathway at the edge of a sparkling marina.

Dozens of white boats were docked there, rocking gently in the water to our left. To our right was a row of restaurants, each packed with tourists relaxing on the half-shaded patios. The salty air was warm and dry with the lingering scent of grilled fish and garlic.

I shoved Ah-Puch in the shoulder. "You didn't let me say good-bye!"

"She'll forgive you," Ah-Puch said, looking around. "Maybe."

He didn't know Brooks. Maybe she'd understand me leaving without saying good-bye. Quinn might be able to smooth it over. But she'd *never* understand me leaving with the god of death.

Ren patted my arm. "Zane, you have to stay focused."

"But..." I felt my insides slowly collapsing. Rosie grunted a trail of smoke like she was telling me Ren was right. Thinking about Brooks hating me wasn't going to help me stay clear-headed.

Ah-Puch stretched his arms in front of him and popped his creaky elbows. "That gateway took too much energy. I need to eat. Definitely no fish. Preferably, a rib eye. Extra rare."

Rosie licked her chops and whined at the mention of steak.

That's when I noticed the dimming sky. A giant fist got lodged in my throat. "The sun's setting! Wasn't it just dawn?"

"Yes, well, I had to take an under-the-radar gateway, and those can be real time sucks," Ah-Puch said like it was no big deal that we'd lost a whole day. So now I was down to two days and the few hours I had left tonight.

"We didn't have that time to waste!" I growled.

"That's what I said," Ah-Puch agreed. "Time to eat."

"I said time to waste, *not* —"

"Where exactly are we?" Ren asked.

"They call this paradise Cabo San Lucas," Ah-Puch said. "Well, that's not the true name, but history is quite the liar sometimes, isn't she? Just ask the ghosts of the forgotten Pericú people."

"Can we just get to the Fire Keeper?" I asked, trying to keep my cool.

A few tourists cruised by, followed by a skinny dude on a bike pulling a covered carriage. "¿Quieren un aventón?"

"We don't need a ride," I told him, waving him past. "Look," I said to Ah-Puch. "The deal was to take us to the Fire Keeper. Today! So, where is he?"

"Do you mean in this exact moment?"

My hands trembled with the craving to throttle him. "You get what I mean."

"How should I know?" he said. "Give me a break here. You asked to come to Land's End in Cabo San Lucas and I delivered—flawlessly, I might add. Now we just have to narrow things down a bit. Not to worry."

I was definitely going to strangle the god of death. "Then I guess you're going back to the Empty, because the deal was to take me to the Fire Keeper *today.*"

"Then I have until midnight, don't I?" There was a challenge in Ah-Puch's eyes that reminded me of the powerhouse he used to be.

"Can't you call up one of your spies in Xib'alb'a?" Ren asked him.

"I have to be careful how I communicate. If the gods find out a part of me is free..."

I didn't catch the tail end of Ah-Puch's sentence, because a loud and terrible cry came from the palm tree above our heads. I swung my gaze upward. Clinging to the trunk was a blue-haired monkey. His mouth was shaped like a giant O and his scream sounded like a mix of gnashing teeth and a horrifying howl.

I jumped back in case the thing was about to leap onto my head, and nearly tumbled into the water.

"What's wrong?" Ren said, following my gaze.

"That . . ." I said, pointing up.

"The tree?"

"Ren, the monkey. He's pretty hard to miss."

"Zane, there is no monkey. Are you feeling okay? Maybe your blood sugar is dropping, or you're having hallucination side effects. You should eat something."

Was I hallucinating? But the monkey looked so real, and that screech . . . Ah-Puch lifted his gaze and I was sort of hoping he'd point and say *Hey, check out the blue primate*, but his eyes didn't register that he'd seen the monkey either. And then the thing vanished into a cloud of yellowish smoke. I didn't even have time to register *that*, because Ah-Puch sniffed the air hungrily and announced, "I smell fresh blood."

Rosie butted my ribs as Ah-Puch started to take off. I grabbed the god by his scrawny arm, stopping him in his tracks. "I said no killing or devouring, remember?"

Ah-Puch's eyes narrowed. "How accurate is that spear of yours, godborn?"

I gripped Fuego tightly. "Why?"

"Because that blood I smell? It's on its way. And it's going to kill us. Well, mostly you, which I suppose by extension means me."

"What do we do?"

"Run!"

29

"Run?" I shouted. "To where?"

"We have to get to open water," Ah-Puch said. "Hurry!"

"How do I know your nose isn't as bad as your ears?"

"I know blood, godborn."

Okay, that convinced me. Ren and I took off with Rosie a few paces ahead. I glanced over my shoulder to see Ah-Puch dragging himself after us. A part of me wanted to leave him behind, but we'd made a deal, so I backtracked with Rosie.

"Get on Rosie," I said to Ah-Puch.

"I am the god of death! I will *not* ride a hellhound."

"Then I guess it's back to the inferno."

With a scowl, Ah-Puch climbed on Rosie, muttering words I can't repeat.

Once we got to the dock, Ah-Puch herded Ren and me into a sleek powerboat. The kind that's shaped like a bullet and built for speed. He and Rosie hopped in behind us.

Groping through compartments, Ah-Puch finally found the owner's manual. Furiously, he flipped through the pages.

"What are you doing?" I hollered.

"Learning to drive," he said as he fumbled with the ignition.

"We need a key." I looked under the seat and turned over some cushions, hoping to find one hidden.

"Is Ah-Puch joking?" Ren's eyes darted around nervously. "We can't take this boat. We're going to end up in a Mexican jail!"

"Uh, I'm more worried about the blood that's coming," I said.

"What did you mean, blood is on its way?" Ren asked Ah-Puch. But he was too busy starting up the boat to answer. Don't ask me how, since we hadn't found the key.

"I can steer," I said, and as soon as the words left my mouth, my brain sent an all-out panic alert: *WHAT ARE YOU DOING?! You can't sail into open waters with the god of death!*

Ah-Puch waved me off while Rosie leaned over the port side, her tongue hanging out of her mouth like she couldn't wait for the blood to arrive.

Whatever.

"We can't just steal a boat!" Ren hollered over the roar of the engine.

"There was nothing about that in our agreement," Ah-Puch said as we cruised across the harbor and into the open sea. "And unless you want the looming horror we're about to face to show up on the gods' radar, we need to get to open water. Trust me."

"Stop saying that!" I groaned. "I'll never trust you."

It was entirely possible Ah-Puch's sense of smell was way off since he wasn't exactly himself. I mean, here we were, stealing a boat, racing across the ocean, and Rosie wasn't even howling or snarling or foaming at the mouth. If there was any danger, believe me, my hellhound would know. Right?

"How do you know how to drive this thing?" Ren shouted

as we skip-jumped over the water. A nearby tourist was thrown off his Jet Ski in our wake.

Ah-Puch gestured to the owner's manual now tossed to the floor.

Okay, so the guy was some kind of godly speed-reader.

Just then, Ren tugged on my sleeve and pointed across the water. "Here comes the horror." No more than six inches above the ocean's surface, a black cloud the size of Hondo's old truck was zooming toward us.

Ah-Puch glanced up. His few strands of white hair blew wildly around his hollow face. "Zane! I need more nourishment. To fight them off."

"Them? What *is* that thing?"

A strange buzz-hum ricocheted across the sea. The winds reached deafening speeds. Two boats careened, barely missing each other. A parasailer tumbled out of the sky. The black formation was only about fifty feet away, and no matter which direction Ah-Puch spun the boat, the cloud followed, matching our speed easily.

Rosie reared her head and let out an epic roar. Oh sure . . . *now* she warns us of danger! Flames erupted from her eyes and nose and mouth, directed at the cloud, but the thing was fast, instantly ducking Rosie's blazing fire trails.

Ren rushed to the stern, like she wanted to get a better look.

"What are you doing?" I screamed. "Get down!"

The cloud was coming right for her. She stood there frozen.

I launched Fuego over her head. It whizzed across the air, hitting the target, but only managing to split the stupid cloud in half. A few tiny . . . forms fell into the water. Just as Fuego circled back, a horde of what looked like giant bees emerged from what was now two clouds. Their hum-buzzing raised the hairs on my arms and neck.

Crap! They weren't bees.

They were *bats* with curled, flesh-colored claws and crooked fangs, which, by the nasty way, hung out of their hairy mouths. Dozens of the creatures came at us in a frenzy.

"Be still!" Ah-Puch said.

"Are you kidding?"

"The more you move, the more agitated they become, trust me."

If there were a way to remove those last two words from his brain, I would have done it in a flash.

Ah-Puch collapsed to his knees, releasing the wheel and sending the boat skittering sideways. He rolled himself into a ball.

Everything happened at superspeed.

I shoved Ren behind a seat, shouting, "Use the camouflage!"

The only problem? When I twisted my button, *zero* camo. And like before, Ren's didn't work, either. Thanks, Itzel. I was so going to give her a seriously bad review for this.

Ren wailed, cowering and putting her arms over her head to try to protect herself from the bloodsucking beasts that were now swarming the boat.

I dropped to my knees and balled myself up, too.

The bats landed on me. It took every ounce of concentration I had not to move. Their little claws tap-danced all over my back, up my neck, and across my head. Their mouths pressed against my ears and cheeks, breathing hot puffs of air. I squeezed my eyes closed, wondering how long they were going to torture me, and then I glanced out of the corner of my eye. One of the beasts had his mouth wide open, and he plunged a mouthful of fangs into the back of my hand.

"AAAAH!"

I jumped up, sending them into a tizzy. I kicked and punched, jabbing Fuego at them, making contact with their fat hairy bodies, but there were too many. The bats shrieked at a frequency so high I thought my teeth would crumble to dust.

Ah-Puch released a shriek to match, and it sent chills down my spine. He could speak bat?

The beasts swooped in a cloud of hair and teeth and claws. I could feel the skin on my hands and neck splitting open with each bite. They were drinking my blood! I fell down, my heart pounding, my vision fading.

Ren...

Glancing over, I saw her huddled. She wasn't moving. Clearly, she had a lot more self-control than I did. Fury at the bats rose up inside me. A deep orange ember began to glow beneath my skin. The creatures that were terrorizing me retreated with an angry screech as I got to my feet. The entire world took on a faint reddish tint, and I knew my eyes were ablaze, too. Smoke streamed from my fingertips, creating long black trails. I didn't know how it happened, but the smoke took the shape of a giant net, wrapping around Ren. The bats beat against the net, but they couldn't get through.

Rosie launched herself into the air, snatching up a few bats in her mouth as she sailed over the starboard side. I wanted her to barbecue the little beasts, but she'd just as likely set the boat ablaze and everyone with it.

The world lurched. I was growing weaker with each passing second, and soon the smoke-net would vanish. I hated to admit it, but I needed the god of death's help. As I hurried over to him, the bats shrank back. Ah-Puch uncurled himself, heaving. I grabbed his hand, placed the corn in his palm, and shouted, "Take it!"

Shakily, he popped the entire blue seed into his mouth. A millisecond later, he stood upright, seizing the bats out of the air with such incredible speed his arms were only a blur. Faster than I could shout his name, he snapped the creatures' necks and sucked the blood from their bodies.

There was no time to be disgusted.

I didn't see what happened after that, because in a single flash, Rosie leaped back onto the boat. A single line of fire exploded from her mouth, wrapping me in a spinning inferno that didn't touch the floor. I used my last bits of strength to knock the nearby beasts into the flames. Their charred bodies fell around me, and then slowly, the heat drew closer, engulfing me. Instinctively, I leaned into the blaze, and as I did, the puncture wounds on my hands disappeared before my eyes.

Then came the Fire Keeper's voice: *You really need to fight more like a destroyer.*

I didn't register the insult, because I had bigger things on my mind: *Where are you? How do I find you?*

But the inferno died before there was an answer.

I looked up.

Ah-Puch stood over Ren. A sea breeze parted his thick dark hair as he licked the blood from his fingertips. Gone was the little old feeble man. And in his place?

A stronger, very familiar version of the god of death, darkness, and destruction.

30

·

═

I think I'd forgotten how threatening Ah-Puch was. (I know, I know, how could anyone forget such terror?) Not only did the guy tower over me, but there was a fierce darkness and determination in his eyes and in the etched lines of his face that commanded utter dread.

A low rumble emerged from Rosie as she faced Ah-Puch. But she wasn't foaming at the mouth, her eyes weren't glowing red, and she wasn't shooting fireballs. Those were all good signs that Ah-Puch didn't intend to eat us all for dinner.

Ah-Puch raised a single eyebrow and gestured to Ren.

Shaking off my shock, I raced over to her. (Yeah, I had to step over all the blood-drained bat carcasses.) She rolled onto her back, looking up at me wide-eyed.

"Are you all right?" I asked, taking a quick inventory of any wounds. "You...you don't have a single mark." I mean, I know our super Itzel clothing was supposed to be dagger-proof, but what about the exposed skin? Was Ren immune to the bats or something?

"I forced my mind to focus, to visualize the outcome," she said. "Like Hondo showed me."

"They don't like the smell of her blood," Ah-Puch said with a small smile.

I shot him a look over my shoulder. "What's that supposed to mean?"

But I didn't get an answer. Rosie wandered over sheepishly, sniffing Ren as she got to her feet. Ren's eyes were glued to Ah-Puch. "You...you..." For once she was at a loss for words. Finally, she managed, "You ate those bats."

"I didn't eat the bats," he said. "I drank their supernatural blood."

Ren gawked at this version of Ah-Puch. "Is that why you're...?"

"So intimidating?" Ah-Puch offered.

"I was going to say scary," she said.

Ren and I exchanged a worried glance, when Ah-Puch added, "I see your apprehension...but not to worry. This new beautiful form of mine is, sadly, only temporary." He sighed dramatically. "The bats' blood was stolen, not a sacrifice, but even if it had been, part of me is still swimming in the eternal fires Zane created."

"I said no devouring!"

"You said no devouring *anyone*," Ah-Puch reminded me. "That means a person, a human—you didn't say anything about monsters."

Already, he was finding loopholes. "You tricked us—led us right to those things."

"The blood made me do it," he said with a straight face. "I was so hungry, and they were coming no matter what. We just met them halfway. You would have had a harder time fighting them off in town, and all those humans could have been hurt. I did you—*us*—a favor."

"We could have died!" I shouted.

"But you didn't. Plus, having the battle in the open water kept us out of the gods' field of vision. All we need is those idiots descending upon us. Then you really will die."

Ren inched closer to Ah-Puch. "You said we could trust you. No more tricking us so you can drink blood. And no more asking us to follow you, because we won't."

Ah-Puch clenched his jaw.

"And you..." Ren swung her gaze my way. "You were like a walking wall of fire, and that smoke—it...it protected me."

I glanced down at my fingertips, shaking my head. "Yeah, I don't know where that came from."

"Oh, I don't know...maybe because you're the son of fire?" Ah-Puch said, his voice dripping with sarcasm. "Son of the creator *and* destroyer."

Maybe it was the adrenaline, but I felt invincible, like I could seriously take on an entire army of demons or bats or... whatever. "Except I can't control it," I mumbled, thinking no one heard me.

Until Ah-Puch said, "You will."

I stared at him in surprise, wondering what he knew that I didn't.

Ren's gaze fell to the dead creatures scattered around our feet. "I sort of feel sorry for them."

Was she serious? "They tried to kill us!" I reminded her.

"I know, but maybe we should toss them overboard. Like, give them a proper burial at sea or something."

Rosie groaned like she didn't think the little monsters

deserved anything other than what they got. She stood at attention as the last traces of the sun melted into the sea.

"What are they?" I asked Ah-Puch.

"A specific variety of magic," Ah-Puch said, "that I haven't tasted in a thousand years. Quite a delicacy."

"Why were those monsters here?" I said. "How did they even find us?"

Ren cleared her throat. "They came to steal me."

I jerked my attention back to her. "How do you know?"

"Because they kept trying to lift me up." She narrowed her cool eyes. "I think they're the same monsters as the ones the other night, back in Sievers Cove."

Ah-Puch started up the boat and turned us back toward shore. "If you don't mind, I'd like to take a shower, order chef service, and get into a nice clean suit before I tell you a sordid tale about the bats."

"I like sordid," Ren said way too enthusiastically.

"Er...I don't have enough money for chef service," I said. "Maybe some tacos?"

A slow grin spread across Ah-Puch's face. "We don't need money."

We returned the boat to the dock where we'd found it (Ren was a good influence on the god of death) and grabbed a taxi. As soon as we were inside the car, Ah-Puch told the driver "Take us to the most opulent resort in town." Rosie was too big to fit into the backseat, so she ran alongside the cab. A few minutes later, we had zipped through the colorful bustling town and into a torch-lit tunnel dotted with chandeliers.

Emerging from it felt like coming out of a long dream. Rocky hills surrounded us, and the turquoise sea stretched across the horizon as palm trees swayed like they were waving hello. A line of staff waited at the entrance of what looked like a Mediterranean mansion.

Ah-Puch smiled. "Yes, this will do quite nicely."

"Nicely?" Ren's mouth fell open. "This is, like, better than a castle or the White House or . . . Check out the view and—"

"And we need to hurry," I said, reminding them we weren't here on some vacation. I had to find the Fire Keeper. But even I was having a hard time not being totally impressed.

Ah-Puch waltzed inside like he owned the place, and some employee named Javier followed him around like he did. I hung back, watching Ah-Puch flirt with the lady behind the check-in counter. She smiled. No, that's not right. She practically fell over herself trying to find the biggest and most luxurious suite for him. I didn't get it. I mean, he was wearing a dingy white T-shirt that looked like it had shrunk ten sizes, his too-short pants were grubby at best, and he smelled like garlic and old cheese. Maybe the god of death could smooth-talk his way into anything . . . and his new face probably didn't hurt. Whatever.

And when it came time for payment? Ah-Puch just leaned closer and whispered, "Put it on my tab."

I thought I'd misheard, because surely Puke Face didn't have accounts all over the place. Turns out I was right. He used Kukuulkaan's credit. Apparently, my dad's old friend (also known as K'ukumatz, or Mat to his friends) has an arrangement with a five-star hotel in every city in the world. No joke. I guess Mat likes to travel.

The stars blinked awake as the sky darkened and our "concierge" led us to our casita. Personally, I'd call the freestanding two-story house a mini mansion. Not only did we have our own private yard and beach, but the place had high ceilings lined with dark wood beams, French doors, stone floors, two fireplaces, a hot tub, and a killer view of the ocean. Never mind the chips and guacamole that were waiting for us when we got there. Oh, and did I mention the room came with an on-call butler? I was bummed Hondo and Brooks weren't there to see this over-the-top place. Actually, I was bummed they weren't with me for any of this. I bet Brooks would have ripped those bats to shreds. I just hoped that for once she listened to me and went home.

As soon as we were alone, I launched a million questions at Ah-Puch about the monsters and how they'd found us. Ah-Puch just raised a single finger and said, "Not until I am clean and in a decent suit."

I wondered why he couldn't just conjure up a slick suit, like he did when I released him from his prison. Or had that been Muwan's doing?

Within the hour, his new clothes were delivered, everyone had washed up, and room service had brought dinner: quesadillas and papaya and pineapple wedges for me and Ren, five raw steaks for Rosie, and a one-hundred-year-old bottle of tequila for Ah-Puch. I guess the bat blood had been enough to curb his appetite—for the time being.

He quickly told us that the bats were likely the minions of some bat god named Camazotz, who used to live in the House of Bats in Xib'alb'a and whose whole job was to bite off travelers' heads. He'd been exiled for reasons Ah-Puch couldn't remember, and no one had heard from the guy since.

"Camazotz as in the planet in *A Wrinkle in Time*?" asked Ren.

"What's a wrinkle in time?" Ah-Puch looked confused.

"A book," Ren said. "And also a Disney movie."

Ah-Puch raised his eyebrows. "Does this Disney know Camazotz?"

"No, I mean . . ." she faltered. "Did you say bat god?"

"Yes." Ah-Puch adjusted his cuffs and picked a piece of lint off his dark blazer.

"But . . ." Ren picked at her tortilla. "How did they find me?"

"Your magic is pretty thick," Ah-Puch said with a heavy voice. "It attracted them, but it was also why they couldn't hurt you. Even their sharp little teeth can't penetrate that kind of power."

I looked from Ah-Puch to Ren. "Is it like some kind of super Maya magic that protects you, Ren?" Was this what she had been trying to tell me back in San Miguel?

Ah-Puch rubbed his knuckles along with jaw. "Not Maya, but that's not the important question. The better question is, why did Camazotz send his cronies to snatch her? Not that I care, mind you. Just trying to help your tiny human brain stay on track."

"I guess my tiny human brain is still on the *not-Maya* track," I said. "What did you mean?"

"Zane," Ren said, "you look . . . kinda pale and tired. You should go to sleep."

Before I could answer, her arm jerked forward, knocking her glass to the floor, where it shattered. And then she was frozen, locked in one of her trances. Her body slumped, and Ah-Puch caught her before she fell onto the broken glass.

He picked her up and carried her to the sofa, where he laid her down gently, like she was made of china. Stretching his back, his eyes met mine. "No sense having her crack her head open. We're going to need her." But I knew he didn't catch her only because he was thinking about himself. He liked Ren and didn't want to admit it.

Ah-Puch watched as I quickly cleaned up the shards of glass with a thick towel.

"What do you know about her?" I shook the towel over the trash.

"Not my secret to tell," he said. "And before you threaten me with the Empty, telling you other people's business was not part of our deal."

I could feel my blood starting to boil. "She was about to tell me in San Miguel and then you showed up, and I kinda think it's important to know...."

"Why?"

"Because it could be the kind of secret that lands our heads on spikes!"

"Yes, well, lots of scenarios could lead to our heads being put on spikes. For example, the fact that you have not managed to summon and control your fire power." He hardened his gaze and hesitated before adding, "And since I plan to return to my former state of glory, I'm obviously going to have to teach you a thing or two. To keep our heads *off* the spikes."

I took a small step closer. "*You* want to train *me*?"

"Who said anything about 'want' or 'train'?" He folded his arms across his chest.

"Fine, but why did you tell me back on the boat that I'd control the fire soon?" I thought about the smoke that had trailed from my fingers to make a protective net around Ren. How my mind was on auto-don't-die-pilot like it had been back in Xib'alb'a. Was that the secret? Was my power more of an instinct than a skill?

Ah-Puch buttoned his jacket with one hand. "Explaining it to you would be like explaining the universe to a beetle. I am not about to waste my precious short-lived energy on such a task. But I will give you this one free morsel of wisdom: Do not try to *control* the fire. Surrender to it."

He was for sure loco. Loco and confusing, and I couldn't believe I was even entertaining *anything* the god of death told me.

"Yeah, great advice," I said. "I'll just wave a white flag."

"When I acted as the god of death, darkness, and destruction, I surrendered to the power of all three. I became *one* with each in order to reach my fullest potential. Does your human mustard seed of a brain get what I am telling you?"

My cheeks prickled with heat. "My dad said that if I didn't release the fire it would destroy me, and now you're telling me to surrender to it?" Maybe this was his way of doing me in for good.

His expression was blank. "What part don't you understand?"

"How do I let it out *and* surrender at the same time?"

"You are half god. I suggest you start remembering that."

He clapped once. "Well, that's all I've got, because I have to spend my vitality on sniffing out some answers while I still have this beautiful blood magic flowing through my veins."

"Sniff?"

"I, the *true* ruler of the underworld, have the best tracking skills of any of the gods. How do you think I found all those souls trying to hide back when I was reaper? Surely I can unearth the dark mysteries surrounding those bats. And who knows? Maybe I can also find some clues about this Fire Keeper of yours."

"No way. Not without me," I said. I didn't trust him on the loose in the real world. Who knew what kind of trouble he'd cause?

He shook his head. "You'll only be a distraction. Besides, Ren's right. You look awful. You need to"—he looked me up and down—"I don't know . . . take another shower, brush your hair, get some sun."

"It's nighttime."

"Just stick around here, in case more of Zotz's minions head this way. It won't take him long to realize his wretched bats haven't returned with the gold." He nodded toward Ren.

If Ah-Puch was right about who the bats reported to, Camazotz was just another disgruntled god hell-bent on revenge. Was he behind the kidnapping of the other godborns, too? What did he have planned? Something told me we'd only scratched the surface of however many layers deep this went into Maya madness.

"One hour," I said.

I couldn't put all my bets on Ah-Puch succeeding. I had to find my own way and fast.

After he left, I made a quick call to Mom from the hotel phone. Actually, I called the office, because I knew the phone would ring through to voice mail. Trust me, it made things easier if I didn't have to talk to her live.

Mom's cheery voice came on. "You've reached Maya Adventures. We're closed right now, but if you leave a message after the tone, we'll be sure to return your call just as soon as we can." Her message was repeated in Spanish and then came the dreaded beep.

"Hey, Mom. It's me, Zane." What a stupid thing to say. "I, uh...Did you get my email? We're all still okay and should be home soon....Don't be mad. It's really important. I did some stuff, and now people are in trouble because of me, and I have to fix it. You always say I should try to fix my mistakes." I took a shaky breath. Rosie's dark eyes bored into me, and she let out a yelp. "Rosie says hi. Okay, that's all. Light a candle for me. Bye."

I hung up. Rosie licked her chops and let out a long breathy grunt that said *She's so going to kill you.* Yeah, well, she could get in line behind Brooks and Hondo, and maybe even the godborns once they figured out it was my fault they'd been abducted. Then there was the mastermind (most likely Zotz) behind all this, who no doubt wanted to flay me. And let's not forget the death magic that was starting to feel like a noose around my neck, tightening with every second.

Rosie and I headed outside to the fire pit that was already

roaring, thanks to some unseen employee. A bar of moonlight glistened across the dark ocean in a trail of shimmering white.

"The Red Queen said to listen to the flame," I told Rosie as I sat in a wicker chair, setting Fuego down as I leaned close to the fire. Rosie wagged her tail and dove into the pit, grabbing a burning log with her jaws.

"No fire fetch now, girl."

Rosie dropped the log back in, snorted a trail of smoke, and settled onto her belly. The fire crackled and sparked.

"Hello?" I said, now sticking my head into the pit. Maybe I had to be super close to hear the message. (Do not try this at home.)

A tiny flame leaped out of the pit.

I jerked backward and saw it land on a side glass table, where it fizzled, but not before I noticed a leather binder sitting there. Inside were pages of Cabo tour sites and activities.

Flipping through them, I landed on an advertisement. My heart came to a screeching halt.

There, in the back of the book, was a photo of a huge rock formation in the shape of an arch sticking out of the sea. Big gold words were printed across the bottom:

EL ARCO, THE GATEWAY TO ANOTHER WORLD.
COME SEE LAND'S END.

"Rosie!" My palms began to sweat. "The Red Queen told me to go to Land's End, where two worlds meet. This looks pretty much like an entrance, doesn't it?"

She studied the picture, sniffing it suspiciously.

Quickly, I scanned the small print. The tour company was closed for the day. I picked up the outdoor phone and dialed the concierge, hoping someone from the hotel could tell me how to get to Land's End. But the señora who answered told me El Arco was only accessible by boat, and none would run again until the morning. Luckily, it was only a few minutes' cruise from the resort. I could get there myself, as long as I could find a boat or a surfboard or an inner tube or anything that floated.

Rosie whined and danced on her paws impatiently. I knew she wanted to swim me to Land's End. "I can't let you take me," I said, glancing inside the casita. "You need to protect Ren. It's a big job, Rosie. You have to promise me you won't let anything happen to her. I'll hurry back." She blinked slowly like she understood, her soft brown eyes shining in the firelight, and for half a second, I saw the old Rosie. My heart melted. "That's my good girl."

The shore was empty and, you guessed it, there were no boats (or surfboards or inner tubes) anywhere. Maybe I could use a chunk of wood or . . . Just then, I heard a familiar cry-howl-growl in the palm tree above.

Slowly, I looked up.

A banana peel fell onto my face.

The monkey was back. I tossed the stinky peel back at the beast. "You dropped something!"

The monkey flashed its long fangs in a half sneer, half smile. Then he motioned for me to follow him as he leaped to the next tree, using his long tail as a fifth limb.

"Seriously?" I tightened my fingers around Fuego. "You expect me to follow you? I don't even know you!" Maybe hallucinations *were* a side effect of the death magic.

An old couple walked up, eyeing me like I was some wack kid talking to trees.

"Hey, uh..." I said as they were passing, "do you see that monkey up there?"

The couple glanced up, and just when I thought they might shake their heads and call me loco, they smiled, pointed, and said something in French. They snapped a quick picture with their phone and left.

Okay, so I wasn't crazy.

Once they were out of earshot, I looked back at the hairy rascal. "How do I know you're not an evil monkey demon trying to lead me into some awful trap?"

The primate rolled his eyes, palm-smacked his forehead, and threw another banana peel at me. Where in the heck was he getting all these? Did he have a hidden pocket or something?

"Hey!" I held up Fuego. "I've got a killer spear, and I'm not afraid to use it!"

He grunted, climbed down from the tree, and raced out to the darkened shore. I glanced over my shoulder, half expecting an army of apes to be waiting for me. But all was clear, so I followed him to the beach, where a dinghy was waiting. The monkey climbed inside, grabbed the oars (which looked like long bones I really hoped weren't human), and howled at me like I was taking too long. Man, he had big teeth.

"You think I'm going to get in a rowboat with a...?"

When I saw his arm go to his side, I thought he might attack me with another banana, but instead he pulled out a postcard of El Arco and tossed it toward me with an annoyed grunt.

"You're going to Land's End?"

He smacked his lips together and peeled them back, showing all his choppers. *Eee-eee-eee.*

I took that as a yes and climbed into the boat. The monkey scratched his head and began rowing like a champ (he'd for sure done this before). Once we were past the breakers, he stood. Here it was. He was going to pull out a dagger and stab me to death.

I readied Fuego. In a flash of pale blue light, the monkey transformed into a human. The dude had curly black hair that sparkled like each strand was laced with stardust. He was tall, skinny, and wore wire-rimmed glasses with mirrored lenses, so I couldn't see his eyes. Even his long blue robe shimmered, and I thought maybe Ren was right about aliens. This guy looked like he'd come from the moon.

"Who are you?" I saw my own reflection in his glasses, trying not to show fear over being in the middle of the sea with a sparkly dude in a robe.

He didn't answer me. Not at first. Instead he stared—or I guessed he was staring. He sat back down and said in a low voice, "I am Itzamna."

31

"Itz . . . who?" And then I realized I recognized his voice. My insides felt like they were dying a slow death.

He tugged off his glasses. His eyes were as black as a starless sky. But they were circled in a silvery light that matched his sparkling hair. Even his dark skin glittered like quartz. "I am the moon god, bringer of writing and culture, creator of the calendar, and father to the Bakabs. And you are Zane Obispo."

"You're not the Fire Keeper."

"No."

"You . . . you're the one who's been whispering to me."

"In the flesh."

Crap! Crappity crap crap crap! Had I made the worst mistake ever, wasting all this time on a maybe? Quinn's words haunted me: *My dad used to tell me anyone who believes something is foolproof is likely to be proven a fool.* And I was the biggest fool this side of Idiotsville.

I swallowed my disappointment. "Why are you here?"

Was that the right thing to say to a shimmery god you'd never met and who, like the other gods, might want to behead you?

Then the shocking realization hit me like a thirty-foot

wave. He could see me! So much for my so-called "expert" death magic camouflage. *Thanks, Ixtab!* I edged back. "Are you here to . . . kill me?" Might as well get the truth right up front.

Itzamna threw back his head and let out a musical laugh. I swear, that's the best way to describe it. It was like he had a whole symphony in his mouth or something. "No, I am not here to kill you," he said. "If I'd wanted to, I could have struck you down long ago. I've been watching you for some time."

"You were there with me and the Red Queen."

"I was *nearly* there. It really isn't as easy as it sounds, being in more than one place at a time. But I thought I would make a showing, remind her she owed me a debt. And I am flawless at collecting."

"Why? What do you want from her?"

"That doesn't matter. What matters is that you're quite the writer and I'm a fan." He grinned. "I've been following you since you penned your first story, the one my fellow gods forced you to write. They are so clueless—they obviously had no idea of the power they'd given you."

"Power?" Wait . . . did he say *fan*?

"The written word is power. It can change worlds. I always say, rule with wisdom, not war."

His voice was deep and soothing like Jazz's chocolate drink especial. My whole body started to relax as he spoke.

He continued. "When you wrote the first cuento, I, being the god of writing, noticed you. I don't like to get involved with human affairs, or even godly affairs. I'd much rather read great works, write poetry, play the flute, and float across the starry sky." His forehead wrinkled. "But then you began to write again—a second story, using magic ink—and that magic drew me to you. Your words connected us." He sighed and smiled at the same time. "I must say, you are in quite a predicament. Not sure you are making the right choice here—it's pretty risky—but I suppose that's what ups the stakes."

I felt sick. "How come you haven't told the other gods I'm alive?"

He continued rowing slowly, the oars gliding effortlessly through the dark, calm waters. "Why would I tell those unenlightened fools about you?" he said. "So they could destroy a talent as rich as yours as they have so many of my other protégés? I think not. I'll be honest, you do need to work on your phrasing, and perhaps you could use some help with settings, but I know talent when I see it, and you, young man, have a future in words. It would be a travesty for such artistic talent to go to waste. Therefore, I am here to offer my help."

Why did I have the feeling I was being used as a pawn to stick it to the gods once again?

"What kind of help?" I asked.

"My services, to take you under my wing and show you culture, refinement, and—"

"Uh . . . sorry, that sounds like a really good offer and all, but I . . . I, uh, have to get to the Fire Keeper. Now." So what if the Fire Keeper hadn't been trying to talk to me? It didn't mean he wouldn't help me, right? "Did you say going to see him is a bad choice?"

"A risky one, which I prefer," he said. "I know what's at stake. Which is why I have gone through all the trouble to meet you face-to-face. I want you to stay alive, Zane Obispo. So I am breaking my own rule and interfering this one time. But I ask for something in return."

There it was. The fine print, reminding me that Maya gods never give anything away for free. "Okay?"

"You must continue to write. No matter what happens, you must share your story with the world."

That's it? I thought. I really appreciated that this guy liked my story so much, but there are a million writers in the world. "Yeah, okay . . ." Seemed an easy enough request, right? But remember what I told you. Things are never what they seem when it comes to the Maya gods. "But why?"

Itzamna stopped rowing and leaned forward. "Because the world was born on the back of a story, and the world might be saved—" He cleared his throat. "I have said too much. I am glad we have a deal. Now, I will do what I can to help you stay alive, and if you do your part, you will win a lifetime's supply of the greatest variety of magic paper ever written upon."

Great. A lifetime supply of paper. Lucky me. "Maybe you could just take me to the Fire Keeper?" I remembered what the Red Queen had said about going alone, but I bet that didn't include gods. "I mean, since you're already here and everything."

"Ah, that would be too easy. All good stories have peril and risks, stakes so great that the reader shivers in their bed, wondering what will happen to the young hero. Worrying that the young hero has made a grave error in judgment." He quivered dramatically. "Will he survive? Will good triumph over evil? Will he get the girl?" Itzamna pushed his glasses up his long nose. "So, no, I will not make this journey easy for you. I am much more interested in a grand tale. Something to make all the senses come to life. Aren't you?"

Uh, that would be a big fat NO! "I'd rather keep my head and my organs and my skin attached to me." I glanced at the black sky and back to Itzamna. "Am I... making a mistake?"

"Things will get tricky, you have a very high likelihood of death, and in the event that such a tragedy occurs, I have taken it upon my generous self to carry you to Xib'alb'a, where you can pen the ending to this tale."

I dug my feet into the boat. "I don't plan to die."

"No one ever does."

I stared at him in disbelief. "So that's it? You came here to tell me to write a good story?"

"Of course not. I came here to wish you luck. Make the story fuerte! Interesting!"

Itzamna set his glasses back on. In the reflective lenses, I saw a massive and seriously awesome dragon with blue, green, and red scales. It wore a wreath made of gold feathers around its neck. But that wasn't the most freaking amazing part: the dragon's mouth was open, but instead of flames, a hand was coming out. And in its grasp? A pen.

"Whoa!" I fell back. "That's... Wait... Did it eat a writer?"

"I'll add metaphor to our list of studies. If you live."

"Is it real? Does it fly?"

"Obviously." Itzamna stood. "It is my faithful companion, and all the writers I deem worthy have the power of the dragon. Now, I must go."

"What?!" My voice flew across the water. "Power of the

dragon? What does that even mean?" My mind was spinning faster than a blender blade, slicing my thoughts to bits so nothing made any sense.

Itzamna pressed a finger to his lips and looked around like he'd heard something. "Good luck. Make your story a worthy one, young man."

He and his bone oars turned to shimmering dust and blew out to the dark sea.

32

Perfect.
There I was, floating in the middle of the Sea of Cortés, no oars, no map, no idea how to get to Land's End. The barely there moon floated behind a bank of clouds, plunging me into utter darkness. (Really, Itzamna? You couldn't even give me a single oar?)

I peered through the night, scanning in every direction. In the distance, a massive rock formation stuck out of the sea awkwardly. The thing looked like a giant stegosaurus dipping its head into the water for a drink. The grande space between its neck and body must have been the famous arch, and to the left of that was a narrow beach.

Quickly, I stuck Fuego into the water, trying to use him as an oar. (Yeah, I know, dumb idea, but you do stupid things when you're desperate, okay?) I was only about fifty yards from the arch, but I might as well have been a million, because the tide quickly shifted, dragging me away from Land's End.

I leaped into the cool water. Gripping the edge of the dinghy, I began to kick with all my might. But it was useless. The power of the current was too great. Why did I have the feeling Itzamna was turning the tides to make for a better story?

No way was I going to be this close and get shoved back now. I had to think quick. *If only Brooks were here, she could fly me.* But the Red Queen had been clear. I had to take this journey alone. Was that why Itzamna had bailed?

I closed my eyes and focused on my godborn leg, willing it to do something. Anything. I'd barreled through water like a supersonic engine before, I could do it again. I *had* to do it again.

Focus. Focus.

I dug deep, deep into where the shadow memories of all the hurt and anger I'd ever felt were buried. As Ah-Puch had said, I reminded myself, *You're half god.* A burning sensation coursed through my storm runner leg. A second later, it was like lightning ripped through every cell in my body, igniting something I couldn't name, and an overwhelming power rocketed me forward.

"Woo-hoo!"

But I'd celebrated too soon. Just as I was speeding across the sea, Land's End started moving. That's right! The huge dinosaurish rock formation reared its head, looked in my direction, and began to glide *away*.

"NO!" I shouted. "Wait!"

Crap! It was moving too fast. It would soon vanish into the horizon if I didn't do something pronto. Maybe it was a long shot, but . . .

I hopped back into the boat, tied the rope around the end of Fuego, shifted it into spear mode, and said, "Fly like you've never flown before." Then I launched it toward the rock. I watched the rope unravel, and at the last second, I grabbed hold of its end. Then, with a sudden jerk, I was launched into the air, flying behind my handy spear.

Things were pretty awesome. At first. But then stupid gravity got in the way and... *splash!*

I plummeted into the sea, holding tight to the rope that was still jerking me forward. Salt water sprayed up my nose and into my mouth. It was just like the first time I had tried to Jet Ski back at Isla Holbox and forgot to let go of the line when I crashed. Who knew Fuego could go so fast? I choked and heaved, my eyes burned, and it was impossible to see anything. Like whether I was headed into the mouth of a giant shark or something.

With a sudden jolt, I was reeled out of the water. I stared in horror as I headed straight for a massive rock wall. Or was that a leg? With a second to spare, I released the rope, wind-milled through the air, and crash-landed on a sandy shore.

Sucking air, I rolled to my knees and looked around for Fuego. It was stuck in the rock.... I take it back. It was stuck in a huge dinosaur's mouth!

The stone stegosaurus grunted, spraying a gush of slimy ocean water from his nose into my face. The impact sent me stumbling back. Gross! Did a four-hundred-foot rock dinosaur seriously just shower me in mocos?

I wiped the slimy boogers off my face and out of my eyes. Since I'm all about giving you an honest account, yeah, some got in my mouth. Okay, a lot. But I was a little more worried about the fact that the humpback rock was alive and still had Fuego locked in his stony jaws.

"Hey!" I shouted. "Let it go." I must have looked like an ant to this thing, and I knew better than to think it was going to listen to me, but no one messes with Fuego.

The rock dinosaur grumbled, and I ducked for cover. When I looked back, Fuego was glowing blue. Bright, electric blue. Old Steggy must not have liked that, because he wailed and dropped Fuego, which sailed back to me. With my spear safely in my grasp, I inched back. The stone monster winced. Wait a second. He was afraid of *me*? No, he was afraid of *Fuego*, but this dinosaur thing could crush us with half a step, so what was its deal?

That's when I heard the whistling. Distant at first, then so close I was sure someone was within arm's reach, but when I looked around, I was alone with only Fuego and shadows for company.

There it was again. The sad blues tune . . . it was so familiar. Sickeningly familiar. The whistling grew louder. Then came a deep, low voice I'd never wanted to hear again.

"The prophesied days are a-comin'. . . . Oh, they are a-comin'. Find the shadows and hide, for the days are a-comin'. . . ."

It couldn't be . . .

A long moonlit shadow crept up in my peripheral vision. I turned to see a man with long locs step from behind Steggy's back leg.

"The boy with many troubles," he said in the same thick accent as that day I'd encountered him on Venice Beach. "I still have your future in my pocket."

The world spun so fast I wasn't sure I was actually seeing the tarot-card-reading, guitar-strumming dude who had tried to read my future so many months ago. The same guy who'd said the Prophecy of Fire *was only the beginning. But fire spreads. Until it burns everything in its path.*

"You...What the—?" The words got jammed in my throat. "You're...the Fire Keeper?"

The man half grinned like he wasn't sure I was worth an entire smile. His gold front teeth glinted in the moonlight. He looked just like I remembered. His eyebrows were burned off like before. He wore a plain orange T-shirt with a pair of long shorts and had a half-chewed pencil tucked behind his ear. His left leg was inked with a red tattoo: a winged panther breathing fire from its mouth.

"I am Antonio Marcel De La Vega." Jazz had called him Santiago before...but it made sense that the Fire Keeper wouldn't go by his real name. He patted the rock monster. "It's okay, Chiquita. I'll write you a song later. And don't worry, he's not staying long. Our business will be over soon enough."

"Uh...my dad, Hurakan...he told me about you, and so did the Red Queen."

Antonio scratched the back of his neck and said, "You think I don't know that?" He eyed Fuego, still in my hand. "I don't like visitors who burn my baby's mouth."

"Baby? That—" I stopped myself before I called her a monster. "She's, like, hundreds of feet tall and made of solid stone!"

"Her name is Chiquita, and you owe her an apology."

Chiquita whined and tears (more like mini waterfalls) streamed down her craggy face. Seriously? She was going to pull the crying card?

"Fine," I said. "Sorry, Chiquita ... Fuego's sorry, too. We thought you were going to eat us."

This must have pleased the giant stone monster, because she dipped her long neck, sniffed me once, and let out a light whimper.

The Fire Keeper patted her again, then said to me, "I was in the middle of a smokin' jam session before you interrupted me and attacked Chiquita."

"I didn't attack—" As soon as his face hardened, I switched gears. "Sorry, but—"

"Everyone's always sorry. Cheap word." He shook his head. "Hey, that might make a good lyric." He tapped his fingers on his leg and sang to a hip-hop beat, *"Everyone's sorry. Cheap words. Cheaper hearts."* He eyed me. "Less bebop, right? Maybe more rhythm and blues. You got a pen on you?"

Was he serious? "Uh, you have a pencil behind your ear."

His eyes flashed surprised as he reached for it and patted his short pockets. "Man, no paper. Make sure you remember that line—it's a good one. *Cheap words. Cheaper hearts,*" he repeated. Chiquita let out a noise that sounded like something between a purr and a soft grunt. I guess she liked his word choices.

I shifted my feet. "Right, so back to why I'm here ..."

"Maybe you shoulda listened to me back at the playa. Coulda avoided all this wasted time. But no, you thought you had all the answers, and now there are consequences to your inaction." He opened both palms and blew his breath across them. Instantly, a wall of purple flames rose into the air, engulfing both of us.

The next thing I knew, we were standing in a large candle-lit room with barreled stone ceilings and a concrete floor. There were rows and rows of record albums on a tall rickety bookshelf to my left, and to my right was a glass case filled with all types of guitars in every color and sheen. Some even had signatures on them. A stick of incense that smelled like desert rain burned on a glass table nearby. Beyond that were two worn barstools with a couple of acoustic guitars leaning against each.

Antonio followed my gaze back to the case. "Those fine pieces of musical art were touched by the greatest hands in history," he said. "Hendrix, Cobain, Richards, Clapton, Santana." Hondo would have flipped if he could have seen all those guitars.

"Where are we?" I asked.

"This is my jam pad."

A tall, skinny dude with long blond hair and too many nose piercings to count poked his head through a door and said, "Dude, come on. We ain't got all day."

"Actually, we do. I'll be right there," Antonio said.

The guy glanced at me before looking at Antonio and rolling his eyes in a slow sweep. "If I lose the rhythm because of you..."

"No one's losing rhythm," said the Fire Keeper. "Have a cerveza while you wait."

With a huff, the guy slammed the door.

"Who's that?"

"A new guy in our band. He's a little skittish. What do you expect? He's a drummer," he said. "He doesn't like to take breaks and for sure doesn't like anyone new at a jam. Thinks it's bad luck."

"Oh, so, like, do you live here?" I thought a little bit of small talk might warm the guy up.

"Nah . . . I just feed the eternal flame here."

I studied the place more closely, looking for fire somewhere. Scraps of paper and cigarette butts littered the floor. Tall iron candelabras filled with half-melted candles lit the space. But other than that, I saw nada. I don't know what I'd been expecting, but it wasn't this.

"So where is this *eternal* flame?" I asked, trying to ease into it.

He laughed and patted his chest. "In here."

I must have given him an *are-you-kidding-me?* look, because he added, "You think the great fire keepers would let such an important flame burn in the open?"

Okay, well, I'd for sure heard crazier things. Couldn't think of any in that exact moment, but I had a lot on my mind, like an exact address of the godborns and how to save my dad. It was time to get down to business.

"I need your help."

"No kidding."

I explained that the godborns had been taken and the great Hurakan needed rescuing. "I thought that you could tell me where the godborns are and how to stop Hurakan's execution."

Antonio swept a loc out of his face, unfazed. "Do I look like your personal nine-one-one?"

Was this guy for real? "My dad mentioned . . ."

He gave me a sly grin like he knew exactly what Hurakan had said: *run.* "Yeah, well, your old man is decomposing at the bottom of a nasty prison, and the universe is changing. If you'd come a few days ago, no problem. For a high price, maybe I could have changed some things. But now? You'll be lucky if I can locate these godborns."

"What do you mean 'the universe is changing'? Does this have to do with the sobrenaturals' powers getting weaker?"

He ran his long fingers over the guitar frets and said, "Dark days. Dark war. Only the shadows can hide us." He picked up a scrap of paper and scribbled something on it. "That's good," he mumbled.

I waved a ribbon of incense smoke out of my face.

"Ah, I see from your expression that you came here on a whim with no real knowledge of how this all works. You don't know your father gave humans fire. He took a piece of it and created the first fire keeper to protect the magic of the Maya, because he believed in balance above all else. He worried about what would happen if the gods held all the power. You know one hundred percent of nothing."

"Hang on! My dad wanted to protect sobrenatural magic? Why?"

"To create a more even playing field. To make sure the gods never destroyed the world again." He shook his head. "Up until a few days ago, I could see past, present, and a blink of the future in a single ember's flicker. I could see every possibility of every decision you might make." He laughed harshly and strummed a low E chord to make his point.

A lump throbbed in my throat. Was I really too late? Had

I come all this way for nothing? "Tell me about the dark war. Is that why the demons in Xib'alb'a are training?"

Antonio began to strum the guitar, slow, then fast—so fast his fingers smoked and small flames appeared on each of the strings. I have to admit, it was seriously awesome. With sweat dripping down the side of his face, he stopped playing and swayed like he might collapse. Then, breathlessly, he said, "I see seventy-six and a half possibilities leading to a *potential* war. All dependent on certain decisions made during Wayeb. Or maybe the war is going to start during that time. I can't be sure."

"Wayeb? You mean the five days of doom?"

"Ah, so the boy knows *some* things. That period is also known as 'the days without names,' or as I like to call it, 'the days without souls.' It's exactly four months from today."

He was talking about one of the three Maya calendars: the Haab', a 365-day calendar that is divided into eighteen months of twenty days each. It includes one month with five extra days at the end, which is the Wayeb.

"Hold up. If the sobrenaturals' magic is weakening, and *you* control the flame that gives them power . . ." I swallowed hard. "Are you the one who's . . . ?"

"Stealing their power?" A slow and glittery grin spread across his face.

33

Antonio let out a deep laugh. "Get your head on straight, man. I'm the protector, not the thief. The magic flame began to sputter a few days ago. I sense it's because your father is getting weaker by the minute."

I felt like I wanted to blow something up. "Are you saying the fire dies if he dies?"

"And without Hurakan to feed the flame . . ." Antonio said.

"The sobrenaturals aren't so super."

Slowly, the pieces began to click together. Stolen godborns. Weakening magic. My dad's sudden execution. War. Was Zotz, the bat god, masterminding everything? Whoever was behind this was behind *all* of it. Which meant that the godborns and soon-to-be-broken sobrenaturals were going to be pawns in this war. And the Maya gods didn't even see it coming.

My hands pulsated with sudden heat. "I'm the son of fire. Maybe . . ." It was a long shot, but I had to try. "Maybe *I* can feed the flame." If I could make it strong enough so Antonio could change the outcome of my dad's execution, he could tell me exactly where to find the godborns. Maybe I could save the magic.

Antonio raised a doubtful eyebrow.

"Let me try, at least."

His dark eyes glistened in the dim light. "But, my man, you can't even control your own fire. How, then, do you expect to be able to give power to the greatest fire magic in history?"

A thick, lava-like heat raced up my storm runner leg. I was sick of half truths, half strengths, half a life. "How do you know I can't?" Maybe this was the reason I was here.

Antonio shrugged. "I don't. But someone else might."

With the wave of his hand, he drew a trail of incense smoke to him, then tapped his fingers across the air as the smoke took the faint shape of . . . a human heart? I stood frozen as the heart began to beat slowly, echoing across the room with a *thud thud thud*. A small flame grew from its center, and, without thinking, I drew it to me and spun it in a small ball on my open palm. The orb rotated like a planet on its axis, growing bigger and bigger. So big it burst into a wall of blue flames, blocking Antonio from my view. Before I knew it, I was swallowed in a huge, soundless inferno.

Instinctively, I stepped into it, searching. *Dad?*

I knew he was close. I could sense it. The flames engulfed me, and for the first time in days, I felt safe, like here nothing could touch me.

Zane. You didn't run.

You didn't tell me they're going to kill you.

Silence.

I took a steady breath. *How do I strengthen the flame?*

I hoped, if you ran away, it would change things, take you out of the equation.

We were wasting time. *Right now I really need you to tell me how to feed the flame. Please.*

The flames grew taller. *It will take great sacrifice, and even then, Zane, the outcome may not be what you expect.*

Okay, but what do I do?

The inferno began to die, and the last word Hurakan spoke was *blood.*

The fire disappeared. I fell against the wall, coughing up trails of smoke.

Antonio was strumming a guitar casually like he was used to people being swallowed by flames in his studio. "What did the old man tell you?"

"I think he said I can strengthen the flame with blood."

"That ain't right. Unless you've got some of Hurakan's blood."

"He's my dad! I . . . I can give some of mine. Same thing, right?"

"*Pura* sangre," Antonio said slowly in his thick accent. His expression was blank. Or maybe resigned. "Only the pure blood of the creator god of fire can strengthen the flame."

And there it was, the reason Hurakan was being put to death: so he could never protect the magic of the Maya again. The enemy had thought of all the loopholes. A terrible sinking feeling gripped me, and I leaned against Fuego for support.

Then slowly . . . so slowly I was afraid the idea would disappear if I thought about it too long, the answer came to me. "My cane . . . spear—the Sparkstriker infused it with . . . Hurakan's blood."

Antonio jumped up from the stool (dropping another guitar). "Then split it open!"

Fuego began to glow a bright turquoise color like the October New Mexico sky. I felt the sudden need to protect my cane. "No! I mean, if we split it open, all its magic...my spear, everything will be gone."

"But if you don't break it, all the magic of the Maya will be gone and with it so many possibilities. This could be the answer to making the flame stronger. To helping you on this quest."

Panic gripped me so hard I thought I might pass out. "But the Sparkstriker said Fuego's indestructible."

Antonio inched closer. "I know the magic.... This weapon is indestructible to everyone *except* its master."

I collapsed to my knees, staring at Fuego in my hands. I know it was just a tool, but there was something so real about it, like it was alive. And it had saved me. How could I just sacrifice it like that? Fuego had never failed me. But what choice did I have?

"There has to be another way."

"There are always other choices, my man. Other choices, different outcomes. But time is running out. The flame is weakening. And once the magic is gone, nothing will bring it back. Do you get what I'm telling you?"

"Can't you find enough power to change Hurakan's execution, and then he can give his blood and ..."

"The flame is too weak. But maybe this will strengthen it enough."

How could I kill Fuego on a *maybe*? My stomach twisted so tight I could barely breathe. Tears stung my eyes. "Sorry,

Fuego." I set the cane on the floor and drew a flame from the candlelight, expanding it across my hands. Then, before I could reconsider what I was about to do, I knelt down, pressed the flame against Fuego, and watched it burn.

34

The whole scene was like watching a film in reverse. A single stream of dark blood rose up from Fuego, snaking toward a small flame that pulsed in Antonio's hand. The blaze sparked, popped, and turned deep blue before it expanded so much it consumed him.

A second later, the fire disappeared. I was glad to see Antonio still intact and untouched by the flames. But when I looked down at Fuego, I saw nothing but a pool of silver and its jade handle. Antonio kneeled next to me. "The Prophecy of Days is a-comin', and your sacrifice won't be forgotten."

I was too stunned to speak. Too stunned to feel anything. It was like I'd lost a piece of myself and I was never going to get it back. Like something had gone dark and cold inside of me.

I got to my feet shakily, wiping ash across my jeans, pulling myself together. And yeah, trying not to cry. I stuffed the jade handle in my pocket. "Well? Was it enough to change the future?"

Antonio's expression was grim, and all the color drained from his face. "My man." He pressed his hand against his chest. "The fire expanded some."

"Some?"

"It's still weak."

"I . . . I stole the life from my . . ." It sounded so much worse out loud. Antonio wouldn't understand. No one would. I felt like a murderer. "I sacrificed Fuego for nothing!" I'd come here for nothing!

"Not for nothing. You came with a single purpose, one goal. But goals change, whether we like it or not. The hand of destiny is strong, and you came here to give enough life to the flame to buy us some time. To save centuries of magic from being destroyed. That ain't nothin'."

"The Red Queen lied. She told me that if I came here I . . . I would change the future for the better."

"How do you know you haven't? That's why it's called the future. We can't see what's around the bend." Antonio picked up another guitar and strummed some chords. "Let's say I could've granted you one wish and one only. Even if I had the power to change Hurakan's execution, would you have used your one request to save his life? Or the godborns? Your own life? Would you have chosen to end wars and stop bloodshed? Which future would you choose to change? Just remember . . . one wrong choice, no matter how pure your intentions, can lead to disaster. It's called cause and effect, my man, and it can be brutal."

My voice rose a couple of notches. "You did this for you!" I cried. Smoke trailed from my mouth and nose. "Because if the flame dies, you probably do, too."

"Death is only another form of being. My job isn't to get all hung up on what happens to me or how this all ends. Get it?" Antonio's fingers plucked the air. "Now, you must play the notes to hear the song. But I can tell you this. Beware. There is a traitor among you."

"Who?" It had to be Ah-Puch! Then another horrible thought occurred to me. My heart sank to the lowest level of Xib'alb'a. Ren wasn't the traitor, was she? Was this what she'd been trying to tell me back in San Miguel? Did it have something to do with her special magic?

"I will try to keep the flame going for as long as I can. I cannot tell you more without affecting decisions and consequences," Antonio said. "But I can give you this."

He opened his palm and blew into it. A tiny vortex of smoke swirled to life like a mini hurricane. Slowly, it spun toward me in dizzying circles. I ducked to avoid a collision, but it was too late. The smoke swirled up my nose. My brain fired off a burst of white light behind my eyes, and, in an instant, I knew not only the exact location of where the godborns were being kept, but also the details of how to get in and out. They were a couple hundred miles from my old backyard in New Mexico. Then the picture changed, and I saw Hurakan kneeling on the top of a rounded pyramid under a starless sky. Two shadowy figures stood over him.

One held a gleaming ax.

35

I floated away from Land's End on Chiquita's back with two distinct sounds ringing in my ears: Antonio's stupid words, and some very loud guitar banging. It might sound like fun to cruise on a massive stone dinosaur across the Sea of Cortés.... It wasn't. Not when your brain feels like it's got a slow leak and, with every mile, the memories of Antonio, his place, Fuego...all seemed to drift farther and farther away. It was like walking backward through a hazy dream. All I could remember when I finally collapsed on the beach was that something had been broken and something had been repaired. Two words drifted into my subconscious: *creator* and *destroyer*.

This next part isn't from my own memory. I pretty much had to take Ren's and Ah-Puch's word for it. They said they found me at dawn, passed out on the beach. I (supposedly) woke up mumbling stuff about wars, blood, paper, dragons, and the Beast.

The first thing I remember was waking up on the sofa back in our hotel room. I sat up, rubbing my head, trying to recall what had happened and how I'd gotten there. I was relieved when I heard Ren's voice.

"He's awake."

She leaned over me. Rosie was sniffing and grunting trails of thick smoke while licking my face.

"What . . . what happened?" My mouth was as dry as a cotton ball and tasted like I'd eaten out of a dirty ashtray.

Ah-Puch sighed. "It's about time you decided to wake up. We've been under siege, and you sleep?"

"Siege?"

"More bats," Ren said. "Rosie incinerated most of them down on the beach. And A.P. wouldn't even let me give them a funeral."

A.P.? She had a nickname for the god of death?

"Burned the beasts so bad, there was no blood left for me," Ah-Puch complained. He looked around anxiously. "We need to go now, and quickly. Where to?"

The words came without me even thinking about them. "New Mexico."

Ah-Puch muttered, "Such cruelty."

"Are you sure?" Ren asked me. "How do you know?"

I stretched my memory in four different directions, searching for the answer. The last thing I remembered was a boat and a dramatic, over-the-top god. . . . What was his name?

Ah-Puch frowned and looked around nervously. He'd aged again. I mean, not as bad as the little bald viejo coughing up blood. More like a leather-skinned middle-aged dude with a really bad receding hairline who'd smoked and drunk all his days away.

"What happened with the Fire Keeper?" Ren asked.

"Can we have this conversation somewhere else?" Ah-Puch

was worried. "After we're through a gateway, perhaps? Far, far away? I sense danger."

"More bats?" I asked.

"More danger."

I checked my hands. They were pale with greenish veins bulging out of thin skin. It was only the second day of the death magic, and I was looking more and more like a zombie.

"Fire Keeper..." I whispered. It felt like my brain was drowning at the bottom of the sea. Something about dinosaurs and shadows. Or was it guitars? I reached into my pocket and pulled out the jade handle that used to be attached to Fuego.

The memories of last night came flooding back all at once, suffocating me under the weight of the awful truth. Rosie came over and nuzzled me with her nose like she knew what I'd had to let go of. What I'd destroyed.

I sucked in a sharp breath.

"What happened last night?" Ren asked.

I walked into the living area, trying to cool off. "You want to know what happened with the Fire Keeper?" I asked with unexpected fury. Hondo once told me anger is the easiest emotion of all. It's sudden and powerful. My eyes flashed from Ah-Puch to Ren. "He said there's a traitor in our midst. So how about you tell me about this magic of yours and why you really showed up the night before the mud person came, and why shadows surround you, and—"

"You think...?" Ren shook her head in disbelief. "You think I'm a traitor?" Her lower lip trembled and tears pooled in her eyes.

"I don't know *what* to think."

"*I* think we should go," Ah-Puch said.

With fists on her hips, Ren glared at me and said, "I never lied. I already told you I have magic from my Mexican side of the family. I never lied," she repeated.

"I'm not going anywhere until you tell me everything. You said something about your family's blood...." My words hung in the air.

Ren shot Ah-Puch a side-glance. "Tell him," he said to her. "Quickly."

I braced myself.

Standing straighter, Ren said, "I'm part Mexica."

All eyes were on me. And for a blink it felt like time stood still. "You mean, you're related to those pitiful ghosts?"

Okay, those weren't the words I'd planned to say. I can hear your sighs and groans and *you're-an-idiot* accusations already. What, you've never stuck your big fat foot into your even bigger mouth?

"I didn't mean it like that...." I was backpedaling. Hard. "I meant..."

"Apparently, they're not all ghosts," said Ah-Puch.

"Mi familia, we're the last bruja bloodline of our kind," Ren said. "Some Maya gods didn't want any Mexica magic to survive. If they found out that we had..."

She didn't need to finish her sentence. I knew firsthand how much gods craved power.

"So some Maya goddess..." I tried to choose my words more carefully. "Your mom... she, like, fell for a Mexica?"

Ren frowned. "She fell for my dad."

"That's what I meant." I struggled with what to say next,

because I'd already said too many stupid things. "I'm sorry for what your family's been through. I...I know what it feels like to be hunted...hated for something you didn't even do."

"We definitely didn't have anything to do with this mess," Ren said. "My dad refused to teach me any magic, and now he's gone. So I'm not the traitor, okay?"

I put up my hands. "I get it, I get it. I'm sorry."

"Enough with the repulsive pleasantries," Ah-Puch said with a groan. "They're making me sicker than I already am. We really have to go."

Ignoring him, Ren asked me, "What happened to Fuego?"

"I...I broke him....I had to." I told her and Ah-Puch what had happened.

Ren paced. "So, whoever's behind stealing godborns, getting your dad executed, draining Maya magic...it's all for some war?"

"They're taking out all the Maya weapons." I sounded like Hondo, except he probably would have figured all this out sooner.

"It's what I would do," Ah-Puch said. "Brilliant strategy, if you ask me."

My eyes met his. "How do I know *you're* not a part of all this?"

"Because whoever is behind it can't free me," he said. "I align with whoever can benefit me most, and right now that's you."

"Then what would be your next move?" I asked, figuring I might as well pick the twisted god's brain. If anyone knew a villain's mind, it was Ah-Puch.

He seemed surprised by the question. "Do the unexpected."

"Zane already *has* done the unexpected," said Ren, "by feeding the Fire Keeper's flame."

"I only bought us some time," I said, glancing at the wall clock. The second hand wasn't ticking. "Their powers aren't permanent—yet."

"This kind of mastermind will have a backup for every contingency," Ah-Puch said.

"Could it be Zotz?"

"Camazotz is a natural-born killer," Ah-Puch said. "He is cunning and smart, but he's not this smart. If he's behind it, he's working with someone, and whoever that is, they know the Maya gods will call on any and all magic to win, which is why they are destroying it all."

Ren scowled. "Those Maya gods have a lot of nerve if they think they can call on godborns to help after how mean they've been to us."

Just then, the door swung open.

We all recoiled.

Two stocky resort security guards stood there, guns pointed at us. "¡Pongan sus manos sobre sus cabezas! Están bajo arresto," the bald one said.

"What are the charges?" Ah-Puch growled like he'd had experience in getting arrested.

"Robo. Incendio provocado. Fraude."

"I told you we shouldn't have stolen that boat," I said with a groan, putting my hands behind my head.

"Or fried those bats," Ren said, eyeing Rosie.

Ah-Puch backed up with his hands in the air. "I am the

great Maya god of death, darkness, and destruction, and if
you don't want to wear a curse for a millennium, you should
let us go."

One of the guards lifted his walkie-talkie and spoke
angrily, spitting projectile loogies. He was probably asking
for backup from the loony bin. Then the bald guard scowled
and shouted at us. His gun was still pointed.

Ren inched backward. "I'm not going to jail."

Rosie snorted clouds of smoke and snarled savagely. But
all these guards saw was an angry three-legged boxmatian
who was no threat against a gun. If only I could ask her to
launch fire . . . but these guys were human. I couldn't incinerate them just for doing their job.

Ren asked Ah-Puch, "How about opening a gateway and
getting us out of here?"

"I'm too weak for that."

"What?!" I shouted. "Ugh! Then we have to storm the
guards. We can handle them, Ren. You take the smaller dude
on the right."

"There *is* no smaller dude," she said. "They're both huge
and, um, they have guns."

"Then how about some shadows to, like, knock them out
or smother them or something?"

"¡Silencio!" the bald dude ordered.

Ren's worried expression told me she was less than confident she could get the shadows to listen to her, but she closed
her eyes, clenched her fists, and muttered things I couldn't
make out. A couple of morning shadows swayed, began to
rise, then went kaput. Ren shook out her hands. "I need quiet!"

The guards approached us cautiously, guns still pointed, handcuffs swinging from their belt loops.

"Rosie can get us out of here," I said in a low voice, keeping my eyes on the guards. "On the count of three."

Everything happened faster than thought. Before I knew it, we were all on Rosie's back, bolting out the door to the beach. There was shouting. The guards chased after us, but Rosie was hell-on-wheels fast.

"Go, Rosie!" I shouted from the back.

Ah-Puch was in the middle, shouting things like "I will not perish at the hands of security guards!" Then: "Get us to the cliffs."

Cliffs? He'd rather splatter all over some rocks?

We were cut off at the pass by a new set of guards on dirt bikes. Rosie took a sharp right and raced down a space between two buildings that opened up to a seaside cliff. She came to a halt at the end of the alley. At the same moment, a helicopter approached and circled overhead. I'd seen lots of outcomes for this quest in my mind, but never this—being caught on top of a cliff and wanted for theft, arson, and fraud!

"We're trapped!" Ren shouted.

The helicopter's rotor spun wildly, pushing down a warm and biting wind. Some guy leaned out of it with a huge camera hoisted over his shoulder.

The guards were right behind us, racing forward on their bikes.

"What do we do?" Ren shouted over the helicopter's whirring blades.

"We will have to combine our strength," Ah-Puch cried.

"It will take tremendous concentration and—" His words cut off as he patted Rosie's ribs and my dog took off to the edge of the cliff.

Seriously? She was taking orders from the god of death now?

I was about to argue against death by splatter, when a deep buzzing began in my feet. It snaked up my legs, spreading into my stomach and across my chest. Rosie left us at the cliff's edge, then spun back to face and probably distract the guards. I looked down. The ocean was at least ten feet beyond a colossal rocky outcropping that equaled sure and sudden demise.

The guards were off their motorcycles now, guns pointed. "¡Alto!"

And then Rosie released a growl that would rival a dragon's. Here's where things got really weird, because the guards screamed, the helicopter nearly spun out of control, and steam rose off Rosie's massive body. I knew then that they, as in everyone, could see her as the hellhound she was. Since when could she show her hellish side to humans?

Ah-Puch gripped my hand and tugged me and Ren closer to the edge.

Do you feel it? Ah-Puch asked.

Yes, Ren and I said together. The electrical current was like some kind of shared energy or magnetic pull binding us together. The rushing air pounded us. I looked over my shoulder to see Rosie holding off the guards.

Now imagine a place in New Mexico you know the best, Ah-Puch said, jerking my attention back.

No, we have to go directly to the godborns!

For this to work, you have to have spent a lot of time where we're going.

Ren said, *Hurry!*

I pictured the mesa where the Beast used to be. *Now what?*

Jump!

36

The three of us plummeted toward the rocks a few hundred feet below, and all I kept thinking was *I just jumped off a cliff because the god of death told me to.*

"Open the gateway!" Ren screamed.

Concentrate harder! Ah-Puch said, still managing to grip our hands. It was as if the current that ran through us also tied us together with some kind of invisible rope.

At the same moment, Rosie's howl echoed. She tumbled through the air toward us.

"Focus!" Ah-Puch shouted.

Ren's way-too-calm voice broke into my mind. *Zane, don't look down.*

Right, easy for her to say. Or maybe not. I mean, she was headed toward Splatsville, too. How was she talking to me telepathically? We weren't even touching, because Ah-Puch was between us.

Suddenly, a shadow spread beneath us, blocking our view of the ground. Not exactly helpful, since we were still falling toward certain death . . . Then the air shifted—or maybe *thickened* is the right word, because it seemed to wrap tightly around us, slowing our descent. But how was that possible?

It wasn't enough to land us safely but enough to buy us time before our skulls were crushed.

Ren?

Just imagine the volcano. Her words were rushed but calm. *You know it better than anyone.*

I forced my eyes closed, bringing up images of the New Mexico mesa with all its trails. We continued to plunge. Then Hondo's voice broke through my memories: *You have to visualize the outcome you want. You have to feel it.*

Focus. Focus. Focus.

Warm sun and thick dry air.

A coyote's distant howl.

The smell of creosote like desert rain.

Bam. We landed with a *crash, thunk,* and *Oof, my back!* (That last one was Ah-Puch.)

I opened my eyes and sat up. A sharp pain radiated down my right side. But I smiled anyway. "Woot!" I shouted. "We made it. We're alive!"

"That was better than the time I bungee-jumped off a bridge," Ren said while Ah-Puch cursed up a storm about busted spines and broken spirits. Rosie nudged me with her giant paw, like she was saying *I know this place. Get up. Let's explore.*

I scanned the area. Silvery brush dotted the desert leading to the base of the Beast. This was the fake one Ixtab had made so people wouldn't freak and wonder how the heck a whole volcano had disappeared. I had to give Ixtab credit: the volcano was a perfect duplicate, down to the squatty cactus with thorny spines and the zigzagging trail that led to my secret entrance inside.

As I searched the horizon, my heart sank. The houses that used to belong to Mr. Ortiz, Ms. Cab, and my family were nothing but piles of rotted wood, destroyed in the flood Ixtab had sent. Too many emotions battled inside me, and all I was left with was a weird kind of sadness at how fast a life can just disappear.

The sun was halfway across the sky, which told me it was close to noon. I only had part of today and tomorrow before Hurakan was scheduled for execution and I had to get back to the underworld.

Ren swept sand off her back and yanked mesquite twigs from her hair, which was now sticking up in every direction. Her right cheek had a short, jagged cut. Rosie healed it with a slobbery lick that made Ren giggle.

Ah-Puch groaned as he rolled over, sucking wind. Ren was at his side in two seconds, helping him sit up. She asked the question that was on the tip of my tongue: "How did we do that? I mean, the shadow... And, Zane"—her eyes slid to mine—"you opened a gateway!"

"We bound our magic together," Ah-Puch said with an annoyed tone. "Well, technically, *I* did it. And the connection made..." He inhaled sharply and winced. "It made our power stronger." He leveled us with a threatening stare. "It's an ancient godly secret, and if you ever tell anyone I showed it to you, I will rip out your spines and send you spiraling into the darkest depths of Xib'alb'a."

Ah-Puch's threat didn't even faze Ren. She stared at her open hands, smiling. "I felt, like, electricity between us."

"Is that how you made the shadows listen to you?" I asked. "They slowed our fall, right?"

"I don't know. I just focused really hard and I imagined them and there they were." She shrugged. "Like Hondo taught me."

"This is so very cruel." Ah-Puch shook his balding head. "Bitter and cruel, forcing me to return to my four-hundred-year-old prison—with godborns, no less." He turned his back to the volcano.

"This isn't the real volcano, A.P.," Ren said, trying to make him feel better. She wandered a few feet away, checking things out.

"We've got to get to the others—now."

"I need a moment's rest." Ah-Puch coughed. "Though I really hate this place."

"Zane?" Ren's voice quivered.

I went over to where she was pointing at the sand. There were several rounded paw prints (like those of a massive wolf) with four long claws on each. But they were staggered in such a way I wasn't sure that whatever made these prints had four legs.

Rosie growled, foam oozing from her mouth as she sniffed and scratched at each.

"Hellhound?" I guessed.

"Aliens," Ren whispered.

"Neither." Ah-Puch stood next to us. He tilted his head and

took a deep breath. "Smells like Ahuitzotl." He pronounced it *Ah-weet-so-tul.*

"What's that?" Ren's eyes widened, but not from fear—more like fascination.

"A Mexica water monster with an ugly, lopsided face, spiked fur along its spine, and a lizard tail with a freakish hand at the end to drag around its screaming victims."

"Victims?" Ren's eyes widened.

"Ahuitzotl likes to eat humans—especially nails, eyes, and teeth." Then, more to himself, he muttered, "So, someone found a way to bring back the monsters. . . ."

My heart pounded in my ears. "Why was it here?"

Ren nodded. "And where did it go?"

Rosie sniffed the ground ferociously, each breath getting shorter and more pronounced until she poked her head beneath a mesquite bush. She let out a long woeful whine, backing out with something in her mouth. *Please don't be a hand or a foot or an eyeball,* I thought.

"What'd you find, girl?"

In her mouth was one of Brooks's demon-fighting flashlights, and it was still on (in non-demon-killing mode), which told me it had been dropped recently. The shock hit me like a sledgehammer to the gut, and my knees nearly gave out. It was impossible. Brooks had come here. How?

I scrambled beneath the bush and came back with her torn backpack. The gateway map was still inside. She would never have left this behind. Not unless she was forced to.

That's when I noticed, beyond the bush, a cow skull stuck

on top of a branch that had been rammed into the earth. Something was attached to the skull. I tried to hurry over for a better look but was slowed down by my limp. I'd gotten so used to walking straight and fast with the help of Fuego, I'd forgotten what *this* felt like. Drawing closer, I saw what was tied to the skull. A brown hawk feather. Brooks's feather. And if she had been here, my guess was that Hondo had, too.

I looked around frantically for their footprints. And then I saw the blood—a trail in the sand like it had just been spilled. My legs shook.

"Where are they?!" I demanded from Ah-Puch, who now stood next to me. As if he had the answers.

"That could be anyone's blood," he said.

Rosie sniffed the fresh sangre, gave me a mournful look, then threw back her head and let out a howl.

I held my breath. "Show me smoke if it's Hondo's blood and fire if it's Brooks's."

Rosie blinked as a plume of smoke trailed out of her nose.

I fell to one knee.

"Zane," Ren said quietly, "you need to keep your cool... so we can think this through."

She sounded like Brooks. Always ready to make a plan, but what good were plans? They burned faster than brushwood no matter how hard you tried to keep them away from the fire.

Heat pulsed painfully in my limbs. I was chasing a monster I didn't know, an enemy without a face. And my uncle was hurt.

"They were ambushed," I hissed as I stood. Why hadn't Brooks and Hondo listened and just gone home? "What if the monster . . . ?" I didn't even want to finish my thought.

"It didn't kill them," Ah-Puch said.

"How do you know?!"

"Let me rephrase that. It didn't kill them *here*. Because if it had, I would smell the leftover death," he said, licking his lips hungrily. "Zane, think with the god part of your brain."

"But . . . how did this monster know they were here?" Ren asked.

"We're in enemy territory," Ah-Puch said. "Security was probably set up, just in case Zane ever came back."

"That's a big 'in case,'" I said. It was like whoever was behind all this could see our every move.

"The enemy is luring you to wherever they are. They are playing head games, relying on your ridiculous human emotions. It's a trap. It's always been a trap. And now we need to figure out its trigger."

"Yeah, well, I know where they are," I said, seeing the location of the godborns Antonio had planted in my brain. "They won't be expecting that, and trap or not, we have to hurry. Or did you forget our deal?"

Ah-Puch sighed. "Do you have exact coordinates? We have to be very precise about where we open the gateway. One wrong move and we may find ourselves right in the middle of the enemy's den, which is not a place I plan to be."

I stuffed the map in my back pocket and walked my memory through the images Antonio had given me, including the trail that led to where the godborns were being kept.

There was a shady tree-lined cliff that overlooked the valley campsite. I didn't know if it would work, but I took hold of Ah-Puch's elbow and opened my mind so he could see where we needed to go.

"Something isn't right with that forest," he said.

"What do you mean 'not right'?" Ren asked.

"I don't know." Ah-Puch groaned. "I blame it on the puny brain that's feeding me these visions."

I didn't bother wasting time with a comeback. "How far out will guards be posted?" I asked.

Ah-Puch's mouth tugged into a half grin. "Not guards. Magic. And I, for one, have a godly form to return to, so if you don't mind, I'd rather not waltz into their little snare."

"We made a deal," I reminded him. "So, if you really want that godly form back, we still have some rescuing to do."

He glared as his shoulders sagged with defeat. "Deals really are the devil when you're on the weaker end," he muttered.

"How are we going to get inside with . . . with magic surrounding the place?" Ren asked.

If Hondo were here, he'd say to visualize the outcome, then he'd ask for an arsenal of weapons and he'd go in swinging. Brooks would tell me to plan, to wait for the exact right time to strike. But when was that?

"At least be on the lookout for the trap's trigger," Ah-Puch said. "I don't want to get caught like a rat."

Just then, Brooks's feather glistened in the sun. Golden specks of dust whirled around it like a mini Dirt Devil. I reached out.

"Zane, NO!" Ah-Puch shouted.

But it was too late—the feather was in my hand. The cow skull split open, and a torrent of wind formed a tunnel that sucked me inside. Shadows wrapped themselves around me so tightly I felt like my lungs were being crushed under the weight of dirt-packed earth. No air. No light. But instead of being buried, I was being driven up, up, up.

Itzamna's voice broke through. *It's going to hurt, but don't tell them anything. Do you hear me? Trust no one.*

Hurt? What's going to hurt? You said you were going to help me!

This IS me helping you.

I blacked out.

When I came to, I couldn't open my eyes. I was blindfolded. I couldn't move, either—my hands and feet were bound to some kind of tree or wooden pole.

A cold wind whipped around me. Leaves rustled. Birds chirped.

"And the prince awakens," a woman's voice said.

I squirmed uselessly. "Who are you? Where am I?"

"Oh, we'll get to that," she cooed. "But first, young prince, the snake."

37

It's pretty hard to write about what happened
next. Because I'd rather put it out of my mind forever. I used
to think fear was a feeling—a blood-pounding, heart-racing,
fight-or-flight response. But you know what? It's a thing. A
living, breathing thing with teeth and claws and hate so dark
it can tear you to pieces if you let it.

Maybe that's why Itzamna had said it was going to hurt.
He wasn't talking about getting hit over the head or thrown
off a cliff. He meant the fear. And he was right.

I cursed myself for being so stupid, for walking right into
the trap Ah-Puch had just told me to avoid.

The woman ripped off my blindfold. I blinked in the sudden light, and once my eyes adjusted, I saw I was in a grassy
field surrounded by forest and weathered canyon walls. The
air was chilly and smelled like a blend of pine and horses.
But something about the place wasn't real, like it had been
stitched together with scraps of fabric made to look like the
world. Ixtab would have called it a poor imitation.

"Ah, the son of fire. Welcome."

The lady was of medium height, with hair twisted into
two long white braids. She had pale gray eyes, and a sagging
face that reminded me of a wet tea bag. Her hands were large

and beefy, with hairy knuckles—the same hands I'd seen in the scrying pool taking the godborns. *She* was the abductor?

"Where are Brooks and Hondo?" I asked, trying to keep the strain out of my voice. It was a stupid question. I could tell by looking at her that she wasn't in charge. She blinked too much and paced too quickly, leaving a trail of wet clay behind. Great! Another mud person, here to serve. I tried to draw on fire, to burn through these stupid ropes, but I couldn't find a heat source.

"We'll get to that," she said. "But first, introductions. You can call me Gee, like the letter. Oh, and before you try to burn anyone down, your powers have been locked by the masters." She smiled and waved a hand through the air. "Now let's have you meet the godborns."

A group of ten kids stepped out of the forest in unison. They each wore a black sweat suit and marched stiffly like a soldier. I wanted to throw a fist pump and shout, *Guys, I'm totally here to save you! I mean, once I'm not tied to this pole.*

Why were they glaring at me like that?

I spotted the girl with short, honey-colored hair, brown skin, and hooded, suspicious eyes. She was the first godborn I'd seen in the Eternity pool when I was in Xib'alb'a. The same girl who had walked down a littered school hallway with her head down but her gaze turned up. Her head wasn't bowed now.

Gee gestured to the girl, who immediately began to walk toward me. Still glaring.

"Zane, this is Serena. She, like the others, has a gift for you."

"Gift?" Why did I have a feeling that wasn't the right word?

"Boys and girls." Gee swept her arms wide, and flakes of dried mud fell from her pits. "Please come forward when called to bestow your offering. Remember what I taught you. Self-control above all else. Zane must understand if he is to join us."

Okay, this lady was cracked. Literally. Every time she made an expression, her face looked like it might crumble. *Join them?* Weren't the godborns prisoners waiting to be rescued? Except they didn't look like prisoners. They looked like... recruits.

Serena opened her hands and a cloud of red mist appeared, taking the shape of a snake. A big, fat, murderous-looking snake with beady black eyes and a forked tongue pointed in my direction. If I weren't tied to a pole, I would have jumped ten feet.

"Thief," Serena whispered as she set the snake on the ground. The serpent slid through the dried grass, right in my direction.

"Hey!" I squirmed. "Is that thing poisonous?"

Gee snorted like it was too much effort to laugh.

The snake slithered toward my shorter leg. Sweat dripped from my neck, trickling down my back. My chest tightened. *This is not how I'm going to die,* I told myself, trying to draw the heat of the sun so I could burn this place down, but I was in serious panic mode because... well, the snake! Which was now about to wrap itself around my ankle. But the second the serpent touched my leg, it hissed and recoiled.

Gee frowned, staring down at the red monster like this

wasn't part of the plan. "The show must go on," she whispered as the snake melted into the ground in a sizzling cloud of steam. Quickly, she motioned for the next godborn to come forward. Serena fell back in line with the others.

Where were Ah-Puch and Ren and Rosie? Had I left them behind? My eyes darted around the field, searching for them or any sign of Brooks and Hondo.

"How about you untie me?" I suggested, hoping Gee's mud brain might work to my advantage. "We can talk about all this. Uh, maybe come to an agreement."

Gee ignored me. I wondered how long it would be before I had to face her creator, whoever that was.

Itzamna whispered in my mind, *Remember, Zane, darkness is Deception's mistress.*

I'm tied up in enemy camp with dozens of hateful eyes wanting to scorch off my face, and you're telling me about Deception's mistress? Seriously? How about some of that help you promised?

Look closely.

What?! I mean real help, like cutting these ropes, or getting me out of here, or . . . ? Hello? Itzamna?

Make the story worth it.

I'm not your stupid entertainment!

A short round dude with high-water pants walked toward me. Gee introduced him as Louie.

Louie frowned at me. "Traitor," he said flatly.

I wanted so badly to shout, *I'm not a traitor! I came all this way to help you! Dude, I'm risking my life here. And I'm writing, like, a whole book for you guys. Does that sound like a traitor to you?* But there was no reason to show all my cards to the ringmaster of this ridiculous circus. Whoever it was clearly had a thing for theatrics.

Louie turned up his palms. I held my breath. *Please don't sic something on me that sucks blood or has big teeth and claws,* I thought.

Thunder boomed, echoing through the canyon walls so loud the earth trembled. A long shiver ran up my spine. Lightning cut across the darkening sky and a torrential rain began to fall. The trees bent under the force of it, and I thought the rain would wash me away if it hammered too long.

I struggled against the rope, but it only cut deeper into my skin.

The next godborn stepped onto the field and began to walk toward me. This time, Gee made no introduction. The person's hood was pulled up as the rain pelted them. Even when the rain stopped suddenly, their face was a blurry haze.

"This one's special," Gee said, making space.

The godborn stood right in front of me. Dark curls spilled out of the hood. The face looked up, and eyes flashed amber. My heart stopped beating.

"Brooks?"

"Liar," she whispered.

I thrashed against the stupid rope. "Brooks, it's me. I didn't lie!"

With her lips pressed together, she smiled. But then her face mutated, like her features were being erased right before my eyes. "What the ... ?"

A scar appeared on her chin, then a nose, and small green eyes that were bright against his light brown skin. That's right—*his*. This dude's face was appearing like a sketch on paper. I knew him. He was the guy with bleached hair who had cruised down a city street while the wind pounded him. He hadn't screamed when he was abducted—he'd fought back like a madman.

"This is Marco," Gee said proudly.

Marco gave me a stony stare.

"I'm not the enemy," I said, but he didn't even blink.

"Aren't their gifts incredible?" Gee squealed. "Imagine how powerful we'll be once we put them to good use."

Good use? For what? The war Zotz and whoever else wanted to have with the Maya gods? I considered what I'd seen so far. The snake girl, the rain guy, and the creepy morphing/disappearing face dude. How could the godborns be using these powers if they hadn't been claimed? What was I missing?

Look closely.

"Would you like to see more?" Gee asked proudly.

"That's enough," came a familiar voice, a voice I thought I'd never hear again.

Footsteps sounded behind me. Gee lowered her gaze and cowered like a scared dog before she slunk into the forest with the godborns.

"Hello, Zane."

My heart crawled up my throat.

Jordan (aka the evil hero twin Xb'alamkej) stepped around the pole and stood in front of me. Yep, he looked just as tall, just as ferocious, just as cruel as the first time I'd met him at his magic mafia fiesta back in Los Angeles, except he'd swapped his dark suit for a gray long-sleeved T-shirt and a pair of dark jeans.

"You?" I choked out. *"You're* the one who took the godborns? You're supposed to be—"

"Poisoned and paralyzed by La Muerta? Suffocated and crushed between Usukun's greasy wings?" Jordan ground out the words like he'd been practicing this for a while. "Left to rot in a cage made of blood and bones?" He wrapped his large hand around my throat. His ring stabbed my skin. His black eyes were cold and flat as river stones. "I could snap your neck right now."

So Jordan was the traitor Antonio had warned me about. A godborn who was a traitor to other godborns, casting a bad light on all of us.

A column of colorless dust rose from the ground. Out of it stepped Bird, Jordan's twin, otherwise known as Jun'ajpu'. His face was solid granite, like the first time I had met him.

"He doesn't deserve to die, brother."

My hope flared. But it was immediately extinguished when Jordan continued:

"Not quite yet."

38

"You look a lot worse than the last time I saw
you," Bird said, eyeing me. His voice was smooth and cold like
ice. Could he sense the death magic?

"Where are Brooks and Hondo?" I asked through clenched
teeth.

Bird crossed his arms over his chest and ran his thumb
over a half smile. "You're not in any position to ask questions,
godborn."

Yeah, I guess he was still holding on to that little fact, and
maybe also resentment that I'd led Ah-Puch to their hiding
spot and revealed their existence to the Maya gods. The twins
were the very first godborns, and it was because of their trickery that the Sacred Oath had been decreed and the rest of us
weren't supposed to exist.

"You really think you can beat the Maya gods?" I asked,
thinking how quickly enemies can become allies under the
right circumstances.

"Okay, Obispo. Settle down now." Jordan chuckled.

Bird unbuttoned his dark suit jacket. Did this guy ever
go casual? I wondered. "It's been fun keeping you as a pet,
Zane. Just like a little mouse, placed in a maze we built, you

fell into every single trap we set for you," he said. "From the mud person to the images of this place the beetles planted in your brain—"

"The beetles . . . ? But how did you find me on Holbox?"

"I admit, it was pretty hit-or-miss." Jordan smirked. "But then came a beautiful blip on the radar—the message with Jazz's magic swirling all around it. Led us right to you." He clasped his hands. "Gotta hand it to Ixtab. Her shadow magic is strong—it really messed with our connection. And once you left the safety of your little hideaway, we had to modify the maze a bit. When our guards at the volcano caught Brooks and Hondo, that was icing on the cake." He gave me a glacial stare. "In the end, we were able to get you to come right to us."

I felt like the biggest idiot on the planet. No matter what, I would have ended up at the Beast. If I didn't come for the godborns, they knew I would come for Brooks and Hondo.

As much as I wanted to bury my head and pretend I wasn't there, I had to learn everything they were willing to tell me so I could find the exit from their little maze. "You kidnapped the godborns just to get *me* here? Wow, I'm super flattered you guys like me that much."

"Actually, we hate you," Bird said.

"Huh, doesn't seem that way."

Bird opened his mouth to speak, when Jordan patted his shoulder and said to me, "You don't think we're going to give away all our secrets, do you?"

Okay, so that wasn't going to work. Time for plan B—run

away. I twisted my hands back and forth hoping to loosen the rope, but it was a solid knot.

"Don't bother," Jordan said. "You can't get loose."

"You won't win." I jerked forward with a hunger to wipe the smug expressions off their faces.

"Doesn't look like anyone's going to stop us," Bird said.

I glanced at the tree line, scanning furiously for the other godborns.

"Imagine our surprise that night in LA when Ah-Puch revealed that *you* are a godborn," Jordan said, twisting a fat silver skull ring around his finger.

"We sat in our prison for months." Bird's expression was flat and cold. "Day after day we lived off our revenge, planning our next move against the gods who'd turned their backs on us. You should be thanking us. We could have ratted you out, hermano. Told the gods you were alive and then watched the murder show."

"I'm not your brother."

"Aren't you?" Jordan said. "A brother in a common cause, that is. The final piece..."

Bird shot him a glare, silencing him. *The final piece of what?* I wondered.

"I'll never help you!"

Bird paced slowly in front of me, thumbing his scruffy chin. He was enjoying this and, knowing these guys, they were going to draw this out as long as possible. I needed to find Brooks and Hondo. Hondo! A sour taste climbed up my throat when I thought of how they'd nearly killed my uncle last time. Man, if he knew these guys were still around, he'd put up the fight of his life. But they'd tear him to bits without blinking an eye.

I searched the forest for any sign of Ah-Puch or Rosie or Ren. That's when I noticed that the trees looked odd, their trunks and branches misshapen. The sky was distorted, too, like puzzle pieces put together all wrong.

Look closely.

This place wasn't real! It was just like the twins' illusory world back in Los Angeles, and if I was right, this probably wasn't even the Gila Forest.

Crap!

If this wasn't the real Gila, how would Ah-Puch and Ren ever find me? The twins really were masterminds (sick and twisted, but still masterful). What was their endgame?

Anger pulsed slowly beneath my skin as my mind went to work, trying to break down their plan. They had tricked me off the island, luring me on a hunt for the godborns. But why? Why did I matter so much? It couldn't be just for revenge. Hondo would tell me that revenge is built on anger, and anger is irrational, and irrational always loses.

Last time I went up against these guys, I'd played their egos. Maybe it would work again. "You caught me," I said through gritted teeth. "You caught Brooks and Hondo and the godborns. Good for you. How did you manage to do it?"

"When we found out about you," Bird said, "we knew there had to be others, because the gods are deceitful, and no way did only *one* god defy the oath. So, we set out to escape, and we finally did with the help of . . ." He hesitated.

"Who?" I blurted. Who would ever help these jerks? Camazotz?

"That's not the important part." He stepped closer. "What mattered was finding the godborns and putting our plan in motion. But guess what?"

"You're crazy?"

Unfazed, Bird went on. "We didn't have a clue where to start, and then—"

"Don't give it all away." Jordan stretched his neck like a wound-up athlete. "I'd rather watch him squirm."

"I know all about your *plan*." I sat up taller, hoping I could play them stake for stake and ruin their element of surprise. "The sobrenaturals, the godborns, the execution." Then, just to see how they reacted, I threw in, "The Mexica ghosts." I stopped short of mentioning the war.

The twins looked at each other, and I could tell I'd hit a nerve. Then, to my total surprise, they busted up laughing. Had I gotten something wrong? My cheeks flushed, and fury boiled beneath my skin.

"You're *half*way smart," Bird said after he'd caught his breath. "I'll give you that."

"You mean he has *half* a brain," Jordan muttered.

The twins needed something from me or they wouldn't have gone through all this trouble to get me there, and they hadn't gutted me yet. Whatever that something was, I had to use it as leverage to free everyone. And I had to do it in the next twenty-four hours, before my dad was gone forever. Swallowing a boatload of pride, I said, "What do you want

from me? You think I'm going to join you? Fight with you?
Go against the Maya gods for you?"

Bird wagged a finger in my face. "Not for us. No, of course
not. But you'll do anything for your girlfriend and uncle."

39

The forest rippled like water.

The ground shifted and groaned. White and black ashes fluttered like snowflakes from the sky, draining the whole world of color. The forest shrank to a place made of iron and darkness and fear.

I barely had time to blink before I found myself in a cage not tall enough to stand upright in, but at least I wasn't tied up anymore. The smell of gasoline and old tires hit me first. Was this place an auto shop? I looked around the prison for any clue as to where I was. My cell was positioned above a row of twelve cages about six feet below me on the opposite wall. Their iron bars dripped with a thick substance that looked like honey and crawled with winged scorpion-like insects. On each of the cells' barred doors there was a dark shield, hiding whoever was inside. I tried to adjust my eyes to the night, to see beyond the tinted glass, but it didn't work.

Jordan and Bird appeared on a shallow ledge in front of my cell.

"How do you like your new home?" Jordan asked with a sick smile I wanted to wipe right off his face.

"You should be thankful. This is a lot better than where we

spent the last seven months," Bird said. "Which speaks to our generosity." He pounded his fist on the cement above the cell door. "We built your cage special, to give you an unobstructed view. But it has its drawbacks. Like, don't bother trying to use any of your godborn abilities to escape. Only our powers are effective here. So, unless you have a key, you're stuck."

A single light went on in one of the cells below, and I could see beyond the shield.

I jumped and my head smashed against the cement ceiling, sending a wicked pain down my neck and spine.

"Hondo!" I shouted, gripping the sticky bars.

The winged scorpions whipped their tails ferociously, stinging my skin. I jerked back. My hands seized with pain, then went cold and rigid, hanging off my wrists like ice bags.

"Oh, we forgot to mention, you probably shouldn't touch the bars." Jordan's eyes hardened. "Paralysis, even temporary, is a terrible, terrible condition."

"What did you do to him?" I stared wide-eyed at my uncle, slumped in his cell, staring straight ahead. Sweat beaded on his forehead. A bloody cut ran down the length of his forearm.

"*We* didn't do anything," Bird said. "No matter how many times we warned him, he shook the bars like a madman, screaming for Brooks and making all sorts of empty threats and . . . well, this is the consequence."

"Hondo!" I screamed again.

"He can't hear you," Jordan said. "He can't even see you through the shield."

My heart shrank to the size of a walnut. Hondo hates

small spaces. I could only imagine his panic. I had to fight the urge to reach through the magic-coated bars and rip off the twins' heads.

The only problem was, my hands were still locked like claws and completely useless.

Another light came on in the cell next to Hondo's. I wanted to look away, scared of what I was going to see, but I didn't. A small, battered hawk hopped on one leg, holding a wing close to its body.

Brooks!

An intense rage gripped me so hard, fire burst from my eyes. The flames hit the magic-coated bars and ricocheted on me.

With a twisted laugh, Jordan said, "You can try to burn the place down with your flimsy fire skills, but no way are you strong enough to break through *our* magic. And that substance on the bars? One touch of flame, and hallucinogenic gas is emitted into the cells below."

I watched in horror as Brooks shrank into a corner, pressing her beak into the wall to try to avoid the sickly green smoke infiltrating her cage. Hondo just lay there helplessly breathing in the poison.

"No!" I screamed.

Bird smiled as he watched the agony unfold all around him. "We really went to great lengths to build your prison *uniquely* for you."

"You're sick!" I said.

"And you're doomed," Bird said.

I struggled to find my breath and the words, but all

that came out was "Wh-why?" My voice cut off in a swell of emotion.

"We told you," he said. "We have a plan—a very big plan. And to think that your godborn-ness, the thing we despised you for, will be what gives rise to our new empire." He let out a small laugh. "It's so poetic, isn't it, Jordan?"

"I will never help you!" I screamed. But that was a lie. I'd do anything to save Brooks or Hondo.

"You're such an egotistical fool," Bird spat. "We don't need *your* help. Nor do we want it."

Then why was I there? Just so they could torment me?

He straightened his sleeves, spun to leave, then turned back and looked me straight in the eye. "Have you ever heard what the ancient Maya did to the enemies they captured?"

I could barely look at this guy, never mind talk to him.

"Have you?" he demanded.

I kept my eyes on the floor.

He leaned closer and whispered, "They fed their hearts to the gods."

Silence pressed in on the cold cage, and I stumbled back. "You . . . you want to sacrifice me to the Maya gods? For what? You think I'm some kind of prize? That they'll forgive you or something?"

Bird gripped the bars. The scorpions fell dead to the ground instantly. "Such a small mind," he said. "Why would we *ever* honor the Maya gods with your blood—or anyone's? No, you're even more valuable than *that*."

Hondo used to tell me that learning what your enemy *doesn't* want can be as valuable as learning what they *do* want.

Now at least I knew they didn't want me to fight for them and they didn't want to feed me to the gods. Maybe they just wanted the thrill of murdering me in my sleep? Nah, they were the kind of guys who would want my eyes wide open while they stuck the dagger in my heart.

Jordan looked at his watch. "Time's up. We can't be late to your father's execution."

"What?!" I lunged, stopping inches from the bars. "No! The execution's not until tomorrow."

Bird's eyes flashed with some kind of victory. "Seems you've lost time in our world. 'Tomorrow' is today."

The twins hadn't been gone two seconds, when the fire spread through my veins, hot and searing. Hate and panic and darkness and revenge were causing it to build up in me. My body went rigid with pain. I tried to push the fire down, to swallow it whole. But it pulsed and thrashed and raced inside.

The air felt thick and charged. Sweat trickled down my neck. Tears stung my eyes. All my senses shrank down to this: the living fire wanted out.

Breathe. Breathe. Breathe.

I squeezed my eyes shut, digging the heels of my palms against my temple. Spikes of fear pounded into my heart.

And then Ah-Puch's words found me: *Do not try to control the fire.... Surrender to it.*

Okay, maybe it wasn't a good idea to take advice from the god of death, but if I didn't do something fast, I knew the fire would consume me.

I heard another spark of a memory, a distant voice—
Hurakan's. That day in the Empty he had said, The fire *will
destroy you if you don't release its power.*

But what about Brooks and Hondo? They'd get poisoned
by the gas....

Regardless of my doubts, the heat and power ripped
through me, fast and furious like a bullet. My eyes blazed,
coloring the world bloodred. Smoke trailed from my nose and
mouth. Turning away from the bars, I took a deep breath and
pressed my hands into the back wall.

Then, with everything I had, I screamed and let the
fire out.

40

••

⬭

Blue flames engulfed me, creating a spinning inferno with me in the center, and the harder I tried to shrink away, the tighter it squeezed. When I breathed, the fire breathed. When I moved, the fire moved.

I let it burn. Man, did I let it burn. I watched in awe as the blue fire (the hottest part of a flame) spread. The concrete around my prison cell melted, running like colorless lava. I let the fire rage and quickly realized that a magical thread connected my walls to all the others. Carefully, I drew the flame's energy back, tamping it down until it liquefied into pools of blue at my feet and seeped into the ground with a hissing gurgle.

Out of breath and exhausted, I found myself in a weed-choked wrecking yard. There were ten-foot-high stacks of rusted cars, heaps of old tires, and piles of scrap metal everywhere. No wonder the prison had smelled like rubber and gas.

A swollen moon floated over the dark woods that outlined the yard. The lifeless trees were angled all wrong and had sharp, grasping claws.

I blinked in astonishment. I had obliterated the twins' imagined world. And that's when I knew: I had finally become one with the fire. But what did it matter? I was still locked up behind the magic bars that hadn't melted. So was everyone else.

My eyes quickly found Brooks the hawk, shivering in her cell near a corroded van balanced on cinder blocks. Hondo was laid out flat in his enclosure, unmoving. The godborns' cages were scattered across the yard. I didn't understand it. They had been free before, part of the twins' army. Why lock them up now? The cells' shields were gone, and for the first time, I wished I couldn't see through the dark. Each of the godborns was staring up at the sky with their mouth open. Except for that Marco dude. He was on his knees, reaching for a screwdriver on the ground outside of his cage.

I followed their gazes.

The moon cast enough light for everyone to be able to see hundreds of bats clustered together, hanging from a green wrecking crane, their heads tucked beneath their shiny black wings.

They looked just like the vile little creatures that had tried to kill us back in Cabo. And in the center of them all was a dark bulging shape, a mega bat at least ten feet tall, suspended by its claws, swinging gently in the breeze. Its rubbery wings were wrapped tightly around its swollen body. And its head? Human . . . ish. The face had a creepy masklike look—grayish skin pulled too tight like overcooked chicken. The eyes were closed.

Camazotz. And here I'd thought the *demon runners* were repulsive.

I had just melted the twins' stage set, and these bats were snoozing away like they were hibernating. Could we be so lucky?

As much as I wanted to call out to my uncle, to Brooks, and to the godborns, I couldn't risk waking up King Batman.

Marco caught my eye. He was clutching his screwdriver like a knife and jabbing it in the air, pointing at the bats.

Wait a second. Why would he want to kill the bats? Wasn't he on the twins' side? Hadn't he morphed his face to look like Brooks just to throw me off guard?

I shook my head and held my finger to my lips in a *be-quiet* gesture.

He frowned and stuck the tool into the keyhole, making the metal *clang*. He stilled immediately.

We all glanced up. The bats didn't stir.

Serena drew her hands to her mouth and quickly extended them out, fingers spread, like she was miming *breathe fire*, or maybe it was *I'm going to vomit*. The others followed her lead, and before I knew it, all the godborns were sweeping their hands in the air, clutching their throats, fake-dying, and desperately pointing at the creatures.

I leaned closer to the redheaded girl in the cage next to mine and whispered, "How could you ally yourself with the twins?"

She jerked backward and gave me a *what-the-Xib'alb'a-are-you-talking-about?* look. "We're *prisoners.*"

"Really?" I said in a sarcastic voice so low I wasn't sure she would hear me. "Because that Marco guy changed his face,

and Serena over there tried to kill me with a snake, and..."
I looked around for Louie. His cage was right next to mine
on the other side. He stood in the corner and kicked the dirt
mindlessly. "He made it rain."

"What are you talking about?" The girl looked at the others, confused. "We've been stuck in these cages."

Was she telling the truth? Had Jordan and Bird used clones
to trick me into believing the godborns were against me? Was
everything I'd seen just another sick little magic show they
had made up?

I thought I'd been afraid earlier. But that was nothing
compared to the cold terror pressing on my bones now. And
not because of the very likely possibility I might get eaten
by a giant bat with a human face, but because people were
depending on me. I'd been so confident I could do this, sure I
could save my dad *and* the godborns. They were all looking
at me expectantly, like *Are you listening? You're the guy who
got us into this mess, so get us out.* Only problem was, I had no
idea how. I'd melted the prison walls, but I still couldn't melt
these blasted bars. The twins hadn't lied about one thing: no
Maya powers were going to unlock these cages.

As I was racking my brain over how we were going to
escape the bat-god-guarded junkyard and get to the execution
before my dad's head rolled, the air rippled about ten feet away
from me. And there, next to a taxi with a busted-out windshield, a gateway opened, and out stepped the most unlikely
allies: Ren, Ah-Puch, and my faithful hellhound.

I nearly shouted Ren's name but stopped myself just in

time. Thankfully, her eyes found mine. I pointed at wannabe Batman with one hand, and with the other, I pressed my finger to my lips.

Everyone's gaze floated up. Ren's eyes widened. Rosie started to growl, but Ren petted her flank and whispered something, quieting her.

Do NOT wake him, she mouthed to me.

Ya think? I mouthed back.

The trio navigated the metal minefield stealthily, trying to avoid kicking hubcaps, carburetors, or any other metal junk that would make a noise.

Ah-Puch looked frail and weathered, like he could blow away on a light gust.

Once they got to my cage, the god of death whispered, "You're a lot more trouble than you're worth."

I gripped their shoulders.

My telepathic voice was a rush of panic that to me sounded like coherent sentences but probably came out more like *Brooks . . . Hondo . . . evil twins . . . godborns . . . trap . . . execution. Hurry!*

Ah-Puch's jaw clenched.

The hero twins? Ren looked at the other cages and a tortured look passed over her face. *Zane, we need to—*

A tall girl with short brown hair, a face full of freckles, and a fuzzy pink sweater sneezed.

We all froze. The crane screeched as it moved slightly in the wind.

Ren looked at Ah-Puch. His bald head was bent to one side

and his shoulders sagged like he had no bones to hold him up. *Do you have enough strength to open these cages?* Ren asked him with a note of sadness, and urgency.

He can't help, I said before the god of death could answer. *The twins put a no-Maya-magic security system on the cages. I... I melted their pretend world, but I couldn't destroy the cage.*

Their ridiculous magic can't stop me, Ah-Puch said. Even his thoughts sounded raspy. *I am a god.*

A dying god, I thought to myself. How had he gotten so weak so quickly?

As if Ren had read my mind, she said, *He used a lot of energy finding you through the jade and then opening a gateway.*

I put a protective hand on the pendant around my neck and looked at Ah-Puch. *But, before, you said you couldn't—*

Ren did the heavy lifting, he said.

Threads of shame and anger tightened inside of me. If I hadn't fallen for the hawk-feather trap, he would still have enough strength to keep his end of the deal. *Thank you,* I said, two words I never expected to say to the god of death. *Now hurry. I have to get to the execution!*

Ah-Puch took a wheezing breath. *This pathetic body is too drained to unlock the cages.* He stared at me, and I knew what he wanted. The jade.

No way, I said. *Not until the godborns are free and my dad... You know the deal.*

Deals change.

I can do it, Ren said.

I just told you, no Maya magic.

I don't need Maya magic. I've got Mexica *magic.*

Oh.

Yessss! I was pretty sure this was what Ah-Puch had meant by *Do the unexpected.* Ha! Looked like Jordan and Bird hadn't thought of *everything.*

Ren clenched her fists and closed her eyes. Nothing happened. I was about to nudge her, when a small moon shadow peeled itself off a dented car hood. The sombra drifted across the yard, turning in slow circles. A puff of wind blew across the space. The crane swayed, and metal grinded against metal.

Screeech.

Zotz stretched his neck. We all froze. A fat piece of drool dribbled from his mouth. My heart pounded like a jackhammer as the monster settled back into his slumber.

Ren's shadow, a round blob, floated in front of my cage, slowly taking the shape of ... a bumblebee?

"Ren?" I whispered.

She opened her eyes. *KEY, not BEE!*

The shadow bee zipped into my cage, where it landed on my head. I gripped her arm.

Come on, Ren. We have to hurry. Focus.

I am focused!

Use some of my powers, like we did on the roof in Cabo.

But you said no Maya magic.

My power isn't going to open the lock—it's going to increase your power. Get it?

Okay, she said, closing her eyes again. I felt the power channeling between us like a rush of fire speeding through my blood. Goose bumps appeared on Ren's arms, and the bee flew back to her, circled her head, and took the shape of a large skeleton key, too large to open the . . .

The sombra drifted into the keyhole. The bars shook. I held my breath.

Ka-click.

The door opened, and I rushed out, breaking my connection with Ren. She stared down at her hands in fascination and then gave me a confident nod that she had enough power left over to unlock the other cells.

Ah-Puch's legs buckled. My arms shot out to catch him before he collapsed. "I can walk . . ." he whispered. His voice trailed off into a sputtering cough.

Crap! Did he really have to cough up a lung now? He seriously had the worst timing.

One by one, the godborns tumbled out of their prisons looking shell-shocked. I understood—I mean, this was a lot to take, and who knows what had happened to them after they were abducted.

Brooks's and Hondo's cages were the last to be unlocked.

I started toward them, when Ah-Puch grabbed hold of my arm. *Do not be fooled by anything you see here,* he said. *The twins' mother, Ixkik', is the master of deception, so it's in their blood.* He glanced up at creepy bat dude. *Except him. He's very real.*

Just then, a hubcap went whizzing through the air, directly toward Zotz. Miraculously, it landed soundlessly on a soft piece of dirt.

The world stopped.

Chest heaving, Marco stood outside his cage, scowling at

the bat with a madman's eyes. He picked up a hammer next and hurled it at the sleeping monster. I wanted to lunge for him, but it was too late.

The hammer fell short and smashed into a windshield. *Craccckkk.*

Everyone froze. Marco stared at the destruction like he couldn't believe what he'd done.

Zotz opened his eyes. He stretched his wings. His hairy little minions took flight simultaneously, creating a shadow big enough to blot out the moon.

"Rosie!" I shouted. "Get to Hondo!" She took off to his now opened cell, where I knew she would use her healing saliva to restore him to a 100 percent lean, mean fighting warrior.

I hurried toward Brooks's cage, but my limp slowed me down. More than ever I missed Fuego, but I could do this. I concentrated on my storm runner leg, willing its power to carry me faster.

Brooks was pressed into the corner. The second she saw me, she began to screech and flap her wings crazily.

"Seriously?" I said. "I don't think this is the time to chew me out."

Her eyes flashed yellow, and I guessed she couldn't shift back to human because her magic was still weak. My heart sank as I realized the twisted truth. My dad's blood hadn't been enough to help the sobrenaturals. I really had destroyed Fuego for nothing.

Out of the corner of my eye, I caught a glimpse of limbs, claws, and shining teeth. A dark laugh filled the air, followed by a sickening chorus of bat screeches.

I dropped to my knees, soldier-crawled across the dirt, and scooped Brooks into my arms. She thrashed, driving her beak and claws into my wrists, hands, and neck.

Rosie released a chilling wail. A pile of cars came crashing down, metal grinding on metal. Screams and shouts rose into the chaos.

"Zane!" Hondo hollered from somewhere. I glanced over to see him herding the godborns together.

We needed a gateway and fast.

"Ah-Puch!" I shouted, getting to my feet. "We have to get out of here!"

The voice was sudden, dark, and terrifying. "You're not going anywhere."

41

··

·

We all watched in horror as the bat dude made a sweeping arc and landed right in front of us, standing at least four feet taller than me. He rubbed his hands together as he spread his wannabe Batman wings. On their undersides were tiny fanged mouths opening and closing like piranhas, hissing words I couldn't make out. His bat army circled overhead as though they were waiting for his command to drain every ounce of our blood.

My stomach turned as I pressed the godborns, now huddled behind me, back. Hondo took Brooks from me and joined the crowd. Rosie followed, no doubt to heal Brooks's wing.

"Who is rattling the cages?" the bat said in a deep gravelly voice. Was he really trying to sound like Christian Bale from *The Dark Knight*?

A cold feeling spread through me. I didn't like the looks of this guy. I'd fought monsters before, but there was something extra cruel and savage about this one. Something predatory, like he'd kill just for the sport of it. Or because someone dared him to. So, what do you say to a monster like that?

"Er . . . sorry," I said. "We were just leaving."

He smiled, showing a row of glistening fangs. "You didn't

hear me. No one is leaving. But I do enjoy a good hunt if you want to run."

"Camazotz." Ah-Puch's voice crept up behind me.

"Ah-Puch, old friend."

Old friend?

"I was wondering if my offering in Cabo would be enough to lure you here," Camazotz said. "By the looks of you, maybe I should have sent more."

All the air went out of me. This guy was lying. Ah-Puch couldn't be helping him, could he? "You sent those bats?" I asked. "They tried to kill us."

"They get a little carried away sometimes." The giant bat shrugged. "But they weren't there for you. They were for my comrade here," Camazotz said. "You looked pretty weak, Ah-Puch. And how I pitied you for having to babysit these kids." His sickly green eyes met mine.

"Your bats tried to abduct me!" Ren growled.

"Call it a dual mission. Snatch you and fortify my friend."

"You sensed my presence. Good." Ah-Puch kept his steely gaze on Camazotz. "The bats were delicious. But as you can see, I need something more."

"What's he talking about, A.P.?" Ren asked as Rosie stepped to my side.

My muscles tensed.

"Oh, he didn't tell you?" Camazotz said to Ren with a gleeful stupid smile. "We have a long history from our time hanging out in Xib'alb'a. Well, I did most of the hanging. Ha. Get it? Ah, so many late-night parties when he was the king and hell was wretched. Now it's gone soft and vegan and..." He sighed. "What matters is that I had to make sure he got you here safely, Zane. You kept taking annoying little detours and that made me nervous, so I sent blood. Because blood is always the answer."

My head broke through the earth's atmosphere and was going to burn up in three...two...one.

Ren gasped. "Ah-Puch would never work with you!"

Camazotz tucked his wings to his side. His bats swooped into the trees, where their eyes glowed in the waiting shadows. "Let's get these monsters back in their cages, Ah-Puch, and then we can talk terms."

"Talk is cheap, old friend," Ah-Puch said. "Show me my prize."

"Quit calling him *friend*," I blurted out.

Hondo growled, "A snake is always a snake."

Ignoring my uncle (and maybe the terrible truth), Ren tugged on Ah-Puch's sleeve. "Don't let the bat bully you, A.P."

Ah-Puch inched toward his "old friend." "Don't be fools, Ren and Zane," he said. "The second those bats arrived in Cabo, I knew I had a real chance at freedom and could finally be done with both of you."

"No!" Ren's eyes filled with tears. "After everything...I... we helped you and—" Her voice cut off in a choked sob.

Ah-Puch's face tightened with impatience. "Did you really think we stood a chance to save these wretched godborns *and* Hurakan?" he said. "I knew it was a doomed effort from the start, so when you told me bats had come for you, Ren, I put two and two together. But it wasn't until Zotz's blood gift made its way to me that I was sure of what I had to do." He looked down at his weathered hands. "Don't you see? This is about me, and I *always* choose the winning team."

Searing heat gripped my bones. "Then *you* can rot in your inferno! I'll never save you now. Never."

Camazotz smiled as Ah-Puch kneeled in front of him, his head bent like some kind of beggar. "I humbly ask to join your cause, and I commit my loyalty and service for all eternity."

"A.P.!" Ren screamed.

"You delivered my second most valuable asset," Zotz said to Ah-Puch. "So, I accept your offer. I need a brilliant godly mind to help keep those insufferable and impetuous twins in line. And their mother?" He sighed. "Don't even get me started on her demands. Now we can be kings together. I grant your request to trade your bones for glory."

"No!" I shouted at Camazotz. "Only I can give him back his power." Did he say "second most valuable asset"? What was the first?

Ah-Puch's face was so tense I thought it might crack if he so much as flinched. "There is going to be a new world order, Zane," he said, getting to his feet weakly. "And the blood sacrifices made will be great enough to raise me from the inferno. Don't you see? I don't need you anymore."

One of the godborns muttered, "Why did you ever trust this guy?"

Rosie growled and released a firestorm at the huge bat. Camazotz threw his wings up, instantly extinguishing the fire. "Tell your dog to settle down," he said to me. "Does she not know who I am, what I am capable of? I am the great bat god. I am the night."

Oh, geez. Now he was *quoting* Batman?

Hondo shifted his feet into a warrior stance, white-knuckling the crowbar now in his hands. Where was Brooks? Had he hidden her somewhere? Had she flown away? "Aren't you gods sick of wanting to end the world?" he asked. "Like, come on, dudes. Come up with a more original plan already."

"Who said anything about ending the world?" Camazotz asked. "Been there, done that. So boring and unimaginative. Now, be good little thugs and get back into your cages. Or do we have to drag you kicking and screaming?"

"If you don't want to end the world, then what do you want?" I asked. It wasn't to make me their soldier, and it wasn't to sacrifice me to the Maya gods. . . . I thought about what the twins had said, *Why would we* ever *honor the Maya gods with your blood or anyone's? No, you're even more valuable than that.*

Ren leaned against me, trembling. *He isn't going to let us go,* she said. *We have to fight this monster.*

Monster. The way the word bounced off my mind reminded me of something Ah-Puch had said back at the Beast when he told us about Ahuitzotl. *So, someone found a way to bring back the monsters. . . .* The plan unfolded in my mind and it began to make perfect, sick sense. *I get it!* I communicated to Ren. *Jordan and Bird want revenge, a new order that they can rule over.*

We already know that, Ren said.

They want to bring back the monsters.

Ren gasped, squeezing my hand so tight I was sure the blood stopped flowing. *Not just the monsters, Zane.*

My stomach writhed as the realization hit me. *You're right! The twins told me they would never waste my blood or anyone's on the Maya gods but. . . crap!*

If the blood sacrifice is enough to raise Ah-Puch, then . . .

Ren dropped my hand and blurted to Zotz, "You want to sacrifice us to wake up the Mexica gods?"

Camazotz raised an eyebrow and laughed, which sounded more like he was gargling acid.

"Your blood is valuable," Camazotz said to Ren, "but it isn't *that* valuable. Or at least not enough to set off our chain reaction. You see, first we need to awaken a Mexica god of our choosing. Then. . ." He frowned. "You. . . none of you little thugs are enough."

I bet they wanted to wake up that earth goddess Ixtab told me about. The devourer who still had followers. What was her name? Tlaltecuhtli.

Then another thought occurred to me. If *we* weren't enough to awaken a Mexica goddess, who. . . ?

The shock nearly toppled me over. "But the blood of a *god* is enough," I said. Hurakan's execution wasn't an execution at all—it was a *sacrifice* to raise the first Mexica god!

Camazotz tilted his head and studied me. I couldn't even look at Ah-Puch, but I could feel his eyes burning a hole in my chest. I stepped closer to the giant bat. Rosie was right behind me, dripping puddles of foam into the dirt. "If we're going to die," I said, "at least tell us what our deaths are for, what they mean."

"First the father's blood," Ah-Puch said. "Then the next-best thing: his claimed son's."

"Ah-Puch . . ." Camazotz's tone was one of warning.

"The boy should know what his sacrifice is for," Ah-Puch said. "Once we awaken the greatest of the Mexica deities, something only the blood of another god can do, we will use your heart, Zane, to feed and strengthen her. Only then can we begin the ritual to rouse the others." His cowardly eyes roved over the godborns. "And a newly risen army of gods and monsters nourished on the blood of innocents is more powerful than you can possibly imagine."

Gasps and sobs sounded behind me.

"But why?" Ren cried.

Camazotz didn't hesitate. "I will never be powerless again. I will be the new king, and the Maya gods will know my fury."

The tips of my fingers ignited into blue flames. Streaks of red colored my vision as I glared at Ah-Puch. "I knew I could never trust you."

"Then why did you?"

"Just for fun," the bat god interrupted, "why don't I give you all a demonstration of the power of sangre?" Camazotz spread his wings again, showing the hungry mouths. Three mouse-size bats slithered out of one of the mouths. Ah-Puch grabbed them in one hand, snapped their necks, and turned his back to us as he drank their blood.

A few groans and moans echoed across the junkyard.

Someone barfed behind me. Ah-Puch turned slowly. Like before, he stood taller and stronger. His eyes flashed silver, zeroing in on Rosie. But he still wasn't a full god. Not yet.

"I'd rather die fighting," Hondo said in a low voice to me.

"Me too," one of the godborns said. Another voice rose up, then another and another.

"Fight."

"Fight."

"Fight."

"Come now." Camazotz shook his head. "You cannot win. If you resist, we will hurt you. Bones can be broken without bringing about death. Without precious blood being spilled. You will suffer in your cages, broken and beaten, until the time comes to feed your hearts to the gods. Is that what you want?"

My gut clenched. So this was the end. It had all come down to this terrible moment. I glanced at Hondo. He blinked and tipped his head down. If he could speak to me telepathically, I knew he would be saying, *Give Batman a smackdown he'll never forget, kid.*

I tugged on Rosie's neck and with a deep breath shouted, "DEAD!"

Rosie launched herself at the bat god. Teeth flashed. Claws sliced. Fire exploded. Camazotz bolted into the sky out of Rosie's reach. His bats zipped from the trees and came at us in a whirlwind of death, splitting off and circling us from different directions.

Hondo whirled, did a backflip, and kicked a few of the bloodsucking beasts in midair before landing. He punched with one hand and jabbed his crowbar with another. The guy was a ninja, but his blows dizzied them at best. I had never been more grateful for Itzel's armored clothing than at that moment.

The godborns ran and ducked for cover behind an old truck. Wrenches, a pair of motorcycle handlebars, side mirrors, and all sorts of junk came hurtling out of the truck bed. A valiant effort, but, um, we were dealing with a bat god from hell?

Even in all the commotion, I looked around for Ah-Puch. Where was he? Too weak and cowardly to fight?

Ren's fingers danced in the air like she was playing an invisible piano. Shadows rose up and wrapped themselves around her as she hurried over to join the godborns behind the truck. At the same time, Rosie propelled herself into the air, caught a handful of the bats in her mouth, snapped them in half, and dropped them to the ground, where they squirmed. Faster than thought, I shot a river of fire from my hands, incinerating a trail of the monsters to keep them away from the godborns.

Kee-eeeee-ar!

My heart stopped. I looked up and saw Brooks attacking a few bats in the air. Even in her small hawk form, she was fierce.

Hondo swung his crowbar mightily, but he was losing. The bats attacked him claws-first, tearing at his cheeks and neck. "No!" I shouted as I drop-rolled, coming up on my knees with my arms extended. Thick ropes of smoke trailed from my eyes and hands, speeding toward my uncle, wrapping around him like a net that the bats couldn't penetrate.

Camazotz returned, zooming straight for me. He clutched something in his claws.

My stomach dropped.

"Brooks!" I screamed, holding back the fire that wanted to burn through Zotz's heart.

Hondo stumbled back, raising his crowbar. The smoke net was beginning to vanish.

"Give her back NOW!" I growled.

Camazotz landed in front of me and shifted Brooks to his humanish hands. The minion bats ceased their attack, hovering in the air over their god. "I will kill your friends one by one," he said, "until you give up this wasted effort and accept your fate."

"You can't kill us," I cried. "You need us!"

"I don't need your uncle. And I certainly don't need this half nawal." Brooks the hawk struggled against him. "One wrong move and her heart is my dinner."

I stared into his eyes, looking for some sign of weakness. Anything to give us a glimmer of hope. But they were completely vacant.

Then, in a whirl of shadow and dust, Ah-Puch surfaced and blindsided the bat god with a massive shard of glass, driving it deep into the bat's ribs and slicing upward with a nauseating *ripppppp*.

"Run!" Ah-Puch shouted just as a gateway opened a few feet away.

Clutching his gushing side, Camazotz fell to the ground, shrieking. The bats cried and raced toward him, melting into his flesh as Brooks tumbled out of his grasp. Hondo snatched her up, tucking her between his arms before he took off running toward the gateway with the godborns and Ren.

Rosie was there in a flash, and I jumped onto her back, ready to race toward the gateway.

Strengthened by his bats, Camazotz was able to get to his feet. "You chose wrong this time, Ah-Puch." His eyes flashed triumph as he leaped at the god of death, fangs bared. His claws slashed, ripping Ah-Puch like paper. Thick blood spilled onto the dirt.

I leaped off Rosie and lunged for Ah-Puch. His body collapsed like an empty sack in my arms. Fire ignited inside of me. Smoke curled from my mouth and nose.

"One shot of fire from you and my bats will kill another needless life," Camazotz warned. His chest heaved.

"NO!" Ren broke off from the others and ran back to us.

Camazotz spun toward her and smiled viciously. "Fine. Another kill it is." He moved like a flash of liquid shadow. In the space of two blinks, he had Ren ensnared in his wings, and all I could see were her red boots kicking at the bat god's hairy legs.

Ah-Puch's bleeding chest was still. He wasn't breathing. I felt like I had just walked off a cliff and was spinning down, down, down. Forever falling toward nothing, no earth to crush my bones and end this misery.

Camazotz sniffed the air. "Well, well, what do we have here? Mexica *and* Maya blood?" His laugh reverberated across the corroded world. "You will make an excellent sacrifice," he said to Ren.

I hated to admit it, but I didn't see a way out, a way to beat this guy. He was too powerful.

I glanced up. The gateway had closed. Of course it had—Ah-Puch was dead, and without his power to keep it open . . . Hondo and the godborns stood waiting, looking stunned. Why hadn't they left when they had the chance?

"Such a shame." Camazotz sighed. "Ah-Puch would have been such a formidable addition to my new world."

Then it came to me—my last resort. Quickly, I ripped the jade off my neck and placed it in Ah-Puch's limp hand. With a deep, shaky breath, I said, "I give you back your life as a god. Don't make me regret this."

42

••
••

Instantly, darkness swallowed the world. The ground shuddered. And then came ringing silence, like the aftermath of an explosion right next to my ear.

I peered through the dark. Ah-Puch's borrowed and broken body vanished in a trail of silvery dust. And in its place, raw god power appeared in a perfect human form. He wore his signature black suit. His face was a mask of anger and death. Around his neck was a yellow serpent with glowing green eyes and black stripes that seemed to breathe.

I stumbled back. Camazotz crouched and balanced on the balls of his feet, wearing a wicked smile. He had Ren by the throat. She must have been in one of her trances, because her eyes were glazed over.

"You had me fooled, old friend," said the bat. "I truly admire your deception. But what was it for? These worthless thugs?"

Ah-Puch's jaw tensed as he glanced around casually, like he was sizing up the place. "Let the girl go and I may not make this supremely painful."

"Where would be the fun in that?" Camazotz squeezed Ren's neck tighter.

I shot fire bullets from my hands, aiming precisely for the guy's eyes. His bat wings didn't deflect them fast enough this time. He screamed, shook his head, and looked back at us with empty, scorched sockets. "I don't need eyes when I can smell you," he hissed.

Ah-Puch placed his hand on my arm. *I can only buy you minutes. Go now!* he said.

A shimmering light caught my attention—Ah-Puch had reopened the gateway near the crane. With a mere flick of his wrist, he sent the entire army of bats tumbling into the night sky.

"I'm not leaving without Ren!" I said.

Camazotz let out a twisted laugh. His eye sockets smoked, and the smell of burning flesh rose in the air, turning my stomach. "You'll never save Hurakan in time! And in the end, your blood *will* be mine."

The godborns, Hondo (with Brooks still in hand), and Rosie waited at the portal.

"Get out of here!" I yelled to them.

"Enough talk," Ah-Puch said flatly. At the same moment, his snake split into hundreds and they shot forward, taking Camazotz by surprise. They ripped Ren from his grasp and wrapped themselves around her protectively. As one large serpentine form made of many smaller ones, they slithered her over to the gateway before vanishing into yellow smoke.

The bat god released a terrifying screech. His wings grew wider and his fangs longer as he charged at me.

"Go!" Ah-Puch yelled. He shot a gust of wind beneath my feet that whisked me toward the gateway and out of Camazotz's claws.

Hondo stood at the gateway's edge, waiting for me as the

last of the godborns stepped inside. Rosie howled as if to say *Hurry it up!*

I balanced easily on the wind, like I was riding a surfboard in raging waters. Hondo went through, then Rosie, then me. I glanced over my shoulder just as the wrecking yard exploded into shrieks and fury and flames.

We landed on a dirt road in the middle of a dense jungle. Drums boomed in the distance. The godborns stared at me blankly. Breathless, I spun to face Hondo. Brooks the hawk was still cradled in his arms. I stroked the top of her head and my gut clenched. Would she ever return to human form? Was Camazotz right? Would I be too late to save my dad?

The execution was scheduled for midnight, but I had no idea what time it was. "Does anyone have a watch or a cell or—?"

Ren said, "It's eleven twenty-seven p.m."

"How do you know? You're not even wearing a watch."

Ren glanced around at the shadowed faces and shrugged. "I have a crazy precise sense of time."

At that moment, I had an inkling of who her mom was. But this wasn't the moment to go into it. If she was right, I only had thirty-three minutes to stop the execution and get back to the underworld before I died permanently.

I tugged the gateway map out of my back pocket, hoping it might tell me something about how close we were, or if there was another gateway that might get us to the pyramid faster.

"That was a bold move," Hondo said, "raising your enemy from the d—" He stopped himself, looking at Rosie.

Pure shock buzzed through me. Had the god of death just saved our lives?

The map blinked all haywire-like, making it impossible to read.

Brooks blinked. Her glowing eyes, golden like a cat's, studied me like she recognized who I was. For a hopeful second, I thought she might shift and yell at me, or slug my arm. Instead, she wriggled out of Hondo's grasp, snatched the map out of my hands, and took off into the night sky.

My lungs caved in as I watched her go, not knowing if I would ever see her again.

"Zane, are you okay?" Ren asked.

It took a moment for me to catch my breath. I shook my head, then changed it to a nod so she wouldn't worry. "Ah-Puch said he could only buy me a few minutes," I said. "We need to get moving."

The godborns' panicked voices spilled across the dark:

"Where are we?"

"That bat god was twisted."

"Did you see his fangs?"

"That *other* dude was Ah-Puch?"

"Can we go home now?"

"I'm getting the hell out of here." I was pretty sure that was Marco.

There was a chorus of huddled whispers and hushed words among the godborns as Hondo started to explain everything to them. I had just climbed onto Rosie's back, when Ren tugged my arm.

"Ah-Puch—you gave him the jade," she cried. "He saved us."

There wasn't time to talk. I had to stop the execution, or Hurakan would die and the sobrenaturals' magic would be gone forever. "I have to go. Now."

She wiped her tears and pulled herself together. Red splotches spread across her cheeks. "I'm coming."

Smoke curled from Rosie's snout as she lowered herself for Ren to climb on. I knew it wouldn't do any good to argue.

"We're coming, too," Marco said, leading the pack. What was it with this kid and a death wish?

"It's too dangerous," I argued.

"Danger?" Serena said. "Did you see what we've been through? Caged, tormented by that . . . that bat god, and those awful—"

"Twins," Louie finished her thought.

"We deserve to know who we belong to," the redheaded girl said to me as the others nodded in the shadows.

Marco crossed his arms. "Even if they want to kill us."

They'd waited at the gateway when they could have escaped, and they'd risked their lives to see this through. It wasn't up to me to tell them what they could and couldn't do. Gritting my teeth, I said, "Fine. Just hang back. Once I give the signal, you can face the gods yourselves." Then I made eye contact with Marco. "Can you do that without trying to get killed?"

"Probably."

"And by the way . . ." I said, looking across their faces. "Thanks."

Hondo patted my leg and glanced up. He looked like he was about to say something mushy like *I love you*.

"Shoot to kill," he said.

Okay, maybe not.

Rosie took off toward the sound of the drums as the others followed in our tracks. And all I kept thinking was *I hope Ren's right about the time and I'm not too late.*

43

••
•••

The dark trees passed by in a blur as Rosie sped stealthily over the earth. My palms were sweating as I tried to keep hold of her thick neck, but more than anything, I felt like my heart had tumbled right out of my chest half a mile back. Brooks hadn't come with us.

A woman's hard-boiled voice boomed through a loudspeaker, echoing through the trees. Rosie slowed her pace cautiously as we drew closer.

"Such a deliciousss roasssting," she sang. "Who knew the almighty, sanctimonious, intense, storm-provoking Hurakan was actually a fun dude to have around?"

The crowd erupted in laughter. A few people heckled, calling out, "He's a bore. Let the god die!"

Though I was annoyed by the comments, relief flooded my body. Hurakan hadn't been executed yet!

Rosie's ears twitched as she flew toward a row of big, colorful tents that blocked our view of the commotion beyond. Only the top of the pyramid was visible. Rosie cut through a narrow gap and we landed on a grassy plaza filled with giants, demons, aluxes, regular-looking humans, and other creatures I had never seen before. Dozens of flickering blue-white globes shimmered in midair. Some people were decked out in tuxes and gowns while others wore cutoff jean shorts and baseball caps. The scents of smoked meats and popcorn filled the air, and for half a second, I felt like I was at the state fair back in New Mexico. Inside the tents, vendors sold Hurakan bobbleheads, refrigerator magnets, coffee mugs, and T-shirts with sayings like NACHO REGULAR GOD.

Ren tugged on the back of my shirt and whispered, "What now?"

We were about a hundred yards from the pyramid steps. The structure looked like a Lego-stacked mountain with rounded edges and a dangerously steep hundred-foot incline. At the very top was a temple on a platform, and that's where the action was taking place. But there was no way to see it from where we were, which was why big screens had been set up at the far end of the field. I guess the gods wanted everyone to witness the grisly details of Hurakan's death up close and personal. I felt sick.

The screens blinked awake. Seven figures emerged from the stone doorway at the top of the pyramid, each wearing a dark robe or a cape. A sudden silence fell over the place like the flu as everyone waited anxiously.

One by one I identified the loser gods for Ren telepathically: *The first guy is Kukuulkaan, god of the sea, feathered serpent (and traitor). You know Ixtab (deceiver). The ballerina-looking one is Ixkakaw, goddess of chocolate (and manipulator). The guy in the leather robe? That's Nakon, god of war (and fighter). The next dude is Alom, god of the sky (judge) and . . . I don't know those last two. . . . Wait!*

What?!

That last guy ... the one whose hair sparkles?

The stocky one with the big nose?

The tall, skinny one in the purple silk robe! That's Itzamna, the writing magician/dragon-god dude I told you about.

I bet that's not his official title.

What was *he* doing here? Since when was he on the council?

The woman's voice carried over the PA system: "Please remember to turn off all cell phones. Photography is strictly prohibited during the event. Any illegal filming or rebroadcasting will result in slow dismemberment."

Everyone held their breath, as if waiting for the greatest rock star of all time to be introduced. I wondered if the gods were always so dramatic. Probably.

The woman's voice echoed across the field again. "I give you the one, the only ..." She paused—for effect, no doubt. "The formidable king, the master of all, the god of rain—Chaac!"

The crowd went crazy, cheering, whistling, and stomping their feet. The earth vibrated.

The pudgy guy stepped onto the platform. He wore a pale blue robe that glistened like moonlit rain. "We glorious gods grace you with our presence for a solemn affair." His voice carried like he was speaking through a microphone. "To say good-bye to a god of great feats, of both creation and destruction. We say farewell to a god who will be remembered as a legend."

Applause and chants of "Chaac! Chaac! Chaac!" were heard.

He held up his beefy hands to quiet the crowd. "Do not

dare applaud again until I give you permission. Do you understand?" Thunder cracked across the sky like a whip, a warning from the rain god.

There was immediate silence.

"And why must we kill one of our own?" he said. "He broke the Sacred Oath. He fathered a threat to our way of life, a threat we had to kill. You all remember Zane Obispo."

My heart stalled at the mention of my name. Man, I was *so* glad for the death magic hiding me from the gods.

"He, too, served as an example," Chaac said. "Like father, like son." He turned his gaze to the sky with a pleading expression.

Is he trying out for a telenovela? Ren said.

Do you see my dad or the twins?

She shook her head as Chaac went on.

"And, with the awesome responsibilities we all carry, we cannot have gods in our ranks who break the bonds of trust and brotherhood."

Ixtab cleared her throat.

"And *sisterhood*," Chaac corrected himself with a barely there eye roll.

"So let this be a warning to everyone here. When you defy the gods—even if you are a deity yourself—you will pay the price. If you do not honor us, pray to us, make sacrifices to us, we will punish you."

Wow! This guy had a seriously huge ego, and he was starting to get on my nerves. My gaze bounced around the place as I semi-listened to him thunder on about how great he and the other gods were. That's when I spotted a familiar eye (yes, just one) staring at me from a few feet away.

Jazz!

My giant friend. His eye grew three sizes too big and he started to come over, but I shook my head and pressed a finger to my lips. He stared at Ren, then looked around. I knew he was searching for Brooks, and my heart split a hundred different ways. I didn't know where she was.

Ren pointed. *Look.*

On the screen, I watched as two figures appeared in a column of mist on the pyramid's platform. They wore gold jaguar masks with red-feather headdresses.

It's the twins, Ren said.

How do you know? I asked.

For the ceremony to mean anything, they have to do the deed themselves, to make sure it's a sacrifice and not an execution.

Hurakan rose up from the platform like there was a secret mechanical trap door. He was chained upright on a wooden wall, and he wore only a loincloth. His entire body, including his face, was painted blue. I hate to say this, but my dad looked kinda like a Smurf. Even so, he held his head high and his eyes glistened with the defiance of a thousand suns.

What's the plan? Ren said. *There's at least a couple hundred feet from here to the pyramid, and all those stairs? How will we ever reach Hurakan without the gods chopping off our heads?*

You think you can manage some shadows? I said.

I'll try. Ren put her arms around my waist. *No, I take that back. I can. I can do this. It's why I'm here. This is the destiny my abuelo told me about, I know it. Just let your power flow into me and think about shadows instead of fire. Got it?*

Great. Now I was totally going to think about fire.

Ren borrowed a shadow from a dark corner of the Turkey on a Stick booth. A second later, the sombra wrapped itself around us like a thick blanket.

I'll hold it as long as I can. Even telepathically, her voice held a tremor that made me nervous.

"Let us begin," Chaac said, stepping back without so much as a glance at my dad. I bet this guy was the school bully when he was a kid. I already hated him.

Rosie walked slowly at first so no one would notice a big misshapen shadow gliding through the blood-hungry crowd. She maneuvered like a lion on the hunt, measured and alert, careful not to bump into people. *If only she could teleport with us on her back,* I thought, but I guessed there were limitations even to what hellhounds could do. I tried to steady my breathing, but the shadow was thick and heavy, and it felt like trying to inhale and exhale under a wool blanket.

As we moved past Jazz, he stepped aside like he felt our presence. With a single stride, he took the lead and marched ahead, making a wider path for us.

"Hey!" someone called. "Giants in the back. You'll block the view."

"How about I shove a brick up your nose?" Jazz said, punching his fist into his palm. No one argued. And then I saw what his strategy was. His more-than-seven-foot frame looked like *it* was casting the shadow.

On the screens, Chaac asked Hurakan, "Do you have any last words?"

Hurakan stared straight ahead, his face unmoving.

Faster, Rosie!

A low hum rose from the crowd and my heart hammered so hard my bones shook.

"No words?" Chaac said.

Kukuulkaan's eyes shifted like he was looking for someone in the crowd, but who? And Ixtab? She stared at her nails with a slight frown, as if she didn't like the color anymore. I wanted to scream, but from this distance, it was too risky. I had to be close enough to make the gods listen to me. Any wrong move now would for sure equal instant death and likely force the twins' hand too early.

We were only a few feet from the bottom of the pyramid stairs when smoke began to trail from Rosie's nose and rise past the shadow into the air.

"Kill Hurakan!" someone shouted.

Chaac snorted. "Are you ready to see *a dead god*?"

Rosie stiffened. "No, Rosie," I said. "Don't listen. It's just a word." But it was too late. She'd heard the command. She shot fire from her mouth and eyes, instantly incinerating the center screen.

Ren's shadow collapsed.

The crowd screamed.

"STEAK!" I shouted.

Of course, Rosie didn't obey. I extended both hands toward the fire my hellhound was still streaming and drew it to me. The force of the heat's impact flung me and Ren off Rosie's back. My whole body smoked like a chargrilled chicken breast, but it didn't burn, and Ren's clothing protected her.

Jazz quickly lifted Ren and put her on his shoulders, out of the crowd's reach. Then he turned to me. "Man, kid. Do you always have to get into so much trouble?" He shook his head. "Why are you just standing there? Hustle!"

Seeing that the immediate danger was over, people began shouting at me.

"Spy!"

"Traitor!"

I jumped onto Rosie's back, and she bolted up the stone stairs. I turned to see Jazz with his hands high in the air, shouting, "Folks! It's all part of the show. Don't you watch reality TV?"

"That's the girl from the news!" someone screamed.

News? Then I remembered the helicopter cameraperson back in Cabo, and my heart did a backflip. Who else had seen us on the news? Did that mean the gods knew I was alive? No, they would have come for my head—and Ixtab's—by now. I bet they only watched Netflix.

A dense fog rolled in so fast I barely had time to see the last of the crowd get swallowed up by it. Everything fell silent, as if the mob had disappeared. Jazz (with Ren still on his shoulders) rushed up the steps behind me, running from the fog headed our way.

"¡Ándale, Rosie!" I cried.

My hellhound bolted up the steps three at a time, but the mist was faster. It curled all around us. Alien-looking hands with long, spindly fingers grew out of the fog, reaching for us, shoving us so hard that Rosie tripped, and I tumbled off her back, scraping the side of my face against the stone. A shroud of gray tightened around me.

"Rosie!"

The only answer was silence.

"You cannot win, you little fool," a woman's voice said.

I pressed on up the stairs, crawling on all fours because it was faster than trying to get to the top with my bum leg. Why weren't the gods doing anything? Didn't they notice the fog? Or that the crowd had disappeared behind it? Hadn't they wanted a public execution?

The woman laughed. "You'll never make it in time."

I spun onto my back and shot a river of fire into the air toward the voice. "Hey!" I screamed, hoping the gods could hear me. "It's me, Zane Obispo. You're being tricked! Stop!"

"How about I let you watch?" The woman laughed.

Bird's dreaded words echoed down the stairs. "We offer you the blood and heart of the god of storm, fire, and wind—the great Hurakan!"

I whipped around and looked up. The fog thinned.

Jordan raised the ax. It was pointed right at my dad's neck.

"NO!" I screamed.

The ax came down with an unbearable blow.

44

••

••••

Instantly, the world went black, so black even I couldn't see through its darkness. My heart pounded *no-no, no-no.*

Shock rippled through me.

This wasn't happening. This wasn't happening.

Is that all you have? Itzamna's voice rammed against my skull. *Not very hero-like.*

That did it. Every cell in my body exploded with rage. I felt a burst of blinding power. My blood flowed like hot lava, my lungs seized, my muscles contracted. My storm runner leg jolted awake.

I raced through the dark and up the steps with lightning speed.

Just as I reached the platform, the darkness vanished. I heard a piercing cry. Brooks? I saw her glowing eyes first, cutting through the fog like twin candles. She dove straight for the twins, ripping off their masks with a single bloody swipe.

Jordan and Bird stumbled back, looking stunned. Then a thicker blanket of mist wrapped around them, making it impossible to see them.

Brooks screeched.

Forget the hawk, the woman's voice said. *Run!*

Since the fog blocked the gods, I have no idea what they were doing at that moment—probably standing around taking a vote about what to do. Someone really should write a letter of complaint about their lack of leadership.

Panic gripped me. Hurakan. Where was Hurakan? I nearly slipped on a pool of blood. The world slanted. I hate to be so morbid, but I looked around for his severed head. Stupid mist! I couldn't see anything. I fell to my knees and groped through the haze. I stumbled on the ax. And Hurakan's chains, but they were empty. What the heck?

The woman's voice drew closer, like she was right behind me, but when I spun, there was nothing. Then the mist parted enough for me to see the twins glaring at me. Long fangs protruded from their foaming mouths and . . . I blinked. Had they sprouted wings? Bat wings?

"Hurry, boys," the woman warned. "The mist will only blind the gods for so long."

"We're going to kill him first, Mother!" Jordan screamed.

Bird stretched his wings. His human arms were extended underneath them, but instead of hands, he had scaly black claws. "You're going to pay, Obispo."

"Think of the bigger plan, you fools!" the woman, who I now knew was Ixkik', shouted.

The twin bats launched into the sky, splitting off in opposite directions and disappearing into the fog. A second later, they emerged again, looking bigger, stronger, and more dangerous. The only recognizable part of them now was their faces—the rest of their humanness had been consumed by their bat selves. I went after them, shooting dozens of fire bullets from my hands and nailing them in the chest, but it didn't stop their rage. Or their momentum.

My visibility was three feet at best, which put me at a serious disadvantage. It was impossible to know where I stood on the platform and how close to the edge I was.

Just then, Rosie appeared by my side, blue flames exploding from her mouth as Jordan swept down with ferocious speed, slicing my neck with a razor-sharp claw.

I lost my balance and staggered back, gripping the wound. Rosie howled.

But her warning was too late. I stumbled over the side of the pyramid. My arms shot out to catch myself, but I was already in free fall, tumbling through the misty air as Jordan and Bird shrieked in celebration above.

The terror of the moment gripped me so hard, I almost passed out. Instead . . .

I landed clumsily on a feathered surface. As I rolled to the edge, it lifted, catching me before I fell off the side of . . . Brooks. She was in grande hawk form. My mind spun, coming to the realization that the only way she could be back to her all-powerful nawal self was if the flame had been fed. That meant Hurakan had to be alive. But how?

Brooks!

God, Obispo. You really are a pain. Worse than a pain, and when this is all over . . .

I had never been so happy to be insulted in my whole life.

I missed you, too.

And then I realized she was flying away from the pyramid. "Wait! We have to go back."

There's a gateway nearby and you only have thirteen minutes to get to the underworld, Zane, before you're permanently dead. And if you don't mind, I like you better alive.

Is that why she had seized the map? To find a way back to the underworld? To save me?

Brooks . . . we still have time. Let's finish this. We won't get the chance again.

No! The gods are up there, and so are those vile . . . She hesitated, then shifted direction back toward the platform. *You're right. I only need two minutes to rip off the twins' faces.*

I clung to her feathery neck as we broke through the thick fog. *Since when are the twins bats?*

In exchange for Zotz's help and protection, they agreed to become part of his nasty, hairy army.

How do you know?

You learn a lot when you're a prisoner.

Guilt punched a hole in my chest. *I'm sorry.*

Through the haze, four glowing yellow eyes zoomed toward us—the twins' bat selves taking shape as they drew nearer. Brooks didn't pull up—she didn't even hesitate, just flew straight for them.

I hurled fireballs in their direction. Brooks's screech echoed through the haze. The twins did a one-eighty back to the platform. Brooks pursued. She was bigger and faster than they were. And let's be honest—fiercer.

But why were they fleeing, when just two seconds ago they wanted to kill me?

We landed on the platform. The thick mist wrapped cold arms around us. Then slowly, as if by design, it parted enough for us to see the backs of Jordan and Bird, once again in full human form, at the side edge of the pyramid. They half spun to face me, their eyes filled with hate and defiance.

Why were they just standing there?

Brooks jerked forward, but something was holding her back. *I can't move through this mist,* she said.

I shot ribbons of flame, but the mist remained strong.

I kept my gaze on Jordan and Bird. "Too afraid to face us?" I shouted.

"Too many gods here for our liking." Bird sneered. "Soon enough."

Then they smiled and jumped off the edge.

I heard Ixkik' whisper in my ear, so close I was sure she was standing right next to me. "Someday, when you least expect it, you'll pay with your blood for this. My sons will show no mercy. Nor will I." And then she was gone.

The air cleared instantly.

A commotion of godly voices and growls rose up behind us.

It's a trap! Brooks shouted.

"Stop him!" someone shouted. "Stop Zane!" It sounded a whole lot like Nakon.

Really? Stop *me*? How about the loser twins who had duped the gods yet again?

Just as Brooks took off with me still on board, a giant net

dropped out of nowhere, stopping us in our tracks. I tried to incinerate the thing, but the stupid nonflammable trap only tightened around us more. Brooks flapped her wings wildly, to no avail. She shifted into human form.

Together we turned and saw some seriously angry gods glaring at us.

I remembered what Fausto had said about the death magic making me undetectable to the gods unless I walked right up to them.

I'd planned for this moment, what I was going to say, how I was going to get them to hear me out. It was pretty masterful. It went something like this:

"You guys suck!"

Okay, that wasn't the plan. But let's be real. For all-powerful beings, they do tend to fail miserably. How could they have let Jordan and Bird escape from prison? And again, tonight, when the twins were right under their stupid noses?

I glanced down the pyramid steps. The crowd stirred restlessly, like they had no idea what was happening.

Nakon tugged off his robe (he had on his cliché leather biker outfit underneath). "I told you all this was a bad strategy, a bad plan. Bad outfits. Bad everything."

Chaac shook his head with disgust. "You've made us look like fools, boy."

"Let's all remain calm, shall we?" Itzamna said. "After the fog lifted, I ran a feedback loop on the screens so no one saw what really happened. They all still think they're waiting for an execution."

"Then let's give them one," Ixkakaw said, looking at me

with a catlike sneer. I was definitely going to give up chocolate. Forever.

Struggling against the net, I said, "Before you kill me, you should listen to what I have to say...."

"Or you're all going to die," Brooks added.

"Are you threatening us?" Alom said.

Brooks looked like she was about to nod yes when I grabbed her hand and said, *We need to be calm. No fights with the gods.*

Since when?

But I didn't answer, because Nakon had narrowed his already beady eyes and stepped closer. I could tell something was dawning on him. "If you're alive, that means..." He turned to glare at Ixtab.

"I escaped Xib'alb'a!" I shouted. "I'm just a ghost...still dead." I pointed to my face. "See?"

"Who gave you this death magic?" Chaac asked.

Ixtab looked at her watch and smirked. "Six minutes," she muttered casually like those minutes weren't the last of my life.

I didn't have much time to convince the gods to let me go, tell them about the evil plan, find Hurakan, and... "Where's my dad?" I demanded.

The gods looked at each other like they were only now noticing he was missing. A flurry of accusations started: "I thought you had him." "You were supposed to be watching him." "You idiot!"

"Should have been paying attention," Brooks muttered in a singsong voice.

Ixtab raised her hands and stepped next to me. She winked before turning to face the gods. She tilted her eyes to Nakon and, with a single touch, vanished the net. "Zane didn't escape Xib'alb'a," she said. "Because he didn't die all those months ago in the Old World." Her red painted lips parted into a smile, and if I didn't know any better, I'd think she had been waiting for this moment for a long time. "I shielded him," she continued. "I defied you all. And do you want to know why? How? Because you have become complacent, lazy, so absorbed with yourselves you cannot see the truth. You cannot see what's coming."

Kukuulkaan spoke for the first time. "She speaks the truth. I helped her."

"Just hear me out," I said. "Camazotz is plotting with the twins, and Ixkik'—"

The gods inched back, eyes wide, like they were seeing ghosts or . . . I don't know—whatever would scare all-powerful Maya gods.

I whirled around to see Jazz, Ren, Hondo, and Rosie.

But that wasn't what had the gods so freaked. It was the godborns who stood behind them.

And I could tell by the gods' shocked faces that they recognized their own kids. Well, not Itzamna. He just stood back and watched like he was thoroughly entertained by all of this. Ixtab's eyes roved over the group, and a look of utter sadness crossed her face. I could tell she was looking for someone who wasn't there.

"Did you say Camazotz?" Nakon asked with disgust, like he couldn't believe he had to talk to me.

But before I could answer, a familiar voice rang out.

"Well, well, well . . ." Ah-Puch said. "I don't think I've ever seen such astonishment, such speechless bewilderment. Have you, my friend?"

We all looked up to see him standing on top of the temple with my dad. I never thought I would ever in a million years say this, but boy, was I happy to see the god of death alive.

"A.P.!" Ren squealed.

I was even gladder to see Hurakan next to him, clearly restored to his godly strength, but not nearly as formally dressed as Ah-Puch, who was in his expensive custom-tailored suit. My dad wore a pair of jeans and a navy shirt with a gray collarless blazer.

A smile tugged at my mouth. Then Hurakan's eyes found mine, and for a split second, I thought he might smile, too. He didn't, and there was no *Hey, son, thanks for everything. You're a true warrior.* Instead, he said, "Today is the day of reckoning."

Chaac cast a bolt of lightning right above Ah-Puch's head. But Ah-Puch only sighed and said, "Thought you'd gotten rid of me? Sorry to disappoint."

"Please, let's be civil," Itzamna said. "Hurakan is right. Everyone here is guilty of breaking the Sacred Oath. Well, not me. I haven't fathered any human children."

Rolling her eyes, Ixtab said, "The boy has minutes to live and a story to tell, and if you want to hear it, I suggest you follow me to hell."

45

..

—

With two minutes to spare, Ixtab opened a gateway to the underworld so I could live long enough to tell probably the greatest Maya tale of all time. (That is not hyperbole, Itzamna!)

Everyone traveled through the gateway. Except Jazz, who politely said, "Hell? Thanks, but no thanks. See you on the other side." The minute we stepped into Xib'alb'a, I felt a rush of cool air in my lungs and a warming under my skin. I looked down at my hands, and they were back to normal, no more thin-skinned, veiny hands. The death magic was gone.

Who knew going to hell could have such a rejuvenating effect?

We ended up in a massive conference room with carved stone beams, animal-skin rugs, chandeliers made of bones, and a long table with a mirrored top that ran the length of the space. My friends, Hondo, and the godborns were told to wait outside along with Rosie. Unless she wandered off for more snake heads.

While the gods sat at the table, I stood before them and spilled every single detail—from Camazotz's alliance with the twins and their evil plot to awaken the Mexica gods to Ah-Puch's heroism when he didn't have to help us. He'd even taken my dad—just before Jordan's ax fell—to the Fire Keeper, to reinstate the Maya magic.

It was high time the gods knew everything. When I was done, no one spoke, or harrumphed, or threw a knife at me. The room was utterly quiet.

I was the one who broke the silence. "Why so glum, everyone? The twins failed."

Nakon stood and stabbed a steak knife into the table. "Momentary failure does not have the finality of true failure. There is always more than one road to victory. They won't stop trying to find a way to awaken the Mexica, to begin this war they so desperately seek."

"Never could trust Camazotz or Ixkik'," Ixkakaw said. "Her beady eyes should have been the first clue. And now they've escaped."

Ah-Puch pushed back his chair and stood. Slowly, he rounded the table and came closer to me. "Camazotz is hurt. I made sure of it. But he will heal. He will come back—with a vengeance."

"They can't awaken a Mexica god without *our* blood," Chaac said (squeamishly, if you ask me).

"We must unite," Hurakan said. "We can no longer afford to fight within our ranks. There is a greater enemy now."

Nakon stood and clapped. "I will begin strategic planning, counterstrike analysis . . ." His voice trailed off in a cloud of glee.

"Right," I said. "Um . . . but what about your kids? They aren't safe, not with our enemies at large."

"What do you expect us to do? Take care of them?" That was Alom.

Ah-Puch's eyes flashed around the room. "Such a bad renovation," he said. "What happened to all the demon skins? And the skull chandeliers?"

"They cannot spend their lives in hiding," Kukuulkaan said.

"Are we talking about the skulls, or the godborns?" Nakon said.

"What do you know of hiding?" Ixkakaw sneered.

Kukuulkaan started to speak but was interrupted by a familiar voice.

"I know *everything* about hiding."

We all turned to see Pacific standing in the threshold.

I think everyone's hearts stopped beating. At least mine did.

Pacific, goddess of time, had been wiped from memory because she'd once told a prophecy about me the gods didn't want to hear. They'd been led to believe my dad had executed her, but instead he and Kukuulkaan had hidden her beneath the ocean, where she'd spent the last several hundred years. Yeah, she knew a thing or two about living in hiding.

She stood there with her locs and leopard cape, holding a golden rope in her hands. The time rope. Her blue eyes were fierce—they had a look that said *Don't mess with me. I have a time rope and I know how to use it.* Her expression reminded me of the nuns at church—rigid and unpredictable.

The gods began shouting. Insults zoomed, faces reddened, spit flew. They pounded their fists. There might have been some lightning and bursts of fire, too.

With a wave of her hands, Ixtab commanded everyone's

attention. "It is time we come together in peace, without secrets, without grudges, without hate. Only then can we defeat our enemies." That sounded crazy coming from the queen of secrets.

My head was ringing.

Pacific lifted her chin and her hard gaze, and she spoke so softly everyone had to shut up to hear her. "I will never hide again. Not from you, not from anyone. So if you want to kill me," she said, "do so knowing that you are destroying a tremendous power that could help vanquish your foes."

Oh wow. That was a pretty good line.

The gods, shocked into silence, stared hard at Pacific. At first, I thought maybe they were deciding how they might kill Hurakan or Kukuulkaan for their betrayal. But then I saw that they were processing Pacific's value—to them, to their futures. They couldn't afford to imprison, kill, or punish any more gods.

I knew the moment the gods had decided the goddess would live, because a calm fell over the room. Pacific stepped closer to the table as she answered the questions that began to fly at her.

Hurakan stood and came over to me, letting them have at it. "I am sure the gods will do the right thing. They will claim their children and grant them their full birthright of godly powers. It's in their best interests, after all."

"But won't that make the godborns more valuable? I mean, as sacrifices?"

"To leave them without any defenses would be worse," he said.

Ah-Puch joined us, still shaking his head over the room decor. "Where are all the cobwebs?"

"Nice last-minute swoop before the ax came down," Hurakan said to Ah-Puch.

"If only I'd had time to rip off the twins' heads," Ah-Puch said. "I was tempted. *Very* tempted, but a deal is a deal." Then his eyes met mine and it was like a thousand words passed between us. But the only ones that mattered were these: *we're good.*

I nodded. We were more than good.

"A new treaty will be signed today," Itzamna said as everyone finally quieted down. "We will work together to defeat our enemies. Ah-Puch and Hurakan and Pacific shall live. We will need their strength as we will need the godborns'. Those who choose not to join us will be exiled. Now, let us vote."

That was my cue to leave.

The godborns were waiting in the hall outside, along with Hondo, Rosie, Ren, and Brooks, who all hung back. Louie, Serena, and Marco walked straight toward me like they might knock me off my feet.

"We wanted to say thanks," Serena said.

"I don't," Marco said. "It's your fault we're in this"—he glanced around—"hellhole."

Coming to my defense, Louie said, "He could have left us on top of that pyramid." He looked around skittishly like he was waiting for someone or something to jump out and attack him.

Brooks stepped forward and stared hard at Marco. "Would you rather live a lie?"

"I'd rather live, period," Marco said.

"Then say thank you." Her eyes flashed yellow, a warning that forced Marco to inch back.

"It's okay," I said. "Marco's right. But so are you, Brooks." I turned to the godborns. "My magic called to you guys, but I didn't know that would mean putting your lives at risk. I thought you'd rather know who you really are."

"I would," Serena said, keeping her eyes on the door to the conference room.

Louie raised his hand. "Me too. Also, do you know if they have any food around here?"

The other godborns nodded silently. I didn't blame them for being so quiet. I mean, they had been abducted, caged, and informed they were godborns, and they were now standing in the underworld waiting to meet their godly mom or dad.

Hondo rubbed his hands together. "You think they'd let me teach at that school Ixtab mentioned? The Shaman Institute of Higher-Order Magic? It needs a new name, but I could teach the godborns some moves and meditations. Stuff like that."

Ren nodded enthusiastically. "Your meditations definitely helped me with the shadows." The godborns flocked to Ren as she explained her take on how to control magic, using the "visualization" techniques Hondo had taught her.

Marco lifted his chin and motioned me to the side, away from the group. Brooks kept her hawk eyes on us. "I hope you fight better than you write. This doesn't sound like it's over."

"Where are you from?" I asked.

"Don't try to distract me. I know what's up."

"You're right. Camazotz and the twins . . . they'll be back.

But maybe, if we're lucky, it'll be a hundred years from now and it'll be a problem for the gods to worry about."

"I'm not stupid." He gave me a slight nod, backing away. "But you'll find that out in the Tree."

Tree?

Ren hurried over. "Do you think my mom is in there with the gods?"

Just then, the doors—very grandes, by the way—flew open, and the godborns were summoned. I peeked into the room to see that even more gods and goddesses had arrived since I'd stepped out. I wanted to stick around to see who belonged to whom, but I wasn't allowed inside.

While we waited in the hallway, Hondo and Rosie played fetch with a bone that looked like it had come from a large animal. Or a . . . Never mind.

Brooks kept pressing her ear to the wooden door. "How thick is this? I can't hear anything!"

"I think that's the point," I said.

"You're such a killjoy, Obispo."

A few minutes later, Hurakan emerged. He asked Brooks to excuse us and took me out to a small bone garden. (Yes, bone garden. Like spines that grew out of the ground in tall columns, and rib cages that lined the walkways. Did I mention the stepping-stones made of skulls?)

"They all signed the treaty," he said, sitting on a bench made of what looked like femurs.

Three reddish moons hung low, casting a pinkish glow over everything.

"Why did so many gods lie about breaking the Sacred Oath?" I asked, taking a seat next to him. "And almost let you die for something they did, too?"

"The gods are not easily understood, Zane. Perhaps they believed that by condemning me, they could erase their own guilt. Self-righteousness is always blind."

It sounded like some pretty twisted logic, but whatever. "So, what happens now?" I asked.

He stretched his long legs in front of him. "Ixchel, the moon goddess, has agreed to oversee the Shaman Institute of Higher-Order Magic. We will train you all, teach you how to control and use your powers. Determine your strengths."

I wanted to be happy. My dad and the godborns were all alive. We were going to get the training we needed. The gods had made a truce. But I knew deep down that the only reason for the peace between the gods and their kids was the threat of war.

"And you," Hurakan said, "you will help train the godborns."

I froze. Me? A trainer? Of other kids? I didn't even like school. I mean, not in the traditional sense. I'd been taking online classes because Mom had said that even if I *am* a godborn I still needed an education.

"You look stunned," Hurakan said.

"I, uh...yeah." I pushed my shoulders back. "Why not? Sounds good." I knew Hurakan wasn't asking my permission, and you know what? The more I thought about it, the cooler it sounded. I mean, I *did* know a whole heck of a lot about the gods and their tricky ways.

"Then we're all set."

"What about Pacific?" I asked. "Does she get to come out of hiding now?"

"All debts have been erased, all grievances buried." Hurakan's mouth turned up, but I wouldn't exactly call it a smile. "She has been reunited with her daughter, Ren."

"I knew it!" I froze. "But wait . . . If Pacific's been in hiding, how . . . ?"

Hurakan folded his arms across his chest. "She was angry and wanted to get back at the gods, so she had an affair with a Mexica brujo. When she gave birth, she left Ren with him, knowing she couldn't hide her in the ocean."

"She abandoned her."

"She *protected* her. Like I . . ." Was that a tremble I heard in his voice? "Like I tried to protect you."

"You told me to run." The words weren't planned, but I'd been carrying them around for a while. "If I'd listened to you, people would have been hurt."

Hurakan clasped his hands, hesitating. "I wanted *you* to be safe. It isn't in my nature to care about the others. I'm not made that way, Zane."

Right. I had to remember that the gods weren't humans. They didn't have thoughts and feelings like ours. It made me even more grateful for my mom's big heart. I'd inherited some awesome powers from my dad, but the stuff she had taught me was just as important.

"And the gods . . . do they know?" I took a quick breath. "I mean, about Ren being part Mexica?"

Hurakan stared out across the garden. "She is very powerful. They may see her as a threat someday, but for now she is safe."

"Someday? Do you mean when war breaks out?"

"We must find the twins and Ixkik', and Zotz, and anyone else who is a traitor. We must put an end to their plans."

"You think there are more helping them?"

"The Maya have a lot of enemies."

My stomach turned.

He cast a side-glance my way. "You and the fire are one now. I can sense it."

I stared down at my hands. The last few times I'd called on the fire, it had felt so natural, like breathing. Ah-Puch had been right—I just needed to surrender to it.

Hurakan stood and placed his hand on my shoulder. "Your power will continue to grow, son."

My heart stalled, as in went kaput in the middle of the garden path. Did he just call me *son*? My face got all hot and buzzy. "Ah-Puch . . . he helped me. I mean, to understand the fire."

Hurakan scratched his chin and nodded thoughtfully. "Enemies who become friends, friends who become enemies."

Was the god of death my friend? "Does he want hell back?" I asked. Even though it had been part of our deal that he wouldn't try to reclaim the underworld, you never know with Maya gods.

"He and Ixtab came to an agreement," he said. "She will continue as goddess of the underworld, and he will get his

own layer of hell, one without her fingerprints all over it."
His mouth turned up into an almost smile. "He's also going
to teach at SHIHOM."

I almost busted up. "The god of death...a teacher?"

Hurakan told me that the training school would be set up
near Itzamna's tree, mostly because it would be a safe place,
guarded by the oldest and strongest Maya magic. So that's
what Marco had meant when he'd said *But you'll find that out
in the Tree.*

"You mean the tree of Itzam-yée'," I said.

"Same thing. Itzam-yée' is the god-bird version of Itzamna."

How come old Itzamna hadn't mentioned that little detail?
My mind raced back to the messenger bird with the anvil-
shaped head. Nah, couldn't be. Could it?

My dad stood and turned to me. "You defied me. You chose
your own path. You put yourself and others in danger."

My eyes met his. "And I'd do it again."

"Worst of all, you gave my jade to Ah-Puch!" This time
Hurakan really did smile. (Okay, it was small, but it was
something.) He looked like he might say *Thank you* or *Good
job*, but he didn't. Instead he said, "I have to go."

"Where?"

Patting my shoulder, he said, "There's someone I need to
see."

46

I knew my dad was going to see my mom, and something about that felt right. Who knew what would happen, but I bet they had some stuff to work out.

We didn't stay in the underworld long, only long enough for the reunions. Turns out Nakon, god of war, is Marco's dad. Big surprise. Serena's mom is Ixchel, the moon goddess; and Louie's dad is Chaac, the mighty rain god. Ren was so happy to meet Pacific she couldn't stop talking about it in the magical cab ride all the way back to Isla Holbox.

I worried my family would have to leave the island since Bird and Jordan knew where we were, but Hurakan said the twins wouldn't be foolish enough to come back. The island would be too protected now (as in *godly* protection), and the risk would be too great for them. No, our enemies' attention would be on a counterstrike, on gaining access to power.

The godborns got to go back to their homes, too. They were each given a golden jaguar charm to protect and shield them, and act as an instant (better than speed-dial) call button to their godly parent. The cops were given all sorts of excuses for the godborns' abductions—everything from cross-country joyrides to "I hit my head and got amnesia."

* * *

Quinn was waiting for us on the beach.

Hondo smiled so big I thought his face would split open. "You're here to welcome the heroes home," he said.

She rolled her eyes and said, "I'm not here for you. I'm here for my sister."

"I don't care why you're here," he said. "As long as you're here."

I was shocked. Cool dude had left the building! And guess what? Quinn smiled. Okay, it was only half of one, but still, it was something.

She told us that the spectators at the execution had been sent home after they were told that the gods had changed their minds, and if anyone had a problem with it, they could file a complaint in one of the six fatal houses of the underworld.

"At least they each got a free bobblehead," Quinn said.

"I bet no one files a complaint," Hondo muttered to me.

Mom was hyperexcited to see me—*after* she chewed me up and down for leaving on such a dangerous quest.

"I had to save him!" I argued once we were alone in my room.

"You could have been killed."

"But I wasn't."

She hugged me again, even tighter this time, then pulled back and pointed to my bed where a box sat, along with a manila envelope.

"Who are they from?"

"No idea. I'll call for some pizza. You must be starving."

"Mom?"

"Yes?"

"Did he come here? To see you?"

I knew the answer before she said anything, because her whole face lit up. "Yes, he came to see me, and also to deliver this." She reached into my top dresser drawer and pulled out something—something I never thought I'd see again.

I blinked in astonishment. "Is that . . . ?"

She held up Fuego—perfectly restored, shining, blue-glowing Fuego! I patted the pocket where I'd been keeping the jade handle. It was empty. How in the heck had Hurakan snatched it? So my dad was a pickpocket, too?

I grabbed the cane/spear from her, smiling so wide my cheeks hurt, turning it in my hands like glass that would break if I held it too tight.

"Hurakan did say to be careful," Mom said. "This is the two-point-oh version, whatever that means."

After Mom left my room, I inspected Fuego. It looked the same but felt different, like the power that pulsed in it was greater, stronger. I wondered if the letter-opener feature was still a thing. The second I tried it out—*poof!* the cane disappeared. I looked around frantically, patting my chest, my jean pockets. Nothing. And then I noticed the back of my hand: there was a quarter-size tattoo of a jaguar profile, black with golden eyes.

"Fuego?"

With a single thought, the cane appeared back in my hand and the tattoo was gone. "Okay, then," I exhaled slowly, and smiled. "Totally better than a letter opener. Thanks, Dad."

I couldn't wait to try out Fuego's power, but I needed a wide-open space so I didn't incinerate anything.

Quickly, I opened the box on my bed and found six gold-wrapped chocolate bars and a stack of plain white paper with a note that read:

Zane,
    A deal is a deal. This is storytelling paper. A story isn't over until it's been told. And don't try and skimp on the details—the paper won't let you. But it will allow you to make the words your own. Make them count.
    See you in the Tree,
    Itzamna.

P.S. The bars are from Ixkakaw. She said every writer needs divine chocolate.

Great! While everyone else was going to be learning warfare and other cool stuff, I was going to be taking writing lessons. Ugh!

Before dinner, I found Quinn walking the shore alone. I still had a big unanswered question for her. I didn't think she would give me a straight answer, her being a spy and all, but I had to try.

"You said the Sparkstriker sent you undercover to the underworld," I said. "Why?"

Quinn tossed a twig into the oncoming waves, and just when I thought she was going to say, *That's none of your business, Obispo,* she said, "The Sparkstriker saw something evil in her lightning pool, something that scared her. I've never seen her frightened. She said the seeds of this evil could only be discovered in the underworld."

"What do you mean, 'seeds'?"

"She didn't tell me, just said to keep my eyes open. But maybe it was Camazotz, since he's from there, or ..."

"Or maybe Ixtab has more secrets we don't know about."

Quinn let out a light laugh. "Oh, you can bet on that. Come on. I'm starving!"

We all sat on the back patio—Mom, Hondo, Brooks, Quinn, Ren, Ren's abuelo, and me—telling stories over pepperoni pizza. I watched as Brooks and Quinn spoke to each other in low whispers, and wished I knew what they were saying. Mostly because Brooks's face was filled with worry—but about what?

Pacific even showed up to say hi to Ren's abuelo, who, by the way, looked too young to be someone's grandfather. He must have had some powerful anti-wrinkle magic in him.

After dinner, Ren and I walked Pacific back to the sea.

"You're the one who helped Ren get here," I said.

Pacific nodded, pulling her leopard hood over her locs. "I knew you would need her. And she would need you."

"You saw the future?" Ren asked.

"Only a glimpse," Pacific said. "It was enough." She wrapped a slim gold watch around Ren's wrist. "We're supposed to wait until the claiming ceremony to bestow our gifts, but"—she smiled—"I'm too impatient for that. This will keep the right time—the true time for you." She dipped her toes into the sea. "You, being my daughter, might disturb the threads of time. Nothing too big, just a few lost minutes here and there."

That's when I remembered Ixtab's broken watch, the stopped clock at the church, and the busted one in Cabo. And in San Miguel, Quinn had thought more time should have passed. Had that all been Ren's doing? Then there was the waterfall in the underworld that froze for a nanosecond, and my mind skidded right into the moment we tumbled over the cliff and the world had seemed to slow.

When I mentioned all this, Pacific nodded. "And the absence seizures . . ." She looked at Ren. "Trances are the gateway to your godborn power."

Ren blinked slowly, her gaze on the sand like she was taking it all in. "That's how I always know what time it is." She looked up at Pacific. "Can I like . . ." She hesitated. "Can I control time?"

"Not yet. Maybe never. But one thing is certain. You are deeply connected to time, and with training you will no doubt learn some powerful skills, but we'll know more soon." And with that Pacific walked into the waves and disappeared.

I guess she'd gotten used to living there after all these years.

"Now I get why I love the sky and aliens and stuff," Ren

said, still staring at the sea. "My mom's the great sky-watcher. She taught the people how to read the stars. She said she'll teach me, too."

"Did she tell you if aliens are real?"

"I haven't had a chance to ask her yet." Ren danced excitedly. "I can't wait to find out!"

The claiming ceremony was planned for June, a few months from now, to allow enough time to find any other godborns before the twins did. I knew Ixtab wouldn't stop looking until she found her offspring.

I finally understood. She had told me about the godborns all those months ago because she knew I'd go looking for them—she knew I would lead her right to her daughter. Except I hadn't done that, and now I wanted to. I wanted to help find each and every godborn still out there. It was hard to imagine what it would be like to train side by side with them, to see all their powers emerge, and to work with the gods instead of against them.

For me, the story ends here. Or at least what I would consider the "public" part. But after I finished writing, Itzamna's paper added more sentences. It was like there was some ghost looking over my shoulder and, if I left out a detail, *whish*—the words appeared on the page. So annoying.

Anyhow, I'd rather the whole story, even the private stuff, come from me and not some controlling paper (it *is* controlling, Itzamna). So, if you're interested, here's how this story *really* ends. . . .

POSTSCRIPT

Rosie and I took a hike that night (it felt great having Fuego again), going all the way to the beach on the east side of the island. The sky was moonless, and even the stars seemed too far away.

"You were a real champ on this quest," I told her.

She walked slowly beside me, and at first I thought she was ignoring my comment. Then she looked at me out of the corner of her eye, snorted, and nudged me with her nose, as if to say *You weren't so bad yourself.*

It was one of those moments you know you'll never forget, all warm and fuzzy and PERSONAL. "Love you, girl."

Rosie raised up on her hind legs and whined like a puppy. I laughed and high-fived her paw as she came down. She might never go back to being the dog I had found all those years ago, but I realized that underneath her tough hellhound exterior she was still Rosie, just as my being a godborn didn't change who I was deep down.

I peered across the beach and saw a small beam of light.

Brooks was sitting on the sand with a flashlight. She had a book in her hands. *My* book.

Crap!

I was backing up, intending to leave before she saw me,

when Rosie took off toward her, tongue hanging out the side of her mouth.

Brooks looked up and smiled. "Hey, girl." She scratched Rosie's leg. She'd already seen me by then, so I couldn't slink back into the dark and pretend I wasn't there.

"Hey," I said, gripping Fuego as Brooks tossed a stick into the waves for Rosie. My hellhound took off after it.

Brooks's eyes fell to my cane/spear. "You got it back."

Eager to see what this 2.0 version could do, I launched Fuego over the waves. It streaked blue across the sky and appeared back in my hand before I could blink twice. I stared down, catching my breath. "Whoa!"

"Yeah," Brooks said as she stood and came closer to inspect him. "Whoa! Even faster than"—she held up the book—"before."

I felt pressure in my chest like I'd just run up a mountain. Why was it so hard to breathe? "Pretty boring, huh?"

"It reminded me of how nasty Ah-Puch was back then. And now he's . . ."

"Yeah."

"It was hard to see you take off with him."

"I know. But I needed his help."

"I get it." She shrugged. "I would have done the same thing."

"Really?"

"Well, no. I would have told you—*not* left a worthless note." Her amber eyes flashed. "You should have trusted me."

"You wouldn't have let me go alone."

She paced. "It makes sense now."

Oh gods—was she going to call me out on all the other

reckless things she'd read about? I groaned inwardly, thinking of the PRIVATE thoughts she'd seen by now, about her
being beautiful, and her smile, and . . . Stupid truth paper!
Heat rushed into my face. Man, I hoped my skin wasn't glowing with fire.

"'All roads lead to the gods' angry wrath,'" she quoted.
"The ancestors' message—they meant the Mexica gods."

I let out a tense breath. "Not the Maya."

She nodded, clutching the book. "It's not bad."

I didn't know if she was talking about the message or
the book, and if she was talking about the book, I wanted
to change the subject. "I didn't get to tell you, but that was a
good move, ripping off Jordan's and Bird's masks, and then—"

"Saving you?"

"Again."

"Too bad I didn't get in more clawing." She smiled, adding,
"Next time you take off and don't want to be found, you might
want to erase your Google search history."

"*That's* why you went to the volcano?"

"We saw the images and figured if you went back to New
Mexico you might start at the Beast. Thankfully, we found a
nearby gateway."

I toed the sand, thinking Brooks would make an excellent
spy. Then my mind drifted back to Jordan and Bird. "Do you
think the gods will find the twins?"

Brooks frowned. "I don't know. Those guys are pretty
shrewd, and now they're getting help from their mom. And
that creepy Zotz. . . ."

"But we have all the Maya gods on our side."

"No, Zane—we're on *their* side. Don't forget who's boss."

We stood like that, staring at the ocean, neither one of us knowing what to say next. She reached for my hand. *Things are going to get . . .*

Dangerous?

Serious.

Then she a took a deep breath and said, "Zane, I . . ." She hesitated and dropped my hand.

"What?"

"I have to go."

"Like, back to the house?"

Her words came out in a single rush. "Back to where I came from. To be with my sister. And . . ." She hesitated and took a deep breath. "My dad is sick."

Her dad? The guy who had left her and Quinn for some new family? I wanted to ask that, but I knew this wasn't the right time. "What kind of sick?"

"When Hurakan renewed the Maya magic, my dad's nawal power didn't come back all the way. Quinn thinks it's because he was already sick. Anyways, he needs our help." She squeezed her hands together. "I can't just leave him alone."

So that's what the sisters had been talking about over dinner.

I felt like a giant fist had punched a hole in my chest. Brooks gone? I was so used to her being here, bossing me around. Telling it to me straight. Being my best friend. I wanted to beg her to stay, but I'd be a world-class jerk to hold her back. She belonged with her family.

"It's not for forever," she said. "Ixtab is letting me train with the godborns this summer. I'll see you then, right?""

I turned to face her. "In the Tree."

She looked up at me, pushing a stray curl from her face. "In the Tree."

The waves rolled. The sea breeze wound between us. I stepped closer to her, holding my breath. She didn't punch me. I found myself tilting my face toward her, getting near enough to...

Brooks closed her eyes.

A burst of flame startled us and pulled us apart. Rosie's fireball rolled to my feet.

Stepping back, Brooks laughed. "Want to play some fire fetch, girl?"

I picked up the fireball and tossed it down the beach. Rosie tore after it. When I turned back, Brooks socked me in the arm and said, "Your face is kind of on fire." And then she shifted into hawk form and took off, flying directly over my hellhound like she wanted to race.

My hands flew to my cheeks. Yep, they were blazing hot. With Fuego in hand, I raced into the sea and dove beneath the breakers, where the only sound was the pounding surf. I launched myself to the surface and looked up to see Brooks soaring overhead in a wide circle. Watching her, my heart pretty much expanded three sizes. "You're still a show-off!" I hollered, smiling.

I knew these moments of peace wouldn't last. Jordan, Bird, and Camazotz wouldn't stay gone forever. They'd been plotting revenge for hundreds of years, and they weren't about to stop now. They'd try to raise the Mexica gods, and monsters, and who knew what else.

But the difference this time? I had the fire. I still had a lot to learn, but I'd be ready. *We'd* be ready. Me, the godborns, the sobrenaturals, and the Maya gods. For whenever that someday might come.

For now? I'd count the days till summer.

One . . .

EL FIN

GLOSSARY

Dear Reader:

This glossary is meant to provide some context for Zane's story. It in no way represents the *many* Maya mythologies, cultures, languages, pronunciations, and geographies. That would take an entire library. Instead, this offers a snapshot of how *I* understand the myths and terms, and what *I* learned during my research for this book. Simply put, myths are stories handed down from one generation to the next. While growing up near the Tijuana border, I was fascinated by the Maya (as well as the Aztec) mythologies, and I was absolutely *sure* that my ancestors were related to the gods. Each time I've visited the Maya pyramids in Yucatán, I've listened for whispers in the breeze (and I just might've heard them). My grandmother used to speak of spirits, brujos, gods, and the magic of ancient civilizations, further igniting my curiosity for and love of myth and magic. I hope this is the beginning (or continuation) of your own curiosity and journey.

Ah-Puch (*ah-POOCH*) god of death, darkness, and destruction. Sometimes he's called the Stinking One or Flatulent One (Oy!). He is often depicted as a skeleton wearing a collar of dangling eyeballs from those he's killed. No wonder he doesn't have any friends.

Ahuitzotl (*ah-WEET-so-tul*) a Mexica water monster with a lopsided face, spiked fur along its spine, and a lizard tail with a hand at the end to drag around its screaming victims. It eats humans.

Alom (*ah-LOME*) god of the sky

alux (*ah-LOOSH*) a knee-high dwarf-like creature molded out of clay or stone for a specific purpose. The creator of an alux must provide offerings to it. Otherwise it might get mad and take revenge on its owner. Sounds kind of risky, if you ask me.

Aztec (*AZ-tek*) a group of people indigenous to Mexico before the Spanish conquest of the sixteenth century. The word means *coming from Aztlán*, their legendary place of origin.

Bakab (*bah-KAHB*) four divine brothers who hold up the corners of the world, and all without complaining about having tired arms

Camazotz (*KAH-mah-sots*) a Maya bat god who, before he was exiled, lived in the House of Bats in Xib'alb'a, where his job was to bite off travelers' heads

Ceiba Tree (*SAY-bah*) the World Tree or Tree of Life. Its roots begin in the underworld, grow up through the earth, and continue into paradise.

Chaac (*CHAHK*) the Maya rain god

Hurakan (*hoor-ah-KAHN*) god of wind, storm, and fire. Also known as Heart of the Sky and One Leg. Hurakan is one of the gods who helped create humans four different times. Some believe he is responsible for giving humans the gift of fire.

Itzamna (*IT-sahm-na*) a Maya creator god associated with writing

Itzam-yée' (*eet-sahm-YEE*) a bird deity that sits atop the World Tree and can see all three planes: the underworld, earth, and paradise. Imagine the stories he could tell.

Ixkakaw (*eesh-ka-KOW*) goddess of the cacao tree and chocolate

Ixkik' (*sh-KEEK*) mother of the hero twins, Jun'ajpu' and Xb'alamkej; also known as the Blood Moon goddess and Blood Maiden. She is the daughter of one of the lords of the underworld.

Ixtab (*eesh-TAHB*) goddess (and often caretaker) of people who were sacrificed or died a violent death

Jun'ajpu' (*HOON-ah-POO*) one of the hero twins; his brother is Xb'alamkej. These brothers were the second generation of hero twins. They were raised by their mother (Ixkik') and grandmother. They were really good ballplayers, and one day they played so loudly, the lords of the underworld got annoyed and asked them to come down to Xib'alb'a for a visit (no thanks!). They accepted the invitation and had to face a series of tests and trials. Luckily for them, they were clever and passed each test, eventually avenging their father and uncle, whom the lords of the underworld had killed.

K'ukumatz (*koo-koo-MATS*) (also known as Kukuulkaan) one of the creator gods. He is said to have come from the sea to teach humans his knowledge. Then he went back to the ocean, promising to return one day. As Kukuulkaan, he is known as the Feathered Serpent. According to legend, he slithers down the steps of the great pyramid El Castillo at Chichén Itzá in Yucatán, Mexico, on the spring and autumn equinoxes; festivals are held in his honor there to this day. El Castillo is definitely a cool—but also hair-raising and bone-chilling—place to visit.

Kukuulkaan (*koo-kool-KAHN*) see Kʼukumatz

Mexica (*meh-SHEE-ka*) a Nahuatl-speaking group of people indigenous to Mexico before the Spanish conquest of the sixteenth century. Also referred to as the rulers of the Aztec empire.

Muwan (*moo-AHN*) a screech owl that Ah-Puch used to send messages from the underworld (good thing she couldn't text!)

Nakon (*nah-CONE*) god of war

nawal (*nah-WAHL*) a human with the ability to change into an animal, sometimes called a shape-shifter

nikʼ wachinel (*nikh watch-een-EL*) a Maya seer, a diviner who can forecast the future

Tlaltecuhtli (*tlah-tek-OOT-lee*) the Mexica earth goddess, whose name means *the one who gives and devours life*

Xbʼalamkej (*sh-bah-lam-KEH*) one of the hero twins; see Junʼajpuʼ

Xibʼalbʼa (*shee-bahl-BAH*) the Maya underworld, a land of darkness and fear where the soul has to travel before reaching paradise. If the soul fails, it must stay in the underworld and hang out with demons. Yikes!

Yum Balam (*YOOM bah-LAHM*) *Lord Jaguar* in Mayan; a wildlife preserve in tropical Mexico

ACKNOWLEDGMENTS

Writing is a solitary act, but bringing a book to life takes an entire team. Heartfelt thanks to my amazing agent, Holly Root. Your guidance, wisdom, and support are more grounding than you know. To Steph Lurie for your mad editing skills and brilliant sound effects; you've got the brass key to unlocking stories. To the incredible Disney Hyperion team: from copyediting, book design, school and library marketing, publicity, and everything in between—I appreciate and admire each of you and your imaginations. To Irvin Rodriguez, who creates mesmerizing, on-point cover art. To Rick Riordan, your enthusiasm is unparalleled. It is such an honor to work with you.

No writer shines (or stays composed) without outstanding, generous, brilliant crit/readers. I'm looking at you, Janet Fox, Lucia DiStefano, and the ever-shining AMC. And to David Bowles. Your mind is a world all its own. Gracias for your expertise.

To my father, who trained me night and day. Yes, I won the jacket, but in the end, I got something better: resilience and a stubborn spirit. I am incredibly blessed to have the unwavering support of my parents, who are always more excited than I am for each new bend in the road. And to my forever loyal, big-hearted family: Joe, Alex, Bella, and Jules. You four are the moon and the stars and my everything.

To all the teachers and librarians who put books into the hands of kids and nurture their love of story. To my readers: There are no words to thank you enough for choosing to follow Zane on his adventures. (Both he and Rosie are beyond grateful, too.)

And as always, I thank God for this incredible journey.

Coming in Fall 2020

The Shadow Crosser

A Storm Runner Novel
Book 3